A SYMPHONY OF STARLIGHT

ALLISON PANG

ALSO BY ALLISON PANG

THE ABBY SINCLAIR SERIES
A Brush of Darkness
A Sliver of Shadow
A Trace of Moonlight
A Duet with Darkness
(a prequel short story in the *Carniepunk* anthology)

THE IRONHEART CHRONICLES
Magpie's Song
Magpie's Fall

STANDALONES
Respawn, Reboot
(a short story in the *Out of Tune, Book 2* anthology)
The Wind in Her Hair
(a comic in the *Womanthology: Space* anthology)
A Dream Most Ancient and Alone
(a short story in the *Tales From the Lake, Vol. 5* anthology)

WEBCOMICS
Fox & Willow

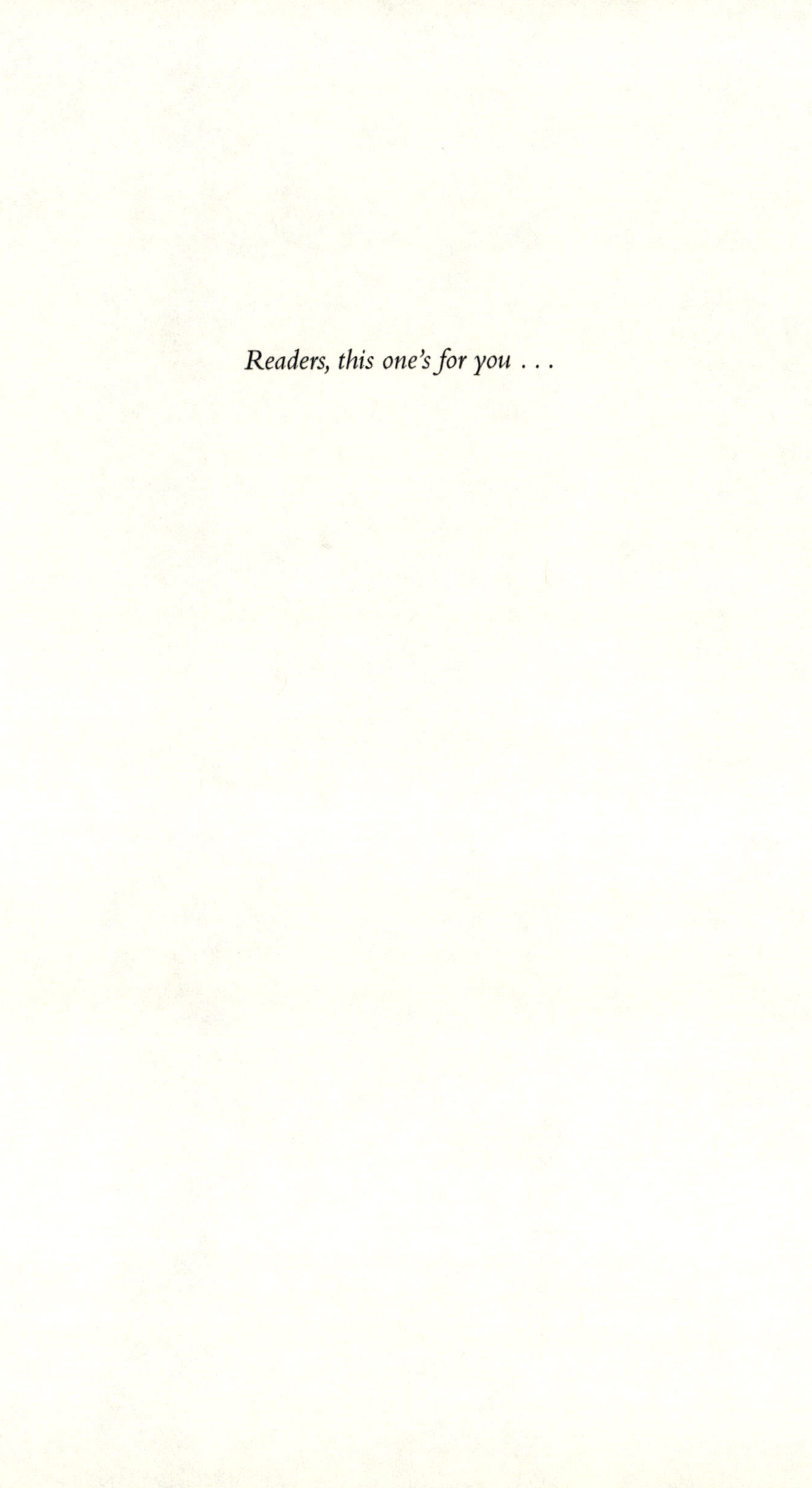

Readers, this one's for you . . .

CHAPTER 1

"YOU'RE TROUBLED." BRYSTION LIFTED HIS head from my shoulder and blew gently against my ear. I shivered and leaned against him, warmed by the chuckle rumbling from his chest.

"Maybe a bit." I stared out over the hillside, the mist rolling through the tall grass as though it wanted to block my vision. I eyed the incubus sourly. His doing, perhaps. He was never particularly subtle when he wanted to keep my attention, especially when he was hungry. As an incubus, Ion had to feed off of sex—specifically orgasms. More specifically, mine.

It didn't surprise me that he might try to take advantage of my distraction for a bit of a snack while he had the chance.

His ebony skin glittered, the moonlight illuminating the pale, silvery markings etched over his body in elegant relief. Everything about his satyrine appearance screamed "old-world godling," from the cloven hooves and furred legs to the tufted lion's tail and crystalline antlers that burst from his brow to crown him in wild beauty. Even the cupped ears that flickered back and forth to catch the lowest hint of my voice were those of a deer, silver hoops jangling. And in the tangle of his long black hair, a bell chimed plaintively, braided into the dark strands with red thread. The proud thrust of his jaw spoke volumes of his arrogance, and his eyes turned golden as he angled toward me to catch my gaze the way a snake hypnotizes a mouse. I froze for a second and then snorted, waving my hand so the mist disappeared.

He let out a disappointed chuff as the rest of the hill appeared beneath the moonlight. The center of my Dreaming Heart was in the form of the old Victorian house I'd grown up in—my grandmother's house—surrounded by a lush garden. My childhood memories had rooted themselves here as a place of solace and comfort. At the entrance stood the gates that allowed entry into this place and beyond . . . Well, if I squinted hard enough from here I could see them, the webs of silver and gold stretched out from this place into the void, a tangle of connections linking me to those I cared about.

Or really, to their Dreaming Hearts.

All mortals have them, though most have no memories of it. It's an abstract residence of sorts, full of dreams and nightmares and whatever bits and pieces that make a person . . . well, a person. The fact that I had the ability to visit and interact with my Dreaming Heart at will was what made me a Dreamer. It only made sense that I would have taken an incubus for a lover. At least, as one of them.

I stared out at the connections all around me that sprouted from my Dreaming Heart—my friends and my family. And on a short silver cord moored not far off my own was my unborn daughter. I glanced down at my mostly flat stomach. Pregnant or not in the real world, sometimes my body didn't seem to show it in the Dreaming, but then I was only a few months along as it was. Dreams weren't always particularly good when it came to accuracy.

Bryston hummed at me when he saw where I was looking. "She seems to be doing well enough," he observed. "That cord will get thinner and longer as she grows. Right now, though, she's tightly tethered to you, as she should be."

"The whole thing feels a bit surreal," I said, taking a few steps away from him, his fingers trailing against my palm. Far beyond my daughter's Dreaming Heart lay another, smaller than mine and drifting about like a boat tethered off a dock. From here, I could only make out the faintest bit of light pulsing on a cord that split toward both mine and my daughter's. "And yours?"

The incubus smiled ruefully, flashing his teeth. "Ah, well, I was never meant to have such a thing. It's still here, though. Still trying to exist, in whatever way it can."

"Like all of us, I suppose," I said. As a creature made of the Dreaming itself, Ion had never had a Dreaming Heart of his own. He'd been spun into existence by chance via a Dreamer like me who'd had no idea what she'd done. But months ago, in an effort to save me from wandering the Dreaming forever, he had become mortal for a time, which not only freed me but granted him his own Dreaming Heart. But how long it would last was anyone's guess.

The fact that his Heart was connected to mine and my daughter's was at least a fairly good indication that she was his. She'd been conceived during that period, as well, though the waters were a bit muddied, as I'd had a husband at the time.

I still did actually.

Complications upon complications. But at least I wasn't try-ing to save the world now. Being able to appreciate the mundane problems of relationships and family was a gift I'd wanted for a long time. Seemed a bit rude to be vexed about it.

His clawed hand pressed against my forehead. "Worrying like that's going to give you wrinkles, you know."

"The horror," I retorted. Before I could say anything else, his mouth captured mine. It was always, *always,* so damned satisfying to sink into him, each casual touch a featherlight stroke of heat that sparked an answering shiver across my skin.

But I wasn't that easy these days.

He pressed his tongue deeper, and I let him linger there, swirling over my lower lip, before giving him a light shove. Startled, he blinked at me, his eyes narrowing as I snorted and turned to run away. I took one step, then two, and the ground parted slightly to capture my feet like quicksand.

"Cheater." I grunted, my knees bending as I struggled to free my legs.

"Always," he said, lips pursing.

I flipped him the bird and then shifted into a hawk, launching myself skyward. This being a dreamscape, I'd learned over the last few years how to control a number of things, including my form and the very shape of my Dreaming Heart.

He laughed and did the same, only he became a coyote, loping beneath my shadow with an easy grace.

I had nowhere near the control he did. Dreaming Heart or no, as an incubus, he innately understood it. What was a struggle for me was as natural as breathing for him. But this was still my place, and it had its own protections that he couldn't always breach.

As I flapped my wings and rose higher and higher into the sky, the Dreaming stretched out all around me. The silver lines reminded me of the CrossRoads, the ley lines woven around the world that connected the metaphysical realms to the world of humans.

Heaven. Hell. Faerie. They were the three main Paths of the CrossRoads under which most of the OtherFolk were categorized. Some were obvious: Angels and such could only be from Heaven, even while an incubus like Brystion had powers of a more daemonic nature. Elves and Fae were square in the middle, and everything else fell on either side depending on their motivations and magical tendencies.

Most people couldn't see OtherFolk so they had no knowledge or understanding of such things beyond Disney movies or Grimm's Fairy Tales. But mythology and legends hold certain truths, a fact I was more than intimately aware of. When I'd arrived in the town of Portsmyth several years ago, I'd had no idea what I was in for, and once I'd gotten involved with the OtherFolk living there, there had been no going back.

Thump!

I dropped a few feet in surprise as something small landed on me. "You're not paying attention." Brystion clacked his beak. He'd taken the form of a crow and was now hitching a ride on my back.

"Pay attention to this, then." I banked sharply and veered toward the ground, shifting into an armadillo as I curled into a ball.

He snickered, barely fluttering up before becoming a butterfly. We went back and forth like that for a while, shifting in a magical give-and-take. From deer to fox to hare, switching from predator to prey in an instant. Somewhere along the way, Ion grew impatient, catching me and us both tumbling into the long grass, our bodies entwined and breathless. His erection was pressed into my thigh, but he merely looked down at me, his face unreadable.

"Sometimes I forget," he murmured.

"Forget what?" I reached up to tangle my fingers in his hair, twirling his braid carelessly.

"How insanely in love with you I am." His hand crept over my belly possessively. "This shouldn't even be possible, but here we are."

"Here we are." I shifted, suddenly uncomfortable. "Uh, I hate to ruin the mood, but . . ."

One brow arched at me in amusement. "But . . . ?"

"I really gotta pee," I muttered. "Like in the real world."

He let out a long-suffering sigh and flopped onto his back in mock frustration. "All that foreplay undone in a moment of mundane bodily functions. How irritatingly mortal."

I shoved him with my foot. "Dude, you try growing another person inside you and tell me how it goes. All I know is I've got garbage coming out of me from both ends, and if I'm not puking, I'm pissing. So if you don't mind?"

"Ever the romantic, Abby. I'll be by shortly to check up on you." He snorted and leaned forward to press a kiss upon my cheek, his eyes flaring gold with power. "Wake up."

I jerked out of bed, tossing aside the covers in a rush and pelting into the bathroom. Relief shuddered through me as I emptied my bladder, washing my hands and splashing a bit of cool water on my face. A quick glance in the mirror only showed a faint flush on my cheeks from the Dreaming's wanderings. It wasn't too bad, I supposed. On the occasions I'd had dream sex with the incubus, I usually pulled him straight from the Dreaming into my bed.

I glanced over at said piece of furniture and chewed on my lower lip. That part of my life was a bit troublesome these days. And crowded. I shuffled toward the bed, ignoring the grumbling of a certain tiny unicorn, and shoveled my way beneath the sheets.

"Blanket hog," Phineas said, yawning. When I flopped over on my side, he shook out his mane and leaned up against the inside of my knees. About the size of a cat, the little shit had a penchant for biting people on the ass and relieving his amorous urges in my panty drawer. About the only time he could be counted on to be polite was when he was asleep, and even then, he was fairly obnoxious.

"Says the one who jacked off into my bath towel this morning," I snarled. "I saw the glitter."

The unicorn let out a solitary giggle, and then all I could hear was the sound of snoring. I rolled my eyes and debated what would happen if I kicked him across the room, but I decided the fallout would probably not be worth it. Not tonight, anyway.

"*Mmmph.* Everything all right?" Talivar's voice was hoarse and gravelly with sleep.

"Pee break. Again." My elvish husband blinked his one good eye blearily in the glow of the nightlight I'd left plugged in. I'd been getting up more frequently these days and had thought it at least somewhat prudent to keep myself from tripping over things like shoes or small, perverted unicorns who couldn't keep their junk to themselves.

"Sounds troublesome." He reached out to stroke my shoulder. "And the incubus?" He asked it lightly enough, but there was always a tension in his voice, as though he didn't want to know the answer but couldn't quite help asking the question.

"Mostly talking," I said, squeezing his hand. "Mostly."

He slid a little closer to me, ignoring an outburst from Phineas as he was abruptly displaced from his nest behind my knee. "I suppose I should be grateful he isn't here as well." He frowned. "I'm sorry. Such petty emotions should be beneath me. And yet . . ."

"I know. It's complicated." That was a lie. It was an emotional clusterfuck of epic proportions, but I was trying to be polite about it. But politeness doesn't change facts, no matter how dressed up they are in pretty words or veiled phrasings. I'd been handfasted to Talivar for nearly a year— partially out of love, partially out of necessity.

It was supposed to only last a year and a day, and then we could decide what we wanted to do from there. But my pregnancy sealed the marriage contract, so to speak. The fact that Talivar was king of the Unseelie Court only added another layer of entanglements. According to Fae marriage laws, it didn't matter that the child I was carrying was probably Ion's. Talivar and I were now bound as husband and wife, and my daughter was quite possibly the heir to his throne, regardless of true parentage.

"You've a gift for understatement." He let out a barking laugh as he stretched out beside me with careless abandon, clad in nothing but scars and the gold torc around his neck. The aura of royalty weighed heavy upon him. His features were more delicate than Brystion's, but he was no less a warrior from the blue swirls tattooed on his cheeks to the missing eye and damaged leg he carefully bent beneath him. "But we can talk about it another time. You need your rest, and I need to figure out how to better balance my time between here and my kingdom."

"Talivar," I chided gently, not wanting to get into this particular argument again. Married or not, I wasn't technically a queen. There had been no coronation as of yet, and to be honest, I wasn't exactly gunning for the position. That left me as his consort, though I knew he wanted to change that.

He flushed. "Well, it would make things simpler. Even you have to admit that. At least we'd all know where we stood. A few weeks ago, you didn't even know if . . . if he could return from Hell. He was gone for months, and now he's back and it's like you and I are nothing at all."

I sat up, flinching away from him. "Wait, what?"

"It's not like I *wanted* to be gone." As though he'd been waiting for the perfect moment to make an entrance, Brystion strode into the bedroom. "Hell runs on its own schedule, and its rules are not mine to break." He'd glamoured himself into his usual human appearance, all pale skin and a broody mouth, with cheekbones you could cut yourself on and a tangle of ebony hair aching for a comb. "Oh, and weren't you waiting in the wings to swoop her up in her time of need?"

"I wouldn't have had to if you hadn't taken so long," Talivar snapped. I could tell he had more to say, but he went quiet when I placed my palm on his chest.

"You try hauling the soul of the man responsible for nearly destroying the CrossRoads to Hell and tell me how long you think it should take." The incubus gestured at me. "And she already died once under your watch, if you recall, so I wouldn't say your track record is much better."

Talivar ground his teeth hard enough to make his jaw pop. I could nearly picture the two of them as children fighting over a sandbox, but the image didn't do any of us any favors. Was I the sandbox? The shovel? Neither was particularly flattering.

But we'd had this argument before, round and round, and there were never any clear ways out of it. Undoubtedly, we were going to have it again, but not tonight.

I pinched the bridge of my nose as a flash of anger sparked in my gut. "Gentlemen, I love you both, but it is two in the morning. I am not doing this now, so either shut up or get out. Actually, no, both of you get out."

Both men blinked at me. "Abby," Brystion said, reaching toward me.

"No. You both have valid points and the whole thing sucks, but I need to go to bed." I'd been avoiding dealing with this issue since the incubus had come home, somehow hoping we could fumble our way through the tangled webs of our relationships without too much fuss. But clearly that wasn't going to be good enough, and I couldn't put my head in the sand about it any longer.

Beside me, Talivar got up, casually putting on his clothes, ignoring us both. He quickly covered his pointed ears with a wool cap that was far too warm for the weather outside, but he wasn't particularly fond of glamours and preferred to hide his OtherFolk characteristics more naturally.

"Nice going, numbnuts," Phin piped up from the foot of the bed. "Now none of us get any sleep."

I pointed at him, his slightly smug tone setting me on edge. "That goes for you as well. There's far too much testosterone in this room."

Crestfallen, the unicorn shuffled his way to the floor, his hooves tapping against the hardwood. "I'm too old for this bullshit," he mumbled, pattering out the door. A guilty twinge twisted through my gut because he was probably right, but I was cranky enough not to be able to pull the words back.

Bryston pursed his mouth. "There's an all-night drink special going on at the Hallows. Sonja invited me to tag along. Think I'll take her up on it."

"I'm sorry . . . To both of you." I tugged on my hair. "I've got some thinking to do, and I can't do it with you guys looming over me like this."

"I know. Perhaps a bit of space would be a good thing for all of us." Ion's eyes dropped to my belly with a hint of amusement. "I'll see you at work tomorrow, if I don't find you before then."

Talivar sighed. "I'll catch up with you later," he said, glancing at me and then the incubus with a shake of his head before slipping away.

Ion followed suit, leaving me to the quiet of my bed and my apartment and to a whirlwind of thoughts drifting across my mind like tumbleweeds before a tornado.

"Baaaaabbbbbyyyy shark, doo doo doo doo doo doo . . ." My enchanted iPod chugged along, music piping out of one of the nearby speakers set against the far side of my kitchen counter.

"That's quite enough of that," I said impatiently, relaxing as the music paused and then shifted over to something classical, a lone piano plinking out Brahms's "Lullaby" quietly. I rolled my eyes but said nothing. It was far more tolerable than the alternative, especially this early in the morning.

"Are you sure you're getting enough sleep? You look tired." Melanie eyed me from over her cup of tea, as though daring me to lie. "And irritated."

"Ask me if I care." I shoveled the oatmeal around my bowl and scowled at the iPod. "Sorry. I had a shitty night, that's all. And that infernal device will not . . . Stop. Playing. Nursery. Music." To be fair, it had always had a mind of its own since I accidentally magicked it up several years ago. Some things about it were convenient. It never needed charging, for example. On the other hand, it had been awfully enthusiastic about this baby thing and almost all of my playlists had been replaced by songs about animals, diapers, and the wonders of sleeping in cradles.

"Oh, I've no doubt." Mel sipped the tea, pushing her violet teashades a little farther up her nose. We were planted at my kitchen table this morning, enjoying the bit of sunlight pouring through the blinds. The golden hue lit up the red waves of her hair like an inferno, fiery and brilliant. She stared absently at her fingernails, rubbing at the chipped black polish with her thumb.

"You don't sound particularly surprised," I pointed out, piling on another teaspoon of sugar. I didn't always like sweet things, but since getting pregnant, my taste buds were unable to tolerate even the blandest of foods.

"*Mmmph.* Well, I had a visitor in the wee hours after my last gig finished up at the Hallows." Her eyes flicked toward her violin case, which was covered with a riot of stickers—clubs she'd played at, countries she'd visited, other bands she liked. A skeleton Hello Kitty. Abbey Road.

Punk Beethoven. Bits and pieces of her history had been slapped on the case of an instrument worth her soul.

"Which one? I kicked both of them out last night when we started sniping at one another." I sipped some orange juice, wrinkling my nose at the tartness.

"Ion went off with his sister somewhere before I finished playing. But . . . yeah. A certain elvish king appears to have taken up residence on my couch." She snorted. "Incidentally, he was rather drunk, but he held it together well enough to get to my apartment. I suspect he'll have a bit of a hangover when he wakes up, but nothing he can't handle." She set her cup down on the table. "Must have been one hell of an argument."

I shrugged, ignoring the heated flush creeping up my neck. "Ah, you know. It's not like they weren't possessive before, but this baby has screwed everything right up."

"Or maybe you didn't notice it as much before. The last few months have been hectic, not even counting the fact that you're pregnant. It's kind of hard to care who's knocking boots with who when you're trying to save the world from a madman with delusions of supreme power. Or whatever Maurice's deal was," she said, shuddering.

"I'd almost rather not think about it." And I didn't. I'd died, been brought back, lost my memories, and found myself pregnant over the span of a few months. Not to mention getting involved with the Wild Hunt, being Tithed to Hell, and watching Eildon Tree—aka the World Tree—burn to the ground, thereby throwing the Cross-Roads into chaos. It had taken the cooperation of all four Paths to bring Maurice to justice and the memories of those events had scarred us all.

"Yeah, same. Except, well, you know . . ." She stole a piece of toast from the plate on the center of the table and buttered it fiercely. "You remember what it was like the first year at Julliard? When the world was simple and there was nothing more to do than remember to get to class on time? Before all this OtherFolk garbage and magic violins and saving the world?"

I snorted, rubbing the side of my head. There was a metal plate on the side of it, the scar tucked neatly away beneath my hair. "Before," I murmured, not finishing the sentence, but I didn't have to. Before a car accident had stolen my mother's life, ruined my ballet career, and destroyed my health?

Yes, I remembered all too well.

My fingers crept over the slight curve of my belly. Without such things, though, I wouldn't be here, and neither would my baby. Trade-offs sometimes had very interesting results.

Melanie gave me a tight smile and paused before taking a bite of her toast, her eyes dropping from mine. "Did Ion ever mention what happened when he was in Hell?"

It was asked so casually, but I knew what she wanted was information on her lover, Nobu. He'd accompanied Ion to Hell with Maurice's soul, but Nobu hadn't returned. "I'm surprised you didn't ask him," I said. The two of them had been close friends and were former bandmates. The incubus could be a jerk, but they had a history that involved some pretty crazy shit.

"I did. He wasn't particularly forthcoming. Just said he and Nobu had been separated when they arrived, and Ion hasn't seen him since. No one's heard anything." She sighed. "I guess I was hoping he might have told you more, but it's not the first time Nobu has been gone so long."

I shook my head and finished the last of my orange juice. "No, he didn't say anything else to me. I'd tell you in a heartbeat if I knew. Honestly, Ion doesn't talk to me about it either, but he understands how much Nobu means to you. He would have said something to me by now, even if it wasn't good news." I hesitated as Melanie flinched. I was treading on delicate ground here. Her relationship with Nobu was even more complicated than mine was with Brystion and Talivar, but for far different reasons.

"I think you're reading too much into it. Not everything needs to be a shared experience, even between couples. And I suspect he was trying to spare you the worst of it." Phineas trotted into the kitchen and jumped onto one of the seats at the table. "It's not as though Hell is a place people visit for fu—" He cut off his words abruptly as I shoved the chair, my eyes darting to Melanie, who was staring at her hands with an empty expression.

Shut up, I mouthed at him.

Phin winced and then coughed, his ears flattening. His eyes glittered at me expectantly as he changed the subject with all the grace of a sledgehammer to the face. "Where's breakfast? And I don't mean this porridge garbage you're eating."

"Feel free to help yourself to whatever's in the fridge, Phin. I'm not inclined to cook this morning." Between the morning sickness and my exhaustion after last night, I hadn't been in the mood to eat much, *period*, let alone my bacon-filled meals of the past.

"I see how it is," he said, his tone becoming aggrieved. "Kicked out of your bed. Left to starve in the streets. What's a mythological beast to do?"

"You could always sell your body," Melanie suggested, glancing up from her now-empty teacup. "Or I could play and you could dance for tips like a little monkey."

"You wish." He dragged a piece of toast from her plate with a delicately cloven hoof and gobbled it up without another word, crumbs tumbling into his beard.

The three of us ate in silence for the next few minutes, each lost in our own thoughts until there was a sharp rapping at the door. I glanced at Phin. "Are we expecting anyone?"

"Not that I know of. The other two wouldn't have knocked anyway." He shrugged. "Maybe don't answer. I'm not in the mood for another crisis at this point."

I was half-inclined to agree with him, but the knocking grew more insistent. I gave up and answered the door.

"Kitsune?"

Dressed in a brilliant viridian kimono with a dark-blue obi, the silk painted with crimson cranes that seemed to move over the folds and seams like a living entity, the fox-woman stood on the doorstep. She was Talivar's distant cousin and the former leader of the Barras, a roaming tent city that currently served as the location of the Unseelie Court.

Something between outrage and bemusement flicked over the perfect sereneness of her face when she saw me, but the crystalline sharpness of her golden eyes gave away nothing. Her furred ears twitched, her long, black hair hanging almost to her ankles. Her fluffy fox tail wagged slightly. "Ah, good. You are awake."

"More or less . . ." I hesitated, wondering if I should let her in or not, but manners and all. I gestured for her to enter. "Please come in and have a seat."

Melanie had gathered her things already, her violin case slung over her shoulder. She shrugged at me, making as though she might slip out the door without being seen.

Kitsune shook her head and took a seat at the kitchen table, one slightly clawed hand emerging from the sleeves of her kimono. "Stay. I think this concerns you too."

"Can it wait? I'd really like to get some sleep. I was play-ing all night," Melanie said, irritation edging her voice.

"Patience. I'd rather not chase you down later if you're already here." Kitsune's tone had a steely clip to it. I'd yet to meet anyone who could go up against it, and even Melanie slumped into her chair.

I shook my head, giving Kitsune a wan smile as I paused

the iPod and poured her a cup of tea from the still-warm kettle. I sat in the seat across from her. "I'm sorry I don't have more to offer in the way of hospitality." I paused a beat, but she didn't respond. "If you're looking for Talivar, he isn't here right now."

Her eyes glinted in amused understanding. "Ah yes. Talivar has been rather . . . irritated as of late. Which brings me to my reason for coming." She folded her hands neatly before her on the table. "We need a kingdom."

I frowned. "I don't understand. I thought the Unseelie Court was already a kingdom."

"Well, on paper, I suppose we are, but since Talivar's coronation and subsequent takeover of the ruling body, a number of us feel it's time for us to be recalled from our banishment. Especially considering he has taken a wife." She inclined her head at me. "And said wife is expecting."

"So why aren't you asking Talivar about this directly?" I asked. "Seems to me he would be the best person to make this sort of request to. King and all that."

"I have. Several times." Kitsune raised a perfectly arched brow at me. "But when the man will not hear with his ears, we must beseech his heart."

I flushed despite myself. "I have no desire to become queen," I reminded her, my tone a bit sharper than I'd intended.

"And yet here I am. And here you are."

"I have no influence over those things. Not here, and certainly not in Faerie." I tapped my fingers on the table, not liking where this conversation was heading.

"Bitch, please." Phineas snorted. "You're married to the king of the Unseelie Court, you're the half sister of the princess-heir of the Seelie Court, *and* you're the daughter of True Thomas the Rhymer, current consort to the actual Faery queen. If you got any more related to the royalty side of things we'd be in Narnia."

I flushed. A tangled spider's web had nothing on my personal life. "All right fine. Point taken. But so what? The Faery queen hates me; she has no qualms about showing that. As for Moira . . . Maybe I could talk to her, but she's been stupid busy every time I've seen her recently. Not to mention the split between the two Courts happened long before I was ever part of the picture. I hardly think anyone would listen to my opinion of what to do about it."

"I'm aware of that." Kitsune sipped her tea. "I was there, after all. As was your husband," she reminded me. "I'm not expecting you to interject your opinion into the Faery queen's ear, simply to remind her son that one of his duties is to restore the Unseelie Court to its former glory." Her eyes locked on mine. "We need a permanent kingdom, one on par with the Seelie Court. It is very difficult to arrange things like trade, and other aspects of a political nature, without it."

"I can only imagine," I said dryly. And I could. The Barras was never in the same place twice and was filled with denizens of the Unseelie Court in a sprawling maze of constant chaos. They hadn't had a king in a long time, so Kitsune had been running the day-to-day operations until Talivar had stepped up to take the position. It made sense for her to want a bit more order.

She sighed. "In truth, I am tired of wandering. Those who wish to keep the Barras running are free to do so, of course. But I think it would be best if Talivar was centrally located so he could be found on a more regular basis. As a king should be." Her teeth gleamed in a little smile as she said it, irritation radiating off her in waves.

Melanie and I exchanged a doubtful look. While I was all for Talivar taking on his responsibilities, I wasn't sure I wanted him to confront Kitsune in his currently hungover state. From Melanie's expression, I could tell she felt the same. She stood up abruptly. "Well, I'll tell him if I see him," she said, sliding her violin over her shoulder. "But in the meantime, I need to get some sleep."

Kitsune cocked her head at Melanie. "I need a Door before you go."

Melanie hesitated and then shrugged. "Where do you want it? There's a Door right out in the garden, isn't there?"

"Yes, but I have no TouchStone, and I don't want to wait. There are things I need to get in order before I meet with Talivar." Her eyes slid toward me. "Hopefully soon."

The CrossRoads could be traversed by the OtherFolk to take them to the various realms, including the mortal one, but to cross over from one location to the other they needed a Door. Most Doors were permanent, built into structures with a great deal of history or mystical power. The kicker was that the OtherFolk could only use them at four different times each day: Dawn, dusk, midnight, and noon.

Unless they had a mortal TouchStone, which required a Contract between a human and an OtherFolk being, usually involving an exchange of some sort of magical power—a wish, for example. And in return, the OtherFolk could use the mortal to access the Doors whenever they wanted. Contracts were usually nothing more than business transactions, and often short-term, though they could also be romantically linked and more permanent, like the one between me and Ion.

In Melanie's case, she could *create* temporary Doors on the fly for whomever she was TouchStoned to, and she often did so in exchange for favors. To be honest, having OtherFolk indebted to you is a pretty sweet deal. They aren't all particularly kind to humans, and having OtherFolk to back you up when the shit hits the fan was invaluable.

But Melanie hesitated, glancing at her wristwatch. "Are you sure you can't wait another couple of hours?"

I frowned at her. She might be tired, but I'd never seen her turn down a Contract, especially from someone as highly ranked as Kitsune.

"I insist," Kitsune said, her eyes narrowing at Mel before her attention flickered toward me, lingering at the base of my throat. "You no longer wear the Key to the Cross-Roads, I see. I cannot sense it, even beneath its glamour."

I shook my head. "We decided it was too dangerous, particularly in my condition. Talivar thought it would make me a target." An ancient elven artifact, the Key to the CrossRoads allowed its mortal wearer to open any Door at any time. It had been gifted to my mother by my father and passed to me, but its power came at a terrible price. It could only be removed upon the death of the wearer, which I learned firsthand when Maurice killed me for it. Once the TouchStone of my half sister, Moira, Maurice had gone power-mad, trying everything from kidnapping to murder in an effort to retain his status. Once the Key was in his possession, he'd been nearly unstoppable, jumping from Door to Door all along the CrossRoads with an army of daemons who were completely loyal to him.

Kitsune's ears flattened. "He said no such thing to me. Surely if you weren't going to wear it, you could have given it to me for safekeeping."

I shrugged. "Ah, well, the three of us thought it better if no one knew where it was. Besides, he can't even get to it."

"How does that make you less of a target?" Melanie asked, clearly unconvinced.

"Because it's tucked away in the Dreaming," I said. "It's not on any of the mortal planes or the CrossRoads, and only I know where to find it. If they kill me to get it, well . . . I suppose it will be lost forever."

Phineas let out a low whistle. "Clever girl."

"It seemed to be the safest course of action," I said. "At least for now."

"Fair enough." Kitsune coughed politely, turning toward Melanie with an expectant gaze.

Melanie dug into her purse, pulling out a small notebook of parchment about the size of a pad of Post-its. Carefully she tore off a piece and tossed it on the table. The script on it was elegant and crisp, embossed with the seal of the Fae Protectorate who ensured OtherFolk Contracts were written correctly.

"You know the drill," Melanie said, handing it to the fox-woman and then fussing with the violin case.

Kitsune gently scratched the tip of her index finger with one of her sharp nails, watching impassively when a drop of blood beaded up, shining crimson in the midmorning light. She pressed her finger into the Contract, leaving a bloody smear behind.

The paper shimmered slightly, and Melanie scooped it up. "Contract accepted." She folded it and slid it into her pocket before setting her violin case on the table and popping it open. "There's just one little problem."

"And what's that?" Kitsune looked inside, her eyes widening.

"Yeah." Melanie gave me a half smile, but I could see the tremor in her lower lip. "I think it's broken."

CHAPTER 2

"I DON'T UNDERSTAND. WEREN'T YOU PLAY-ING it last night?" I leaned over for a closer look. From this angle it looked the same to me as it always had, the wood glimmering with a silvery sheen that screamed magic. Which it should, considering she'd sold her soul for it. Not on purpose, exactly, but several years ago, she'd gotten into a dueling-banjos situation with the TouchStone of the Devil himself to try to win it, not realizing what the ultimate cost would be.

And she had lost.

Or rather, she had won the violin, but her soul was now the Devil's to claim. Nobu had traded himself to pay Melanie's soul debt, but in return, he'd had to leave her, to serve in Hell beneath the Devil's watchful eye. His self-enforced separation from her had been for her protection, but sometimes love has a way of messing with the best of intentions, and we all knew she was on borrowed time, at best. Sooner or later, the Devil would call her home.

Melanie hissed and rubbed at the violinist hickey on her chin as though to hide her suddenly shaking hands. "Yeah, it plays regular music okay, but the Wild Magic . . . I don't know. Something is off."

Kitsune stretched out her hand as though to touch it and then drew back. Phineas hopped onto the table, sniffing at the bow.

"*Off* might be the wrong term," Melanie said, pulling the violin out and raising it to her chin. She slid her bow over the strings. A quick succession of notes followed suit, the beginning of "Bittersweet Symphony" resonating in my little kitchen for a few seconds. "See, that's regular music and it's fine. But when I try to tap into the Wild Magic . . ."

She sucked in a deep breath and played the same song, but this time the vibrato was richer, the air thick and heavy, wrapping about us like a fur coat. If I concentrated, I could almost see it: A riot of fiery colors swirling up the bow and around the violin, shivering with potential. It was this power that allowed Melanie to create Doors, manipulating time and space for the span of a few moments. But she could only do it for those she TouchStoned—never for herself.

And then the sound changed, the notes curdling like sour milk. Sweat broke out on her forehead, her mouth curling into an uncharacteristic snarl. Abruptly, she stiffened and the music seemed to right itself, the dark feeling receding until all that was left was the normal thrum of the Wild Magic dripping from the strings like golden butterflies.

She stopped, her green eyes opening in a hazy fog, as though she couldn't quite see clearly. "I have to fight it," she said. "I've never had to do that. Not like this. I mean, it's not a dog you can call to come to you on command; it takes convincing sometimes. But now it feels as though it might bite my hand off. I know that doesn't make sense, but that's about the best I can do."

Kitsune pointed at the underside. "Turn it over. The side there—is there something on the wood?"

Melanie twisted the instrument in her hand, biting hard on her lower lip. "What is that?"

"Corruption," Phineas said gravely, gesturing at me to take a closer look. Sure enough, there was a blemish on the wood near where she rested her chin. It was the color of an old scab.

Mel's face had paled into a ghostly whiteness. She pulled her sleeve down over her palm, frantically rubbing at the spot.

Kitsune laid her clawed fingers over Melanie's wrist. "That needs tending to, Door Maker. How long have you been like this?"

Melanie stilled, sighing in relief as the spot disappeared, melting away as though it hadn't existed. "I don't know when it started. After I helped restore Eildon Tree, maybe? The Wild Magic required was insane, even with the other Paths helping. Maybe there was some sort of backlash. I don't know. At first I thought it was an anomaly, but now it comes and goes. I keep thinking it will somehow get better if I simply ignore it." She rubbed at her forehead and let out a mocking little laugh. "Did you want that Door now? The Contract is still open, but we can terminate it."

Kitsune's mouth pursed shrewdly. "Prudence would dictate that would be risky, but I confess I'm rather curious to see if the Door itself has changed. Perhaps if I can see that, I might be able to assist in determining the cause of your . . . weakness, for lack of a better term."

"For something in return, I'm sure," Melanie said dryly. Kitsune almost never did anything without a catch, but frankly, that was true for most of the OtherFolk. Altruism wasn't exactly a popular currency on the CrossRoads.

The fox-woman inclined her head. "That goes without saying."

"You know, I *could* just TouchStone you myself and we could avoid doing this in my apartment," I said. Unlike most mortals, I didn't need a written Contract. I could TouchStone OtherFolk on contact, though I usually tried to avoid it.

"Of course not. Not in your condition," Kitsune said

primly, staring at my belly. "No need to put additional strain on your body. No, we'll do it this way."

"Your funeral," Phineas said, leaping down to the floor and making himself scarce. I decided to follow suit, retreating to the main door of the apartment. I craned my neck so I could still see into the kitchen. If the shit hit the fan, I'd have to bail. It wasn't like I had any way of stopping it if she lost control.

Melanie nodded. "All right. You've done this part before. Think about where you want to go, and I'll try to make the Door. But if it looks like it's going to be unstable, I'm stopping."

"Of course." Kitsune's tail twitched. "I'm ready, whenever you are."

Melanie sucked in a deep breath and raised the violin to her chin again. This time, the notes came much easier, transitioning into the Wild Magic with a harmonious echo that reverberated through the apartment. It wasn't a song that I could name per se, but there was something familiar and primal about it, as if she were tapping into the very fabric of our souls.

The doorway between the kitchen and the living room shimmered, silver vines of power scaling either side and meeting at the top, tendrils twining together as the music hummed beneath it, the Wild Magic bending to her will.

"My thanks." Kitsune bowed slightly and stepped lightly through the Door. A shimmer of sparkles erupted at her passing, and she faded from view. Melanie finished up the song with a little flourish, and the music and magic ebbed away until there was no sign the Door had ever existed.

She sagged as I approached her, slumping into one of the chairs. "That could have gone worse," she muttered.

"I'm glad you didn't . . . I don't know . . . make my apartment implode? I've got enough problems right now without having to find a new place to live." I nudged her when she said nothing. "I'm joking."

"I know, I know." She returned the violin and bow to the case and snapped it shut carefully. "If there is something really wrong, I don't even know where to start looking, Abby."

"We'll figure it out," I assured her, giving her a quick hug. She leaned into me, her demeanor a far cry from her usual robust cheekiness. "Kitsune is wise when it comes to this sort of shit. She'll be able to think of something. But I would talk to Talivar about it too. You were TouchStones once, and I know he's been relying on your services for some of the transportation issues around the Barras. It's only fair he knows."

"You're right. And I will. But after a nap and something to eat." She stood up and shouldered her bag. "I'll be by the Midnight Marketplace tonight, and I'll make sure Talivar comes along. Sounds like you two have some talking to do, and this way you can tell him what Kitsune wants."

"Gee, thanks," I said.

"I always aim to please." She gave a little bow as I followed her toward the front door. There was no sign of Phin, but that wasn't overly unusual. Fucker was probably hiding out in my underwear drawer again.

"Get some rest, and I'll see you later," I called after her. The screen door shut with a click, and I heard her booted feet trudge down the steps as she made her way up the path to the back alley and the street that would take her home. Somehow it felt as though I was about to lose something precious. And when I looked out the window into the courtyard below, she was already gone.

" . . . and then she rubbed her silky thighs over his chest, whickering softly. *The end.*" Phin's hooves typed out the words in dainty fashion as he repeated the sentence aloud.

"There now. First draft of *The Girl of Horns and Bites* is finished."

I glanced up from my copy of *Baby Bumps in the Night: Tips for the Preternaturally Pregnant.* "Sounds like a bestseller. For Furries."

"Damn straight." The unicorn adjusted his tiny spectacles and peered at the laptop screen. "And you know, I don't think you even need that book you're reading. After all, Ion was mortal at the time of conception, wasn't he?"

"Sure." I continued to sift through the pages, choosing not to linger over the chapter titled "What to Do When Your Baby Decides to Eat Its Way Out." Blanching, I shut the book with a snap. "But I might not have been. After all, I was carrying some of his incubus powers then."

Phineas paused, his mouth open, and then he shrugged. "Fair enough. Still a bit early, though. You're not even showing much."

I supposed that was sort of true. Maybe things weren't changing to the outside world, but inside, it was very different. I was rounding that third month of what all the baby books indicated was the end of morning sickness and the beginning of something called "the Golden Trimester" or some such bullshit.

Nothing golden about it from what I could see. Just a never-ending run of tightening clothes and sore boobs. And as of now, the morning sickness was less of a morning thing and more of a whenever-I-stepped-in-the-kitchen thing.

I nestled into the overstuffed sitting chair, my legs stretched out on the matching ottoman as I watched Ion wipe down the counter with brutal efficiency. The Midnight Marketplace had closed nearly an hour ago, but even so, there were stragglers finishing up the last of their strawberry tarts or lingonberry pies, taking a last shot of espresso for the road before disappearing into places unknown. A drunken elf here; a yawning nymph there. A severely happy vampire who wouldn't stop giggling at a pocket mirror he kept pulling out and gleefully staring into with abandon. I couldn't imagine how chemically enhanced such a creature would have to be to see his own reflection, but I wasn't going to interrupt him either.

Phin's usual writing groupies had long since left, which is probably why he managed to finish the thing. Normally he let himself be willingly distracted by a bevy of female creatures, both humanoid and not, nipping asses and generally being his obnoxious self, but he seemed a bit more restrained this evening.

And of course, Melanie still sat on the small stage, playing her violin slowly. There wasn't any sign of her earlier troubles from this morning, her eyes closed and her face smooth. The notes trickled from the bow, puddling at her feet with the distinctive vibrato of enchantment. But it was lonely tonight, aching and soft and full of want.

The Marketplace itself had started out as a sort of OtherFolk goods shop, owned by my half sister, Moira, when she had been the Faery Protectorate of Portsmyth. I'd been her TouchStone at the time, running the Marketplace in the wee hours and a dilapidated used bookstore during the day.

When things finally settled down after the incident with Maurice and the Eildon Tree, I converted it to a coffee shop. Moira had moved on to more royal duties in Faerie anyway, and I found I rather liked the laid-back atmosphere over the hustle of nonstop inventory and disgruntled buyers.

When the last of the song faded away, so did my OtherFolk customers. They stumbled out the door and into the early light of dawn—or wherever the CrossRoads would take them. Melanie stretched, craning her neck back and forth before putting the violin in its case and slipping on her Dr. Martens. She'd taken them off hours ago, prancing about the stage in her rainbow-striped thigh-high stockings, but she didn't seem tired as she took a seat at the counter.

Ion slid her a mug of something hot and steaming, the scent rich and spicy. She dipped a finger in the foam and snorted. "Your dick drawings are getting better."

"I do try," he admitted as she took a long sip, glancing over at me with a wry smile. "Don't I?"

"When it suits you," I agreed, sliding off my chair to take a seat at the bar next to Melanie. He tipped an imaginary hat at me before disappearing into the back with a tray of dirty plates.

"You've domesticated him," Melanie murmured. "I never thought I'd see the day. Probably a good thing with the baby and all."

I snorted. "Probably. And no, we haven't had time to talk since I opened tonight. It's been stupid busy. I was hoping Talivar would be here too so we could hash things out after everyone leaves."

"I did tell him. He left in the afternoon after a shower and some lunch. I was still napping so I don't know what time exactly, but he was gone when I got up." She shrugged. "Maybe he went to the Barras first."

"Yeah. Knowing Kitsune, she's probably been talking his ears off for the last few hours. It's not like he doesn't have a phone at this point. He could have texted." Not that he was particularly good at it, even in the best of times. Technology was not Talivar's strong suit. "Did you, uh, tell him about your violin?"

Her eyes slid sideways. "Eh. Not in so many words. I mentioned there was a problem, but we didn't get into specifics. And I was napping, like I said."

"What's this about your violin?" Ion had remerged from the kitchen, his apron hanging over his arm. His dark gaze darted between the two of us with a resigned expression. But then he glanced sharply at Melanie, reaching out to turn her head. She didn't pull away, but there was a visible twitch when he ran his finger over the violinist hickey on her jaw.

Melanie had always been sensitive about it. The Devil's Mark, she called it. But even though she sometimes kept it hidden beneath clever foundation, it often hurt her, burning whenever the Devil thought of her—or so she claimed.

"It's getting worse," she said. "Each passing day, the burning grows. He's thinking of me a very great deal, I suspect."

Ion's eyes narrowed. He'd been there with her when she had lost her soul and had helped her clean up the pieces when Nobu left, so he was rather intimately familiar with her issues.

"Always keeping this to yourself," he said, snarling. "When will you learn that your friends are here for you?"

"I know. But I—"

"Have somewhere else to be?" The raspy voice came from behind us in a panicked rush as we all swiveled toward the entrance of the Marketplace. Ion launched himself over the glass cake counter and toward the door. My mouth dropped open when he staggered back, his arms full of feathers and . . .

Nobu.

Melanie let out a startled cry as she rushed forward to take Nobu from Ion. Her lover's blue-black wings sagged to the floor as the crimson stains grew larger. I barely had time to take in his wild appearance—the sunken cheeks and the tangled mess of hair, the golden skin checkered with bruises and cuts.

"No time to explain," he gasped. "They're tailing me pretty hard." His mouth quirked up at Melanie with a tired smile. "Little bird, we have to go."

"But you're hurt!" I said, grabbing some napkins from the counter and passing them to Melanie. She pressed them against a gash in his forehead.

"It's not deep," he said. "Just bleeding a lot."

Ion held out a hand to pull Nobu up. "Peacock," he said, his tone oddly gentle.

"Dream-eater," Nobu replied, limping toward the counter.

From there, I got a better look at his wounds. He'd claimed to be a fallen angel when we first met, though he'd never fully explained what that entailed. And to be honest, we hadn't been on the best of terms then, so I hadn't pressed the issue. As long as he was good to Melanie, that was about all I could ask for.

He wasn't as tall as Ion, but his hair stood up in a spiky Mohawk in a riot of dyed purples and blues. His leather pants were torn, and there wasn't much left of his shirt, perhaps due to the enormous green–black wings arching from his back. He had a wiry build and dark eyes, and the cut of his jaw dripped arrogance though the effect was somewhat ruined by the swelling cheekbone and bruised neck. His expression softened when it fell on Melanie, who was quickly gathering up her purse and tightening the laces of her boots.

"I see Hell finally released you," Ion observed. "I was beginning to worry."

Nobu shook his head. "I wouldn't say *released*. More like they weren't paying attention and I slipped away. But that's not the point. They're not really after *me*. They're after *her*." He thrust his chin at Melanie. "We need to go. Right now."

"We don't have a back door," I pointed out. The Marketplace wasn't actually on the CrossRoads, but it wasn't entirely in the mortal world either. More like a little pocket of enchantment connected to the mortal realm via a Door that could be accessed in the courtyard below my apartment. Moira's doing, I supposed. It had been here long before I'd met her, anyway, and I'd never had time to sit down and ask her how it had been done.

"Since when has that ever stopped my little bird?" he asked softly, limping over to her. When the two of them looked at each other, it was as though the rest of us faded away. Like I was looking at an old photo of some friends—perfectly still, perfectly real, but nothing more than distant memories of some forgotten time, immortalized in something as mundane as a picture.

"Nobu," Melanie said, her voice strangled. "You need to understand. The violin isn't working properly. The Wild Magic . . ."

Nobu pressed a finger to her lips, staring at the entrance to the Marketplace. "If we don't get out of here right now, the Devil's TouchStone will be prancing in here any moment to take you back to Hell. The Wild Magic will be fine."

I exchanged a look with Ion, but his face darkened. "So you bring trouble to our doorstep and dump it like a bag of dog shit on the stoop while you flitter off?"

Nobu's upper lip curled. "You took my quarry from me, dream-eater. I think I've earned the right to cause a little trouble. Had I been the one to capture Maurice, our positions would be quite reversed. Think on that a bit."

Phineas's ears flattened. "If your goal is to get out of here, you might consider zipping your mouth shut and save the pissing match for later, yes?"

Ion shook his head. "Fine. We'll stall them as best we can."

Melanie threw herself at me and gave me a tight hug. "Be safe," she whispered. "I'll contact you as soon as I can."

"You too," I murmured, lightly shoving her toward Nobu. Without another word, she dug her Contract pad out of her purse and shoved it at Nobu. Wiping his thumb through the gash on his head, he pressed a bloody print upon the paper. He staggered, leaning hard on Ion even as she raised the bow to the strings, hovering above them.

"Where do you want to go, Peacock?" His dark eyes lit up, burning with an intensity that threatened to set the entire place on fire.

"My home," he said. "My people will be able to protect us for a time, I think. Though we can't get there directly via a Door. Get us on the CrossRoads for now. If we can find a safe space until I catch my breath, we can figure it out then."

"I know where." She lifted the violin to her cheek, the first notes already slipping from the strings in a flurry of silver. Corrupted or not, the Wild Magic flooded the coffee shop with an urgency I'd never heard before, Melanie's face flushed with emotion.

I opened my mouth to say something, but Ion clamped a hand on my shoulder, shaking his head. "Let them go," he said, lowering his face to my ear. "We'll only slow them down."

The doorway to the kitchen lit up with a silver brilliance. Without missing a beat, Nobu snatched up Melanie's violin case, going through the motions as though he'd done it a thousand times before. Perhaps he had.

Together, they slipped through the Door to whatever location she'd chosen, leaving only a flurry of sparkling snowflakes in their wake. The music faded with a lingering flourish, leaving Ion and me alone with Phin. The three of us turned toward the front door, waiting.

The usual giveaway that daemons are near is the smell. At least the ones that are fresh from Hell have an odor of sulfur, thick and cloying. So when the scent of rotten eggs rolled under the door to sift through the room, I was not particularly surprised.

My pregnant stomach roiled beneath the taste of it. Ion shimmered, his body blurring into something dark and shadowy. I know without looking that he's transformed into his original shape—midnight black and antlered, cloven hooves and golden eyes. For him to rely on his daemonic form before we had even seen what was chasing Nobu spoke volumes.

"What is it?" A ripple of fear worked its way down my spine.

Ion waved me away, his eyes still fixed on the door. "Shh. Go wait in the back. Whatever is coming, I'd rather it not be aware that you're here."

His jaw locked into place, lion's tail lashing. Brystion might be a daemon, but an incubus isn't meant for fighting. His magic relied on other means.

"The hell I will," I snapped. He turned, his face a mixture of anger and fear, even as whatever it was strode through the door. Ion snatched my shoulders so I was forced to look in his direction.

"Incubus!" The voice rolled the word with an insidious twang, setting my legs to quaking, as though a deep darkness slithered past us like the reptilian tongue of some ancient snake.

"Don't move," Ion breathed at me, his teeth bared in a snarl, the glittering marks on his skin flaring to life. His head lowered in the slightest of bows. "Collector." There was a tight politeness to his demeanor I had never seen before, and it was both fascinating and horrifying all at once.

From the corner of my eye, this mysterious "Collector" came into view. It appeared to be a nebulous shadow, fading in and out of my vision. There was a hint of something made of fangs, an infinite sharpness that reminded me of my shark nightmares: The gullet that can never be filled, will never grow tired, of dead eyes that will never stop searching for its prey, like the weight of a thousand dying infants, lost souls wailing in terror.

The mass giggled, high-pitched and terrible. "Ah, I see there is more than just you here. How droll." The shadow shifted closer, its presence pressing down upon me, as though I were trapped in a coffin, the very air seeming to compress in my lungs.

Phineas trotted across the pie counter, his entire body shimmering in a silvery-white light. The nub of his horn seemed to grow sharper and the air grew lighter. "That's quite close enough," the unicorn snapped. The shadow halted abruptly. "You are not welcome here, no matter what form you take."

"Big words," the darkness sneered, a familiar lilt to its voice. It had grown softer, more feminine. Coaxing and warm. "Perhaps Abby should be the one to decide that? If she'd do me the simple courtesy of facing me."

A shudder ran through me. It was almost the same cadence as my mother's voice, but I'd confronted the memory of her long ago. A daemon wearing her shape was not a new monster to me, by any stretch.

Ion stomped a cloven hoof in warning, and I knew better than to acknowledge whatever this creature was. I shut my eyes instead. Not out of fear per se, but to try to ignore its presence. I couldn't be tempted by what I refused to see. "How does it know my name?" I mumbled.

The answer was a burbling chuckle vibrating through my bones. "My master knows everything about you, Abby Sinclair: Key to the CrossRoads, Dreamer, daughter of True Thomas the Rhymer . . . My master bears you no ill will, given your service in the restoration of Eildon Tree and your subsequent escape from the Devil's Tithe. However," it hissed, "your companion, the Door Maker . . ."

" . . . is becoming vexing." Another voice, one I didn't

recognize, smoothly butted in.

"The Devil's TouchStone," Brystion said, lowering his antlered head a second time. His mouth brushed against my ear. "Stalling for time," he murmured.

"Paganini," I breathed, my jaw tilting slightly to catch a glimpse of the newcomer. I'd only seen him once, when all four Paths met at Eildon Tree to weave it together, growing the new tree in its place. Eildon Tree was the lynchpin to the entire CrossRoads. The very center of it, in fact, four roads stemming from its roots the start of each OtherFolk Path.

Paganini bowed with a little flourish, his mouth curving into a charming smile. "In the flesh," he said, turning toward the shadowy form of the Collector. "You may go. Your presence here will only serve to attract attention we don't need."

"But I was just getting to the good part," it burbled, pouting.

"I insist," pressed Paganini. "Besides, our quarry has gone to ground, and we have no quarrel with these people. So run along. I'll join you soon."

The Collector vanished in a puff of noxious smoke, setting me to gagging. I doubled over, dry heaving as I attempted to not lose my dinner.

"My apologies," said the violinist. "Sometimes the methods are not worth the price."

The incubus bared his teeth in a snarl as he handed me a glass of water. "Whatever he says, do *not* make a bargain with him."

I had no plans to anyway, and sipping the water gave me an excuse not to answer Paganini at all. I studied him over the rim of the glass as he aimlessly walked about the coffee shop, pausing here or there to admire some of the elvish art on the wall.

He was a tall man, lanky by any measure, with shoulder-length wavy hair and a proud nose perched above a sensual set of lips. His gaze grew disdainful when he saw me, his cheek twitching in some personal amusement I wanted no part of.

"What do you want?" Brystion demanded, warily eyeing the violin dangling from the other man's hands. Melanie's fingers had always appeared graceful and strong to me, but Paganini's fingers were monstrously long, almost inhuman.

"Well, the Door Maker, of course," Paganini admitted. "Though that is neither here nor there. And that paramour of hers . . . He's got a bit of a price on his head as well." He stooped and swiftly picked something off the floor. My heart sank as I realized it was one of Nobu's feathers.

No way to feign ignorance now.

"Why?" The question escapes me before I can stop it, blowing right past Ion's impatient tsk. "I thought there was some sort of deal in place."

Paganini's eyes lit up, eerie and sinister, and he twiddled the feather between his thumb and forefinger before tucking it neatly into his waistcoat. For the briefest of breaths, I thought perhaps some other entity was staring out at me, and I swallowed hard. I stepped backward, jumping when I realized I was already pressed up against the counter.

"Well and that may be so." I couldn't quite look away from the mesmerizing way he began to caress the strings with those long fingers. "Tell me, KeyStone. How does that poem by your father go? You know, the one about 'fair Elfland'?"

"What, all of it?" I scoffed. "I'm not going to recite it for you, if that's what you're asking." Even as many times as I'd read it over the years, I probably knew it by heart, but I wasn't sure what he was getting at.

"No, not all of it. Just the important part about the CrossRoads." He was practically purring the words now, and I knew this was some sort of trap. "The verses that talk about the path of righteousness and the thorns and briars and all that sort of nonsense."

Ion shrugged at me, glancing at the place Melanie had made the Door, and I knew he wanted me to keep Paganini busy. The longer we delayed, the longer Melanie would have to escape. Fair enough. I chewed on my lower lip and began:

"O see ye not yon narrow road,
So thick beset wi' thorns and briers?
That is the Path of Righteousness,
Though after it but few inquires.
"And see not ye that braid, braid road,
That lies across the lily leven?
That is the Path of Wickedness,
Though some call it the Road to Heaven.
"And see ye not that bonny—"

My words were cut off with a hideous shriek as Paganini suddenly drew the bow across the strings. Wild Magic dripped from the instrument, but unlike the silver melodies that Melanie captured, this was dark and shadowed and full of evil.

"That one!" he snapped. "The one about the road to Hell. What's so important about it?"

"'Braid, braid road'? It means it's easy to walk. Unlike the road to Heaven, but so what?"

"It isn't," he said softly, sliding the bow against the strings again, coaxing a sound from it that I could only describe as the aborted love child of a train and a chalkboard. I clapped my hands over my ears, my entire body shivering in response.

"Isn't what?" Brystion asked desperately, looking as though he might vibrate straight out of his skin.

"Easy to walk," said Paganini. "Not anymore. Not since *she* changed it." He coughed, his face flushing. "When we restored Eildon Tree. I seem to recall you being there, correct? Each of us took a Path. Melanie should have represented the Mortal Path, as I did for Dark Path of Hell."

"Right," I said slowly. "But I don't understand. Melanie changed the Path to Hell? But how? You were there. The angel Gabriel was there for Heaven. My father was there for the Fae . . . I thought you were all working together to rebuild the tree with the Wild Magic."

"And so we were. Perhaps she herself doesn't know or understand why, but somehow during the weaving of our music she did something to the Path to Hell, and it's a complete— How would you say it now? Clusterfuck? Souls are getting tangled and trapped, daemons are taking a very long time to get their tasks done. In short, Hell is in a sort of hell. Gridlock, I suppose you'd say."

"How ironic," I said, trying to wrap my brain around it.

Phineas snorted. "Well it makes sense, doesn't it? I mean, what's she most terrified of?"

"The deal she made with . . ." My voice trailed away as I looked at Paganini. "Well, you know."

"Right," Phineas said, rolling his eyes. "So use your heads. If you knew you were going to have to end up going someplace you didn't want to be, so much that you were in complete denial about it for years and you had that kind of power? I mean, even if she didn't do it on purpose, she was using the Wild Magic."

"So maybe it was trying to help her by making it so she *couldn't* go there." Ion's upper lip curled at Paganini. "You'd think *He* would keep better track of that sort of thing. I don't recall it being that difficult when I last took that road."

"It wasn't overnight," Paganini admitted. "Things happened slowly enough that none of us noticed until recently. And it seems to be happening faster and faster. Before long it's going to be so overgrown no one will be able to walk it." He shuddered. "The paperwork for this is going to be nearly insurmountable as it is. She needs to undo what has been done."

"You've got access to the Wild Magic," I countered, pointing at his violin. "Why don't you do it?"

"Because I can't," he snapped. "No one can. Only the Door Maker can tap into whatever she did. And she must."

I sipped the rest of my water, resting the glass on the counter. "Why? Seems to me like she's managed to outwit you. She hasn't broken whatever agreement you all had, and unless you specified that she needed to play a certain way when you rebuilt the Paths . . . Well, I'd say she's free and clear."

Brystion squeezed my arm, his clawed fingers almost painfully tight. "That's enough," he said gruffly, as though to hammer the point home. "What do you want from us? The Door Maker is gone, and we have no idea where she went."

"Not that we would tell you, even if we did," I muttered under my breath, earning me another sharp squeeze from the incubus.

Paganini's eyes narrowed. "Listen, we know her violin is breaking down. The magic that holds her soul inside the instrument is unraveling. It was never meant to last as long as it did, so it's rather a bit of a miracle that she's still able to use the thing. Token of her will, I suppose." He pulled out the feather again, looking at it. "Our dear Nobu, so gallant to try to run away with her again, but it's a lost cause. Eventually, the enchantment will wear off, and she will die. Unless she decides to honor her deal with the Devil, that is."

The words stung me hard, but Melanie had her own way of doing things. She always had. I was not going to gainsay her in what was most likely going to be the fight of her life. And certainly not with this douchebag.

"Melanie can do what she likes," I said softly. "It's her

choice. She knows the stakes and so does Nobu, so I can't imagine what it is you expect from me."

Paganini's eyes lit up. "Why a bargain, of course. That's what we do, isn't it? I've heard tell you can open any Door on the CrossRoads. Simply go find her and bring her back." He cocked his head, rubbing his cheek with the edge of his bow. "I suppose you could let me go after her, but I suspect this news would be better accepted if it came from a friend."

I shook my head. "I don't wear the Key to the Cross-Roads anymore. Even if I wanted to, I couldn't do as you ask right now." Technically it was true, even if I knew where it was. But Dark Path OtherFolk knew a lie better than anyone, and I needed to phrase my words very carefully, even if it was to simply omit certain things. After all, I never said I didn't know *where* it was.

He snarled. "Well, then why am I talking to you?"

"Search me. I'm officially retired." I patted my belly, rewarding him with a wan smile. "You know how it is, I'm sure. Off to be a soccer mom or something, right? Although, that does bring up a good point. Did you get permits for bringing that Collector fellow here?"

"Permits . . ." Paganini's voice trailed away in confusion.

"Mmm. Yeah. The entire town of Portsmyth is under the jurisdiction of the Faery Protectorate. That used to be Tali-var, but now it's Roweena du Mont, and I'm pretty sure it's a bit of a no-no to bring a lesser Lord of Hell into town. I mean, the optics of having the Mouth of Sauron waltzing about the farmers market are pretty bad. It has a tendency to muck with the heads of the Muggles, and that leads to a lot of questions."

Paganini backed up before my onslaught of legal jargon, helplessly glancing over at Ion.

The incubus snorted and shrugged. "And now you see why I love her."

"But . . . but . . . the Master insists the Door Maker fix her mistake. Look, if she will at least agree to that, we'll lift the spell on the violin. It won't control the Wild Magic anymore, but her contract with the Master will be null and void. At least let her know what's on the table before she makes a decision."

My eyes narrowed. The phrase "lift the spell" sounded vague enough that it could mean damn near anything. After all, killing her probably would remove the spell too, but without specifics it was hard to determine whether the offer was genuine or not. "I'll be sure to mention it to her when I see her again. Can't make any promises she'll do it, though," I clarified. "But next time, you better come through the proper channels."

"Such as they are," Brystion said.

"Indeed. I shall do so within the hour. By the time approval comes through, that should give you a few days head start to find her. I'll be following up as soon as I can." He frowned, fingers stroking the violin idly. "In the meantime, I suggest you make your plans accordingly, Ms. Abby Sinclair. This was the polite way of asking. Should we meet again under these circumstances, I suspect you will find it much less pleasant."

He turned then, the violin still clasped in his hand and absently tapped the bow upon his knee as though trying to decide something. But in the end, he left.

I sagged into a chair the instant his figure disappeared through the door, cupping my face in my hands. "Nothing like veiled threats for breakfast. Now what?"

Ion shimmered, his glamour returning him to his human form. "Now I head off to the Barras to find Talivar and let him know what's going on. Moira should be told as well. Despite what Paganini said about bargains, word will get out soon enough. Before long, anyone in need of a favor from Hell will be hunting her down."

I crossed my arms. "Charming."

"Despite the fairy tales, the CrossRoads aren't all rainbows and magic sparkles." He gave me a wan smile. "Nobu will make sure the two of them lie low, but I can guess where they'll head."

I crossed my arms. "And that would be . . . ?"

"Japan," Phineas chimed in. "Duh."

I blinked. "Japan?"

"Well, it *is* where Nobu's from originally," Ion pointed out. "He'll have resources there that he wouldn't have access to here."

"So assuming they go to Japan, will they be safe? Except for the whole violin-soul issue," I added.

"'Safe' is a relative word," Ion said, pouring himself a glass of bourbon. I eyed the drink jealously. "But to be fair, I'm not entirely sure. I think they can hide themselves there for a while, but the Paths are fickle things. Sooner or later, the highest bidder will win out. It's simply a question of when." He let out a bitter laugh. "The house always wins, you know."

I shuddered, not wanting to think on it. "So what's the plan? I mean, we can try calling Mel's cell, but I suspect she'll have it turned off. I suppose I could try to reach her in her dreams tonight, but that's assuming we're even asleep at the same time. Failing that . . ." I chewed on my lower lip. "Maybe we'll need the Key, after all."

"No," Ion snapped. "You are not putting on that ridiculous necklace again, not after everything we went through last time. It's safe enough where it is." His eyes flared gold, and he shook his head. "Even if you did put it on, what were you planning to do? Simply head to a country where you don't speak the language, full of an OtherFolk culture you've never seen before, and what? Waltz right through Tokyo asking if anyone knows a guy named Nobu?"

I flushed. "Not really, no."

"Yes, that was exactly what you were going to do." He shook his head. "I don't know. Maybe Kitsune can guide us there. It's her country too."

"So we'll have to go to the Barras regardless," I said.

Brystion gave me a wan smile. "I think you'll be sitting this one out, Abby. You've given up plenty to save them before. This much stress can't be good for you or the baby. Chasing them down on the CrossRoads? No. You can leave that part to me."

"She's my best friend. I can't simply abandon her. Where would I be without her? Where would any of us be?" In my gut, I knew he was right, but that didn't make it any easier.

"Who said anything about abandoning her?" Phineas mumbled into my arm with a yawn. "There's plenty you can do from here, even if it's coordinating everyone else so we're not going in circles."

"All right. Fine. At least, I can contact Roweena and let her know the situation. Maybe I'll stop by the Hallows, see if anyone there might be willing to help."

"I'll head to the Barras," Ion said. "Even if I can't find Talivar there, someone can take the message to Moira and the others. And then you're going to rest, understood?"

I saluted him. "Aye, aye, sir."

"That's 'aye, aye, sexy sir' to you," he said, rewarding me with a sly smile.

A moment later, he had disappeared through the Door, the silver pattern of the CrossRoads illuminating the café for the briefest of heartbeats. I sighed and picked up the phone.

CHAPTER 3

"OH, ABBY! GOOD TO SEE you!" Brandon grinned at me from behind the bar, his tongue lolling out between a set of pearly canines. For a werewolf, the owner of the Hallows was almost amazingly laid-back, but sometimes I couldn't tell if that was really part of his nature or if it was the nearly perpetual doggy grin he was always sporting. And he was only truly laid-back when Katy, his girlfriend, was in town. For now, she was at college, so if his grin grew a bit more strained than usual, it was probably understandable.

I thanked him when he set a glass of ginger ale on the bar in front of me. Thoughtful fellow, as always. I sipped my drink, the other patrons swirling about me in a mix of feathers and glitter, cloven hooves and pointed ears. The music from the sound system thumped in time to the witchlights dotting the ceiling, illuminating everyone in a haze of soft pastels and silver sparkles.

"Seen Charlie anywhere?" I asked him, glancing at my watch. It was about noon now. After Ion had left, I'd texted Roweena du Mont to give her a heads-up, promising to give the full details to her representative as soon as I could. As another human TouchStoned to an OtherFolk lover, Charlie had a lot of experience in such relationships—and she was a dear friend to both me and Melanie. Surely she'd want to know the situation between Melanie and Nobu, even if she didn't have specific advice for the situation.

I would have called her earlier, but I'd crashed for a few hours in my apartment. After working a full shift at the Midnight Marketplace until the wee hours and all the excitement with Paganini, I'd needed a bit of a rest and something to eat.

But the Hallows was definitely the place to go to get and give information, so I'd headed there shortly after I'd awakened. I might not be able to help directly on the CrossRoads, but at least I could try to pass along information to those who could.

Brandon shook his head. "She doesn't stop by much these days. Not since becoming a full-time mother. Babies and bars don't mix."

I rubbed my belly. "Tell me about it."

"Tell you about what?" Robert's thick Boston accent rumbled beside me as the angel slid onto the stool next to mine. "Roweena sent me, by the way. Said you had some information to share?" Blond, blue-eyed, and graced with the body of a powerlifter, Robert was known mostly for his muscle and his explosive temper. He'd been Moira's bodyguard when she had held the position of Protector-ate in Portsmyth, and that had apparently transitioned into something similar for Roweena. He was also Charlie's hus-band and had a lethal streak ten miles wide when it came to protecting her and his son, Benjamin. OtherFolk rela-tionships were nothing if not complicated when it came to mortal paramours.

Brandon's ears flickered with interest. I had briefly men-tioned the Melanie issue to him over the phone but hadn't given him specific details—only that she would most likely be gone for an extended period. She played regularly onstage at the Hallows. I didn't know if she'd had time to cancel any gigs or what, but it couldn't hurt to at least let people know.

He'd seemed unsurprised. Melanie did have a habit of drifting in and out of our lives. In some ways, she'd always been like the sea, and nearly as hard to capture. For as long as I had known her, she'd had secrets. Private scars she didn't show anyone. Whatever she was looking for, I could only hope that one day she would find it. And maybe Nobu would be part of that.

"Paganini's in town. Melanie's in trouble. Nobu's returned from Hell, and they're trying to outrun the Collector." I ticked off my fingers, one at a time as Brandon let out a low whistle. "Oh, and her violin might be broken so she's having problems containing the Wild Magic. How's that for starters?"

The angel's face darkened considerably, and he let out a string of words that were definitely not of the Light Path. The square cut of his jaw tightened. "Did you say the Collector?"

"Shadowy dude. Lots of teeth. Ion wouldn't let me look at him when Paganini showed up at the Marketplace." I rattled off the story, pretending not to notice as his knuckles began popping when he suddenly balled them into a tight fist, then slammed it against the bar hard enough to rattle the walls.

"Paganini can do what he likes. He's a dick, but he's mortal, so Devil's TouchStone or not, as long as he's not directly being an asshole, there's not much I can do. But to send the Collector?" He looked ill. "That's a serious breach of protocol. Roweena is gonna be pissed."

He snarled something else under his breath, and I was rather glad I was no longer part of the Protectorate dynamic. "What about Melanie?" He shook his head. "It's unfortunate, but I don't think we can interfere. She has a contract with the Devil, and it's no different from sending metaphysical repo men. The Collector aside, there's definitely going to be a fine imposed."

"Well, shit," I muttered. Somehow I'd been hoping for a bit more of an emotional reaction than that. Melanie had been his friend too.

He laid a meaty hand on my shoulder. "That's the official position. Unofficially . . . well, I'll see if I can't knock a few heads together and slow Paganini down a bit. Without being too obvious," he added as if he'd read my mind. "Roweena will understand if I'm discreet about it. I'll tie him up with paperwork."

"Best I can hope for, I guess. Not much else I can do but wait." I flicked my glass in irritation.

"In your condition, that's not a bad thing," Robert pointed out gently. "Charlie wants to throw you a baby shower, by the way. And she's got some things of Benjamin's that she can pass on to you, if you're interested."

"All right. I'll give her a call later," I said as he stood and gave my shoulder a squeeze.

"Sounds good. I'll get back to Roweena and let you know if there's anything else you need to do. If you see that Paganini asshole again, call me. I mean it." His eyes blazed in fury. Robert and I hadn't always gotten along, but there was something reassuring about having him on my side this time.

He gave me a sharp nod of farewell and slipped into the dancing crowd and out the front door. I sipped my ginger ale, wincing at the sharp sting scuttling across my ankle. "Really?"

"About time you noticed me," Phin piped up from the floor. "I've been trying to get your attention for the last five minutes."

"You didn't have to resort to biting, jackhole." I rubbed at my ankle. "A simple nudge would have been enough."

"I could have bitten your ass," he noted sourly, his ears perking up when he flagged down Brandon. "Whiskey," he demanded, humming when the werewolf poured him a small bowl.

"Little early to be partaking, don't you think?"

"Speak for yourself." He shuddered. "If I have to deal with whatever shitstorm is coming—and there will be one, I'm sure—I have no plans to do it sober."

"Another apocalypse in the making. Sounds like a Tuesday," I said ruefully. "But I get what you mean."

"I don't know." He shoved his muzzle into the bowl for a deep drink, tongue lapping up the droplets around his whiskers. "Something feels wrong somehow. Like it's all ending."

"Or maybe it's beginning," I mused, rolling my palm over my stomach. For all that I'm not technically showing, I can feel it, as if my skin doesn't seem quite as flat as it used to be. To imagine myself toward the end was terrifying, if I admitted it to myself.

As for the thought of being a mother . . . I wavered between horror and elation, not knowing if I could even manage it. Oh, I'd done well enough looking after Benjamin for those long months last year, but this was different.

"Ah, yes. Sorry about that." Phineas had the grace to at least look a bit chagrined at his words. "I keep forgetting."

Digging through my coat, I pulled out my phone, but there were no calls or texts from Melanie. Not surprising. The signal on the CrossRoads was notoriously spotty.

I called her again anyway, hanging up when it went to voice mail. "It's like watching a technological pot trying to boil. And about as useful."

"Speaking of useful technology . . ." Brandon said, his ears sheepish.

"Oh gods, now what?" Brandon and Katy had started a small TouchStone-matching service last year. Business had been up, from what I had heard, particularly when the queen of Faerie had closed the CrossRoads completely.

Cut off from the source of magic they needed to survive, OtherFolk had been fading at a remarkably fast rate until they could be TouchStoned to a mortal.

"Well, we were thinking of expanding into dating apps. Not necessarily between mortal and OtherFolk, though. As a bartender, I hear a lot of stories of lonely people, and well . . . you know."

"I don't, but I'm sure I will shortly. How is this going to work?"

"Probably a lot like that Tinder thing. Swipe left or right—very simple. Although ideally, I'd want it to be a bit more in depth than a picture. Glamours and what not tend to make things complicated sometimes, and not every magical creature is compatible with every other."

"Speak for yourself," Phineas said, sniffing.

"Well, you're an outlier," I said. "And there's no accounting for *your* taste."

"I wouldn't brag." He waggled his beard at me, and I let it go. I supposed he was right, though I'd never proclaimed an interest in banging wombats or hedgehogs.

"So what's this magical app going to be called? And how do I tie into it?" I took another sip of ginger ale, waiting for the other shoe to drop.

"Well, I thought we might call it Finder," Brandon started. "But I'm not sure if that would be too derivative."

"*Phinder*, you mean." Phineas stood up, his eyes very bright as he stared the werewolf down. "It's only fair since I'm a silent partner in all this."

I blinked. "Wait, what?"

"I put up the cash for the first few iterations," the unicorn mumbled, looking away quickly. "And I made a lot of suggestions. A *lot*. It's only fair that the product bears my name in some fashion, and I rather like the play on words, don't you? Like Tinder . . . but more *me*."

I pinched the bridge of my nose. "Okay. And what else?"

"Well, I was kind of hoping you might give us a shout-out. Or maybe a little commercial on YouTube. You know, a TouchStone's seal of approval?" Brandon was talking very fast now, and I felt a small vein explode on the side of my face.

"I hardly think a pregnant woman is what you want for the face of your fuck app." I tried to keep the edge out of my voice, but I was pretty sure I was failing.

"Well, no, that's the nice thing. I mean, cross-species fertilization . . ."

"And whose idea was *that*, I wonder." My eyes slid over to where Phineas had been sitting. The unicorn was tiptoeing off the barstool and onto the dance floor, the white tuft of his lion's tale slipping into the crowd.

"We didn't mean any disrespect, Abby," Brandon said softly.

"I don't know . . . I don't have any objections to your app, but I don't want anything to do with the marketing. And I don't think Talivar would be too keen on it either." I paused. "Brystion might, but he's an incubus so anything to do with sex is probably fine. On the other hand—"

Someone tugged at my arm, interrupting my words. "Oi, Absinthe."

A smile broke over my face when I saw the little pig-man stooping beside the barstools. "Jimmy!"

I'd met Jimmy Squarefoot some time ago on the Cross-Roads. He'd rescued me, in fact, and we'd formed a rather interesting friendship after that. I didn't normally see him outside the Barras, and certainly not since Eildon Tree had been restored. His sudden appearance here wasn't a particularly good sign.

A quick check of my phone showed nothing from either Ion or Talivar, or anyone else for that matter, though time did pass differently on the CrossRoads.

Unease rippled in my gut, my smile fading away. "Everything all right, Jimmy?" Now that I took a closer look, he did look a bit paler than usual, his pig's snout trembling something awful.

"I'm so sorry to bother ye here, but I'm afraid there's somewhat trouble at the Barras. Thought it might be best if ye came directly."

Dread swept over me. "What's going on?"

His beady little eyes looked up at me, full of a shaking sort of terror. "The Barras . . ." He snuffled. "It's been destroyed."

I blinked, my head cocked as though I hadn't heard him quite right. "What?"

"The Barras." His voice trembled, his hand clenching mine tightly. "It's . . . it's gone. I came as soon as I could use the noon Doors. King Talivar ordered it," Jimmy said dully, a tear rolling down his bristled cheek. "The Door Maker," he sobbed. "She destroyed it."

"That's impossible." My brain struggled sluggishly with this bit of information. "Melanie loves the Barras—and she would never do something like that even if she didn't."

"I don't know." Jimmy swallowed hard. "They were arguing, her and that winged fellow, and then Talivar was there, and the next minute . . . the next minute she pulls out that violin and starts playing it. We thought she was making a Door, ye ken? But the music was wrong." He clapped his gnarled fingers over his pig ears. "All wrong. Discordant and awful. And then there was this great noise. Like the wind screaming. But it was the tents and the homes, the wood cracking like bones."

"Little pig, little pig, let me come in," Brandon murmured, earning him a sharp look from me. He flushed.

"I passed out, I think. I don't know. I don't remember much after that, but when I woke up, everything was just .

. . gone." Jimmy stared blankly ahead, eyes unfocused.

My stomach roiled, and for a few seconds I wanted to puke. Melanie wouldn't have done something like this—not on purpose. But watching her play yesterday, the way she had to fight the Wild Magic . . .

I shoved the memory away, something snapping in my brain as I tried to keep the rising panic down. I needed to get to the Barras first to take stock of what happened. Pregnant or not, I wasn't going to sit here and wait when they needed me. "What about the people? Kitsune?" With the TouchStone bonds between me, Ion, and Talivar, surely if something had happened to them I would have known, but the others . . .

"They're all right. But I think ye should go there. We need yer wisdom. Please," he begged. "I'll take ye there."

"I hardly think I have anything to offer that constitutes wisdom," I said, wondering what sort of shitshow I'd be walking into. I sucked in a deep breath. "But I'll do my best. Give me a chance to round up Phineas."

"Don't take too long, Absinthe." The pig-man rubbed his eyes.

I gestured at Brandon. "Get him anything he wants and put it on my tab. And, I don't know, maybe a couple of sandwiches for the road?" His golden eyes darted between me and Jimmy, but he nodded.

I ducked through the crowd of OtherFolk, narrowly escaping being elbowed by a centaur trying to dab, heading for the bathroom first. Pregnancy and peeing went hand-in-hand, and I could hardly drink anything these days without it running straight through me.

"Plans, plans," I mumbled to myself as I finished up in the stall. If what Jimmy said was true, there would be a lot of displaced and injured OtherFolk, and not the sort who everyone would necessarily welcome with open arms.

Moira's kingdom might not take them in. The Barras was

part of the Unseelie Court, and it and the Seelie Court were about as compatible as oil and water, to be cliché.

So where would they go? Obviously, it would be more Talivar's decision than mine, but it wouldn't be a bad thing to look at setting up some shelters here, just in case. With doctors or a Faery healer or whatever.

I was still pondering the reality of such logistics when I made my way to the bar. I glanced toward the dance floor in time to see Phin waggling his beard at one of the many nymphs twirling about. She sniffed and turned on her heel, giggling at one of her friends as they moved closer to the center. The unicorn looked a bit dejected, but Phin shook himself, his face perking up when he saw me.

"Come on." I scooped him into my arms before he had a chance to say anything. "We have to go. There's an emergency at the Barras."

He frowned, but whatever he was going to say died away when he saw Jimmy pounding shot after shot at the bar. Brandon gave me a look of desperation. "He's, uh, ready to go, I think," the werewolf said. "I'm already out of my stock of whiskey for the next week and he's not showing signs of stopping."

"On it," I said. "You have those sandwiches?"

His wide-eyed stare focused on Jimmy again and he coughed out an affirmation. I placed my hand on Jimmy's shoulder. "Come on, Jimmy. You can't guide me if you're drunk, right?" Inside, I couldn't help but wonder how bad the damage at the Barras was. I'd been at Eildon Tree when the thing blew up, but even aside from that level of horror, it's still shocking to have your home destroyed.

Spittle foaming at the corner of the pig-man's mouth. "Aye, Absinthe. I'm sorry. It's just . . . I'm just trying to shut it out a bit, that's all."

His nose quivered when Brandon thrust the bag of sandwiches at me. I wanted to let Jimmy carry them, but I suspected if I did so, they'd be gone in fairly short order, so I tucked them into my hobo purse instead.

I exhaled sharply and gestured at Brandon. "Can you pass on a message for me? I need you to contact Robert or Roweena. It wouldn't hurt to set up a triage at the Portsmyth Catholic Church, like we did when the Cross-Roads shut down. Hopefully we won't need it, but . . ."

"Better safe than sorry," Brandon agreed, picking up his phone. "I'm on it. Let me know if you need anything else."

"Thanks." Jimmy's porcine face was miserable. "Where's the nearest Door?"

Brandon gestured at us. "Come on. This way."

"But your bar . . ."

"I do have employees, you know," he pointed out. "It's not like I run this place completely automated or anything. I'll call Roweena when I get back."

The werewolf whistled someone over to his side—a vampire, I guessed, based on his lack of reflection in the mirror behind him. I didn't like vampires much, but this one at least appeared to be professional as he smoothly slid behind the bar, patting down his apron and rewarding me with a quiet smile.

Brandon crossed his arms in satisfaction. "We'll use the Door in my private office. Fewer questions that way."

The three of us followed him across the dance floor, Jimmy clutching my sleeve as he stumbled beside me. The thumping of the music seemed to disorient him, or maybe it was the alcohol. Brandon didn't pay any attention to any of it, ushering us through a locked door next to the restrooms and shutting it quickly behind us.

I'd never been in Brandon's office before so I wasn't sure what to expect, but it was almost disappointing in its normalcy. At least for a werewolf. Just the usual office stuff—laptop, sagging couch, posters of . . . wolves on the wall.

Was that a nature appreciation thing? Or the werewolf equivalent of *Sports Illustrated Swimsuit*? I stifled a shudder and decided I didn't want to know. If Katy was cool with it, that was all that mattered.

Brandon cocked an ear. "All those short-term Contracts with Mel made me lazy. It was way easier to have her simply make a Door that went where I wanted to go, you know? Ah, well." He tapped on the edges of a closet, the entrance flaring to life with a shimmer of silver.

"I didn't even know this Door was here," Phineas said.

"Ah, it's more of an escape room than anything," Brandon explained. "I had it installed after I started dating Katy . . . Well, that and after my bar was nearly destroyed—*twice*. Had to take a second mortgage out on this place to pay for it, but if it provides us a bit more safety, well, it's worth it."

"You could have asked Moira to do it. I'm sure she would have been happy to, especially since she paid for all the other renovations," I said. And it was true: Moira had inadvertently been part of the reason the bar had gotten partially destroyed a few years ago. Whatever else she was, the Faerie princess was very good at paying her debts.

Brandon's lips pulled back in a snarling, lopsided smile. "Ah, well. There's such a thing as owing the Fae a little too much, you know. The bar was fair, so I took her offer. But this . . . this is personal. And I'd like it to stay that way."

"You mean you don't want anyone else to know about it," Phineas said, snorting.

"Maybe that too," the werewolf admitted. "Let's go."

He waved us across the threshold, and I stepped through, still holding Jimmy's trembling hand. Phin tapped along at our heels and Brandon brought up the rear.

Walking through Doors never got old for me. No matter how nonchalant the OtherFolk were about it, the ripple of cold magic that shunted over my skin, illuminating us all in crystalline haze so that everything glowed, my hair lighting up like a tree on Christmas . . .

It was over in seconds, and then we were standing upon the silver-dusted cobblestones of the CrossRoads.

Brandon craned his neck and pointed at the road in front of us. "All right, then. If you follow that path, it will eventually take you to the Borderlands. As for the Barras . . . I'm not entirely sure where they are right now." He tapped Jimmy on the shoulder. "Do you?"

The Barras moved every day, traveling along the Cross-Roads in some magical fashion that made it rather difficult to pin down. That was one of its defense mechanisms, according to Talivar. Being mostly made up by the remnants of the Unseelie Court and other "undesirables" meant that it was a ripe target for Faerie's wrath. And given that it had already been destroyed once, the moving part at least made it more difficult to stage a coordinated attack.

Jimmy blinked his dark, piggish eyes at me as though suddenly realizing he'd been asked a question. "Aye," he mumbled. "I ken where it was when I left it. I don't ken if it can still move, to be honest."

"Jesus, Jimmy." A renewed wave of horror washed over me.

He refused to speak after that, and we were left to follow in his footsteps in silence. I picked up Phin out of habit, clutching him tightly against me. Normally he would have said something rude, but this time, he simply let me hug him. He knew I was heartsick, though I was doing my best not to show it. Not only for Talivar's, Ion's, and Kitsune's sakes, but to think that my best friend would have been capable of such a thing?

"That can't be right," I said. "I won't believe it until I can talk to her. There must a be a reason . . ."

"A reason to destroy the home of thousands of innocents? Aye, I cannot wait to hear it." Jimmy sniffed, blinking back another round of tears.

I didn't know what else to say, so I followed along, my sandals scuffing silver dust along the path until my toes were nearly coated with it. My thoughts churned like mad hamster wheels that spun and spun, but I still couldn't come up with a reason why Melanie would do something like this.

"Nobu," I whispered to myself. They were half-mad for each other as it was. With his escape from Hell and the two of them on the run, what wouldn't she do to save him?

The thought terrified me.

I nearly bumped into Jimmy and realized we'd slowed down. I moved to avoid a piece of debris on the road, my ankle wobbling.

Phin wriggled out of my arms. "You don't need me weighing you down. Pay attention to the path." He kicked at a bit of wood, sending it skittering into the grass.

His tone came off far brusquer than I would have expected from him, and I could only imagine what was running through his mind. In some ways, his silence on the matter was far more frightening than his usual sarcastic or perverted remarks.

I smelled the smoke long before we came across the Barras. But it wasn't the normal scent I would have associated with a regular fire. This was oily and full of—

"Magic," Phineas said. "The air is thick with it. We're going to have to get it cleaned up, or it will start attracting things best left unseen."

I thought of Paganini and his pet daemon, and I shuddered. The last thing I wanted was another encounter with him—or something worse. Though the Unseelie Court was filled with malevolent creatures as well, it was unlikely they'd do anything to destroy their own homes.

As we rounded a gentle bend in the road, a bit of greenery flushed up on both sides, and I knew we were about to leave the CrossRoads. The smoke was cloying, though a stiff breeze was doing its very best to move it along. Normally, there would be a cacophony of sound by now: Voices shouting, animals, children, sellers, and buyers, stray bits of music threading through the crowds. Not to mention the scents of various foods, herbs, and perfumes that were usually in the air . . . In short, chaos.

But now there was barely any sound at all, only a lone sob rising and falling.

"Banshee," Brandon said quietly. "Try not to make eye contact if we see her."

"Yikes. No thanks." I placed my hand on my belly almost instinctively.

We left the path as we drew closer to the Barras, debris scattered over the road like the cast-off bones of some dead animal. Something soft squelched under my feet, but I tried not to look too closely at it, keeping my face resolutely pointed in the direction we were walking.

OtherFolk emerged from the haze, staggering past us as they search through the wreckage all around us. Their faces were hollow, eyes blank, and skin smudged. I let out a soft cry when I saw one of the silkworm ladies who had helped me out on my first trip here—or had helped the Faery Court, anyway, and that was near enough. She was lying on her side, her sister weeping next to her.

I stepped toward them, ready to lay a hand upon the weeping woman's shoulder, but Phin let out a warning grumble. The silkworm raised her head, milky tears streaming down her face, but her expression was empty, as though she wasn't seeing me at all.

"You should have been here," she said finally. "If you had been a proper consort, a proper queen, you would have been here."

The words punched me in the gut with all the grace of a sledgehammer. "I'm sorry." I didn't know what else to say or whether her accusations were warranted or not, but now was not the time to make a fuss about it. Not that I had any idea what I could have done about it, but grief makes you lash out. Everything and everyone becomes a target.

She turned away, dismissing me with a wave of her antennae.

I swallowed against a heavy lump in my throat and let Jimmy lead us through the growing crowd. Before long, we were in the middle of it all with pixies sorting through rubble, insect-men chewing through broken huts looking for survivors, bloody clothes, and horrendous injuries everywhere.

My nostrils flared. This was far worse than I'd thought. "Brandon," I murmured. "When you get back, please get ahold of Roweena *immediately*. We're going to need more than a temporary shelter beneath the church. This is . . . This is . . ."

"I'm on it," he said grimly. "I'll do a blood drive or something at the Hallows too. We're going to need a lot of it and from a lot of different species."

"You'd think we could get some Faery healers out this way—Talivar should be working on that." I sighed, but I knew it would be a bit of a long shot. Far too much bad blood between the two Courts to set aside for the mere evisceration of an entire community.

"You think I haven't tried?" Talivar emerged from between the remainder of two food stalls, his one good eye bloodshot from the smoke. I threw myself at him, a wave of hopelessness sweeping over me as I took in the devastation around us. He pressed his mouth to the top of my head, his arms tight around me. His heart hammered against me, matched by the pulse at his neck to give lie to his outward calmness.

"I'm sorry," I whispered. "I'm so, so sorry."

He hugged me tighter, as though he couldn't quite manage words, his body going perfectly still. I knew he was pushing down whatever emotions he was feeling to deal with later, and he wrapped his royalty around him like a cloak. "I've sent word to the Seelie Court multiple times. So far they've only sent a token group—not nearly enough for everyone here."

I frowned, still trying to make sense of it all. "I can't believe Moira would do that. If you want, I can go ask her directly?" I didn't exactly relish the thought of visiting Faerie proper, but I'd do it if it would help these people.

He shook his head. "It's not Moira's doing. My mother still retains some control, and the councilors are easily swayed. Moira is the one who sent the few we do have; I imagine she'll be sending more as she can, but this is the best she can do right now."

"I'm on it." The werewolf shivered briefly, his human form melting away into a gray wolf. Without a sound, he loped away in the direction we had come, slipping into the smoky shadows.

I took Talivar's arm. "He's going to talk to Roweena. I've asked that the Portsmyth Council offer the church as sanctuary."

Relief flashed over his face. "That will be no small thing. Roweena is formidable in her own right. And while she will not work directly against the queen, I think she will manage to at least assist us. Simply having the shelter will be a big step; at least I would have somewhere to send those who are too badly injured to be healed here."

"And what should I do, Majesty?" Jimmy Squarefoot bowed his head before his king. It made my heart hurt to look at him. Even in his misery, he was still willing to follow Talivar's command.

Talivar looked at him gravely. "Arise, Jimmy. Does that snout of yours still work, even in all this smoke?"

Jimmy nodded. "Aye. It's yours, for whatever it's worth."

"Thank you, Jimmy," Talivar replied. "Now, there's a tri-age tent set up on the far side. Go there and ask the healers if they need anything—herbs or whatnot. If you can procure them, sniff them out on the hillside or the forest, whatever you can do."

Jimmy bowed again. "Aye, Majesty. I'll check in later." He snuffled once and then squeezed my hand. "Absinthe." And then he was gone, shuffling away with a snorting sneeze.

Talivar rubbed his temples. "It won't be much, but he needs to keep busy until things are sorted out. Afterward we'll have a funeral, I guess."

I blinked back a wave of tears as I reached up to place my palm against his cheek. He captured my hand, closing his eye for a moment. "Maybe if I had been here . . ."

"No." He shook his head, kissing my knuckles. "No. It's better you were not. This isn't even the worst of it. Kitsune took the brunt of the attack herself. She's injured, Abby. Very, very badly. Ion is with her now. I came out to look for help." His mouth curved into a faint smile. "And here I've found you."

Phin stood beside my ankles, and I nudged him. "Any chance you can take a look?"

The unicorn grimaced. "I can, but it will probably be at least a hundred years before I recover the power to resurrect people from the dead. I used up that shot on you."

"Understood." Talivar held out his hand to me. "Let's go see her, and then we can try to figure something out."

CHAPTER 4

THE FOX-WOMAN LAY ON HER side upon whatever was left of a futon beneath the ragged remains of a tent. One furred ear was shredded almost beyond recognition, the burns on her face were an angry red, and the silk of her kimono was in tatters. But even aside from that, a dark-greenish color oozed beneath the skin of her abdomen like a living, rippling bruise. The hair from the right side of her head was gone, and her skull seemed to press against the burns as though it were trying to escape. I clapped a hand to my mouth, turning away as I dry heaved.

"Why did you bring her here?" Ion snapped from where he was soaking bandages in what appeared to be an herb-based concoction in a bronze pot. A stout little Faery woman clucked at him, stirring the pot with a wooden spoon, and he frowned at her. "I'm going as fast as I can. Leave off."

I sank to my knees beside Kitsune. "Is she awake?"

"No. Whatever she did to try to stop Melanie must have backfired because it hit her full on and knocked her out." Talivar exhaled sharply. "It's probably a blessing to be honest. The pain must be horrifying."

I studied the ravages of his face, wondering if he was remembering his own torture by his father, which had left him with permanent scars on his body.

"Where is Melanie now?" I asked it quietly, and yet it felt as though my voice had somehow pierced the space inside the tent. From the way they both flinched, you'd have thought I had bellowed the words off a cliff.

"Well, she . . . That is, Nobu . . ." Talivar began, giving a helpless glance to Ion.

Brystion caught my gaze with his, without even a hint of irony or gold to be seen. "She came here to ask Kitsune for help. I don't know the specific details, but when Kitsune refused, Melanie used the Wild Magic to attack her. The destruction of the Barras was accidental, I think. Maybe an offshoot of whatever magic Kitsune had used to deflect the attack." His voice was emotionless and matter-of-fact, as though he merely recited a passage from a book, but even so, it was far shakier than I'd ever heard it.

"But surely—" My voice cracked around a thick sob stuck in my throat, icy horror taking root in my spine, spreading through my belly. I shook my head in denial. "No. Not Melanie. It's impossible."

"No, Abby. I was here. I saw it happen. There was no mistake." He sighed, his face troubled. "Melanie attacked Kitsune with the Wild Magic. There's no way to simply explain it away."

I sank onto what was left of Kitsune's tea table, my legs somehow suddenly unable to support me. "That's not possible," I whispered. "She would never do something like that."

Brystion wet another rag to press upon Kitsune's forehead. "I think," he said carefully, "that we really have no idea what she can or can't do. I suspect whatever power she has via that violin has been rather violently suppressed over the last few years, and now that she's been backed into that last corner, it's exploding out of her." His lips pressed together grimly. "At least that is the only rational explanation I can come up with that doesn't make me want to puke."

The words sat there like lead weights sinking into my gut. I hadn't wanted to consider it like that. And part of me still didn't. Still wouldn't until I saw her with my own eyes, asked her with my own mouth, heard her with my own ears.

I could only hope I would get the chance to do so.

"Let's concentrate on what we can actually do, shall we?" Phineas wriggled onto my lap. "Woolgathering is for when we have the luxury of time, and that is something she doesn't have at all."

"Of course." I flushed, nudging Brystion gently with my foot. "What is that . . . thing under her skin?" Kitsune's abdomen now pulsed with a sinister purple miasma that swirled like a miniature whirlpool, small red-tipped fingers arcing out in various directions.

"I don't know. When I found her . . . after, she was unconscious. Obviously, she's been burned, but beside that and a broken wrist, it's hard to say." Brystion's eyes softened, and he reached out to squeeze my hand. "Are you all right? You look awfully pale."

I waved him off. "Fine. I'll be fine."

Phin reared up on his hind legs to get a better look at Kitsune, his nostrils flaring wide as he sniffed the swirling bruise, wrinkling his nose. "That's not a normal wound. Some kind of corruption, I think. Almost like there's magic trapped inside her. It looks like it's trying to get out."

"Can you fix it?" I already knew the answer would be no when I asked it, and he would have said something snarky about it, if he could have. But when Phineas was fully serious . . .

He shook his head. "Maybe if my horn were restored fully. Proof against death and all that, you know. But as it stands now? No." He poked at the darkening skin with a cloven hoof, the color retreating from his touch. Kitsune moaned in her sleep, and he immediately withdrew it.

"See that? We fuck with it too much and it's probably going to kill her."

I stared at the woman in abject misery. "So what do we do? Everything's a mess, and I don't even know where to start to try to make things right."

"Well technically, you already have," Phineas pointed out. "Roweena will step up, I'm sure, and Brandon will spread the word. Talivar has some healers here. If we can gather everyone and move them to the church in Portsmyth temporarily, that will at least be something."

"There's an awful lot of property here to sift through. I'm not sure everyone will want to go anywhere," Ion pointed out.

"Their choice." Phineas waggled his beard. "There will undoubtedly be looters coming along at some point, but that's something for Talivar to figure out. It's his kingdom, after all."

"Indeed." Talivar gestured to an old elvish woman who had waddled into view with a little flourish. "Madam Twinkle was one of Faerie's best healers in the old days. Moira managed to pull some strings to get her temporarily out of retirement."

I blinked at the name but said nothing. The Fae could be rather fickle when it came to names. I doubted it was her real one, but it didn't matter. She was short and squat, her face a flat pile of wrinkles, and one eye was milky with cataracts.

I'd thought Roweena was the oldest Fae I'd ever seen, but this woman wasn't even pretending to be anything other than ancient.

She trundled forward toward Kitsune, snapping her fingers so that a ball of witchlight burst from her palm. Carefully, she walked around the futon, never touching it, but made lots of *hmmms* from deep in her throat. When she saw the moving bruise, she paused, her hands hovering above it.

A ripple of blueish-white color slipped from her fingertips, bathing the fox-woman's skin. The bruise stopped wriggling as though it was encased in the icy power. Madame Twinkle grunted and continued her examination, but this time she touched Kitsune, carefully checking her joints, pressing her hands along her body.

Each time she paused, a bit of power seemed to drain from her, but I could see the effect it had on Kitsune. By the time Madame Twinkle was done, the burns were fading, a bit of new fur was growing on the tattered ear, and the swelling in her wrist had gone down.

The old woman sagged with a groan. "That is all that I can do. The superficial wounds will heal well enough on their own, but as to the rest of it . . ." She shook her head. "Magic that has become corrupted is not easy to undo. And this wound was caused by Wild Magic. The best I could do was seal it away for a time. But even that will not be enough. Eventually, it will kill her."

Talivar inclined his head gratefully. "You have my thanks," he said. "Anything you ask for will be yours, should I have the power to grant it."

Madame Twinkle grunted, gently slapping his crippled leg. "Should have called me when your father did that to you instead of sulking off somewhere. I've never forgiven him for that, you know. Or myself. Consider this a repayment of sorts."

Talivar inclined his head gravely. "As you will, Lady Healer."

I reached out to stroke Kitsune's forehead, marveling at the brightness of the new skin. "So what now? Will she wake?"

"If she is strong enough," the old Fae said, picking up her satchel. "But more than that, I cannot say. I have done what

I can. Let me see if there are others I might assist."

"Of course. We've set up a triage in what's left of the main part of the Hive. I'll escort you there." Talivar held his arm out to her.

"Pish. I know my way around the Barras, boy. I'll find it. Just send me some whiskey later. I suspect I'll need it." She paused, her eyes narrowing at me. "Remember to eat, milady. Your baby will thank you for it."

"Yes, ma'am," I demurred. She stumped off, grumbling something beneath her breath. Talivar stared after her ruefully, and I shrugged. "But more to the point, we need to find Melanie—or at least find out where she went."

"You'll forgive me if I'm not particularly interested in tracking her down right now," Talivar said darkly. "My people need me, and Melanie . . . is going to have to handle her own problems."

I bit my lower lip, tasting blood. "I know. I'm sorry."

"I suppose the Wild Hunt is always an option," Talivar mused, though his eye flashed miserably as he said it.

"Only as a last resort." I exhaled sharply, hoping it would never come to that. A mystical hunting party made up of magical white hunting dogs and black horses with unknown riders, the Wild Hunt was a tool of the Unseelie Court. Once started, the Wild Hunt could not stop until it caught its quarry. Talivar had taken on the burden of leading the Hunt to try to capture Maurice months ago, but the price for such power was steep, and the magic that allowed the Hunt to exist would eventually kill him. It would have killed him by now, but during Eildon Tree's re-creation, all magic stemming from the CrossRoads had been reset, including the Hunt, giving Talivar a second chance. But I would be happy to never see the Wild Hunt again.

"What about that mixed military group Kitsune was working on? What was it called? TouchStone Tactical? You know, the one that was pairing military TouchStones to likeminded OtherFolk? Do we have a way to reach anyone from there?" I gestured at the wreckage all around us. "If nothing else, they could help provide protection to the property here and maybe assist in some of the cleanup."

"That was definitely Kitsune's project. She handled all the day-to-day operations. I don't know how I'd even contact any of them at this point." Talivar gestured at the devastation around us. "Any records she was keeping were probably destroyed. Besides, if they're deployed all over the world, it might be hard to manage."

When the Midnight Marketplace still existed as a storefront selling exotic goods, I'd traded some magical contraband to Kitsune in return for her help against Maurice. It was the same combination that had allowed me to accidentally enchant my iPod, and she'd melded that magic with mundane human technology, allowing for firearms and weapons of a mortal caliber to become available to the citizens of the Barras, but only in limited circumstances. Guns and bullets tended not to do nice things to Fae magic, so my understanding was that they didn't live directly at the Barras but were stationed somewhere in the human world. If I had to guess, Kitsune was essentially creating a standing army reserve that wasn't part of the Barras but could be called in, if needed, without raising the suspicion of the Seelie Court. But unless we could contact them, it wouldn't do us much good.

"I suppose it's foolish to think you could just, I don't know, toss up a Bat Signal or something?" The elf king stared at me blankly, and I sighed. I forgot sometimes that he wasn't overly familiar with American pop culture. "Never mind."

My head swirled, and I suddenly slumped, giving Ion a thankful smile when he thrust a cup of water into my hand. "Drink," he commanded. "I'll see if I can find something for you to eat."

I waved him off, digging in my purse. "No, no. Brandon made us sandwiches." We devoured them quick enough, leaving me with little else but to stare mournfully at the empty bag afterward.

I sat on the ground between Ion and Talivar, my shoulders resting against both their arms. Somehow my hands crept into theirs, the three of us leaning on one another as we tried to process everything that had happened. An echo of sadness pinged through my bones in bitter tempo with the Banshee stalking the grounds, wailing as though her heart might break.

"Abby . . ."

I came to with a jerk. Somewhere along the way, I must have fallen asleep and someone had covered me with a coat. Ion's. But the ground made for a poor mattress, and my joints were stiff as I sat up, my name sounding harsh and guttural.

Kitsune.

I lurched upward, my eyes widening when I saw the fox-woman struggling to rise.

"Wait, wait. You've been injured," I babbled at her, reaching to find a bottle of water from my purse. Phineas stood from where he'd been leaning against me. I handed Kitsune the water, kneeling by her side to help her sit. "How are you feeling?"

She cracked the lid from the bottle and took a long pull, breaking into a fit of coughing almost immediately. "Like the floor of a taxicab? Is that how you mortals say it?"

I snorted. "Something like that. Do you remember what happened?"

"Oh, aye," she retorted grimly. "I remember. The Door Maker was here with that . . . *baka* shinigami of hers. He should know better than to come to me."

"Idiot shini-what?" I blinked, trying to remember what little rudimentary Japanese I'd learned from watching anime over the years.

"Shinigami," Kitsune said. "And it's what he is."

"He told us he was a fallen angel," I said, turning toward Ion. "Did you know?"

The incubus shrugged. "Angel. Shinigami. They both have wings, right? What difference does it make?"

Kitsune gave him a wilting stare. "It's a bit more complicated than that, but there isn't a direct comparison between mythologies. Fallen angel is good enough for the moment and we'll leave it at that."

"All right then, but I don't understand. What did they want?" This discussion was making my head hurt, and I needed answers.

"An escape, of course. One only I can currently provide." Her smile became thin and feral. "Not that they could use it. And not that I would allow them to. There is a price for my help, as you well know."

Ion emerged from the smoky haze, carrying a pile of rubble on his shoulders. "And she wouldn't pay it? That doesn't sound like her."

"Destroying the Barras doesn't sound like her either," Phin retorted. I whirled on him, and he flattened his ears. "I'll go find Talivar," he said, trotting off.

"You do that," I said, glaring until he disappeared behind a pile of smoldering planks. "So what was this escape? I can't imagine she needed a Door, seeing as she can make them whenever she's TouchStoned."

"Not a Door," Kitsune said, pulling on what was left of her tent so the cloth shredded, whisking away into the smoke. The tent frame was the only thing left standing, and the entrance was shaped like . . .

"That's a—" I stared at the arch across what was left of

the doorframe, shining in the haze in a deep, blood-orange color. I'd seen them in pictures before, of course, but never in real life. "A torii gate?"

"A *Gate*," she agreed. "Like a Door, but they don't work the same, so her Wild Magic didn't affect it, you see. Not like she's used to." Kitsune touched her burned ear and winced. "She was going to force her way through, like she does everything else, but . . ." She shook her head. "What must it be like, to have such arrogance that you can simply demand your way through an entry you have no right to?"

I blinked. "A metaphoric gaijin smash. That's . . . something." I was the first to admit Melanie could be a bit lofty about her music. Arrogant, maybe, depending on the circumstances. Given what she could do, it probably wasn't difficult to start believing your own press sometimes. But to lash out at Kitsune? To destroy her friend's home so she could escape?

"But I still can't quite buy it—unless there was a horde of daemons on their tail, something to make her so desperate she had no other choice."

Kitsune's grin grew wider, and not in a pleasant way. "Believe it. In the end, I suppose it doesn't matter. It wasn't that she actually attacked me, but that corruption on her violin got away from her, and she lost control. They managed to punch a hole through the Gate anyway when I tried to stop the backlash of her music. That's what destroyed the Barras." She gestured at the bruise skittering beneath her skin and winced. "I can feel the corrupted Wild Magic burning inside me."

I pinched the bridge of my nose. "If she had any idea of what happened here, she wouldn't have gone through. It had to have been an accident."

The fox-woman shrugged. "Maybe so, maybe no. I was too busy trying not to die."

"So where did they go? And why a Gate?" I asked. "We

assumed they would go to Japan, but—"

"Yes. The OtherFolk of Japan, the yokai, use Gates, not Doors. But unlike here, not every Gate can be used. Some require the specific permission of its shrine guardian or god." Kitsune shuffled to her feet. "The rest of the Cross-Roads is much the same. We do use the hours for travel, *Akatsuki, Ōmagatoki*—dawn and dusk—and the like, but the veil is much thinner in Japan than in America, so TouchStones aren't as big of a deal."

She ran her fingers over the diseased skin on her side. "With this much of the Wild Magic trapped inside me, the Gate isn't responding to my summons either."

"And I'm guessing there are no other Gates around."

"No. I wasn't even supposed to have that one," she admitted. "I spirited it away here under great personal cost. My powers here in the Barras have always been somewhat limited. Without a shrine . . . Well, it is only what I deserved, after all."

There was an awful lot in that statement. I wasn't sure if we had time to unpack it, but it did remind me how little I knew about the fox-woman.

She grimaced. "Either way, we will need to find a way there. My only chance at healing lies in my returning home to Japan, and I don't think I have much time. Forgive me, but I will have to change form. I'll be able to stave off the corruption easier that way."

Before I had a chance to even respond, she gave a little shake, the silken rags of her kimono fluttering to the ground as her features melted away, revealing a very large fox. A fox with three tails and a set of almost comically large ears, but a fox, nonetheless, even if she had two more tails than usual. Her fur shone a brilliant white, she had red markings above her eyes, and if her smile had been maniacal in human form, it was downright terrifying in this one.

A kitsune in truth, after all.

Not that I'd had much cause to doubt it before, but seeing it happen in front of me left a rather distinct impression. The fox shifted slightly, turning toward the Gate. From here, I could see the same dark corruption rippling beneath her fur along her right side.

Phineas let out an admiring whistle as he trotted toward us, Talivar tailing him a few steps behind. "Hot mama," Phin crooned, earning a snarl and an eye roll from Kitsune.

"Careful," I warned him. "She might be more inclined to eat you now."

"I'd die happy." The unicorn swooned, arching his neck proudly before shaking his body. "I'm tired."

He stared up at me plaintively, his lashes fluttering. I slung my hobo over my shoulder and reached down to let him clamber into it. I didn't know whether it was his age or he wasn't as energetic without his complete horn. Maybe he was simply lazy, but he seemed to want to be carried a lot more than he used to.

Talivar inclined his head at Kitsune. "Cousin," he murmured.

"It has been a very long time since I have taken this appearance," she rasped, her voice higher pitched that in her human form. "But it is easier to keep the magic at bay. That will have to do for now."

"So how do we get to Japan? Other than flying?" I shuddered at the thought. I'd never been there, but I knew it was a long flight. Trying to keep all of the OtherFolk contained aboard a plane hurtling through the sky for thirteen hours or more would be a nightmare beyond compare. Not to mention needing passports for everyone on short notice. It would be worse than trying to herd cats.

"We'll need to find another Gate," Kitsune said. "Perhaps a Shinto shrine in the mortal world will have one we can use." She bared her teeth. "Though perhaps not. The same corruption keeping me from this one will most likely block me from all of them."

I turned toward Ion. "What about the Dreaming? Could you possibly reach someone there that way? A priest or a shrine maiden or whatever?"

Brystion cocked his head. "It's a thought. If I can find someone there with the ability to open a Gate, I could possibly convince them to do so. A monk, perhaps. Or a . . ."

"Yokai," Kitsune said firmly. "Monks are troublesome at the best of times, at least in today's world." She sniffed.

I looked at my watch, feeling foolish. With time passing differently on the CrossRoads, it was hard to tell how time much was passing in the real world. "There's always the Key," I said. "Seems like this might be a good reason to use it."

Ion's eyes narrowed, and Kitsune shook her head. "I don't know if it will work on the Gate like it does a Door—much like that Wild Magic. And I don't have time to waste on *maybe*."

"Well, I'm running out of ideas. What about the thread?" I asked Kitsune. "You gave me a spool of red thread once to help me find Talivar or my destiny or something like that."

Ion and Talivar blinked at me. "Destiny, is it?" Talivar said wryly.

"It led me to the tent with your horses," I explained. "I'm not sure it worked the way it was supposed to, but you did show up afterward, so who knows?"

Kitsune brightened. "Ah yes. The red thread of Fate. A useful spell at times, though I don't know if it will work for us here. Depends on how entwined you and Melanie are. It might not even lead you through the Gate at all."

She paced, her fur seeming to shimmer slightly, and then one of her tails somehow plucked a spool from the air and deposited it at my feet. I picked it up, Brystion craning to see it curiously.

"And what is that all about?" His eyes narrowed. "I don't like the way it feels."

Kitsune cackled. "Mortals are bound by Fate more so than OtherFolk. It's often wrapped so tightly around them they don't even notice it. You were never one for such things, aye?"

He grunted at her and rolled his eyes. For a heartbeat, I could see his natural form, the dark skin, the antlers, the hooves . . . the bells braided in his hair with *red thread*. My mouth quirked, but I said nothing. Perhaps the incubus was bound more by Fate than he liked.

I rolled the spool in my hands, taking one end of the thread. It shivered between my fingers, almost like touching a live wire, jolts of power zipping beneath my skin.

"Focus," Kitsune snapped. "What is it you really want? Where do you want to go?"

I shut my eyes. *Melanie,* I thought. *I need to find her. I need to fix this. I need to save her.*

The thoughts repeated over and over in my head, and as before, the spool jumped from my hand and rolled across the ground toward the Gate. Talivar skirted out of the way as it hurtled toward him, swearing softly.

The Gate lit up in an instant, the spool shunting through and disappearing in a splash of silver and gold, the red thread trailing like a tail behind it.

The fox limped over to the Gate, sniffing at the corner. The corruption on her side grew more pronounced, but her three tails lashed wildly, coating her fur with a silver light. "Abby! Let's go! Before it closes!"

She shifted slightly, her paws becoming humanoid, and she snatched at the hand holding the thread and pulled me hard, the pair of us tumbling through the Gate. "Wait!" We swept through the entrance, but my voice was enveloped in some sort of film, a quiet I couldn't seem to break through.

I reached for the others, but it was as though I was looking through water, a barrier stretched between us that I couldn't quite reach.

The thread. I clenched my fist. I was still holding the goddamned thread. *What happens when the thread keeping the Gate open goes through, Abby? What?*

"It fucking closes," I said. "That's what."

I struggled against Kitsune's clawed grip. "We have to go back . . . The others . . ."

"There is no time." Her voice was hollow and empty as she staggered beside me. Her tails dragged limply across the ground, the dark magic beginning to move along her fur again. "Must make it . . . Inari."

And then she was tumbling forward, the track we were on abruptly disintegrating beneath our feet. I snatched at her, and the two of us fell, fell, fell, the red thread wrapping around us.

CHAPTER 5

THE MIST THICKENED AROUND ME, the stone path echoing beneath every plaintive footstep. Kitsune, still in fox form, hung limp in my arms, her head resting on my shoulder. I would have thought such a thing would be far beyond her dignity, but if she was remotely conscious, she wasn't showing me a bit of it, except maybe in the subtle twitch of an ear.

Phineas had poked his head out of the hobo for half a second, his eyes rolling as he vomited noisily, leaving a distinctively rainbow-colored puddle at my feet.

"Dude, that's disgusting. Get out next time." I skirted away from the puke, trying to keep my own rebellious stomach from joining him. I patted my belly to soothe it, resting my hand on there as though I could make sure the baby was all right. It had been quite a jump to wherever we were, but everything seemed to be in order.

"Sorry," he gasped. "I feel like I've been riding a roller coaster in space. I don't think we went through the Gate right."

"If you were in space, you wouldn't feel sick since there's no gravity," I said snidely.

"I fucking hate you sometimes." He dry heaved several times before settling down in the bag again. "Next time I come out of here, I'm going to bite someone. Wake me up when we get wherever we're going."

"My noble steed." I shifted Kitsune to my other shoulder and continued onward, the thread still clutched in my hand to guide me. We were walking through Gate after Gate, each of them only a few feet apart, leaping along the tracks from place to place. I lost count of how many we'd gone through. Thousands, maybe—all only a few feet apart. And the entire time the spool continued to wend and unwind, leaving me no choice but to follow.

After a while, I realized we were being followed. Maybe "escorted" was the proper word. I only caught glimpses. Perhaps they were foxes like Kitsune, melting into the haze, or the flap of wings above us, the harsh cry of a crow ushering us along. It left me uneasy, a tightly coiled wire of fear corkscrewing through me. Destiny or not, chasing after my supposed Fate was tiring. It wasn't long before even Kitsune's slight weight grew heavy in my arms. Our escorts had vanished, or at least were hiding themselves better, and when I came to a long set of stairs that appeared to lead to nowhere, I finally stopped, slumping onto the bottom step.

Kitsune stirred. "This chaos is starting to become a habit with you. I had better be careful, or it will rub off on me."

"Tell me about it." Hell, at this point, it was almost as if we were going on a group date. One of us was bound to be kidnapped or lose our memory any moment now. With any luck, it wouldn't be me. I'd more than filled my damsel-in-distress dance card. Enough for several lifetimes over, in fact.

I peered into my hobo, rolling my eyes when I found Phin snoring away inside. "Ah, and Phineas hitched a ride earlier. Though he's not feeling particularly well."

Kitsune grunted and wriggled out of my arms. "We're safe enough for now, though we're not quite where we need to be yet. It has been ages since I've been this way."

She limped up a couple of steps, eyeing the thread. I wasn't about to ask how a spool rolls up a flight of stairs; it was long gone by this point anyway. "We need to keep following this."

"Do you know where it's taking us?" I struggled to my feet, wishing there were some sort of railing to lean on. Now that I'd stopped for a few minutes, I realized how thirsty I was, and my legs began to shake.

I carefully dug into my purse, pulling out the last bottle of water and chugged half of it before offering the rest to Kitsune. The fox shook her head. "I need more than mundane things to help me now."

The dark color had spread along her flank, ebony tentacles pulsating beneath her white fur. She didn't make any sound when she nuzzled it but winced all the same, so I could only imagine how painful it must have been. "As to where it's taking us, well that's easy enough." Her muzzle split into a wide, toothy grin. "It's taking us *up*."

I rolled my eyes, and her mocking laughter rolled over me as she limped her way up the stairs. I followed suit, though my limbs were growing more sluggish by the second. Kitsune eyed me from a few steps above. "If I were in better shape myself, I'd go on ahead and send someone else for you."

"Can't help how I am," I said. "Walking for two now and all that. Three, if you count Phineas." I shifted him in my arms, trying to ignore the way they trembled. My calves were tight, and I paused briefly to stretch them. Sweat had pooled down my spine, and I pulled my shirt away from the stickiness, hating the way it clung to my skin.

"Just so. Well, let's keep going. And do yourself a favor, Abby: Don't look back." The warning was light and lilting, and immediately sent my lizard brain into screaming panic. Don't look back because I might fall? Don't look back because there was an enormous tentacle monster slithering up behind us?

The difference between the two wasn't particularly subtle.

And of course, now all I wanted was to look behind me. But I'd read enough fairy tales to know when an OtherFolk creature tells you to do—or not do—something, going against the grain usually led to something awful.

Like death.

And I might have died before, but that was a one-time shot. I sure wasn't planning on tempting fate a second time. Besides, the spool was going forward, and that was good enough for me.

We started climbing again. I kept my eyes focused mainly on the steps directly in front of me. Trying to find the top in the mist was nothing more than an exercise in futility and depressing as hell.

Kitsune's eyes and body gave off an odd, milky glow, but it was easy enough to follow and that was better than trying to do this completely in the dark. I kept my thoughts on Melanie and Nobu, wondering what they were doing and where they were going, if it was possible they would actually manage to get out of this alive.

What had happened to the Barras, if it was on purpose or not, well . . . Despite everything she'd done for the OtherFolk and the services she'd provided, some things couldn't be forgotten.

Talivar had had his entire little kingdom destroyed in an instant, and Kitsune had lost her home, not to mention all the chaos left in Mel's wake. The damage was far more than merely physical. I didn't know how she would ever be able to make up for it.

Over and over, my thoughts chased each other like chipmunks in a blender, my exhaustion tangling them up until I wasn't entirely sure of anything at all except each step rising above me. I didn't even know how long we'd been walking, only that my feet were burning, my legs were aching something awful, and sweat was pouring from my brow.

"Kitsune," I gasped, sinking to my knees, a head rush making me dizzy. Glancing up, I saw an enormous torii gate above us—obviously the place we were headed. The mist was burning away, and a burst of golden light poured through the clouds to illuminate the staircase. Details of greenery and vines, hydrangeas growing on either side of the steps in brilliant blues and purples, chased by wisteria and honeysuckle. The air grew warm and humid, thick as soup.

"Listen." Kitsune's voice was low and urgent, worried. "We're almost there. When we get to the top, let me do the talking. *Gaijin*—outsiders—are not welcome in this place, particularly mortals. You have been around enough magic that your scent isn't quite evident as fully human, but it will not take them long to figure it out." She hesitated. "Don't use your real name, either."

"I know how the name thing works, more or less. Names have power and all that jazz. Stick with 'Absinthe' for now. I don't think I'll have the energy to speak much anyway." And it was true. I didn't know whether it was the elevation or that we'd been walking for what felt like hours and then climbed a damn step-mountain, but whatever it was, I was done. Fate or destiny or whatever it was be damned.

She gave me a sympathetic look. "I'll need healing at one of the larger temples; I'll make sure they set up a room for you so you can rest until I'm done. I hope. After that, we'll search for the . . . others."

She was being cautious. I was fairly certain our conversation was being listened to, either by those white foxes that had been "escorting" us or by something else. But this was completely new territory for me. I barely understood how the CrossRoads worked, and I knew *nothing* of the Gates.

"You don't sound too confident," I pointed out. "That's not like you."

"Ah, well. It has been awhile since I've been home." Her grin became sadly rueful when she turned toward me, her tongue lolling out of her mouth. "One does not anger the gods here lightly, and we approach them in a most direct manner following this path. I would have come another way, if I'd had a choice." Her paw tugged on the thread, and she shook her head. "But that's Fate for you. No matter how much you try to avoid it, eventually it comes for you."

I frowned. "It almost sounds like you were exiled or something."

"Something like that," she admitted. "Spirits in Japanese mythology often walk a fine line between gods and yokai. Sometimes there isn't much difference. It's more along the lines of the different kinds of faeries. They're not necessarily good or bad. Technically, I would be a yokai, though it's possible I might be elevated to a god. All I need is a shrine and some worshippers." She winced again, snapping at the corruption in her side. "Japan has many gods. Over eight million of them—everything from toilet gods, to train gods, to gods of love and health, and nearly anything else you might think of or pray to."

I snorted. "Sounds confusing."

"No more so than any other religion or mythology." Her voice cracked, and she took a few deep breaths, her eyes closing as a series of shudders rippled over her fur. "The true question is whether we were here before mortals or we were brought into being by your prayers, wishes, and hopes. Here, even common objects can grow sentient if given enough time."

"Like the Velveteen Rabbit made real," I said, reaching out as though to pick her up.

"Now you've got it." Her tails swished back and forth,

almost wagging in time as she sidestepped away to mount the stairs again, growing silent as though all her words were used up.

As we approached the top steps, I let out a sigh of relief, though there were no benches of any sort to sit on. I debated the wisdom of simply sagging to the ground, but something told me appearances were extremely important here. The last thing I wanted to do was stick my foot in my mouth on our first meeting with . . . well, with whoever was up here. A sideways glance at Kitsune showed her walking ramrod straight, without a hint of the pain that must be racking her body. The tentacles of the corruption were wrapping around her chest now, convulsing with each breath she took.

The top of the rise was flat and gray, decorated by a lone tree that sported neither leaves nor flowers. Not that I was particularly familiar with trees, but I thought I caught a bit of a song, perhaps—a thrumming similar to that of Eildon Tree.

Beneath the tree were four cloaked beings. Each wore an animal mask, like something out of a Noh performance I'd seen on PBS a long time ago, painted white with red markings. A slightly closer inspection revealed one to be a cat, but I couldn't quite figure the others out. Were they merely decoration in this case or something far more sinister?

"*Sumimasen kamisama . . .*" Kitsune began, bowing deeply. "*Watashi wa—*"

My brain stuttered, trying to understand her words, but the fight was over before it began. In the end, I was left to simply wait, the liquid syllables of her native language washing over me. The four figures remained where they were. Behind their masks, it was nearly impossible to tell what they were thinking, and their lack of response was disturbing.

I swayed on my feet. If I didn't get to sit down shortly, I was going to faint my way to the ground. I stumbled, flailing to keep my balance, only to be lifted by strong hands upon my shoulders. I relaxed as I was straightened, bracing myself for when I was let go.

Except I wasn't set free. In fact, I was still being lifted, my legs dangling off the ground as I rose higher and higher.

"Hey, wait!" I shouted, reaching for the hands holding my shoulders.

No. Not hands. *Talons.* Talons that were gently holding my clothing as opposed to rending my flesh open, but talons all the same. They were thick, black things, the edges curved and wickedly sharp. I didn't want to squirm too much for fear of being skewered. I craned my neck and realized the talons were connected to the feet of a man. Or a man-shaped yokai, anyway.

Judging by the almost obscenely long nose on his mask and the wings, that would have made him a tengu, I guessed. But my knowledge of Japanese OtherFolk or yokai was not great, aside from the fact that they were basically bird spirits who supposedly lived on a high mountain and there weren't any females.

"Absinthe!" Kitsune leaped toward me, her jaws falling just short of my toes.

I struggled briefly and then thought better of it. We were getting awfully high; a tumble from here wasn't going to do my body any favors, let alone my baby. All I could do was look on helplessly at an increasingly rage-filled Kitsune growing smaller and smaller as we sailed up into the clouds.

Her tails lashed as she whirled on the cloaked figures, their masks falling away to reveal monstrous faces. I caught a glimpse of a horned man and something else with wings as they began fighting, even as a wave of white bodies swarmed up the steps in a wave of teeth and tails.

Foxes?

I squinted, but by now we were far too high. "Come on, bird-man, let me down!" His mask didn't move, but I caught the movement of his throat as he mumbled something I couldn't hear.

His wings pumped hard, lifting us higher and higher until we were so far above the mist I couldn't even see the mountain below us. I cried out for Kitsune again, but my voice was torn away in the wind, leaving me with nothing but a hiss in my ears.

My limbs were like ice, and I wrapped my arms around my belly as best I could, the drag of my feet and the breeze on my face sharp and painful. My nostrils flared as I tried not to let the waves of panic running through me distract my focus.

My options for escape were limited, but my communication might not be. If I had a moment or two for sleep, if I could reach the Dreaming, there was a good chance I'd be able to reach Ion there. At the very least, I might be able to pass on a message.

The thought of waiting for a rescue was not particularly appealing, but there was a bit of cold comfort in knowing it was an option, and it wasn't something that would easily be found out by my would-be captor, whoever he was.

On the surface, that wasn't particularly troubling, but as it stood with me being kidnapped—birdnapped?—the potential for a shitshow was growing by the second. Not to mention that it was getting harder to breathe the higher we went. I tapped his clawed hand, foot, whichever it was. "Dude, we gotta land. I'm getting lightheaded."

The tengu didn't slow down in the slightest, muttering something that sounded an awful lot like, "So noisy."

"I'll show you noisy," I snapped. "How'd you like me to reach up there and yank out your tail feathers?"

Something like a snort escaped him but otherwise he

never slowed down. And really, he was right. What was I planning to do even if he did let me go? Falling to my death wasn't exactly a viable plan.

I sucked in a slow deep breath, shivering at the chill. All I could do now was wait.

"Abby! Where the hell are you?" Brystion's clawed fingers dug into my shoulder. I winced away from his angry, frightened tone, and he immediately relaxed his grip. "I'm sorry, I'm sorry."

I was in my Dreaming Heart, standing on the front stoop of the Victorian house, the scent of lilacs and jasmine thick and rich. Flying over mountains or not, somewhere along the way I must have fallen asleep or passed out. I barely had time to collect my thoughts as to whether or not this was a good thing before the incubus wrapped his arms around me, his mouth nipping at my neck almost frantically.

"Shh." My fingers twined in the inky darkness of his hair. Relief washed over me, and I swallowed a sob. That at least I'd been partially found, that I was still alive.

He held me tighter, lowering himself so that his face was against my belly. "Is the baby all right?"

"As far as I know. It's not like I can get an ultrasound anytime soon." The words were sharper than I'd intended.

His golden eyes flared, but he said nothing, his lion's tail twitching in irritation. "Where are you?"

"Got me . . . One minute I was walking up the steps of some giant mountain with Kitsune, and the next thing some bird-winged fucker swept me off the mountainside and carried me off. For all I know I'm still flying." I sobered. "I'm more concerned for Kitsune, though. We were being attacked when I was taken."

"Do you still have the thread?" Ion turned my palms over as though it might be tied to a finger.

"I don't think so. I must have dropped it when I was flailing around."

Bryston's voice dropped low, into an almost-purring hum. "Pull me back with you." The heat of his power slipped over me almost like a second skin, doing terrible, wondrous things between my legs.

"That's not fair," I gasped, a flush of heat spreading from every place his fingers touched. And then his mouth was on mine, his tongue sweeping over my lower lip in a slow, lingering kiss.

"I've never been fair." He let out a chuckle, sweeping me off my feet. "But we'll do this in your bedroom, aye?"

The only answer I could give him was a drawn-out moan when his hand slid down my belly to rest at the junction of my thighs, his knuckles gently teasing at the opening. I let out a half-exasperated laugh as I realized he'd removed my clothing with a mere thought. Not that the Dreaming was real, per se, but it still boggled my mind how easy it was for him to break through even my modest shields. But then again, it wasn't like I was trying to stop him.

It wasn't always a particularly neat solution, but for now I'd take it. Though what we'd do if he manifested while I was still being flown about was another thing all together. The fact that I wasn't in the mood didn't mean a whole lot; if a quickie got me rescued, well, that was simple enough.

My life was messy as hell. Why shouldn't a rescue be the same?

Bryston kicked in the front door to the house with a hard tap of his hooves, easily carrying me up the stairs to the bedroom. The bed was never the same thing twice, especially when he worked his power upon it, transforming it to whatever struck his fancy.

It was simple this time—white sheets, soft pillows, and a hazy light that felt both comforting and warm. He placed me upon the mattress with a delicate, lazy hand, rolling beside me to cup a breast with a possessive growl.

"Pity we don't have time for more of the usual nice-ties." He trailed kisses along the nape of my neck, his teeth brushing the skin harder than his wont.

"Next time." I turned to kiss him, letting him slide me atop him so I was astride, his fingers making little circles on my gently swelling belly to dip a little lower.

I squirmed, his cock rubbing against me insistently as he rhythmically moved his hips in blatant invitation. As I leaned over to kiss him again, he captured a breast in his mouth, his tongue swirling around the hardened nipple. My back arched, and I let out a soft moan, echoed by a satisfied rumble in his own throat. His eyes flared gold, hands slipping over the curve of my ass to bring me closer. Pleasure suffused me all the way to my bones, and I ached with the sudden need to have him inside me.

"Please," I begged against his mouth, letting his laughter at my desperation vibrate over my skin.

"Abby . . ." He breathed my name, and I shivered. "Abby?"

I jolted upright at the panic in his voice. "Wait, what?" I was growing transparent, or maybe he was, or maybe my entire Dreaming Heart was.

"You're waking up," he snapped, grabbing for my hands. Our fingers melded together but he slipped away, and then I was hurtling down, down, down. My ears filled with the ringing of the bells in his hair, like some sort of mythical car alarm.

"Ion!" I screamed. And then there was nothing at all.

CHAPTER 6

" *. . . DAIJOUBU DESU ka?*"

The masculine voice was softer than I expected, but his words were no less confusing. I blinked blearily from where I was lying, not quite ready to risk raising my head, which was spinning nonstop.

Something was pressed against my lips—a cup of some sort, I thought. I gave it a sniff and decided it was only water. My parched tongue strained eagerly, and I quickly sipped it down. The cup was taken from my hand when I finished, the shadow that took it moving away and through a doorway, leaving my eyes to adjust to the relative darkness of wherever I was.

The room was small and cramped. From the dimly lit lanterns, I could see I was sprawled out on a futon. The floors were tatami, and the walls were nothing more than rice paper. Shadows rustled on the other side of the door, moving quietly back and forth. From below came the sound of music and talking, laughter and the clink of drinks. It sounded like one hell of a party either way. Not that I could understand anything that was being said, but merrymaking was probably the same no matter where you were.

Which begged the question . . . where the hell was I now?

My stomach rolled over, reminding me it had been a while since I'd eaten. How long had I been here?

I shifted beneath the thin blanket covering me, realizing my shoes had been removed. My clothes were still here and my cell phone was in my pocket, so I pulled that out, unsurprised when I had no signal.

"Fuck." So close. So *close* to having Brystion here with me. Even if he wasn't a yokai, he had far more power than I did, and in a place like this, it was clear I was going to need some strong allies.

AWAKE. ALIVE. IN SOME SORT OF HOUSE. DON'T KNOW WHERE. WILL TRY TO REACH OUT AGAIN WHEN I CAN.

I texted Ion and Talivar the message. Even if it didn't send right away, maybe I'd be lucky enough to be traveling through a pocket where a Wi-Fi signal would pick it up. At the very least, I could let them know I was all right. My body thrummed impatiently, and I squirmed. All that buildup and nothing to show for it.

And what of Phin? My hobo lay next to the futon, but a quick look inside showed it to be remarkably empty of unicorns. Had he fallen out during the flight? I jerked upright, searching the room for some sign of him. Sagging when I came up empty, I winced at a slight soreness on my backside. My mouth pursed. Unsurprising that I wasn't at least a little hurt. I'd been through a lot but this felt rather specific.

Looking around, I ended up using my phone camera to take a quick shot of the site, snorting when I saw the telltale bite mark. It wasn't as deep as he'd done in the past, but it sure as hell hadn't been there before I'd gone through the Gate with Kitsune. Which could only mean he had to be around here somewhere. As messages went, it was a bit more subtle than I would have liked, but it was better than finding glitter in my purse. Phineas was a sly and crafty little shit. He would lie low until it was safe enough to find me.

I drank the rest of the water and carefully stood up. My bladder twinged. I needed to pee, but there didn't appear to be anything in the room that would help me with that, let alone a toilet. I gently slid open the door on the far side of the wall, catching the barest glimpse of someone walking around the corner, but otherwise the hall was empty. Covered pink lanterns lined the walls, the burnished wood planks of the floor glowing golden in their light.

"Hello?" I said, pitching my voice low. I didn't want to startle anyone, but I also wasn't entirely sure I wanted to be found. Though frankly, if anyone had been going to do anything harmful, surely they would have by now . . .

As I mulled this over and debated my options, a young woman rounded the corner carrying a tray. She was wearing a dark-green kimono but even with her hair bound up neatly, it didn't hide the cat ears or tail poking out from behind her. I waved to catch her attention, and she immediately halted, her face paling.

"Uh, hello? *Konnichiwa?*" I knew approximately three phrases in Japanese. *Hello, good-bye,* and something that would probably be ridiculously rude given the circumstances. "Hello" it would have to be.

Her ears flattened, and she lowered her head, swiftly retreating with a graceful swish of her tail.

I sighed. "And the *gaijin* strikes out again." I closed the door and paced the little room. My shoes were gone, which probably left me with limited options if I did make it outside. So what to do first? Bathroom? Food? Figure out a plan for getting out of here, or at least trying to find out what had happened to Kitsune?

A light tap on the sliding door drew my attention, and I glanced up as it opened, revealing a tall, willowy woman with an oddly long neck. Unlike the cat girl's kimono, which had been on the plainer side, she wore one of gold and crimson, the obi a brilliant blue. Her silver eyes studied me briefly, and then she crooked a finger, gesturing at me to follow her.

She seemed less intimidated by me than the cat girl, and even without words, I'd have little trouble understanding at least the basics. I closed the door behind me. The woman had already swept down the corridor, her body a wonder of silent reproach and exquisite grace, her slippered feet making no sound at all.

She definitely wasn't human, but I had my doubts as whether she was truly that beautiful or it was merely a glamour. OtherFolk were certainly no strangers to such things; I couldn't imagine the yokai here would be any different.

We passed by a number of other . . . servants, I supposed, their heads bowed when they saw her, pausing to let us walk by. I caught a hint of side-eye from a few of them, but if it was fear or disapproval or some heady mixture of both I couldn't tell. I did see the occasional bit of feathers and scales, a hint of fur poking out from some of the kimonos, but it felt impolite to stare so I kept my vision firmly planted on the silver-eyed woman, the silken cloth rippling like water as she floated in front of me. We wended our way through a nearly impossible maze of sliding doors and stairs until we arrived at the entrance of what I could only assume was a bathhouse.

The woman sniffed at me and gestured at one of the servant girls who trembled beneath her gaze. *"Sumimasen."* The girl whispered the polite interruption, bowing her head. I couldn't tell what sort of yokai she was, but it didn't matter. Her amber pupils were slit like a snake, a flush of scales brushing over her cheeks and forehead, glittering like azure diamonds. The silver-eyed woman watched me follow the serpent girl with an interested arch of her brow.

Maybe I should have been screaming in fear, but I'd seen far worse than a few snake scales on people. As long as she wasn't going to try to eat me, we'd be fine. The entryway to the bath had two doors; we went through the red one.

Before I knew it, the serpent girl had somehow persuaded me to shuck the rest of my clothing, pointing me to a row of spigots and buckets. I'd been to a Japanese bath once, though it was more of a spa, really. Melanie had talked me into it when we lived in New York, so I knew the basics. There was even a rudimentary squat toilet behind a screen in the dressing area that I took advantage of almost immediately before claiming one of the stools.

There were other yokai women doing the same, sitting on their stools and washing carefully. The serpent girl provided me with a small towel and a bit of soap. Otherwise, it was the usual scrub and rinse and trying to ignore the fact that I was stark naked in the company of gorgeous OtherFolk.

If they noticed my scars, they were at least polite enough not to say anything. My hair was still colored, though since I'd gotten pregnant, I'd stopped dying my bangs my usual flamboyant pink and blue. Melanie had found some sort of glamour-based color that turned it a more sophisticated aubergine, but I still wasn't sure I liked it. I had let it grow out some too, so it hung past my shoulders, the wet ringlets sticking to my skin.

When I finished, I shut the water off, shivering as I picked up the towel. The other yokai were heading toward a large soaking spring, their hair—if they had any—artfully pulled atop their heads.

The serpent girl gestured that I should follow, but I hesitated. Not that it didn't look tempting. I'd been through an awful lot the last day or so, and my sore muscles were screaming at me for a bit of relief, but somehow, soaking in a hot tub while I had no idea where my friends were or the state of Kitsune's wounds, let alone Melanie's location, was ludicrous. Not to mention my pregnancy. I had no idea how hot those waters were, and I couldn't remember if it was even allowed at this point.

The serpent woman gestured again, more insistently this time. "No," I said sharply, curving my hands around my belly in what I hoped was the universal sign for "bun in the oven." She cocked her scaled head at me and then shrugged.

I shivered again, and she led me to the changing area. My clothes were nowhere to be found, and she handed me a robe instead. A yukata, I realized, recognizing the overall design from my previous spa trip. It wasn't as ornate as a regular kimono, but it was dry and I gratefully accepted it, burrowing my now-chilly limbs as deep into it as I could.

My hair continued to drip, and I squeezed it slightly, surprised when the serpent girl produced a comb and immediately began running it sharply through my hair, hard enough to make me cry out. I nearly snatched it from her hands, but she simply turned my head and continued, ignoring any noises of protest coming from me. When she had completed her task to her satisfaction, the comb disappeared into the sleeve of her kimono and she gestured at me to follow her again.

"Where are my clothes?" Not that I cared so much about them, but my phone had been in the pocket. I crossed my arms, irritated. We were in a different part of the changing area than when we'd come in, but I searched about until I found my basket on one of the shelves. At least I sort of doubted anyone else here had been wearing a bright-pink Deadpool T-shirt with a unicorn crapping out chimichangas. I fished inside the basket, breathing a little easier when I pulled out my phone.

Serpent girl watched all of this silently, her expression

growing even more sour, but I didn't care much. For now, there didn't appear to be any direct danger. After all, why take the time to let me wash if they were planning to kill me? But that didn't mean I was going to leave my only real way of communicating with the rest of the world behind either.

I inclined my head at her once I'd gathered my things, and we marched to where my room had been. I still received nearly as many stares from the others we passed, but at least now I was dressed more appropriately, so it was a little less obvious.

But I still didn't know why I was here . . .

By the time we returned to my room, I was ravenous. The futon was gone when we arrived, leaving me no place to sit but the floor. I awkwardly knelt in the robe, trying to find something to do with my hands.

The serpent girl was gone a moment later, leaving me to a mostly empty room and little else to do except try my phone again. Which was about as useful as the first time, not to mention the battery was running down faster each time I messed with it.

I tapped my fingers on the tatami mat, looking at the pile of my clothes with irritation. I'd move faster if I changed into them, but I'd be way more conspicuous if I did. But the robe didn't lend itself to a lot of maneuvering or even outright running.

Then the door opened again, and the serpent girl entered, followed by the cat girl carrying a tray of covered dishes. My stomach grumbled loudly in response as the scent of whatever it was hit me full-on.

A tiny smile flickered on the cat girl's face, but it was chased away as she set the tray down before me. She backed out of the room, leaving me and the serpent girl to stare at each other.

"Eat." The word dropped from her scaled lips hesitantly,

her gold eyes unblinking.

"Oh, so you can speak English? Why am I here? I need to find my friends. And where exactly am I?" I popped the cover off the largest dish, confronted with a bowl of rice covered with some sort of fried meat.

She blinked at my sudden onslaught of questions and shook her head. She left me then, her expression unreadable as I picked up the chopsticks and proceeded to stuff my face. There was a small bowl of ramen too, and the noodles were ridiculously delicious. It was all gone within minutes, leaving me in the same predicament as before. Alone. With no sign of Phin anywhere.

But the fact that the serpent girl possibly understood me was somewhat comforting, though I was getting tired of not getting any answers. I pushed the tray away, irritated. The room had one window, which was latched in a way I couldn't quite figure out, but I gave it a sharp yank. I immediately was struck by waves of noise from below. I peered out, enchanted by hundreds of red and gold lanterns dotting the sides of an intricate set of wooden balconies, leading out to a main street, crowds of people walking by in purposeful fashion.

Surely someone out there would be able to help me. But if I can't speak their language, what good would it do? Pacing again, I tightened my robe.

"Fuck it. No one's told me I have to stay in here." I ignored the flutter of warning in my belly and peeked out the sliding door again. Empty. Good enough.

I left the room, making a bit of a mark on the paper door with my fingernail so I'd be able to recognize it if I walked by this way again. The chances of me getting lost were pretty high, but I didn't have the red thread of Fate anymore. It was time to make my own.

My slippered feet padded gently on the wood floor. I tried to hide my pounding heart and overall nervousness by trying to imitate the walks of the servants from earlier. My former ballet training would come in handy enough for that: I knew how to keep myself ramrod straight, my legs carefully placing with each step. Hopefully I'd manage to blend in at least a little.

The passages seemed to go on for miles, the lanterns illuminating the halls with a cheerful elegance. From time to time someone would leave a room and make their way past me, occasionally giving me wide berth. Some were dressed in similar robes to mine and others had what I assumed was more traditional clothing. I knew there was a difference in types of kimono, but I couldn't begin to tell what they were: Some had longer sleeves, some had fancy knots in their obi, but nearly all of them were beautiful.

Eventually I came to a staircase. A railing along this side of the hall allowed me to look down into a common room. Laughter and music bubbled up, though I didn't recognize the instrument. A zither maybe?

At least I was headed in the right direction. With any luck I'd be able to find someone willing to help me.

I started down the stairs only to run smack into the serpent girl. She drew herself up and rattled off something at me. I might not have understood the words, but her tone was more than explanatory. Hissing, she snatched my arm and pulled me up the steps.

"Oh no," I said, shaking my head and pointing down. "I'm not staying in my room any longer."

Frustration played over her features. "Wa . . . it." The word hung there, foreign. But she flagged down another servant, whispering something in her ear. The other girl bowed, hurrying down another hallway.

Serpent girl tugged on my robe and then shook her head, pointing at her own dress. I frowned. "Too casual?"

Without ceremony, she led me to my room, but instead of simply shutting the door, she unfolded a simple dressing screen and shoved me behind it, indicating I should remove the robe. I pursed my mouth but did as she asked, even as the room door slid open again.

This time there were three other servant girls, carrying various bundles and a full-on kimono. They swarmed over me despite my protests, pushing and prodding and some-how unwinding the silk so that it draped on my thin frame like liquid. The ocean-blue material was decorated with tiny birds, the obi pale with flowers and gold thread. And somehow it was tied on me in absolute perfection, knotted in a way I'd never be able to manage myself.

I barely had time to look at it before they pulled out a chair and sat me upon it, two girls working on my hair and one on my face. A ripple of confusion washed over me. Was I being made into some sort of geisha? But the makeup artist didn't pull out the white paint I would have normally associated with such things, instead brushing on some sort of golden powder and a mauve eye shadow, and smearing kohl upon my eyelids between blinks.

I closed my eyes, listening to them chatter amongst themselves. I couldn't understand them—and I'm sure whatever they were saying wasn't particularly flattering—but short of manhandling my way past them, I didn't think there was much else I could do. And if looking fancy was my ticket to getting downstairs and out of here, I could masquerade with the best of them. If not, well there was always the gaijin smash.

They finished primping me, but there was no mirror so I had no idea what I looked like. I could only trust they knew what they were doing. Impatiently, I stood up, more than ready to be moving on, and I tucked my phone in the sleeve of the kimono.

Serpent girl finally led me out of the room and down the halls to that flight of stairs that spiraled down and into the bright light of the tea house.

Did I say tea house? I meant *brothel*.

My debut into the carefully constructed chaos on the main level was short-lived. I was ushered almost immediately through the main rooms, where several groups of yokai were being entertained by women dressed like me.

And I use the term "women" lightly. Given the mishmash of horns, scales, and feathers, I wasn't entirely sure if male and female were even the right descriptors. But it fit the stereotype of a tea house anyway, and from what little I knew about Japan's Edo period, there was a fairly good chance the employees here were also prostitutes.

I tugged at my clothing and sighed. Three guesses as to what I was about to be. My eyes tracked the room furtively, looking for something I could use as a weapon. I didn't know how far I'd get if I tried walking out the front door, but damned if I wasn't going to try.

At least, that's what my plan had been until an enormous fellow with horns poking out from the top of his head loomed in front of me. His yellow eyes took my measure with a quick up and down, his voice curt as he addressed the serpent girl.

She led me through the center of the room to another hall. The conversation and laughter became strained, but it was less about the shock of seeing me than seeming to appraise me. I'd been around Ion long enough to know when I was being sized up like some sort of meal, but I would not be cowed by it, keeping my chin lifted as I stared right back. One of them made a crude gesture at me, his drunken friends making it more than obvious what he thought.

I sneered in return. *"Baka,"* I muttered. He made no indication he'd heard me. The serpent girl stiffened but kept her head down, indicating I was supposed to continue following her.

The horned man pointed after her, blocking my way, and in the end, I had no choice. It didn't appear I'd have much luck appealing to the group in here anyway. Before I could do anything else, the serpent girl gave me a little shove into what appeared to be a barred room facing the main street.

"No! I'm not going in there," I refused. "Let me go!"

But the door was slammed shut behind me, the turn of the lock stupidly loud. I turned around, freezing when I saw the eyes of the women sitting in the room before me—dull, dead, and completely uninterested.

Without a word of greeting, they turned their attention to the slatted window. Outside, OtherFolk strolled up and down the street, stopping here and there. A flower shop. Vendors selling meatballs on sticks, candy, and flesh.

I was in a cage, I realized suddenly—one of the pieces for sale. The perfumed air clawed at my throat making it hard for me to breathe. A bitter anger swept over me, both for myself and the others here. I wasn't so blind as to not know such things existed, even in OtherFolk society, but becoming a part of it without even a say in the matter . . .

I winced at the idea, but only because if I thought about it too hard, I'd start screaming. The women around me seemed resigned to their fate, but I pressed forward to test the strength of the slats. If I could manage to break out of here . . . But no. The slats were sturdy, maybe even made of metal, and there was no chance of getting out that way.

One of the women with raccoon ears snorted at my attempts, taking a long draw of her pipe. Her dark hair was drawn up tight, pins hanging delicately from it as she leaned forward toward the window. Her eyes lit up as a man walked by, and she beckoned him closer.

He was cloaked and winged, his bearing ridiculously familiar, but I couldn't quite make out his face through the brassy light. He approached the raccoon woman with a hint of interest but then changed his mind and turning away. Another man bumped into him, pushing him roughly so he was forced to expand his wings for balance. I blinked at iridescent blue-black feathers reflecting the lantern light.

I knew those feathers.

A chill crept over the back of my neck, Melanie and Ion's pet name for the fallen angel . . . errr, shinigami dropping easily from my tongue. "Peacock!"

He stiffened, pulling the hood from his face to reveal his rather distinct set of facial features, set off by a wild burst of makeup, his blue-and-purple-dyed hair spiking high now that it was freed. Our eyes met briefly, a flicker of recognition burning in those dark eyes, and he tipped his head at me.

"Hey!" I shouted. He ducked inside the front door of the tea house, ignoring me completely. The raccoon woman's head snapped toward me, malice dripping from her tight smile.

"*Sumimasen,*" I offered, unsure of what else to say. "I'm sorry." She turned away without responding, but I'd made an enemy for sure. Though if her reaction meant Nobu had been frequenting brothels . . . Well, that was none of my business anyway; Melanie could deal with that.

Mere moments later, the locks were undone on the door. Immediately, the horned daemon overseer poked his head inside, finding me in a matter of seconds and indicating that I should follow him. Ignoring the murmur from the other women, I stood as straight as I could, hoping I wasn't about to get a dagger in the back.

The door was locked behind me, and I was led into a different room. This one was very much like my little bedroom upstairs but much more ornate. Tapestries and shades on the windows, everything dimly lit and intimate. I was made to sit before a table, where tea and an assortment of food had been laid out. A number of instruments lined the wall—to provide other sorts of entertainment, I supposed.

The serpent girl attendant retreated to the far corner of the room, discreetly tugging on a bell pull. Nobu was escorted into the room then, the long-necked proprietress all cheery laughs and smiles as she poured him a full cup of sake. His eyes fixated on me, and he said something curt. Both she and the serpent girl immediately bowed and retreated from the room, any semblance of joviality gone. Nobu and I stared at each other, myriad memories of our shared history pulsating between us.

I'd been TouchStoned to him before—not for very long, but long enough to see how desperately in love with Melanie he was and how far he'd go to make sure she was safe. From here, and in the light, his face was a study of abject misery.

Without his cloak on, I could see he was also wearing a kimono of sorts, but it was much simpler than mine. He had been a musician before he had ended up a servant of the Devil, and there had always been a certain visual kei-glam-rock vibe about his sense of style before. But aside from the guyliner and a few smudges of shadow, most of that was more subdued now.

"That's a new look for you, isn't it?" I asked.

His expression became darkly appraising. "I could say the same about you, Abby Sinclair."

I flushed despite myself. As beautiful as the clothes were, this was *not* a position I'd ever hoped to be in. Ever. I waved him off. "Neither here nor there. Now where the hell is Mel? Why are you here? And what is going on with her?" I leaned forward on the table. "Did you see what happened to the Barras? It's gone—almost completely destroyed. There are so many injuries. And Kitsune . . . I was traveling with her here, and then she got attacked and

I was swept up by some bird-man . . ." I stared at Nobu's wings, eyes narrowing.

He chuckled in amusement, and I gave him a sour smile. "Not quite me, no. And this wouldn't have been my first choice of places to leave you, but I hardly thought you'd volunteer to offer your services. That said, it's rather opportune to simply buy you for the evening. We can converse without anyone knowing the difference."

"I'll bet. How did you 'arrange' all this? How'd you even know where I'd be? That seems awfully convenient."

"I didn't," he admitted. "But I knew you'd come for Mel at some point; the two of you are peas in a pod. I simply left instructions with various allies that if they happened to find you, you were to be brought here. This was the first I heard of your capture." He shifted suddenly, glancing down in anger.

I snorted as a familiar white head emerged from behind the cloak, Phineas spitting out a mouthful of feathers. "You deserved that," I said. "And where the fuck have *you* been? Do you have any idea what it's like being shoved in a cage and sold?"

Phineas trotted over to me with a little shake. "Can't abide liars," he said mildly, ignoring Nobu's indignant stuttering around the room. "And yes, I know exactly what that's like."

I flushed. I'd forgotten that the first time I'd met Phin, he'd been merchandise at the Midnight Marketplace. He'd been delivered in a cat carrier and had hidden his ability to speak, but that didn't change the fact that he surely had a better idea of what it was like to be sold than I did after a few hours stuck in a yokai brothel.

"Point taken," I said, inclining my head.

"Damn straight. And as far as where I went . . . Well, I went to find help. Of course, I found this asshole, but close enough." He smacked his lips at me. "Nice outfit."

I glared at him, pouring myself a cup of tea. "I was hoping if I looked like I fit in here, I'd have a better chance of escaping."

"Not likely." Nobu snorted. "Not dressed like that. You'd be pegged as a lower-class prostitute immediately," he said dryly, gesturing at my kimono. "The belt—your obi—is tied in the front. It's a dead giveaway. You wouldn't have gotten far trying to escape that way." His face grew dark. "And they don't take kindly to runaways in Shimabara, even if it's nothing more than a shadow of the real thing."

"Shimabara? Is that what this place is called?" I asked.

"This part of the city, yes," he said. "It's based off the red-light district of the same name in Kyoto. Established in the seventeenth century, really—though that was before my time." He went silent then, as if lost in his own thoughts. I was pretty sure I didn't want to probe too deeply into them. There were more important things to worry about.

I crossed my arms as Phineas climbed into my lap. "Well, runaway or not, couldn't you have come up with a better way of reaching me? I hardly think being flown over freaking mountains by my shoulders counts as much of an escort," I said. "But more importantly, Kitsune is wounded badly. She took the brunt of Mel's magic when it exploded over the Barras."

"That was . . . unexpected. And not what Mel was trying to do, for the record. Kitsune's stubbornness is frustrating at times, but she would never have done such a thing if she'd been in her right mind." His eyes grew so black they glittered, pinning me in place. "The enchantment on her violin is wearing off, and the Wild Magic is consuming her soul—consuming *her.*"

"Paganini said Mel needed to fix the road to Hell, that she'd done something to it when they healed the Tree." I exhaled sharply. "How much time does she have? Where is she?"

"She's at a local shrine where the priests are attempting to rebind the Wild Magic to the violin. I don't think it's working particularly well, but it's all I have left to try." He bit down hard enough to draw blood from his lower lip. "I cannot lose her again, Abby. I can't. But neither can I hold off her fate. The bargains she has made . . . I cannot stop it."

I made a soft sound at his words, covering my mouth with my hands. "There has to be something we can do."

"I've spent years trying to find a way out of it. There is no back door, no fine print. A contract is a contract, and sooner or later, it must be filled. Otherwise, we would have nothing but chaos left." He pursed his lips. "I'm out of ideas. My little bird needs to face the music, as they say."

"Well, she won't face it alone," I said. "I'm going with her."

Nobu gave me a look of pity. "I hardly think you'll be able to, given your condition." His gaze dropped to my belly, and I instinctively shifted away from him. "If it were up to me, I would not allow it; I highly doubt Ion would either. Or your elf prince, king, whichever he is." His mouth quirked up. "You carry the potential heir to his realm, after all. Why risk that for one mortal's foolish decision?"

"You don't believe that," I said, my hand splaying wide over my belly as though to hide it. "It's not your decision to make. And frankly, I don't care what you say."

"You never do." He tapped his fingernails on the table, the black polish shining. "But that begs the question, how are you going to get out of here?"

I stuck my tongue out at him. "What the hell was the point of sending someone to snatch me just to dump me in a brothel?"

"That was his own initiative, unfortunately. I simply told him to take you somewhere safe—a tea house, a shrine, someplace more friendly to mortals." His mouth kicked up in a half smile. "He said you were so noisy, he couldn't stand it, and since he owed a large debt to this particular place of business, he dropped you off as collateral to work it off."

"What delightful company you keep."

"I could say the same about you." He sighed. "That being said, I do think it would help if you talked to Melanie. She trusts you, you know. Maybe even more than she trusts me."

"Makes two of us." My mouth compressed. "And your tengu friend's 'initiative' means Kitsune was left behind and fighting for her life on top of that mountain. We need to find her, Nobu." I leaned over the table. "You owe me."

"You are right." He stood up, his expression unreadable. "Wait here." With an elegant sweep of his wings, he strode out the door, leaving me to my own devices. Which weren't much, to be honest. In the interest of keeping up my energy, I gobbled up a few dumplings from the tray, wielding my chopsticks like weapons against the hapless balls of pork and dough.

Phineas wriggled into the sleeve of my kimono. "It's probably best the brothel doesn't know I'm here. Keep your arm bent slightly, and I'll hide."

I closed my eyes and counted to ten. "How much money do you owe?"

"Not much," he said quickly. "I simply stopped by the gambling tables for a minute or two before going in search of help. I might have bet on something I shouldn't have. I might have lost. Or won," he added. "Hard to tell when you don't speak the language."

"Uh-huh." I narrowed my eyes at him. "Anyone ever tell you you're a real pain in the ass?"

"All the time. But that's why you love me, isn't it?"

Before I could answer, Nobu returned, followed by the proprietress. Her head bobbled on her elongated neck in astonishment as she saw me, and then her face grew sly. Back and forth they spoke, not that I could understand a word of it, but it sounded an awful lot like an auction to me. They'd settled on something, and now it was time to work out the details.

Nobu's face flashed with frustration, tugging on my robe in sudden emphasis, sliding his fingers through my hair. I tried to pull away, but his dark eyes spun with warning, indicating I needed to stay still.

The proprietress retorted another number, her smile growing toothy as she rounded her hands around her own belly.

Nobu sighed, straightening up and pulling out a small sack from his own robes, tossing it on the table with a thick clink. Money, then.

She retrieved the sack and bowed. "Pleasure doing business with you," she said in perfectly good English, winking at me as she retreated. "Should you find the merchandise lacking, you can look at selling her back. For half the price, of course."

"Of course," Nobu said coolly, tilting his head at her. He rewarded me with a wan smile when she left. "Well, you just cost me a rather pretty penny. Hope you're worth it."

"Take it up with the tengu," I retorted. "It wasn't my idea to be here, and I doubt I was worth all that."

He shrugged. "Value is in the eye of the beholder, I suppose. She knew that."

I wrinkled my upper lip in distaste. "What about my clothes? My normal ones, I mean. I can't walk around in public dressed like this."

"I'm sure they're long gone now. The shrine should have something more appropriate once we get there. The sooner we get out of here, the better."

The door slid open again before I could answer, the proprietress handing Nobu a written note—a receipt I was guessing, proof that I was essentially a free woman. Or at least owned by someone other than her. For now, it was the best I could do. Nobu nodded gravely as he took the paper, tucking it away in his robe, and then gesturing at me to follow. He led me through the common room, ignoring the other patrons, then collected his sword from the front desk, and the two of us made our way out of the tea house.

Along with my missing clothes were my shoes, and the slippers I was wearing weren't meant for walking on the ground. Before long they were almost completely destroyed, my fine kimono getting filthy as it dragged behind me. But for all that, I was mostly ignored as we made our way through the crowds—one more woman owned by a master, and an outsider woman at that. If it hadn't been clear before, the fact that I was worth very little to the people around me had been hammered into me quite hard.

When we arrived at the front gates of the red-light district, Nobu presented his receipt to the guards, and they waved us through.

"Women who are bought usually aren't as flashy in their dress as you are once they've been released," Nobu said, "but it cannot be helped."

"It could have been," I said, shifting uncomfortably.

"And I paid more for you than I should have." Nobu shrugged. "Half the reason negotiations took so long was because she was asking far more than you're worth. You weren't even there long enough to earn a reputation."

"Then I suppose that makes us even." I stretched, ignoring the cat girls scampering by with baskets of flowers on their arms. "Where to now?" Since we'd left the tea house, all the tension seemed to leave my limbs, knowing that even if I wasn't with an ally, I also wasn't with an enemy.

For now, it would do.

"It's a bit of a haul from here," Nobu admitted. "We'll

have to either fly or take Gates."

I shuddered. "Gates please. I've had enough flying around for a lifetime."

"Fair enough. The nearest Gate is on the far side of the city; they didn't want one too close to Shimabara. Keeps people from trying to escape." His mouth pursed. "Not that most of them get past the guards anyway."

"I didn't realize it was such a thing here: OtherFolk keeping OtherFolk as slaves and servants and whatnot."

He let out a bark of laughter. "Don't be on such a high horse, Abby. Your Faery queen is no different. Her people are nothing but whores, turning themselves inside out for her delight. We're simply more honest about it here."

I blinked. "As you say."

He went quiet after that, leaving me to trail behind him as best I could. The city or town or whatever it was had a quaint Japanese feel to it, like something out of a movie or anime. An Edo period thing, I guessed, though I was certainly no expert.

"Why do the yokai live like this?" I asked. "I mean, in such a primitive way? I always thought it would be more like Tokyo—all lights and colors and stuff." My words tried to fill the silence. The less I talked, the more I thought, and the more visions of Melanie and Kitsune and the others ran rampant in my mind without any answers.

Nobu bristled. "I would watch your words, *gaijin*. And it's no different from the Fae living in their silly castles and playing with swords. OtherFolk live as they are most comfortable. The world is changing, after all. Faster than even we can keep up with. And we . . . do not change so quickly. For all our lengthened life spans and magic, we're often reduced to nothing more than mascots for ramen or toilet cleaner. It's frustrating and humiliating. Perhaps living in an environment such as this simply eases our minds, reminding us of who we used to be, when the world was right and we knew our places in it."

"That makes sense," I said slowly, wondering if the OtherFolk of Portsmyth felt the same way. With so much reliance on technology and science, it would be no wonder so many of them were desperate to find TouchStones. Suddenly Katy and Brandon's app didn't seem so foolish. Maybe I was the blind one for not having seen it sooner.

"What shrine is Mel at? And what about Kitsune? Where would she go if she survived the attack?"

"Kitsune will undoubtedly be at Fushimi Inari, the main shrine for foxes. If they cannot help her there, she will not be helped anywhere. Her goddess will most likely step in to assist." He hesitated. "I will see what I can find out, after you've seen Melanie."

After what felt like hours of walking through a maze of buildings and cobbled roads, we arrived at the Gate. Built like so many others, the painted red wood blazed through the mist like a beacon *and* a warning. It spanned the road and then some, providing easy passage for the large groups of OtherFolk walking beneath it—some with carts or animals, some tiny, some ridiculously large.

Nobu glanced over at me. "Ready?"

I swallowed hard, concern for my unborn child swirling in my mind. But I *needed* to see Melanie, to make sure she was all right, to find out how I could help her. So I put on a braver face than I felt, ignoring the trembling low in my gut. "Let's go," I said, holding on to the sleeve of his robe. He cocked a brow but said nothing, and together, we stepped through.

CHAPTER 7

THE SHRINE STOOD AT THE base of a mountain, the path leading to it winding like a ribbon down the hillside and disappearing into the mist. A water fountain flowed into a stone trough of sorts, which stood beneath an awning. The temple proper was beyond it, large ropes hanging down from the eaves.

"We'll pay our respects first," Nobu said, eyeing Phineas, who had wriggled his way out of my kimono sleeve to trot beside us once we'd passed through the Gate. "Have you done this before?"

I shook my head, making my way to the fountain. I was aching with thirst, but he picked up the bamboo ladle and showed me how to wash my hands properly, pouring the water from one hand to the other.

"Not for drinking, I guess," I said as it trickled through my fingers.

He blinked, offended. "Of course not. It's a purification ritual. Now, when you reach the inside of the shrine, bow, put a coin in the box, and then you pull hard on the rope to sound the bells. Bow twice, clap twice. When you finish praying, bow again."

He went through the motions quickly, his wings tucked neatly against his back, and then he handed me a one-hundred-yen coin. He rolled his eyes as he watched me attempt to do as he'd demonstrated, though my shy attempt to pull the rope likely did little to improve his opinion of me.

"This is confusing," I admitted.

"Have you been to a Catholic mass lately?" Phineas waggled his beard at me from where he stood next to the statue of a shrine guardian. Maybe some sort of lion, but I wasn't entirely sure. "Stand, sit, kneel, sit, kneel, stand, eat, drink, stand, kneel . . ."

"Point taken," I said, eyeing Nobu's wings uncertainly. "So just what is a shinigami? Kitsune said that's what you were. A sort of yokai?"

"A death god," he said with a shrug. "Or at least, that's what the word translates to, though it's not quite as simple as that."

"And yet you were working for the Devil when I met you. How does that work?" I frowned at him, still trying to work it out.

"I traded myself for Melanie," he said, his voice growing soft. "I could give two shits what people call me. None of their business anyway."

Something about the tension in his shoulders indicated that this wasn't a particularly good topic of discussion and I abruptly changed it. "So if you are gods, then why pray to yourselves?" I asked dryly. "Seems a little bit like mas-turbation, if you ask me."

"I was merely demonstrating," he said with a flicker of a smile. "You're mortal; it only makes sense that you would at least show us some respect, even if you're not exactly a believer."

"So where's Mel?" I said, getting more impatient. "I've jumped through your hoops."

"All right, then." Something sad flickered over his face. "Try not to be too disappointed," he said finally. "She's got a lot on her mind."

I tightened my jaw, not comforted by his words. He

didn't say anything after that, though, but merely led me through the grounds of the shrine, white rocks crunching beneath our feet. I felt eyes upon us as we crossed the inner courtyard, but whoever was watching us kept themselves well hidden. Save for the barest movement of shadows along the walkways, I had no idea anyone else was there. Perhaps that was the idea.

"How big is this place?" It hadn't appeared overly large from the road, but we'd gone through several courtyards now.

"Part of it extends up into the mountain there," Nobu said. "But that's more for meditation and ceremonial rituals. The priests have Mel here in the infirmary where she can be . . . contained."

It was a cryptically bad word, for all intents and purposes, and not one I wanted to ask about directly. After all, I would see soon enough.

We were met in the next garden by what I assumed was a shrine maiden dressed in red and white. She looked human, though that didn't mean much. She bowed gravely to Nobu.

"How is she?" he asked softly.

"The same, *kamisama*. But she has been growing restless since you left. She is beside the fountain, awaiting your return." Her eyes fell upon Phineas, and her pretty face grew puzzled. "*Kirin*? I thought they were extinct."

"Mmm. I get that a lot. And not quite Kirin . . . They're like distant cousins." Phineas arched his neck and puffed out his chest, winking at her. "I'm rather tired—old bones and all. How about you take me on a tour of your delightful shrine here, and I'll show you how extinct I'm *not*?"

My eyes nearly rolled out of my skull when she let out a little squeal and bent down to pick him up. Phin blew me a kiss as they strolled off. "Later, Toots!"

"Pretty sure defiling shrine maidens is a sin, you know,"

I called after him.

Nobu said nothing at this, walking away quickly, and I struggled to keep up with his longer strides. The inner gardens were full of hydrangea bushes, bursting with blues and purples, and there was a large wisteria tree in the center, its branches so thick and heavy it seemed as though it would be overcome by its own weight.

Beneath it, next to a pond with a bamboo fountain, was a stone bench. And beside that was . . .

"Mel," I breathed when I saw her. She was facing the tree, but there was no mistaking her flaming red hair, the waves flowing down to the small of her back. She was dressed in a turquoise kimono, her feet in geta sandals. It should have been lovely, and from outward appearances it was, but there was something so sinister about the scene, a cloud I couldn't quite see that had somehow cocooned her in a miasma. I shivered to look at her.

Nobu gave me a gentle shove. "Go and see her. Go. I'll watch from here. Sometimes I think my presence agitates her more than not."

"Not reassuring," I said, taking a few steps toward her.

"It wasn't meant to be," he agreed.

The humming of the cicadas became obnoxiously loud, almost deafening, as I approached her. "It reminds me of Eildon Tree," I said softly, not wanting to startle her and unsure of how else to start a conversation. *What the hell were you thinking when you blew up the Barras?* didn't have the right ring to it, even though I had every right to say it, regardless of her intent.

She turned slightly, enough so I could see she was cradling her violin in her arms like a baby. It glittered like it usually did, a soft silver on the burnished wood, but the dark spot on the edge had grown larger. When she faced me, I could see it was black and bubbled, as though something was eating through it.

"Abby," she whispered, her face a wash of confusion and smeared eyeliner. Her lower lip trembled. "I'm so sorry. So sorry. I didn't mean to do it. I didn't know. I didn't . . ." She took a step forward and then another, stumbling into my arms as she pulled me onto the bench. "It's my fault. All of it."

Her face buried its way into my shoulder as she cried, great, gasping sobs that echoed around the garden in rhythmic fashion. Even in her sadness, Mel couldn't stop the music from flowing out of her, in whatever way it could escape. "We'll make it right," I told her. "Somehow."

Yet, in truth, it felt like maybe this wouldn't be that simple. Intentions aside, in the end I simply held her, letting her weep herself empty, my fingers twining through the snarls of her hair and tracing small soothing circles along the edge of her spine.

Nobu watched us with a trace of envy and anguish until I realized she had fallen asleep. He approached when her breathing became slow and calm, her face still pressed against my shoulder.

"She hasn't slept in days," he admitted. "Not since we went through the Gate."

"So what's the plan? Not to be a party pooper, but there's a lot going on. How do we move forward from here?" I chewed on my lower lip, my eyes darting toward the violin. "How do we deal with *that*?"

"My hope is if we can somehow fix it, or at least stop any additional damage, she might be able to repair what she has done." His voice dropped. "Or we could save her life, at the very least."

The tension rose inside me, raging at my own powerlessness in the situation, the fact that there was literally nothing I could do to help.

For myself, I would very much have liked Talivar and Ion to be there with me. I was entirely too far out of my depth, and while I trusted Mel with my life and literally had done so on many occasions, I was a stranger in a strange land. I had no idea what Nobu would be willing to do to make sure Mel survived, but I was pretty sure I didn't want to get between them.

"Kitsune," I said finally. "Go and find Kitsune. She's the reason I even made it this far, and she might know more. But with her injury . . . You owe it to her to find her and make sure she's okay."

He grimaced. "I suppose it would be all right to leave Melanie in your care for a while. The priests here will take care of her basic needs, but having you with her should ease her mind. It will ease mine, at any rate."

"Good enough," I agreed. "And if you can find my better halves along the way . . ." I left the rest of the sentence unsaid. It was unlikely he would simply run into them, and we had more important things to worry about anyway. "Never mind." I stroked Mel's hair. "Just go find Kitsune."

He bowed once and retreated, the rocks crunching lightly beneath his feet as he went. The bamboo fountain trickled beside us, the warm sun seeping into my bones as the cicadas picked up their hypnotic, *wree, wree, wree.*

Mel moaned slightly and turned. Tears rolled down her cheeks and soaked my kimono, though I didn't notice it much between the padding and my own sweat. In the end, there was nothing I could do except rest my head on my arm, dozing off into the hazy afternoon.

"Abby?" Mel's voice startled me awake. I jerked to one side and realized I was indoors now, stretched out over a futon. The relative coolness beneath the shadow of the building made me shiver, despite myself.

The room was even sparser than the one in the brothel, but a sliding door on the far side remained open, allowing for a view of the wisteria tree and a slight breeze to dance about us in playful relief. Mel was kneeling beside me, the violin at her side. I didn't draw attention to it, but simply seeing that she had at least put it down for a while was encouraging.

"I'm awake. What happened?" I stifled a yawn and sat up, taking a cup of lukewarm tea from Mel and sipping it slowly. It was bitter on my tongue, but I was thirsty and it was wet, so it would do.

"You passed out. Maybe we both did," she said, her face showing none of her usual animated snark. Her skin was washed-out, and even her hair hung limp and tangled. Her mouth twitched as her gaze flicked over me. "Nice outfit. You look like a whore."

"I heard they had an opening for one here, but it turns out the position was already taken by the time I arrived," I retorted.

We stared at each other for a moment, and then my face cracked and hers followed suit, the two of us laughing bitterly, my stomach aching with it. I ignored the desperate feeling lurking underneath, like sharks beneath the waves, waiting to rend me with teeth made of doubt and madness. But it lingered anyway, as though nothing would ever be good again, not between us, and it took everything I had to push that horrible empty pit away. I'd been down that road before, and it can never be filled by anything other than despair, a black hole that would become monstrous and overwhelming, consuming everything you used to try to close it.

A hint of color flared to life in Melanie's cheeks, like the frail edge of rose blossoms in the frost. It was a tenuous thing, but I held on to it, hoping beyond hope that she could be saved, that we both could.

When I finally wiped the tears from my eyes, we both sighed. "So aside from my whore clothes, is there anything else I need to be aware of? I wouldn't mind a good bath—get some of this garbage off my face. And, I don't know, a pizza?"

"Well, the bath we can manage. I take one nightly. Not so lucky with the pizza. Get used to rice." Melanie shrugged. "Sometimes I can convince Nobu to duck out and bring me some *kaarage* or something, but he's not inclined to leave me alone much." Her face softened. "He said you'd find your way here, though. He's been watching out for you."

I tugged on my kimono. "That's a rather interesting way of putting it. If by 'watching out' you mean arranging for me to be spirited away via tengu and dropped into a brothel, then yes, I suppose he has been. I'll have to get him one of those 'You Tried' stickers when I get home."

She snorted. "Fair."

I hesitated, not sure I wanted to bring up Kitsune's status yet. Mel was obviously feeling guilty as it was, and it might be better to reestablish our relationship before I started tossing accusations her way.

She bit down hard on her lower lip. "Being here in this shrine or whatever . . . It's only a temporary fix. Whatever spells or charms they're using to slow down the progress of the corruption have to be reapplied every day, and that time seems to be shortening too. Sooner or later, the bindings will wear off, and that will be that."

"And then what? Paganini said you messed up the road to Hell when you helped recreate Eildon Tree. If you fix it, you'll be released from your contract with the Devil."

"I didn't mess up the road on purpose . . . But even if I tried to fix it now, with the violin in the state it is, I might mess it up even more." She picked up the instrument carefully, cradling it against her jaw. She smoothly drew the bow across the strings, the shimmer of the Wild Magic nearly bursting from the violin. The notes hovered there, a focalization of pure musical perfection, beckoning like a promise to fulfill all your dreams, all your hopes, if you'd simply follow it, to let it into your soul.

And then the notes turned sour, shrieking like the cries of the damned. A hint of red, like an inflamed wound, edged around the silver. Mel let out a half sob and lowered the bow. "You see what I mean? Even if I could fix it, I can't hold on to it for long. And it gets worse each time I try to play; it keeps escaping my control."

I stilled, sucking in a deep breath. "Mel, what really happened at the Barras? The stuff about the Gate and your power . . ."

She put the violin down again. "I was so desperate to escape, to force that Gate open, that the power ran ragged over me. I don't know how to explain it. It just . . . exploded, I guess."

"And Kitsune tried to stop it," I added.

Mel nodded miserably. "Yes. She tried to contain the Wild Magic with some sort of barrier, but either it wasn't strong enough or she wasn't fast enough. And the next thing I knew, Nobu had pulled me through the Gate. That's all I remember."

"Must be nice to be so ignorant." Another voice from the open doorway had us both snapping our heads toward it.

"Kistune," Mel said weakly.

"Oh aye, it is me," the fox-woman replied, limping into the room in her human form, clad in a fresh kimono, this one white with pink sakura blossoms. Her tail lashed from side to side, crackling with power, but the rest of her was so still it was as though the air had merely parted to let her through.

I stood, my eyes roaming over her, trying to search out the wound she'd had before, but aside from the slight stiffness in her steps, there wasn't any outward sign. "Are you all right? What happened on top of the mountain? How did you get away?" I babbled the questions at her, relief flooding through me that I hadn't lost another friend.

Kitsune's eyes softened as she stared at me, taking in my kimono with faint amusement. "I can see you've had a time of it yourself," she said. "And I am still healing, but I will manage. I will explain it to you later, but for now . . ." Her voice trailed away before her attention rounded fully on Melanie. To her credit, Mel didn't even try to say anything; she simply sank to her knees and performed *dogeza*, her head dipping forward to rest on the floor.

I'd never actually seen it outside of anime gags and J-dramas, but here it was. Watching my friend prostrate herself before Kitsune made me uneasy, though. To see her so despairing that she would give such a deep apology to anyone.

Kitsune made no motion at all with this particular action by Mel. Nobu lingered in the doorway, his face cement-smooth, but there was a tension about him that didn't seem like it was anchored in reality. It was as though he too might explode any minute, his power rolling over us like a thundercloud.

"You don't need to do that," he said to Mel finally. "It isn't entirely your fault."

"I don't know what else to do," she sobbed. "I don't know how to make it right. I don't know . . ."

He knelt beside her, one wing spread out as if to protect her from Kitsune's stony glare. "Well, this isn't getting us any closer to finding out how to do fix it," he pointed out. Then his head dropped to Mel's ear, and he whispered something only she could hear. She shuddered once and let him draw her to her feet.

Kitsune's brow rose. "Interfering in an apology? That's bold, even for you, shinigami."

"It is not her culture to do so. And I will not have her

abase herself for what she did not mean to do." He snarled at Kitsune, and she bared her fox fangs at him.

"She must still take responsibility for her actions, fault or no," Kitsune insisted. "The injuries to me are grave, but the destruction of the Barras is an affront I cannot allow. That her magic is unraveling is unfortunate, yes, but the innocents who died in that attack were not at fault either, save for the fact that they merely existed."

Mel's eyes widened, turning her face toward me. "Wait, the Barras? What happened to it?"

Nobu shot me a warning look, but I ignored him. "You sort of . . . destroyed it." I hesitated. "There were deaths, Mel. A number of them. Injuries . . ."

"No wonder," she whispered, staring down at her hands. "No wonder you all look at me with those accusing eyes. I couldn't figure it out. I didn't know. I thought I had simply hurt a friend by accident, but this . . . this . . ." Her face paled as she turned to Nobu. "You didn't tell me."

"You weren't in the right frame of mind to hear it," he said softly.

Anger swept across her face. "That's not fair!"

"What's not *fair* is watching you fall apart," he retorted. "Not knowing if you're going to explode with power or implode or waste away." He gestured at the violin but didn't attempt to touch it. "The worst thing you ever did was bargain for *that*. It's coming to roost now, and you have to deal with it, little bird. Running away is no longer an option."

"It's all I've ever done," she whispered, burying her head in her knees. "All I've ever known how to do."

Kitsune's face flattened. "Whether that's true or not is up for debate, but you insult the gods to hide yourself. Why would they give you such power only to have you squander it?" She held out a clawed hand. "Give me the violin."

"But—"

"I'm not going to hurt it," she said impatiently, turning toward Nobu. "All I want to do is assess how bad the damage is now. Your lover wasn't exactly forthcoming about it earlier."

Nobu looked vaguely ill, and I was suddenly very glad I couldn't see her expression. But I felt like a fifth wheel here. Aside from offering moral support, I had no magic, no power, and no way to help my friend. I gathered myself to my feet, wincing at the sudden pulse of pain down the side of my belly. Ligament issues maybe. I seemed to recall that connective tissue got a bit lazy during pregnancy, but it stopped a few seconds later so I wasn't going to worry about it too much. I poured myself another cup of tea and sipped it, trying to ease the tension in my body.

Kitsune hardly paid me any attention at all, and Mel . . . well, Mel sniffled and gave me a red-eyed half smile. "I'm going to go for a walk," I said, not sure if I wanted to be privy to their conversation. "I'm a little stiff."

My hand rolled over my growing belly, fingers white-knuckled and aching as I looked at Melanie again, her misery more apparent by the minute. But I needed time to figure out how best to help her. I stepped through the door, past Nobu, and toward the inner courtyard garden. A wooden trail slipped in and out among the water lilies, fat koi swimming aimlessly. I sat on a bench overlooking the pond, idly tapping my feet. There were soft murmurs coming from the room I'd vacated, but Nobu still stood guard in front of it, giving the women their space while remaining ready to interject if need be.

It wasn't a conversation I needed to be a part of. At least not now.

At some point, I must have drifted off again, the warm sun, the tinkle of the stream, the soft *bub-bub* of the bullfrogs lulling me into a deep sleep. Frankly, it was a wonder anyone ever got anything done here, with how peaceful it was. But I'd had very little peace over the last few months, and I was drinking it up with every drop. Even so, I decided to take advantage of it. Perhaps I'd find more answers in my Dreaming Heart, or at least be able to leave a message for Ion. Nobu hadn't said anything about the boys, after all, and I hardly thought it would be something to slip his mind if he'd figured out where they were.

So that left me.

My Dreaming Heart was as quiet as ever, soft and peaceful beneath the moonlight. But it wasn't particularly empty. Outside the gates, a certain scarlet-winged succubus paced, all pale skin and dark hair and dangerous eyes.

"Sonja," I said, striding toward her.

"And here I thought you trusted me enough to leave the gates open for me," she grumbled. As Ion's sister, she and I had been through quite a lot together, and even if we weren't always particularly close, I knew I could count on her to have my back.

"Well, it's instinctual, I guess. I get nervous when Ion isn't here, maybe." I gestured at the gate, and it opened with a familiar creak. "Don't suppose you've seen him around lately? I seem to have been slightly misplaced."

She snorted. "I'll say. And here I was coming to ask *you* if you'd seen him. He took off yesterday with that elf fellow to head your way—haven't seen either of them since."

"Odd. I told Ion I was in OtherFolk Japan, but without a Gate, I don't think they can get here."

"They went the old-fashioned route." She spread her wings in example.

I blanched. "What, by plane?"

"Yup. I don't know if they would've gotten a direct flight or not, but I suspect they'll be a bit grumpy when they land either way." Her mouth pursed. "Should be a bit of an eye-opener for both of them. I don't think they're particularly used to such mundane means of travel."

"Well, no. Why bother when you can simply take Doors?" I admitted. "But do either of them have any idea what they're doing? Can they speak the language?"

She snickered. "I doubt it. I almost wish I had tagged along. I rather enjoy seeing my brother being taken down a peg or two."

"Well, do you at least know where they're landing? There can't be that many airports in Tokyo."

"Narita, I suspect. Though I could be wrong. Maybe Haneda." She shrugged, her wings shifting in sudden irritation. "They're grown men, Abby. They've got magic. I'm sure they'll be fine. More importantly, how are you?" Her eyes dropped to my belly.

"Well enough. I found Melanie—Kitsune, Nobu, and I are trying to help her, but I'm not sure what else I can do. How are the Barras?" A guilty twinge pinched my gut, remembering Jimmy Squarefoot and the others, the empty loss in their eyes as they tried to rebuild their home.

"They're managing, but it's a bit of a shitshow. It really is. All the tenuous bonds between Paths over the last few years are starting to unravel. You're the common thread, Abby. We need you in Portsmyth to help oversee things." Her mouth quirked up in a tight smile. "It's nice to be wanted, isn't it?"

I let out a sigh. It wasn't me they wanted. It's what I represented—the lynchpin in all these relationships, binding the Paths together. And somehow it had worked. Until now.

"So, what? You all fall apart if I'm not there? What the hell will you all do when I die? Well, I mean, die *again*." I shuddered and waved the thought away. Old history and whatnot. "You're all big boys and girls, like you said. Maybe it's time you started acting like it."

Her lip curled ruefully. "It's not always as simple as that. We're dependent on mortals; we always have been. And that's part of our nature that cannot easily be undone. But I will pass it along as advice, and we'll take it or leave it as we always do." She paused. "That Paganini fellow has been lurking about the Hallows, by the way. No one wants him there. Despite his talent, he's a bit of a buzzkill."

"Go figure. He's probably waiting for me. Or Mel, really. Hopefully he'll simply continue to wait."

"I doubt it," she said cheerfully. "In fact, he's made it rather clear that there's now a substantial reward for finding her—alive, of course. He was very insistent on that part." Her lips parted predatorily, a hint of fang peeking out from between her lips. "Normally I'd say no one would bother, but given what happened to the Barras, there are several who might be having second thoughts. Brandon is doing what he can: The more Paganini drinks, the quieter he is, so we keep plying him with alcohol. And Robert looms passive-aggressively and keeps handing him forms to fill out in triplicate."

Mentally, I felt as though I were simply checking boxes off an imaginary list called 'How can we fuck up Abby's day today?' But I had no simple answers. "All right," I said finally. "Keep me in the loop if anything else pops up. Leave a message here, I guess. I'll do the same."

"Will do," she said before disappearing on the breeze with an echo of laughter. I closed the gate to my Dreaming Heart, slightly disappointed. I'd been on the cusp of asking her to see about finding a Gate in the general area, something that might help us move between realms. But surely Kitsune would have known if there was one like that nearby.

Besides, if we were to find one and use it, it would only be a matter of time before Paganini and the others were to discover it too. So perhaps it was better in the long run to keep things as separate as possible, painful as the traveling might be.

Which only led me to one conclusion: I was going to have to round up the boys myself.

CHAPTER 8

"**I**DON'T KNOW, ABBY. I CAN'T get this thing to react to me. We may have to wait until someone else goes through and follow them." Phineas grumbled at the base of the Gate, his horn rubbing against the red wood without success. "I don't know if I can force it open."

"That's the sort of thinking that got Mel and me in trouble," Nobu said behind me. "And it doesn't work like a Door anyhow. They are two different types of magic and two different sets of transport. The concept is the same, but the currency isn't. Like using a Suica card on the New York City subway."

"And here I thought magic was magic," I said, looking down at the simple kimono I'd borrowed from one of the shrine maidens. It wasn't ideal, and I was sure I'd get some looks strolling around Tokyo—there weren't too many white people in Japan walking casually around in kimonos—but I didn't have a choice. At least I'd washed the makeup from my face and pulled the hairpins out so I could arrange it into something a bit more manageable. My hobo was on my shoulder, though, and I still had my credit cards and phone, so those would get me far enough to start.

The shinigami shook his head as I crossed my arms. "The Gates aren't like Doors on the CrossRoads; yokai can't simply go through them, TouchStones or no. Or at least not all of them. Some of them can only be activated by their spiritual guardians, many of whom have been sleeping for hundreds of years, which makes those Gates effectively closed. The guardians can be rather difficult to awaken." He reached out and laid a hand on the wood, his fingers stroking it gently. "And some only open for their gods."

"Fascinating. But that doesn't help me right now. Talivar and Ion are on their way, and I need to reach them. I don't know when they left or what flight they took, and with the difference in time, there's no way to determine how long ago they even left. I know they're landing in Tokyo. So unless you've got access to a charging station for my phone and some Wi-Fi nestled away in the shrine here, I could use a little help."

Nobu smiled when the Gate lit up like a beacon in the mist as he stroked it. "I can take you as far as Kyoto. If you need to get to Tokyo after that, you will have to board a train, but it won't take more than a couple of hours on the Shinkansen. Assuming you don't make any detours," he added dryly.

"Never," Phineas assured him, looking slightly offended.

Nobu rolled his eyes, but the Gate continued to glow beneath his touch. "And which god does this particular Gate belong to?" I asked.

"Me." Nobu snorted. "I would have thought that would be obvious by now. What did you think a shinigami was? A mere anime character? I assure you we're very real." Amusement flickered over his face when he met my eyes. "Don't look too impressed. There are about eight million of us here; it's not that big a deal. The line between yokai and gods is very, very fine. A few worshippers and a tiny shrine built to a spirit of good luck can elevate us to divin-ity—and just as easily drop us down the moment we're forgotten. Mortals are fickle things," he added dryly.

"And yet you made me *pray* to you," I said, still slightly outraged at the concept.

"Your heart wasn't in it. It doesn't count." His wings unfurled, and he yawned. "Much."

My upper lip curled at him, but I let it go. "So we going or what?"

"Yes. While Mel and Kitsune work on their issues, there isn't much else we can do. Oh, and I need you to pick up a few things for me in Tokyo. Two birds, one stone, right?"

"Demoted to a celebrity shopper. How droll."

His eyes narrowed. "You are more than welcome to switch places with me, Abby. You might find being under His thumb in Hell far more amusing than a couple of errands in Akihabara."

I flushed. "Point taken. What's Akihabara?"

"Electric Town—a weeaboo's wet dream on the east side of Tokyo." He gestured at the torii gate and the edges lit up in a golden hue this time. "Come on."

Barely slowing down, he ducked through the entrance. I hurried along after him, my feet wobbling in my borrowed geta sandals. Phin trotted at my side, his blue eyes pensive. The tracks were still golden, the fog as dark as before, but Nobu strode with a sure sense of purpose, leading us up and down, through tunnels and over bridges, reeds floating in the pools below, until we came to another large Gate, this one far bigger than the one we had come through.

"Heian Shrine," Nobu noted as we emerged outside an enormous courtyard of white stones surrounded by numerous crimson-colored shrine buildings with green rooftops. "There's a tourist bus that stops here regularly. It should be able to take you to the train station, and from there, you can buy a ticket to Tokyo."

"Sounds easy enough, considering I've never been here before," I retorted. "I don't speak the language, but I can read a basic map." Phin pressed up against my legs looking as though he might be sick again. "And I'll have Phin with me, so it's not like I'll be completely alone."

"Depends on your point of view." The unicorn muttered something else beneath his breath, ignoring the way the passersby were staring at us. "Hey, you think they'd make me a god if I farted rainbows or something?"

I scooped him up as quickly as I could and dropped him into the hobo before he could do anything of the sort. We were attracting enough attention as it was with me in my kimono and Nobu looking like a rock star, colored hair, partially shaved head, leather everything. We did not make a particularly good pair, even with his wings glamoured away.

Nobu dug into his jacket pocket and pulled out a wad of cash. "You'll at least need the currency to get around. And *don't* talk to the police. You can get busted if you're not carrying your passport."

"Maybe it would be better if you took me all the way," I said faintly.

"Can't. I'm not welcome in Tokyo right now, and my presence will alert certain untoward yokai to my little bird. I guarantee if I show up there, they'll find their way to her." He grimaced. "We may not truck much with daemons from your realm, but some yokai will be more than willing to sell us out. And given that He wants her so badly ... No." He shook his head. "I will not put the people here in the line of fire for something you can do yourself."

"But you'll put the Barras at risk without a thought, is that it?" I snapped. "Take your high-and-mighty pride and shove it up your ass."

"Ask Kitsune whose fault that was," he said coldly. "If she had just let us through, there wouldn't have been any need for Melanie to even use her violin. Now, if you want to find your lovers and help your friend, you'll head to

Tokyo. Here." He thrust the wad of cash into my hand, watching as I shoved it into the hobo before he wrote something on a piece of paper. "This is the address. Look for Gachapon Hall in Akihabara. There's a yokai there—a kappa. His name is Haru. Give him this, and he'll know what you need."

"Okay." I shrugged. "How hard can it be?"

And the answer was: Not particularly hard at all.

My phone was nearly dead as it was, so I stopped in a McDonald's. At least I knew I could read the basic menu there, but more importantly I could quickly charge my phone while I ate. And I ate *a lot*. However many days I'd spent in yokai land, it was clear I wasn't getting quite enough sustenance, so I quickly wolfed down two burgers and an order of fries, chasing it with a Coke. It might have gone a little further if a certain unicorn wasn't stealing most of the fries, but it was enough.

Once my phone was active, I had a map I could work with. Which helped to a point, but Wi-Fi was a bit scattered and service was currently unavailable. One of these days I was going to have to try to do what I did to my enchanted iPod. If I could somehow replicate it, maybe I could set it up so the phone would never need to be charged and it would always pick up a signal.

I gathered my things, headed outside, and hailed a taxi to the Kyoto train station. The driver was clearly used to picking up clueless tourists, even ones dressed in kimonos. His broken English was more than enough for me to tell him where I wanted to go, though I suspected it wasn't going to be overly cheap.

I flipped through the wad of yen Nobu had given me, trying to figure out how much it was. A million? Was that right?

"Don't get too excited," Phin mumbled from my purse. "It's about a thousand dollars, more or less. Maybe a little more depending on the stock market. Enough to get you to Tokyo and back, for sure, though I don't know about Ion or Talivar." He yawned. "But we can worry about that part later. Besides elves can do that leaf-money trick, right? That thing where they glamour leaves into money and pay for shit, then bail before it reverts? Probably would come in mighty handy for a king."

"Not that he's ever done it," I said. "At least not in front of me. I don't think he considers such things particularly honorable."

"Honor gets you killed," he pointed out. "And sometimes, it's really inconvenient. I'd have thought you would've realized that by now."

"Yeah, yeah. Point taken," I grumbled.

"Wake me up when we get to the station." He disappeared into the purse, and the only sound after that was light snoring.

The entire ride took about twenty minutes, weaving through a mishmash of city streets. I simply watched the buildings go by, wondering at the architecture and the seamless way old and new seemed to blend together. Cliché maybe, but it was true.

In any case, I arrived at the train station without much fuss, though the driver refused any attempts of tipping, and in the end, I wandered about the station trying to figure out where I needed to go. Nobu had mentioned the Shinkansen, so I followed the signs until I found the Japan Rail ticket counter and fumbled my way through the purchase, buying the next ticket to Tokyo.

After that, I bought a bento lunch on Phin's insistence. I wasn't particularly hungry after my McDonald's binge, but even I had to admit the boxed lunches looked divine. They heated it up for me as I waited and by the time it was ready, it was nearly time for my train. I hurried to the platform, finding the unreserved ticket lines and taking a place behind the others who were waiting for the train to arrive.

Scenery rocketed past the windows in a blur, the quiet rush making me sleepy. Being shunted along like this was a bit like blood rushing through a vein. The feeling was vaguely disquieting. But my bento was calling me and I had no seatmates, so a pair of disposable chopsticks later, Phin and I were firmly entrenched in some sort of seafood and noodle dish. Well, to be fair, I ate the noodles and Phin ate the fish, but it was still pretty good all the way around.

I patted the roundness of my belly, polishing off the meal with a bottle of peach-flavored water.

"You know, you're probably going to need to go up a size or two," Phin noted between gulps of his Strong Zero. "You're starting to fill out a bit more."

"Maybe." The kimono hid it well enough for now. But I didn't know how fast these things were supposed to happen. "Dunno if I'll fit in any of the maternity clothes here. I seem to be a bit taller than a lot of the women I've seen. Either way, I'd like to get into something a bit more modern."

"I'm sure Tokyo will have more than enough options," Phin said.

I checked my phone and nearly shouted when I saw the date. Those few days in Yokai-Land appeared to have eaten through several weeks in the mortal realm. I inhaled sharply. If I traveled on the CrossRoads too many times, I'd be giving birth within the month. I touched my stomach. How was this going to affect her development?

"Don't worry about it." Phin rested his head against my belly. "I can hear her heartbeat fine. She's okay."

"Didn't figure you for a midwife. No offense." I appreciated the update, but the whole thing made me dreadfully uneasy. My phone beeped suddenly, distracting me from whatever weird conversation I was about to have. I pulled it out and sighed; it was flooded with texts from Ion and a few from Talivar, mostly from right after I'd been pulled through the Gate with Kitsune.

The last one was from Ion and fairly recent: *Flew to Japan. On our way to you. Don't move.*

Too late. On my way to Tokyo, I responded. *Meet you at . . .*

I hesitated. I didn't know shit about landmarks except what I'd seen in anime, which left what? Tokyo Tower? I elbowed Phin. "Hey, where should we meet them? They're already off the plane."

He blinked up at me, bleary-eyed. "Eh. Akihabara. We have to go there anyway, and I hear they have maid cafés."

I rolled my eyes. "Lecher." I pulled up a map of Akihabara on my phone. I didn't trust myself to find them anywhere in the actual train station, but there was bound to be a landmark somewhere. I scanned through a couple of pictures on Google and texted a shot of a bright-red building, the word "SEGA" emblazoned on the side in large letters.

"That should be obvious enough, eh? Even a color-blind bull wouldn't miss it." I eyed the shop wistfully. Given the circumstances, it wasn't the time to sightsee, but that didn't mean I wouldn't earmark it to visit in the future.

Assuming things with Melanie went well, of course, my inner voice said snidely. If the Devil decided He had a bone to pick with her personally . . . well, that would be another thing altogether.

I sobered immediately at the thought, finished texting Ion, and settled myself in my seat. I was tired, my limbs heavy with fatigue, and I needed to rest while I had the chance. With the lost time on the CrossRoads, I was having a harder time adjusting than usual. It made sense if I really thought about it: Pregnancy was full of changes that happened over a slower period, and by jumping back and forth from the CrossRoads, perhaps my body was jumping forward too, my bones and joints stretching faster than they should.

I stroked my stomach again, as though to reassure myself that it would somehow be all right. But I knew from here on out I would have to stay away from the Gates and stick to mundane travel. At least until the baby was born. Mel would have to face her demons—both literal and figurative—without me. There was no denying that, not with the baby's health taking priority. Still, I seethed with frustration at not being able to do any more than I already had been. Was this how she'd felt about me time and time again? Watching me throw myself off the cliff for the men I loved, the world I needed to protect?

On the whole, it didn't sit well. No wonder she'd taken off when she had thought I'd died. The guilt must have been unimaginable.

I wanted her back—free and smiling, without that dark cloud hanging over her, the despair wrapped tightly around her like a cocoon. *What sort of butterfly could possibly emerge from something like that? But then, I suppose that's what we all wanted.* I tapped my knee in sudden irritation.

"Where do you think we'll find this kappa Nobu was talking about? Akihabara doesn't look that big. A few blocks in either direction isn't too bad, especially if we split up." I pulled out my phone again for another quick Google search. "I don't even know what a kappa is supposed to look like. It's some kind of water spirit, I guess?"

"If it were that simple, Nobu would have come himself," Phin pointed out. "I'm sure it will be a shitshow. Needles and haystacks and all that. If the OtherFolk here are as canny as us, Glamours will be involved in some fashion. Even if we find it, getting in might be another story entirely."

"Like that veil spell on the Door in the Hallows? Ion can be pretty convincing, remember?" I reminded him, remembering a different day where he'd practically seduced an art gallery employee out of her clothes on the spot to help us find a certain kidnapped Fae princess.

"*Mmmph.* I wish we had an actual guide," Phin grumbled. "I feel sorta naked out this way. The magic feels funny. Like it knows I don't belong. Itchy, maybe." He shook himself. "It's not as bad on the train, but that shrine thing was getting a bit ridiculous."

"I didn't realize it was that uncomfortable. I'm sorry I hadn't noticed."

"Yeah, well, you had other things to worry about." He paused. "I wonder if that's how Kitsune and Nobu feel when they're on the CrossRoads." A shudder rippled over him. "Maybe you get used to it after a while."

"Maybe," I said slowly. Nobu was a puzzle I couldn't figure out. Melanie had never told me how they'd met, even. But god or not, he was utterly devoted to her, regardless of the cost. As for Kitsune, she certainly wasn't in particularly good graces with the other yokai from what I could tell, though I could only guess what had happened to her to make her leave Japan. "Or maybe they had no choice. If there are no options, you can learn to live with a lot."

He fell silent after that. I wasn't sure if he was sleeping or lost in his own thoughts. It would be at least another hour before we arrived in Tokyo, so with nothing else to do, I sank into my seat and watched the world rattle by.

"Motherfucker!" Phineas swore from my hobo as I was jostled again. We'd arrived in Tokyo Station just in time for rush hour, and the swarming mass of bodies surrounding us was like swimming upstream in a river of honey. And bees. In fact, a beehive was all I could compare it to.

I earned a few unfriendly looks for getting on the wrong side of the escalator or pausing to try to figure out where to go. My own temper was beginning to fray. I'd been wandering about for nearly forty-five minutes as it was, before even trying to buy a ticket for one of the subway lines. I hoped it would take me toward Akihabara.

Which it didn't. Twenty minutes into it, I realized I was going the wrong direction. I got off as soon as I could, and I was left wandering a miles-long underground shopping mall.

"I'm in hell," I said. "This is hell: A never-ending train station where I can't find the right line and that's filled with a billion people all dressed better than I am. And obscenely cheery music. And Hello Kitty telling me to have a nice day, *onegaishimasu.*"

Phin snorted. "I'll bet you're not half-wrong. Not that I've ever been there," he said, his voice muffled through the fabric. "I hear there's an actual Hello Kitty train out of Osaka, by the way. That's probably the one that takes you straight to the Devil's bedroom."

"Jesus wept." I took refuge in a Beard Papa donut shop and bought at least six of the cream-filled pastries. There wasn't any place to sit down so I spent the next five minutes stress-eating them nearly all at once, crouching against the wall next to a painting of an unhappy egg-looking thing that was picking its nose.

"So much walking." I balled a napkin in my fist. "Why didn't Nobu warn me?"

"Because he's a dick, and you're too stubborn to heed sense anyway. See where all that shit gets you? Shoveling donuts into your craw like some sort of goblin in a Tokyo train station. It's not a good look, Abby."

"You carry a baby in your guts for a while and see how far that argument gets you," I retorted, wiping powdered sugar off my lips with my wrist. "Now where the fuck are we?"

I tried texting Ion again, but none of the Wi-Fi was free and I couldn't get a decent signal. My legs were killing me as I tried standing up again. Surely I used to be in better shape than this? Or maybe what they said about eating for two really was that accurate because all I wanted to do right now was sleep for the next two years. I was going to have to ask for help, but the wave of people hurrying by felt more intimidating than facing down daemons in a bar fight. And I would know. I'd done it.

"There you are, Abby!" A high-pitched voice yanked me from my internal moping, and I blinked. The PETA pixie, Didi, fluttered in front of me dressed like a Harajuku Lolita—one who had vomited a rainbow cloud and decided to wear it, that was.

"Wait," I said, confused. "Why are you here?"

"Hmph!" she grunted. "That's a welcome for you. Your incubus and the elf king asked me for help finding you. Once they learned I come here two or three times a year, it only made sense." She eyed me askance. "They told me what happened. You should have come to me first. I could totally have given you the skinny on traveling here." She sniffed. "I bet you don't even have a Suica card."

"Uh. No. No, I don't. Which is why I'm stuck here. But how the hell would I have known to ask you anyway? Most OtherFolk don't come here from what I can tell."

"Uh, hello? PETA? Greenpeace? Japan's still a whaling country; we try to protest here several times a year, you know. Mermaids and selkies and whatnot—no one likes a slaughter." She gestured at the small trail of animals following her, including beetles and her seal, Seabert. "It's for the greater good, you know."

"Fair enough," I agreed. "Where are the others?"

"Eh, I've got them holed up in a hotel. Believe me, they're not in much better shape than you are."

I frowned. "That doesn't sound like Ion at all. He'd be hot on your heels coming after me, I'm sure of it."

She snorted. "Yeah, well, the two of them don't travel on planes very well, Abby. They're pretty hungover right now—to the point that I had a great deal of trouble even getting them in a taxi." She shuddered. "Cost a fortune, but frankly, the idea of taking the train through rush hour like that was . . . bad."

I exchanged a look with Phineas. "All right. Can you at least tell me where the hell we are?"

"Ikebukuro. There's a good shopping mall up the road—Sunshine City—but I'm guessing you're not in the mood for that right now. Though you look like you could stand a change of clothes. Not sure the traditional look suits you." She shrugged, glancing down at my outfit with a wry smile. "Too bad. I was hoping to hit the Animate store across from the mall, but maybe next time."

"Yeah. I've got slightly bigger issues on my hands. Besides, there's something in Akihabara I'm supposed to get, someone I'm supposed to meet."

"Ah, okay." She brightened. "Not my favorite spot, but it will do in a pinch. Come on. I'll take you to the hotel first. We're staying in Asakusa. You have any money?"

I nodded, suddenly grateful I wasn't going to have to think too hard at least for a few minutes. Having someone lead me around was one less worry, and if it got me to Ion and Talivar, so much the better. Numbly, I let her guide me through the process of buying a Suica card. And with that, the subway became way easier. Even through the remainder of rush hour, I managed to get through crowds, Didi on my shoulder telling me which way to go and Phin in my purse making rude noises at the schoolgirls in their sailor uniforms until I zipped my hobo shut on him.

By the time we made it to the district of Asakusa, with its orange-and-red pagoda nested within the skyscrapers and Skytree lit up like a supernova a few blocks away, I was well and firmly in need of a rest. I'd barely knocked on the hotel door before it opened to reveal Ion's waiting arms. My legs gave way in relief, and I tumbled against the incubus. I was already half-asleep in minutes, dimly aware that he had carried me to a simple bed and wrapped himself around me.

"Talivar's gone out to get us some staples from the local conbini," he told me a short while later when I'd managed to wake up enough to be coherent. I had no idea how long I'd been out for. Minutes? Hours? "Phin and Didi left to go find a bar or something. Some place called Golden Gai, which sounds a bit suspect if you ask me, but I'm just as happy they're gone." He buried his face against my hair. "I'm so sorry we didn't make it through the Gate with you. I'm so sorry it took us so long to find you."

"You're here now," I said. "We're all here." The relief that we were all finally together again, that I didn't have to shoulder this alone, reared up from some hidden place inside me, leaving me weepy and sad. A torrent of tears erupted despite myself, and I wiped at my eyes frantically. "Hormones are a bitch," I muttered, though I didn't know if that was really it or not.

He pulled me closer to him, his hand curving over the edge of my stomach, and then paused. "Is it me, or have you grown substantially . . . larger?" The words were hesitant and delicate.

"Yes," I said simply, knowing there was no way to hide it. "She's growing faster. The time change on the CrossRoads seems normal until I reach the mortal realm again. At least that's my running theory. I don't want to test it again, honestly." I pursed my lips. "I will probably need to sit out the rest of this little adventure once we meet up with the person Nobu told us to find."

"*Mmmph.*" Ion nuzzled my ear. "As long as you're both

healthy. That's all that matters to me."

"All well and good, but I don't want to be dropping and giving birth on the CrossRoads either," I retorted. "Even so, there's too much that needs to be done." I ground my teeth. "Frustrating to not be able to do it."

"You've done enough," he said gruffly. "You found Melanie, you found Nobu, you found Kitsune. The rest of it is up to them."

"That's hardly fair."

"I never claimed to be otherwise," he noted, nibbling on my ear and sending shivers over the nape of my neck.

I snorted, squirming when his hand dropped to the juncture between my thighs. "Really?"

"An appetizer. It's been a few days." His fingers moved softly, questioning, almost hesitant in their motion. The incubus tended to be a bit more proactive, but this felt almost shy.

He kissed me then as I rolled onto my back, my legs spreading automatically while I wriggled beneath the sheets. It's not that I wasn't exhausted; I was. But after the uncertainty of the last few days, even I had to admit I was craving an additional sort of closeness.

His power washed over me as I grunted my consent, sending a rippling wave of heat across my skin, chased by his mouth in soft kisses over my cheeks and neck. I sighed, letting him pamper me in caresses, desire sparking like little lightning bolts with each touch. A soft moan escaped me as he worked his way down, my kimono somehow coming undone in a flurry of expert motions I couldn't quite keep up with. My bra and panties followed suit, and he captured a pert nipple with his mouth, rolling the velvet of his tongue in a series of circles that had me melting.

I squirmed, his other hand slipping beneath my backside to explore between my thighs, dipping into the wetness there with delicate certainty. I vibrated beneath his touch, rocking my hips in encouragement. He chuckled at my impatience, massaging me with a careful knuckle, drawing a high-pitched cry from me with expert motions. The hardness of his erection pressed against my hip, and he rubbed it against my thigh, though he made no attempts to go any further.

When I made a questioning murmur, he kissed me hard, his tongue lapping at the corners of my mouth. "Later," he whispered, sliding a finger inside me, crooking it just *so*, his thumb rolling over my clit. "Come."

The orgasm tumbled through me without warning, the buildup of pleasure suddenly jacking up to eleven, the hum of his magic surging over my skin as I convulsed around him. He captured my soft cries in his mouth, humming in satisfaction as he kept up the gentle thrusting with his fingers.

When I finally came up for air, his golden eyes were glowing and sated. As an incubus, he fed off sex, which sounds more fabulous than it was, at least some of the time. Not that I generally would object to it anyway, but seeing as he needed it to survive, it wasn't like I could deny him. And as much as I appreciated dream sex when we had it, even I had to admit there was something a little more satisfying when it happened in the real world.

"Get everything you need?" I asked.

He removed his hand and gently kissed the roundness of my stomach. "Not that I couldn't go for seconds, but this takes the edge off." He flopped down next to me. "Sleep now. We'll figure out the rest of it in the morning."

Boneless and still trembling with the aftereffects of his love, I was already drifting off, wrapped in the protection of his arms.

CHAPTER 9

THE WATER PELTED HOT AND comforting against my skin as I soaped up and rinsed off quickly. The hotel was Western-style, so the bathroom was familiar enough. Not like the bathhouse in Yokai-Land.

I definitely appreciated the heated toilet seat, though. Perhaps I could get Moira to find me a magical version of something like that for my apartment. First things first, though ...

The evening had passed uneventfully I supposed—though Didi and Phin didn't totter home until the wee hours—they were both snoring away in the corner, stinking like they'd bathed in a brewery. Knowing Phin, perhaps they had.

Talivar must have shown up after I'd fallen asleep. He'd filled the mini fridge with an assortment of snacks, sandwiches, and flavored waters of various sorts. I'd woken up ravenous, so it would certainly do. Whether the time difference or my swelling belly was the cause, I wasn't sure, but it didn't matter.

Talivar had been up early too, leaving before I'd fully awakened, though where he'd run off to, I had no idea. Phin and Didi were gorging themselves on Wasabi KitKats, the thought of which made my stomach roll. Both of them had the bloodshot eyes of the perpetually hungover, but otherwise they didn't appear the worse for wear.

"How was Golden Men or whatever you went to see last night?" I nudged Phin with my foot, earning me a snap of teeth for my trouble.

"Golden Gai," he corrected. "It's not a show. It's an alley. Full of . . . of . . . little bars." He shook his head blearily. "Too many goddamned tourists is what it was full of. I nearly got stepped on three or four times as it was."

"I'm surprised they would even serve you at all," I said. "Unless there are OtherFolk venues there too? Something like the Hallows?"

"Only one they'd let us into," Phin said sullenly. "Apparently the universal language of love isn't so universal here." He crossed his eyes, trying to look at his forehead. "I bet if I still had more of a horn they'd have changed their tune."

Didi shrugged. "Don't let it bother you. Some of these places don't want foreigners as patrons, OtherFolk or not. I know enough of the language to get by, but—"

Phineas let out a sharp bark of laughter. "They won't serve foreigners, but they let a yokai with an eyeball for an anus waltz right up to the bar. Okay. Right."

"Maybe they have actual standards," I said, digging through one of the suitcases. Someone had thought ahead and brought me at least a change of underwear and a couple of fresh shirts, and I changed into them gratefully.

My pants, however . . .

"I think I'm going to need to start looking for something in the maternity section," I said.

"Start? Hell, you better go buy out the whole section." Phin eyed my growing belly warily. "You sure you're not carrying like a litter or something? I mean, he's an incubus: What if instead of one big baby, you've got, like, thirty little peanut-sized daemons?"

"Jesus fuck, Phin!" I barked.

"Sorry, sorry." He dropped his head. "That was wrong

of me."

I picked up a sweatshirt and tied it around my straining jeans, angling it so I could at least unbutton the things without anyone noticing. "I need some fresh air." Before they could say anything else, I snatched a hotel key and let the door slam behind me.

Where I was going, I didn't quite know, but the hotel room had suddenly felt small and cloying and filled with a tension I didn't want to be a part of. The hallways of the hotel weren't air-conditioned, and the warm air hit me full in the face like a brick wall, but all it did was spur me out the door and into the morning streets of Tokyo that much faster.

I wandered about a bit, stopping only to buy some sort of crepe from a café. I escaped across the street to a park, leaning on a bench as I slowly chewed, watching the salary men and the school children walk by, the old grannies on their bikes.

Despite the swarm of humanity, there was something comforting about it. I closed my eyes in the sunshine, for a moment reveling in the sheer normalcy of it all. Different country, different people, but they were mortal, for all that, without a hint of any magic other than that of being human.

I basked in it, imagining what my life would be if I weren't pregnant. If I weren't married to a Faery king. If I weren't TouchStoned to an incubus. If I weren't a Dreamer. If my father weren't True Thomas. If my best friend weren't somehow losing her soul, trapped in a cage of Wild Magic and unable to break free. If my mother hadn't died in that car accident. If I hadn't injured myself to the point of never dancing again.

The thoughts pricked me, biting at my memories like the sharks of my nightmares. I shook my head against it. This train of thought was getting me nowhere, except sending me down a rabbit hole even Alice wouldn't be able to Cheshire her way out of.

Because I was here now, finishing up a crepe on a park bench in the middle of Asakusa Tokyo. But then, everyone else was trying the best they could. I couldn't do any less.

"Have you been here very long?" I startled slightly as Talivar approached from the side, sliding onto the bench next to me. He was dressed in casual clothes, jeans and a plain T-shirt, though he still had his wool cap, eye patch, and gold torc around on his neck. He was clean-shaven, though, and holding a cup of steaming coffee.

My heart ached at the familiarity of him. For the first time in a while he seemed at peace, even if he wasn't entirely happy, and that steadied me.

"Not really. Taking some time for myself is all. It's been a long couple of days." I polished off the rest of the crepe and balled the paper in my fist. "I haven't seen you since you got here. I was worried, you know."

His eye flashed guilty and he gave me a wry smile. "Ah, well, maybe I needed a little time alone too. I haven't exactly been very kingly lately."

"Well, you've had reason. This is uncharted territory—for all of us." I stretched and sank against him so I could rest my head on his shoulder. He turned to catch me against his chest and sighed.

"I'm sorry," he murmured. "The other night, bringing it up like that, it was wrong of me. I just get so frustrated with this. You. Ion. The baby. My thoughts are so tangled up, and I don't know what to do. Do I stay? Go? What would be best?" His fingers crept into mine, entwining briefly.

"I don't want you to go," I said, taking his hand and resting it on the curve of my belly. "I need you, and she will too. We're a family, Talivar. Nothing is going to change that, regardless of who her biological father is."

His fingers curled possessively around my stomach. "She is part of you, and that is all that matters to me, Abby. Whether she becomes my heir or not, I can overlook the realities of her parentage if it means not losing you."

"Even with the rest of it? I have to share my bed with Ion for the rest of my life. Our TouchStone bond is permanent, as least as far as we know. Something about our shared bit of soul maybe, when he became mortal. I'm not entirely sure how it works, but I can't break it like I've broken other Contracts in the past."

"I know." He cupped my cheek, turning my face toward his. "But do not think I will merely wait in the wings as some sort of kept man. I am willing to accept that part of you, but he must accept that you are also part of me. If you share your life with him, I will do so as well, but as *an equal*. Nothing less."

I exhaled sharply as something fluttered in my chest. "I never wanted anything different, but I wasn't sure how to talk about it."

"It has been chaotic," he admitted. "Even for us. If I were more settled within my kingdom, perhaps it would be easier. But it is what it is. I simply want you to be a part of it, to leave your mark upon something greater than both of us."

A hint of sadness crept into his words, and I swallowed hard. We all knew—Ion, Talivar, and me—that I was mortal and would die of old age long before Talivar. I would have assumed the same with the incubus, but now that we were bound permanently, I didn't know what would happen once I was gone. Would he starve to death? Or would my bond transfer my death to him at the same time? Either would mean Talivar would be left alone, most likely for a very long time.

His head dipped down so his mouth was beside my ear. "I want to be able to walk the edges of my kingdom, of my castle, hundreds or thousands of years from now, and see your reflection in the very walls," he whispered.

"Smooth talker," I choked out, my voice trying to form words that made sense even as my eyes swelled with tears. "I— Oh!" I moved his hand a little lower as my stomach rippled with sudden movement.

He pulled back in surprise. "She's quickening?"

I bit down hard on my lip as the baby let out a series of little kicks.

Talivar pressed his face to my stomach, a delighted smile on his face before capturing my mouth in a soft kiss. "Your face, Abby."

"If you say it's glowing, I'll kick you," I said.

He chuckled. "No. But I think she just became very real to you. You look like a deer in headlights, as they say."

"Maybe." I scowled as I realized he was probably right, but that only made him laugh harder.

"I've been in contact with our sister, incidentally. She has taken in those of the Unseelie Court and gotten them settled, both in the church with Roweena and for those who wanted to try living as part of the Seelie Court again, though I don't have much hope for that. A united Court would be the best for all of us, but the divisions run deep. It will take some time to see if it can really happen."

I frowned. "But then what happens to you? To your crown? If the Courts become one . . ."

"Well, my mother won't care for it either way, but Moira and I have already decided if that occurs, we'll rule jointly."

"A regular Narnia," I said, thinking of Phin's earlier words in my kitchen.

"Something like that. Though that, of course, brings up its own issues with succession and all that, but that's something we'll need to figure out anyway." His hand hovered over my belly possessively. "Soon. How far along are you now? Ion did mention something last night about the

CrossRoads and the time change possibly messing with the pregnancy."

"I'm further along than I should be based on mortal time. I should probably get in for an ultrasound or something."

His face grew slightly alarmed. "Of course. I'll see what I can do here about finding a doctor or midwife," he said, fishing his phone from his pocket. "We may have to pull some additional strings if we can't get anyone to help us. I'm not sure how much influence I'll have as some sort of visiting dignitary, but I am technically royalty, after all. I would hope that would count for something."

"Well, we're not getting anywhere sitting here." I nodded toward the street. "Rush hour looks like it's over, so we should head to Akihabara. Nobu gave me a slip of paper with the address of someone he wants us to see. It's up in my things."

"Would have been nice to know about that before," the elf said. "I could have scoped it out earlier this morning when I was out and about."

"Ah, well, I was pretty tired when I got to the hotel yesterday, and Ion . . ." My voice trailed away. "Well, you know."

"Yes, I know. I understand. I don't have to like it, but I understand." He got to his feet and held out his hand to me, gracefully pulling me upright. "Promise me that when all this is over, the three of us can have a bit of a talk. I've got some things to say, and I'd like you both to be there when I do."

"Of course," I said, reaching up to tug on an errant lock of his hair. "I think that would be a very good idea."

"Two prong attack, then. I'm going to see what I need to do to be recognized officially as a visitor. It will take the heat off what you guys are doing, and possibly even from Nobu and Mel. I'll come up with some sort of . . . I don't know. Land grab? Looking for a new place for my kingdom? I'm sure they'll refuse me that, but if we can at least go through the motions, it might allow us a little more freedom."

"I think that is an excellent idea," I said slowly. "And if I need to pull the Wife Card, I can certainly do that as well, though it might be better to keep that part under wraps unless we need it. I can be another servant or something."

"Agreed." He leaned in for another kiss, his beard scratching my face slightly. "We'll meet up for dinner tonight and see what we've found."

"Abby," Phin whispered from my bag, his voice vibrating with excitement. "Abby, do you see what they have? Do you?"

I blinked. "Akihabara has a lot of stuff, Phin. I don't know, what? Maid Cafés? Host Clubs? Manga? Hentai? What are you talking about?"

His blue eyes sparkled up at me. "Hedgehog cafés," he burbled. "They have *hedgehog* cafés. It's like a dating club just for me!"

"I didn't think we were here to find you booty," I observed snidely, craning my neck to get a better look down the crowded streets. Controlled chaos lined each roadway in all directions, a riot of colors and lights clamoring for attention above the sounds of arcades, anime billboards, girls in skimpy maid costumes, electronics, sex shops, and bookstores.

I rubbed my eyes, trying to fight off the beginnings of a headache and wondering how anyone found anything at all, suddenly grateful we had Didi to rely on instead of Google Maps.

"But they also have cat cafés and owl cafés, and I don't know, fox places up north, I think. Bunny Island," he continued.

"If it's small furry creatures you're interested in, I imagine we'd be able to find you someone . . . er, something," Didi said.

The thought of entering these places for the sole purpose of finding something willing to sleep with my unicorn felt wrong on a number of levels, but I knew that look on his face well enough to know there wasn't much point in stopping him. Phin was his own unicorn, after all. It wasn't like I was his mother. Or if I was, I was doing a piss-poor job of keeping him under control.

"Can we at least find this kappa fellow first?" I asked. "You know, saving the world takes priority over getting laid." Ion snorted, and I kicked his shin. "Or at least, it should."

"Speak for yourself," he muttered, but I caught a hint of amusement in his expression even so.

I looked at my watch; it was just past one in the afternoon. "We've got a few hours before we meet up with Talivar—assuming everything goes well on his end. We should probably head over to that gachapon place."

"Kappas like cucumber, so we should get him some as a little gift maybe," Didi noted, perking up. "He might be more likely to help us that way. I'll see if the Lawson has anything that might suit. I don't think it has to be anything fancy." She gestured at Ion. "Come on. I'll need help carrying it."

She flitted across the street, a bemused Ion trailing in her wake, leaving the rest of us to our own devices, mostly of the window-shopping sort. Though Phin desperately begged to go into the Don Quijote for . . . what, I wasn't entirely sure, I concentrated on finding another bathroom. With the slightly larger side of my belly came a rather new and exciting need to take a piss pretty much every time I stood up. But kappa or not, even I felt the pull to go into the seven-story Animate building in the hopes of finding additional anime cuteness. *Next time,* I told myself. Next time I'd come here for a month and do all the shopping.

"So where are we going?" I asked Didi when the two returned with a bag of snacks from Lawson. Ion handed me a bottle of peach water. I sipped it slowly, staring at the confusing sprawl of stores in front of us.

Didi's eyes narrowed as if she were studying something I couldn't see. "Ah, there it is." She fluttered to my shoulder and pointed up the street to a store with a huge yellow sign on top of it.

Inside were rows upon rows of gachapon machines filled with capsules stuffed with a crazy assortment of everything from temporary tattoos to plastic food to knitted caps for cats.

"The weird and the wild." I tossed two hundred yen into one and turned the dial. The plastic capsule emerged, and I opened it to reveal a tiny naked anime figure with tits larger than her head.

"Charming," Ion mused, taking it from me, "if somewhat anatomically impossible." He shivered slightly as though trying to measure if he could transform himself to match.

"Oh come on," Phin piped up. "Don't knock it. Where else you can you find such a mix of shit? Everything from underwear for your drink bottle to rubber poop to naked anime girls. It's like the gods of whimsy took a massive crap when the world was made and this is where it landed."

"Ahem. I'll thank you to kindly keep your opinions to yourself." A small door opened beneath the last gachapon machine in the back row, and a tiny little creature that appeared to be half-turtle and half-frog emerged, smoking a cigarette. He was bowlegged, standing almost to the height of my knee, a shiny turtle shell on his back and an odd little plate on the top of his amphibious head. He jabbed the cigarette at Phineas. "You're a hundred years too early to be talking trash to me in my own house."

"*Sumimasen*," Didi began, holding out the bag of salad and cucumbers she'd picked up at the conbini. "*Ky□ri wa suki desu ka?*"

"Stop." He winced. "Don't hurt yourself. I speak English fine." Ash dropped from his cigarette as he flicked it to the ground. He rolled his eyes. "Tourists."

Didi pouted, lowering the bag. "Do you want these or not?"

"It's vaguely racist, you know. But I'll take them," he grumbled. "Now what is it you want with me? I'm busy."

I glanced down the row of gachapon machines, but the rest of the store was mostly empty except for a cluster of teenage boys standing around a series of machines that sold dubious-looking egg-shaped devices. "I'm not sure we should discuss it here."

"I don't have time for this bullshit." The kappa's eyes went flat. "Get out." He made a little gesture with his stubby fingers. From the corner of my eye, the walls of the store seemed to move, as though the very concrete was filled with shadows.

"Wait!" I thrust the note from Nobu at him. "Here . . . by way of introduction. He said you had something that might help."

The kappa paused, his gaze darting over the scrawling bit of script on the parchment. His nostrils flared, and his turtle mouth grimaced. "So that's how it is." Whirling, he gestured again, the darkness fading until the walls returned to normal. "Step into my office."

He tapped on the wall behind him, and this time the entire thing receded, making an opening large enough for the group of us to fit through. Ion shrugged at me and took my hand, leading me in behind Didi. Phineas brought up the rear, and though I couldn't see anyone following us, the space around us compressed until I almost couldn't breathe.

Ion's hand tightened around mine, and I could almost see his glamour start to shiver, but he held it together. No sense in playing our cards yet. With any luck, the kappa might know he was OtherFolk but not specifically what he was.

A set of curtains blocked the hallway, but the kappa ducked through them easily enough. In fact, it was as though he'd grown a couple of feet in the short time we were walking through the passage. Or maybe it was that we had shrunk?

In either case we emerged into a riot of lights and dinging sounds, cigarette smoke and the raucous chatter of what could only be a pachinko parlor in full swing. Much like the brothel had been, it was full of yokai, plugging their yen into the machines with gusto. Girls in tight dresses waltzed by, taking drink orders and pouring sake, occasionally leading some of the patrons past additional curtains I couldn't see beyond.

The other yokai stared at us out of the corners of their eyes. They weren't trying to hide it, but their attention was fixated more on the kappa in front of us, many of them bowing as we passed by. The kappa didn't bow at all.

When we were firmly ensconced on the second floor in a VIP lounge of some sort, the kappa took a seat beneath an enormous woodcut of erotic samurai art lit up in fluorescent neon. "I suppose introductions are in order. Normally, we'd have done it down below, but this—" he shook the paper at me "—changes things a bit. This particular shinigami and I have a history, and while he owes me money, I owe him a debt far greater than that."

He paused. "My name . . . Well, call me Haru for now. Haru-san, if you feel like you need honorifics," he told Didi, sneering. "But I'll forgive you that for now. Who are you and why are you here?"

I peeked at Ion, unsure of how much to tell our host. Nobu hadn't exactly been forthcoming with information. Ion shook his head, his glamour fading away in a shiver of snowflake glitter. The crystalline horns caught the light, his gold eyes half-lidded and lazy as he smirked at Haru.

"It seems polite to do away with the disguises," he said. "Nobu and I go back a ways as well, but I don't see much point in giving up everything." He gestured to the kappa's arms, which were tattooed in a riot of colors and inks down to his elbow in what was surely a clear sign of the Japanese mafia. "I didn't think the yokai were part of the yakuza."

"Son, I damn near built the yakuza," the kappa snarled. "I may not be the largest, flashiest yokai of the group, but I don't need to be." He gestured at the door we'd come through. "As long as I keep those assholes fat, dumb, and happy, the yen keep pouring into my bank account. Besides, if the shit ever does hit the fan, you think the authorities are gonna look at a low-level yokai like me?" He snorted. "It's the only good thing about my particular stature, to be honest."

I stared at him. "You have a remarkable grasp of English, if you don't mind me saying."

"I *do* mind. And I did my doctorate at UCLA, so I had time to pick up on the particulars." He grunted, his body shifting into something tall and slender and much more human than the odd reptilian thing he'd been before, though there was still a hint of a greenish tint to his skin. "As long as I kept my grades up and the ladies happy, well, no one bothered to look that closely at me."

"Humans rarely do," Ion snorted, his golden eyes flicking sideways at me. "With certain exceptions."

"Truth. So enough with the introductions. Nobu is in a jam again, I suppose." He shook his head. "Too bad that feathered dumbfuck was too much of a coward to come see me directly."

"He's a bit preoccupied," I snapped, bristling at his tone. Ion laid a hand on my shoulder but that irritated me more. "If you have it, fine. If not, simply tell us and we'll be on our way."

Haru's eyes narrowed. "I can't imagine what he needs it for now, but . . ." He shrank down to what I assumed was his normal form. "I'm half-tempted to come with you when you return to wherever he is, but somehow I don't think he'd be too appreciative."

"I have no idea," I said. "But then I don't know what he asked you for. We didn't have time to discuss it."

Haru made a noncommittal noise in the back of his throat and waddled toward a locked closet. He snagged one of the cucumber pieces on the way there, munching it absently. I exchanged a look with Didi, but the pixie only shrugged as he unlocked the closet, revealing an enormous gachapon machine.

It was similar to the ones in the store, but this one glittered as though it was made of gold. Haru turned the dial with a quick twist. For a moment, there was a lot of rattling, like thousands of marbles rolling about a bowl. Didi's mouth dropped open as a capsule fell out. Haru opened it, revealing a small jar with a single white stone nestled inside. A soft glow emanated from it, but it was dim, even as I peered into his hand.

"What is that?" I asked.

The kappa gave me a humorless smile, his toothless grin somehow both innocent and slightly sinister. "Why, his soul, of course."

"Wait, you have his soul? Nobu hardly seems like the type to simply . . . I don't know, leave something like that around. Especially with . . ." My voice faded as I tried to wrap my brain around the idea.

"I stole it from him, duh."

"Stole it how?"

"From his ass. During a card game." He yawned. "Of course, the more I think on it, I suspect he let me do it." His grin grew wider. "It's how I have so much power you know. All those stones in there, each one a soul stone pulled from some mortal's ass."

"You're joking," I whispered, both horrified and fascinated at once.

"I don't think he is," Didi said, her voice cracking, though she looked like she might explode into laughter any second. "Shirikodama, right?"

"Oh, you *are* a weeb, aren't you?" Haru guffawed. "But you're right. Technically, we're supposed to give them as tribute to the Dragon King, but he's been asleep for the last fifty years anyway, so who gives a shit?"

I frowned. "But isn't Nobu a god? How does that even work? You said you only take them from mortals."

"Shinigami were all human once. It's part of the process. Usually they did something horrible in their mortal lives, and when they die, they're given the chance to make up for it by collecting the souls of others." Haru wrinkled his nose. "I suspect Nobu was trying to buck the system. After all, if he has no soul, it makes it a bit harder for him to be controlled."

"Sounds like something he'd do," Ion said, his face pensive. "As long as I've known him, he's always had a scheme of sorts in play. They don't always work, but . . ."

Phineas had been silent the entire time, his eyes sparkling as he listened to the kappa's tale. Finally, he inched forward, his tiny hooves tapping on the floor as he approached Haru's seat on the couch. "Teach me," he whispered, a mad light whirling on his face.

"It's not really a teachable skill," Haru said, seeming alarmed. "You don't look like you have the, er, proper anatomy anyway." He wiggled his fingers.

"Technicality," Phin said dismissively. "After all, I manage to play Fortnite just fine. Never you mind how I'll manage it."

"He *does* manage a lot of things." I shuddered. "But please don't show him that. Please."

"Spoilsport," Phin groused.

"It's a mom thing," I retorted, holding out my hand for the bottle. "So is this it, then? What Nobu sent us here for?"

Haru shrugged. "All that he mentioned in his note. Normally there'd be a fee for it, but like I said, he's done me a few favors in the past, so this should square us up."

Ion stiffened suddenly, his ebony face unreadable. "Hush." He held up a finger. "Listen."

I cocked my head, my ears only picking up the noisy beeps of the pachinko kiosks. "I don't hear anything."

"Enough of this," Haru said. "I've got another meeting, so it's time for you to go."

And then I heard it—or felt it more like. A sweeping brush of magic and music, almost seeming to slither through the room like a snake. It was familiar and sinister, and yet with a hint of discord at the edges, as though it didn't quite belong here and was straining within whatever skin held it together.

Haru jerked his head toward the sound. "What the fuck is that?"

"Paganini." Ion shivered into his human glamour.

"Wild Magic," I said. "From the CrossRoads." I pulled my feet up onto the chair as though to keep it from wrapping around my legs. It wasn't as if I could see it, but I could more sense the way it tendrilled out into the room. "He's the reason Nobu didn't come with us."

Haru's face hardened. "Not in my house, you don't." The kappa strode out through the curtains, the sounds of the pachinko machines blaring loudly as he passed. Didi fluttered around the room. "You think there's another way out of here?"

Phin was already poking about the corners. It wouldn't be the first time he'd been able to fit somewhere we couldn't, and at this point, we were running out of options. The fact that the Devil's TouchStone was here now too was not good. Clearly, He was looking for His due, and our time had run out.

"Stay behind me." Ion pressed his way to front of our group and led us through the curtains. "Maybe we can sneak out while everyone else is preoccupied. The hell I'm going to sit in a cage and wait for it to close in on us."

I only nodded. We had what we came for. However it was going to help us was moot now, but there wasn't any reason to stay. And Haru seemed like he could take care of himself.

The music stopped suddenly as we entered the main parlor. Paganini stood there, his pupils burning into me with an intensity that bordered on psychotic. "Ah, there you are, Ms. Sinclair. How good of you to come out to meet me." He lowered the violin, his bloodshot eyes and haggard face bearing witness to his clear lack of sleep, if nothing else.

"I haven't the foggiest idea of what you're talking about," I said mildly, ignoring Ion's warning squeeze. "I had no intention of meeting you; I thought we'd worked that out already."

"You're taking too long." The violinist sniffed the air as though scenting something, a hint of desperation clouding his face. "That's a soul you've got on you, isn't it?" His eyes narrowed. "What are you playing at? You can't possibly be thinking of substituting her soul for one of these."

I blinked. I hadn't thought of that at all, but by the noise Ion made, it was obvious he certainly had. Was Nobu truly going to make the ultimate sacrifice and exchange his prior mortal soul for Mel's?

Was it even my place to judge?

Haru stepped between us, his squat reptilian body quivering with barely controlled fury. "This is an outrage, and I will not allow it." He gestured to a pair of enormous bouncers, each with a set of sharp horns on their heads and scaled bodies coated in tattoos. "Check the sign on the door outside: FOREIGNERS NOT WELCOME."

"I come on the behalf of one with far more jurisdiction than you," Paganini said simply. He pointed his bow toward me. "Specifically in the case of mortals and souls."

"You're mortal, are you not?" Haru asked mildly, wiggling his fingers. "Perhaps you'd like to offer up your soul while you're here. We have a lovely set of baths downstairs, you know . . ."

"My soul is already spoken for." Paganini said dryly, his voice suddenly sounding tired.

"The only one I pay heed to is the Dragon King." Haru sniffed. "And you and whomever you represent are not him. What you do with my guests once they are off my property is your own business, but as long as they are in this establishment, they fall under his and my protection." He paused, his mouth curling into an eerie smile. "And the souls belong to *him*. I merely steward them until they are required. Believe me, you don't want to see what happens if he wakes up without anything to eat."

I swallowed at the thought. "When was the last time he, uh, awoke?"

Haru gave me a hard look. "None of your business. But let's just say some of those earthquakes we get here . . . Those are caused by his nightmares. Tsunamis are him thrashing about. Frankly, I'd have thought you gaijin would be familiar with him; they certainly made enough movies and TV shows about him."

"I don't know any Japanese dragons who come from the sea and destroy cities . . ." My voice faded into something very small. "Wait . . . You mean Godzilla is *real*?"

The kappa shrugged. "Real enough, even if the movies take a few liberties." He shifted his attention to Paganini. "Do you really want to see what happens when he wakes up grumpy? Because I sure as shit don't."

"I don't either," I said quickly. I shoved the little jar with the soul in it into my back pocket. "I think we're through here."

"Indeed," the kappa agreed pleasantly. "Now all of you, get the fuck out."

The bouncers moved toward Paganini with a menacing glare. The violinist let out a snort, raising his hand to the instrument and pulling the bow across the strings. A shiver of music dripped almost physically to the floor, a golden hue overtaking his hands and filling the air with the promise of sins brought to fruition.

"Try it," Paganini said.

"Drop him, boys." The kappa said something else in Japanese I didn't quite catch, but Didi let out a gasp.

"That was super rude." She fluttered toward the door as the bouncers went to snatch the violin out of Paganini's hands.

"Tsk." Paganini neatly stepped away, moving his body in the same fluid way I remembered Mel doing when she would get into the music she was playing. The two of them were far more alike than I gave them credit for, and the thought was rather disconcerting, if I was being honest with myself.

When the music started up again, pain lanced up my legs, digging into my toes. I clutched my belly in quiet desperation as I tried to move forward and discovered I couldn't. It was as though my feet were nailed to the floor. I let out a sharp cry as I tried not to trip and fall. Ion caught me immediately, his arms holding me upright.

"Dammit," he swore, trying to pick me up.

Fire swept over my feet again, and I screamed.

"It's an illusion, Abby. It's not real," Brystion tried again, and I gasped as my stomach suddenly hardened into a rock beneath his fingers. It startled him enough that he nearly dropped me. "What the hell is that?"

"Braxton-Hicks," I said. "Supposed . . . supposed to be harmless. Practice contractions. Read about them in that book. It doesn't hurt."

"Good enough." He bared his teeth at Paganini, who continued to play. His eyes were closed, but his feet tapped time with the notes. All around him the OtherFolk swayed, unable to move. Haru's eyes were glazed over. Another glance at Ion showed that even he was starting to have trouble shutting it out, the Wild Music luring him forward like the Pied Piper calling his rats. Instinctively, I shoved my fingers in my ears, the music muffling enough to let me catch my thoughts.

Instantly, the burning in my feet receded, and I could wiggle them freely. Mostly. Enough that I could at least take a few steps. Phineas head-butted me through my bag, nudging me along with a snap of teeth, and Ion joined us as we crept behind a row of pachinko machines.

"He's violating a lot of treaties," Phineas said. "I imagine the situation must be rather wretched if he's willing to attempt this."

"Who cares?" Ion pointed to the street beyond the doorway. "Let's get out of here, and *then* we can worry about manners and historical bullshit. We've got what we needed, so let's find Talivar and find our way to wherever Nobu and the rest of them are."

In this, at least, we were all in agreement. But before we could take another step, Haru gasped and made some sort of low humming noise that was a cross between a growl and a bark.

A distinct shudder filled the room, as though the earth

itself was shaking—or maybe it was that the floor was lowering . . . The violin music cut off sharply, and then everything went dark.

CHAPTER 10

"ABBY, WAKE UP." ION'S VOICE. Ion's touch, gently shaking my shoulder.

"This is happening entirely too often," I grumbled, my eyes fluttering open. "Where the hell are we now?" The question was vaguely rhetorical. The bars rippled as though they were made of water, shining beneath the glow of myriad tiny jellyfish rolling past. "Ah. We're in a bubble, I see."

"Something like that," Brystion agreed, shifting to sit beside me. "At least they let the three of us stay together."

"Only three?" I sat up and saw Phin was curled up by my feet. "What about Didi?"

"She got away," Phin said, yawning. "Guess those wings came in handy."

"And we're clearly in a holding cell," Ion said.

I shivered. I had some rather bad memories of being trapped in a bubble like this, hidden within an enchanted painting and unable to free myself, thanks to Maurice. Ion and Melanie had worked together to save me, but I still didn't care for the reminder. Out of instinct, I tried to flatten myself away from the shadows, as if they might contain the sharks of my nightmares. I sagged to the ground when nothing happened. "What about Paganini?" I finally croaked out, turning toward Ion. If I could ignore where we were, I'd manage.

"They took him somewhere else. He was pretty beat to hell when the bouncers dragged him away. I'm not sure what they did with the violin, though I certainly hope they keep it away from him."

"I doubt we're in for anything good," I said. Then I remembered Nobu's soul stone. I jerked my hand to my back pocket and sagged with relief. It was still there, so at least we had that much. I tapped my fingers on my leg and got to my feet. My stomach didn't feel any worse for wear given everything else that had happened, but I needed to pee. There didn't seem to be any facilities for such a thing in this little room, though, so all I could do was hope someone would come for us soon.

"It looks like this is a short-term cell. How long was I out?" I asked.

"About thirty minutes or so." Ion placed a hand on my belly. "They need to bring us something to eat and drink. At least for you. But I think you're right: We're simply waiting for them to release us, or at least tell us what's going on. Maybe Didi was able to find help."

"Well, it's not like there's an OtherFolk embassy. Or is there?" I pondered the thought.

"Yes, actually, there is," Phineas said. "With any luck Didi went straight there. What happened upstairs could potentially be the start of an international incident. We'll need some experts on our side for sure."

"Hopefully the Japanese police won't be officially involved," I said, recalling Nobu's advice to me. "I didn't enter the country legally. I don't even have my passport with me, and it's not like I can simply glamour myself away like you guys can."

We all sighed then. I wasn't above feeling a little sorry for myself, even if I knew it wasn't going to help much. But the thought of staying in here, or someplace worse, for something I hadn't done was intolerable.

"Ahem." The small coughing sound drew our attention toward the far side of the bubble.

"Speak of the devil," I murmured, wincing at my own choice of words.

Haru stood at the other side of the bars, looking distinctively uncomfortable. He bowed deeply, or at least as much as he could being such a squat little creature. "My apologies, Abby-sama."

I frowned at the change of invective. "What's that all about?"

"If I had known—" His words cut off, and he turned his head sharply to the right. "Here, let's get you out of there." With a wave of his fingers, the bars dissolved, and he gave me a rueful smile. "Nobu did not mention who you are in his letter, but I suppose under the circumstances I can understand it."

Ion glared at him as Haru gestured at me to follow. "What are you talking about?"

Haru shook his head. "Sorry, Incubus-san. The request was only for Abby-sama." His eyes narrowed at the way Phin sidled up to my leg. "And her . . . pet."

Phin's ears twisted at the word, and I quickly scooped him into my arms. I still wasn't sure where this was going, but I'd play along. Like hell I'd leave Brystion here, though.

"Well, that's all well and good, but I'm not going without my manservant." I inclined my head toward Ion. His features shifting into something slightly more refined, clothing melting into a formal black suit and white gloves, everything crisp and shiny and pressed so sharply I could cut myself on the edges.

"As my lady wishes." Ion bowed, the hint of a smile twitching the corners of his mouth.

Haru shrugged. "Whatever. I don't care. I want you off my hands and out of my life."

I followed him out of the cell, Brystion tagging along behind me with one hand on the small of my back, gently steering me. I wasn't sure if it was a comfort thing or merely practicality, but I didn't much care.

The hallway was narrow, and we passed several offshoots containing cells similar to the one we had been in. Was Paganini in one of them? I hoped so. The longer he was detained, the better chance we'd have at losing him again. Though it did beg the question of how he'd managed to track us down at all.

"Where are we?" I asked, trying to see past the barrier.

"Underwater," Haru replied shortly. "This particular shitstorm ended up with us in the realm of the Dragon King. Something I usually try to avoid, by the way." His voice was strained, as though he was still attempting to be polite but it wasn't working. He pointed at one juncture where the barrier seemed slightly more transparent. "He's sleeping out there—if you wanted to take a quick look."

I didn't, but my eyes were drawn to the spot as we passed by anyway. I inhaled sharply, my fear of sharks clamping hard on my throat. I'd never seen a dragon before, not a real one. Even among OtherFolk they were rare, and as far as I knew, none of them had ever come to the Midnight Marketplace.

"Ah. It really is a kaiju," I said smartly as I took in the form slumbering beside us, both familiar and yet not, the reality of what it was turning my brain into a gibbering pile of mush. "He looked smaller on TV."

"That's just a stage name." Haru scowled. "And those were models based on incomplete information. For now, his reputation is far larger anyway. We'd like to keep it that way."

I shuddered, imagining the consequences. "So would I."

Brystion let out a small snort but said nothing, continuing to trail me with a politeness that defied explanation.

We mounted a set of stairs to emerge in what appeared to be the great room of a palace, and I suddenly understood what was happening.

Standing in the center, Talivar waited, but whereas he'd been tired and cranky and slightly underdressed as we had eaten our crepes in the park, this time he was impeccable, every inch a king. Dressed in a chic Armani suit, his hair slicked back, except for the beginnings of a braid or two—remnants of when he wore it long and unfettered during his time as prince. He still had the eye patch, the silver earrings adorning his pointed ears, the golden torc around his neck, and the blue tattoos on his cheeks, though. The elf spotted me as we approached the group of yokai paying homage to him, Didi fluttering in his wake.

"Talivar-san," Haru said, pausing as Talivar stepped past him to take my hands in his.

"I appreciate your assistance in this matter," Talivar said to the kappa, his voice cold. "It is fortunate my wife appears to be unharmed."

"Of course, Talivar-sama. My apologies again. Had we known the consort of Your Eminence was here—"

"The visiting king does not need such simpering from the likes of you, criminal." I blinked in pleased surprise as Kitsune strode toward us from the other room, her fox tail twitching slightly. If there was any pain from her previous injury, she was hiding it extremely well.

The kappa paled—or at least became a lighter shade of green—though if it was due to the fact that Kitsune herself was there or the katana at her side, I had no idea. He bowed deeply, rattling off words of what I assumed was an apology.

The other yokai retreated too, her presence radiating outward in a cool, violent sort of way. She stepped past Haru without even acknowledging him, her dark eyes looking me over quickly and lingering on my belly, finally giving me a little nod. "I'm quite glad to see you well, Abby-sama," she said, holding her hand up as though to stop me from saying anything, even as Talivar squeezed my hand in warning at the same time. I inclined my head at her in return but kept my lips shut as tight as I dared.

"We should make sure she sees the midwife immediately," Kitsune murmured to Talivar. "The health of your heir is at stake."

The kappa made a strangled sound, even as I sighed loudly. "I'm not feeling so well at all." I lowered my hands to my belly.

"Of course," Talivar commanded without missing a beat. "My wife must be attended to at once. Please escort her to the car outside; we'll have her taken directly to the hotel."

Kitsune gestured to me and Ion. Ever the consummate actor, the incubus continued his facade of manservant, shadowing my steps with a careful tread. The other yokai bowed, not meeting my eyes.

"Abby-sama!" My entourage paused as Haru waddled toward us. "Please. I have a gift."

Kitsune's eyes narrowed, but she shrugged at me. My call, then.

I waited for him to catch up to us, Didi hovering by my side. "Here," he said, his face miserable. "I would not have this affront be the last thing you remember of me, so please, take this."

"It's dangerous to go alone," Didi quipped, earning her a dirty look from Haru.

His jaw tightened, but he pulled out a gachapon capsule from somewhere inside his shell and held it out to me. "From my personal collection."

"Ah, thank you." I peered through the scuffed-up plastic, blinking when I saw the shadowy outline of a certain Japanese monster, though what I'd do with a rubber Godzilla, I had no idea. I nodded gravely at him and tucked it away in my hobo with Phin. "I'll treasure it."

"You don't need to mock it," he said, suddenly testy. But then he shook his head. "If you find yourself in a pinch, a bad one, open it. But otherwise . . ." He gestured at me to lean closer. "Well, don't mention it to customs, okay?"

"Okay." I blinked at him as my group escorted me away. I risked a careful glance behind us to see Talivar speaking quietly to Haru, but we were well beyond the range of anything I could hear. Didi lingered for a moment and then shrugged, following our little entourage with a flouncing of wings.

I burned with both curiosity and relief, but then we were whisked into an elevator and through a set of doors that led to a statue of an enormous robot. It towered over all of us, looking for all the world to be a life-size Gundum from the anime series of the same name, matching café behind it. Where the hell were we? Not in Akihabara surely. I had no real time to figure it out, though, as Kitsune led us straight to a limousine and quickly tucked all of us inside.

Once seated, Ion immediately poured me a drink of water, and I gulped it down gratefully. Apparently I was more dehydrated than I'd thought. "There's not much in the minibar," he said, tossing me a package of sesame crackers.

"They'll do." I nibbled on my snack. "So what the hell is going on?"

"Talivar is finally acting like a king," Kitsune said. "And about time too. We'll explain everything once he gets here."

I slumped into the seat as I finished the last of the crackers. Phin had already nudged his way into the minibar as well, only he was swallowing down a bottle of vodka as fast as he could, his blue eyes rolling into the back of his head. "What a goddamned nightmare," he snapped, his tail lashing.

Ion snatched the bottle from him before the unicorn

could drop it. "Save some for the rest of us."

"I hardly think drinking yourselves into a stupor is going to help anything," I pointed out, noting with relief that Talivar had exited the building and was making his way over to the car. I moved over as he entered; I barely had any time to say anything before he wrapped his arms about me, kissing me hard on the mouth in a savage claim that left me breathless. It was unusual for him to put on a display like this; of my two lovers, Talivar was much more subdued than Ion, at least in public.

My hands drifted up to his face. "It's all right. I'm all right."

"When Didi said you'd been taken and that bastard Paganini showed up . . ." He shook his head. "It's a good thing I was already at the embassy."

Kitsune rattled off something to the driver—an address, I imagined—before closing the window between us. "Indeed," she said coolly. "Fortunate that I came to look for you there too. I don't think it would have done much for the relationships between countries if you'd unleashed the Wild Hunt here." She shuddered. "The chaos would be terrible."

"Hopefully it won't come to that," Talivar said darkly. He snorted at Ion. "What's with the penguin suit?"

The incubus smiled faintly, his gloved hands making a gesture of apologetic rudeness. "It fit the part. Seeing as I'm a daemon anyway, I guess that makes me one hell of a but—"

He yelped, moving in a most unbutlerlike way as Phineas clambered onto the seat next to him. "Yeah, yeah. Daemon butler. No offense, but those assholes are a dime a dozen here, so dressing like a host club reject isn't going to win you any brownie points."

"One of these days, I'm going to tear off the rest of that horn of yours and shove it up your ass," Ion said pleasantly, his eyes flashing a golden haze of warning. But then he shifted into his normal visage of pale skin and ebony hair, the leather pants, the white T-shirt, and all the rest of his over-the-top aesthetic that I loved so much. He shot me a rueful look as he rubbed his backside.

"You'll have to get in line," Phin retorted, sticking out his tongue.

"So?" Didi nudged. "What the hell just happened?" Her eyes darted toward Talivar.

He grimaced. "I got tired of traveling like a peasant and decided to pull rank. Frankly, as a visiting monarch, I'm technically required to do so; it's good manners. But the yokai here don't like losing face, and having one of their own essentially throw my wife into a dungeon looks bad."

"Almost as bad as having to be rescued from a brothel," I murmured. Kitsune looked at me sharply. "I'll tell you about it later. It was, uh, interesting."

Both Ion and Talivar shared a look that wasn't particularly kind. "What is this about a brothel?" Talivar's tone grew soft and dangerous.

"Ask Nobu," I said darkly, wanting to change the subject. "I don't know about the rest of you, but I could use something to eat. Don't suppose they have drive-throughs around here?" The thought of fast-food wasn't remotely appealing, but exhaustion was setting in and I needed to refuel.

Kitsune shook her head. "There's a good ramen place near the hotel. They know me, so I'll have them bring something to our room." The fox-woman whipped out a phone from somewhere in her kimono, immediately dialing and rattling off a few pleasantries at whomever answered before ordering. "I'll arrange a midwife for you too when we arrive at the hotel. I think you need to be checked out," she said after she hung up.

"Must be some ramen place," I said.

"All this going in and out of the CrossRoads isn't good for you," she said, pointedly looking at my belly. "I think it would at least reassure us all if we knew your baby was safe."

"Are you suggesting she's not?" I bristled, rubbing my hands over my stomach. Had I grown larger yet again?

"I'm suggesting that for *your well-being* and the well-being of your *child* that you see a midwife. Don't be stupid, Abby." The fox-woman sighed. "Some of this is my fault; it only makes sense that I bear some of the responsibility. This is the best way I know how."

"Please. For my sake," Talivar chimed in, pausing as he pointed at Ion. "And for his."

I nodded, unsure of why I was being so stubborn, except that once again I was being pulled in directions I couldn't control or understand. I was going to have to grow up—and real soon.

"All right," I said finally.

Talivar gave my hand a squeeze, and even as Ion's eyes flared gold, he said nothing.

The trip to the hotel was blissfully uneventful and the room an opulent monstrosity. I whistled at Talivar as we entered.

"It's good to be the king," he said with a shrug.

"So I've heard." I sank onto one of the massive beds as Ion opened the curtains to let the lights in the evening sky of Tokyo come in.

A knock at the door revealed room service with our ramen and a number of other treats. Kitsune's eyes lit up when she saw one particular dish, carefully scooping up most of it into a bowl with a dainty hand, her chopsticks making quick work of it. "Inari sushi." She hummed happily. "I've missed it. The CrossRoads tries, but there's truly nothing quite like the taste of home."

I slurped up my ramen, the salty brine filling me with a

warm, contented feeling. Funny how a full belly can suddenly make everything seem manageable. Another knock sounded on the door, and Kitsune shooed everyone else into the sitting room.

"Midwife," she explained. "Allow us some privacy, gentlemen."

"I think we've earned the right to be here," Ion challenged her, but I waved him off.

"I'll let you know right after. I think maybe I'd like a little lady time."

He gave me a look that spoke volumes, but both he and Talivar did as they were asked, leaving me with Kitsune and a rabbit-eared girl with an inquisitive nose and gentle eyes.

"Usagi-san," Kitsune said, her own nose flaring gently. I wondered if there wasn't an element of predator-versus-prey going on, but if the rabbit girl felt any fear, she certainly didn't show it.

She spoke briefly with Kitsune, who gracefully translated the midwife's directions for me. "She wants you to lie down so she can examine you."

I set my bowl on the nightstand and eased onto the bed. The rabbit-girl pulled out what I would consider standard medical instruments—blood pressure cuff, thermometer, the basics. She took my vitals with a nod and then asked some additional questions, translated via Kitsune.

Was I very tired? Was I getting enough rest? Was I eating enough?

Standard and rote, and while I couldn't quite convince myself that I was getting *enough* of any of those things, Usagi-san didn't seem particularly fazed by my answers. And then she leaned forward abruptly, resting her head upon my bulging stomach.

"Um, what is she doing?" I asked Kitsune.

The fox-woman raised a finger to her lips. "Listening to

your baby's heartbeat."

I blinked. It hadn't occurred to me that the ears were anything other than OtherFolk strangeness, but I supposed it made sense. The rabbit-girl changed position several times, her ears twitching softly against my skin. Finally, she sat up and lifted my chin, looking into my eyes with twisted lips, another question falling from her mouth.

Kitsune hesitated. "When were you due, Abby?"

"Were?" I started at the word, my blood chilling. "I knew things were progressing a little faster, but I was about three to four months along when we started all this, and it's been, what? A week? Two? I've sort of lost count."

She shook her head. "Maybe you *were*, but at least a month passed by out here while you were in the brothel and then with Nobu. Between that and the stunt with Haru, Usagi-san suspects you're nearly six months now."

I gaped at her, rolling my hands on my belly. "Six? But I don't feel that much larger. I got new pants yesterday . . ." My voice trailed away as I realized they were definitely stretched more than they had been, the elastic bellyband pushing down lower to fit. I swallowed hard. "What do I do?"

Usagi-san made a little shrugging gesture and said something else to Kitsune who frowned. "Your baby is gestating faster than it should. You'll need to eat and rest more than you might during a regular pregnancy, but above all, you need to stay *off* the CrossRoads."

I stilled, going cold. I'd suspected it, but for some reason I hadn't thought it would affect my pregnancy so drastically. Having Kitsune hammer it home made the whole thing far too real. And yet . . . "But what about Melanie? I can't leave her there."

"She has Nobu," Kitsune reminded me. "And I believe you picked up something of Nobu's, did you not? He will know what to do with it; she is in the best hands possible."

She paused. "Unless you've suddenly started controlling the Wild Magic somehow?"

I shook my head. "I'm as normal as they come now."

"That, I doubt," Kitsune added. She said a few more things to the midwife, and then Usagi-san gathered her things and bowed deeply to both of us before retreating from the bedroom. Kitsune watched her leave, satisfied. "I've retained her services for you as long as you're in Japan. Despite her words of caution, I doubt you'll heed them. Your sort never do. But I think it will ease everyone's mind about all of this if we have someone with us who will know how to handle it, should . . . issues arise."

"Because that doesn't sound ominous at all." I grimaced. "And what happens if I end up on the CrossRoads again? I mean, it wasn't like I was trying to go there on purpose this time anyway. You know how it is."

"Yes. To be honest, I think we should look at sending you home—via mundane means, of course. Or at least hiding you away here until the baby is born."

"I don't remember Moira's son changing so much when Charlie brought him on and off the CrossRoads," I said sullenly.

"Benjamin is OtherFolk," Kitsune said in a gentle voice. "And would age differently from a mortal child regardless. But you're human, Abby. Your baby is human, as far as we know. And I know you want to help your friends—it's what you do, after all—but right now, she has to come first." The fox-woman stood up, taking my now-empty ramen bowl and the rest of the dishes. "I'll send the other two in. I think the three of you need some time to discuss, and we won't be going anywhere until tomorrow anyway. I've put Usagi-san up in the room next door. It's another suite like this one, so I'll share it with her and see you in the morning."

Her hand drifted out to touch my forehead, fingers lingering against my cheek in a tender gesture, but I couldn't begin to guess the meaning of it. Motherly, perhaps. And then she was gone, drifting into the sitting room.

I rolled onto my side, not sure I wanted to talk to anyone, even the two men I loved. Suddenly sweltering, I stood up and opened the sliding doors onto the balcony, letting the rush of sounds and lights wash over me. Skytree was lit up like a beacon in the distance, as if beckoning me with a flush of red against a soft blanket of clouds.

I could hear Kitsune and Talivar talking in hushed tones, and a frustrated helplessness had me pacing. Things were business as usual for everyone else. They could do what they always had and I was limited—by my own body, no less, and on the dependence of the little person I was carrying. I shivered. But wasn't that what being a mother was supposed to be about? I thought of my own mother and how much she'd given up when my father had left us. How frightened she must have been. How sad.

But she'd never said a word against him, not once in all the years after that.

My hands crossed over my belly. At least I wasn't alone. In fact, I had two men willing to play the part of father to this child, to support us, to protect us. Maybe it was time to at least accept some of that instead of constantly forging ahead so recklessly.

Something wet slid off my nose, and I realized I was crying. It wasn't even a sad or happy thing, exactly. My hormones were raging out of control, and it simply felt like a quiet release of everything I couldn't seem to get ahold of, everything that had happened, everything I might stand to gain or lose.

"Abby?"

I turned as the door clicked shut behind me, revealing Talivar and Ion standing side by side. Talivar had removed the business attire and was dressed in comfortable jeans and a T-shirt, Brystion behind him. "Are you all right?" the elf asked.

I wiped the tears away from my face, rewarding them with a half smile. "About the only thing that could fuck up my day more right now is finding out I'm carrying twins," I said. "A real Dr. Phil moment."

Talivar chuckled. The kingly part of him had been stripped away, leaving him nothing more than a man before me. I ached, remembering the way we'd been before he'd ascended to the throne, when he was simply a bodyguard and a friend.

And Ion, my TouchStone incubus, was simply there, the daemonic glamour that usually surrounded him like a cloak of darkness fading away before me to leave him dark skinned and golden eyed, his antlers gleaming in the streetlight from below.

The three of us had been drawn together by something that might not have been Fate, but it may have been more than sheer coincidence. Sometimes relationships are messy, and while we had never really spoken of it, we all knew that, at the heart of it, a triangle needed all three sides to support it.

The two of them had always had a complicated relationship when it came to me. I was never completely sure where I stood except that they both wanted my attention. Aside from a hazy evening where I wasn't entirely cognizant of what they'd discussed, I'd woken up sandwiched between them, roughly aware that they'd worked something out, but they had never spoken of the specifics.

And that would need to change. I'd been walking on eggshells around them, trying not to upset the balance of whatever little dance we were doing, and I didn't have time for that anymore.

The three of us stood there staring at each other for a span of heartbeats, and I raised a brow at them. "Well?"

"Kitsune told us," Brystion said first, shifting his weight uncomfortably. "And I agree with her. Until the baby is born, I think you need to go home via mortal transportation."

"Same." Talivar cocked his head slightly toward the incubus, and they both nodded.

"I see. And what about us?" My heart stuttered, as though it was trying to claw its way out of my throat. Not that I had any illusions. This wasn't some high school drama.

"What *about* us?" Talivar stepped toward me, taking my hand as he sat beside me on the bed. "Abby, suffice it to say, I don't think either of us is going anywhere."

"But the baby . . . It's his," I said softly. "You know this."

He flinched slightly. "Yes. But you're still married to me. More to the point, what is it *you* want to do? We both love you; that much is evident. And you already know my thoughts on the matter."

The comment hung there between us, taut and tense and full of any number of things. If Kitsune had given me a spool of red thread for the three of us, who would it have gone to? One of them? Neither of them? Or was it that we would be so tangled up together we didn't know where any of us began or ended?

I nearly snorted at the thought. For all its romantic implications, being bound to someone forever was a heady burden, and not one that could be treated lightly. A hot prick of tears burned my eyelids as I looked at Ion, standing there like a statue. "And you? What do you think?"

His eyes flared gold and wonderful even as he stamped his hoof on the carpet in impatience. "What I think is of no bearing. Our TouchStone bond should show you all that I am; you simply need to reach out and find it." He sucked in a deep breath. "I'm not much good with sharing, Abby. You know this. He knows it. But if you lose some bit of yourself because of his absence or mine, then he and I have both agreed that it is not worth it."

A half smile kicked up the corner of Talivar's lips. "Life is too short, as they say."

It was an ominous reminder that I was mortal. Despite all the magic I'd had in my life recently, in the end, they would outlive me. "Suppose I could become a vampire." I snorted when alarm swept over his face. "Kidding."

"Ah, yes," he replied weakly. "As tempting a solution as that might be, it would definitely destroy any connection between us. OtherFolk cannot TouchStone one another, after all, and he would starve to death."

My head snapped toward Ion, who shrugged gracelessly. "I'm sure I'd find a way to make it work."

"If by 'making it work' you mean slowing fading away to nothing and disappearing forever, then yes, I suppose you would." Talivar coughed. "So no, that's not an option."

"So that leaves us with . . . sharing?" I rolled the word around on my tongue, still not entirely sure I trusted the meaning. "Which is what? Trading off whose bed I sleep in on various nights? Ménages every month? I attend Faery Court functions three times a week and Dreamer raves every other Thursday?"

I let out a little grunt of frustration. I knew almost nothing about how polygamous relationships worked, let alone with nearly immortal men with various magical abilities. How far could love go when stretched out between multiple people? My previous relationships, at least before I arrived in Portsmyth, had always been run-of-the-mill. Most had broken it off quickly when it became apparent my dancing career was going to come first.

At least until my accident.

And then I'd had no one at all.

"There's no manual for this, is there?" I asked.

"Despite your wishes, not as far as I know." Talivar paused. "As far as how we share, that is entirely up to you. While I don't particularly swing toward men sexually, I can't speak for the incubus." He shrugged. "But neither am I so close-minded not to share a bed with one from time to time."

Brystion's mouth twisted. "I'll sleep with anything. It's not the sex that's the problem."

"I know." My gaze darted away to look at the bulge of my belly. Just another way the two of them were so different. "I don't know what the answer is," I said finally. "I want you both. But TouchStone bonds aside, I don't want some metaphysical force keeping us together forever. I'm not saying we shouldn't commit; if we're going to do this thing, we absolutely should at least make the effort. But . . ." I glanced up at the both of them. "Freely entered, freely given . . . freely ended."

"But the TouchStone bond—" Ion started, his words cutting off when I placed a finger against his lips.

"Circumstances change." I swallowed hard. "Feelings mellow over time. It doesn't mean the love will go away, but I guess what I'm getting at is that I want us to stay together because we want to. Not because of an external force that requires it."

I rubbed my belly uncomfortably. "The marriage thing . . . it's not that I object to it. I never did. But becoming con-sort was never my desire. I don't want to rule a kingdom, to be responsible for so many . . ." I shuddered. "I don't want to give up my life in the mortal world to live in a castle. And now, with her . . ."

"If we dissolve the marriage, I will take another queen," Talivar said softly. "My kingdom will depend on it. Will you be all right with that? My heart will always, always belong to you, but I cannot turn my back on my people. Not even for love."

Ion snorted. "The differences between me and an actual king are not usually so many, but in this . . . well . . ."

"You think with your dick, incubus. I wouldn't expect

you to understand." Talivar's tone became frosty.

I pinched the bridge of my nose. "I don't know. I don't *know*." My mind swirled in a mishmash of confusion: What I wanted, what I needed, what would be best for the baby. But I didn't want to let either of them go. The silkworm's words to me about what a poor consort I was for not being there when they needed me stung me with the suddenness of a needlestick.

"I guess I'm selfish," I said at last, swallowing hard. "I love you both. I want you both. I want to raise this child with us as a family. But I don't know if I can do everything . . . I don't know if—"

My words were cut off as Talivar captured my mouth with his, pressing a gentle kiss against my lips. I thought it would end with that, but he continued on, lightly touching each salty tear on my cheeks, even as a soothing hum vibrated from his throat.

"I would never ask you to take all this on alone, Abby. Neither of us would. All I wanted to hear was this." He pulled me against him and pressed another kiss against my forehead. I let myself sag, the warmth of his scent enveloping me as he smoothed the hair from my face. "So much. You have given me so much. Done so much for our people, so much for your friends. Now it's time for you to let it go for a while. The burdens of leadership are not for you to take on. Let me deal with them accordingly. As long as you're by my side, there is nothing I will want for."

My eyes drifted shut, his fingers trailing along the nape of my neck, and I shivered. The bed shifted behind me, and a brush of darkness swept along my spine as a swell of sexual heat washed across my skin.

Brystion.

My brain stuttered. Was this actually going to happen? Did I want it to? Did they?

Would they be here otherwise? my inner voice pointed out

with a slightly subdued amount of snark.

I raised my arm behind me, fingers finding the curve of Brystion's face. He nibbled on a fingertip, suckling on the tip with a velvet sweep of his tongue. A jolt of pleasure shot straight to my groin, and I let out a little sigh, which was quickly swallowed up by another kiss from Talivar.

My other hand found his jaw, traced the outline of his pointed ear, stroking the edge with a knowing finger. He stiffened, his breath hitching as he pulled away for an instant, his arms growing slack. I seemed to float into the support of the mattress, the elastic waistband of my pants sliding down my belly. I stared up at both of them, Talivar's blue eye intense and heated, Brystion's eyes gold and half-lidded and promising something I couldn't put into words.

And I didn't need to.

"Come and get me, boys," I whispered, my arms outstretched, beckoning them forward.

CHAPTER 11

SENSATIONS SWIRLED IN THE DARKNESS, bodies lit by nothing more than neon lights and shadows drifting in through the windows. I was buoyed along on waves of pleasure, bombarded on all sides by a tender sweep of skin against skin, Talivar on one side of me, Ion on the other. Clothing had disappeared in a whirlwind, Talivar expertly removing whatever he'd had on before casually stripping me of the last of mine.

My stomach felt swollen and huge, an impediment to whatever this was, and I almost shyly drew away, feeling like a rhinoceros in a herd of unicorns. My breasts were larger than they'd ever been, the nipples growing taut and pink and heavy, and I couldn't help but try to block them with my arm, wishing for a bit less light.

Talivar smiled gently, taking my hand in his. "There are no secrets here between us, Abby."

I blinked and realized he'd shed his own glamour, the scars around his face, his abdomen, his crippled knee, which had been badly damaged so very long ago, were all etched in full relief. Brystion stood beside him, his antlers crystalline and glowing, his dark skin tracked with pulses of light that beat with each breath he took, the lion's tail, the cloven hooves, all of it open to my view.

"Trust the TouchStone bonds if you cannot trust your

eyes," Ion added, snaking in for a kiss of his own, the bells in his hair chiming madly. His tongue swirled against mine, teasing a torrent of desire from the motion, and I opened my mouth wider, kissing him back.

Talivar dragged his lips down my neck to my collarbone, nuzzling my breasts and the mounded belly, his gentle caresses so different from the nearly violent clash of Ion's mouth on mine. My eyes snapped open when Talivar latched on to a breast, his teeth kneading with precise motions, lapping at the nipple. He drew a series of moans from me with each flick of his tongue, his face lighting up at each sound I made, even as Ion stifled the noise, capturing them in his mouth.

I went limp, and let the shadows sweep over me.

How much time we spent there I couldn't have said. It was almost as though we'd made a small pocket off the CrossRoads that things like minutes or hours couldn't touch. Ion's golden eyes flared as I ran a curious finger over what looked like an enormous silver bubble around us.

"A shield," he explained. "What we do here is not for anyone but us." His smile grew feral. "We cannot be seen or heard, so I expect you to sing for us. As loud as you like." He lowered his mouth to my ear, nipping at it carelessly. "Until every part of you is begging for it, mindless beyond words or thought."

"Only if you do the same," I grunted, shuddering as Talivar bit my hip. Dimly, I realized the two of them must have worked something out as to how this was going to proceed, but I wasn't entirely sure I wanted to ask.

But then it didn't matter anyway. My mind grew hazy, even as the realities of what we had done, what we were doing, set in.

Fingers sliding over my thighs, my calves, the soles of my feet. Lips trailing down my neck, across my breasts, my belly, my ass. All teasing and light, enough to draw my attention but too numerous for me to pinpoint who was doing what.

The shadows within the shield cocooned us, insulating our movements from the outside world, the realities too harsh to bear. Soft balls of witchlight illuminated us in tiny pinpoints of brilliance, fading in and out like fireflies made of silver snowflakes.

My own hands weren't idle either, reaching out to fist in someone's hair, to tweak an absent nipple, to grasp a *very* firm cock butting against my thigh. A finger was pressed to my lips, and I suckled it eagerly.

The lights began to flash in time, and the touching suddenly became more insistent. Before long, one of my legs was thrown over Ion's shoulder, shuddering as he nipped his way down the inside of my calf.

Talivar had wrapped partway around me to claim my mouth, his hands cupping my jaw tenderly. My hips started moving when he reached down to play with my breasts again, even as Ion moved farther up to the junction of my thighs, to bury his face in the wetness there.

Dual waves of pleasure washed over me, a tongue in my cunt, a tongue in my mouth, opening me wider, exposing everything I was. Ion knew what to do, where all my little pleasure points were, nuzzling and licking, long and slow, soft and fast, plunging shallow and then deep.

Here? Here? How about here?

Talivar paid tribute with slow, languorous kisses and gentle strokes of his hands over my cheeks and jaw. When I reached out to find his cock, he let out a soft moan against my lips, rocking himself toward me in a quiet rhythm. I shifted to take him into my mouth, my tongue slipping over the top, dipping into the tiny entrance, sliding down the shaft, my hand stroking him in tandem. And all the while, Ion kept up his merciless onslaught, pressing a finger inside me, curling up through the soft folds.

Before long, I realized I was doing the same—quick, slow, deep, shallow. Talivar's hips, my hips, moving as one, our moans becoming a duet and then a trio. My eyes fluttered half-open to look at Ion. His mouth kicked up into a half smile at whatever he saw, rising up between my thighs, his hard-on brushing over me with wicked intent. I let out a grunt of encouragement as he settled against me, my legs pale against his ebony skin.

He entered me slow, by inches, slipping forward with ease, and I let out a muffled cry. "Look at me, Abby," he breathed, capturing me with those mesmerizing golden eyes.

Another rush of desire, heady and intense, but he kept his motions slow and even as he thrust in and out, his hands supporting my hips, cradling my backside with an odd sort of reverence. Talivar shifted to change the angle, and I reached for him again, suckling harder, matching every movement Ion made.

There was only the harsh exhalation of my breath, the wet slide of Talivar's cock in my mouth, the slap of Ion's skin against me. Some soft sound vibrated from my throat with each move the incubus made, echoed in the hitch of Talivar's moans in my ear.

Bryston only changed the tempo slightly, rolling his hips, but his eyes never left mine. His nostrils flared wide when I moved against him faster and he increased his pace again, even as Talivar did the same, the three of us growing more insistent, chasing down that perfect wave of release.

"Please," Talivar begged, though if he was talking to me or Ion, I didn't know. And I didn't care. Even Ion was panting now, vocalizing every time he slid home. Again and again and again and . . .

Pleasure, white-hot and brilliant, exploded over me, my belly contracting hard with the ripples of orgasm flooding my senses. A rush of lust seared my skin—Ion's magic through the TouchStone bond, perhaps—tangling around us like a tangible cord.

Both men shuddered. Ion stiffening, his hips jerking forward. Talivar spilling hot across my skin, my mouth, my tongue.

For a moment, the three of us could do nothing but lie there, breathing hard. I was riding the aftershocks, my body continuing to twitch in tiny typhoons. Ion slipped out of me easily enough, though his hands trembled as he cupped my cheek.

The three of us leaned in, sharing an awkwardly leisurely kiss that became a set of shy chuckles and finally an embrace that left me breathless and overwhelmed. The two of them propped me up on the bed, carefully wiping my limbs with a soft towel. My mind rippled with questions, but the words wouldn't seem to form and fled before I could voice them.

Talivar dropped beside me, one arm stretched out over his head. "That was . . ."

"Yeah." I shifted, suddenly slammed with the need to pee. I patted my stomach sourly. Ah, back to the indignities of a mortal body. I felt a small twinge of disappointment as Ion's shield began to dissipate.

It wasn't like we had that much time, but still. "Excuse me," I said, my voice strangely hoarse and husky. Brystion assisted me off the bed, watching me wobble on shaky legs. "You look pleased with yourself."

His only answer was to smile wider, his cheeks darkening with exceptionally good humor. I shook my head and ducked into the bathroom to take care of more intimate cleanup.

I caught a glimpse of myself in the mirror as I washed my

face. My lips were swollen, a flush of color spreading over my chest and cheeks. And of course, there was a sprinkling of assorted love bites and hickeys in various places. I touched one on my right breast bemusedly.

Just my luck that both men were into marking their territories, so to speak. But if it made them happy, I supposed I wouldn't object too much.

I wrapped a robe around me, combing the wild tangle of my hair from my face. If I had any energy, I'd take a shower, but given everything that had happened, I wanted to sleep. Showers could come in the morning.

I emerged from the bathroom to see Brystion and Talivar stretched out on the bed. Brystion had glamoured himself to his mortal visage, but the two of them were murmuring low to each other.

"Am I interrupting, boys?" I asked in a soft drawl.

"Not exactly." Talivar shrugged, his own expression quiet and somewhat sly when he met my gaze.

"We were discussing further . . . arrangements," Brystion said, reaching out to pull me onto the bed between them.

I raised a brow. "You guys want to go another round?"

"Another evening, perhaps," Talivar said regretfully. "Although that was . . . very good."

Ion snorted, looking mildly offended. "Is that all?"

"No. To be honest, I wasn't expecting it . . . At the end, what was that?" He gestured at me. "Surely that wasn't merely a simple reaction."

Brystion shook his head and then shrugged. "My power transferred through TouchStone bonds. From me to her, and then to you through your TouchStone bond with her." He glanced over at me. "To be honest, I've never quite done something like that before. My TouchStones usually receive the benefit of my desire, as you well know, but I've never done it with one who was TouchStoned to another." He looked pensive and then slightly alarmed.

"Do you think that happens to any of your other Touch-Stones when we sleep together?"

I paused, taking a mental tally of all the OtherFolk I'd been TouchStoned to. "Now that's a rather horrifying thought."

Talivar blinked. "Well, it's the first time I've ever experienced something like that." He eyed the door hesitantly. "You'd think if Phin was getting his jollies every time the two of you do the dirty, he'd probably have commented by now."

"I wouldn't be too sure of that," I noted. "He's a pretty big perv. It's entirely possible he'd really enjoy it."

Talivar shrugged. "Well, like I said, I've never felt that before. I don't think Moira has either, and she *definitely* would have said something."

"I'm not sure I even want to know now," I said. "Maybe it depends on physical contact? I mean, I'm as liberal as the next girl, but that's the first three-way I've had."

"Hopefully not the last." Ion ran a suggestive finger up my arm before letting out a wry chuckle. "Maybe later, though."

"That's the first time I've ever seen you turn down an opportunity." I eased against the pillows, suddenly drained.

"Even I have my limits. That was twice as much power as I normally use. But worth it," he admitted. "Even so, sleep sounds like a very good idea. For all of us."

There wasn't any talk of splitting up into different rooms as there may have been before, and somehow, we tucked ourselves in together, a tangle of sheets and limbs and my protruding belly.

I didn't know how long I would last between them. My core temperature seemed to go up and down rather rapidly, and while romantic as hell, being sandwiched between them suddenly felt rather strangling. But I decided to ignore it as best I could. Some things required a bit of sacrifice.

Talivar's hand was resting gently beneath my stomach, thumb idly stroking my skin with careful tenderness. Ion was on the other side, molded to the side of my hip, my head nestled in the crook of his arm. I wasn't even sure if we'd settled anything, our own sexual foibles notwithstanding. But Rome wasn't built in a day, and relationships were ever-fluid. We'd taken an enormous step forward in whatever this was, and for now, that would have to be good enough.

Once the baby was born and the situation with Melanie was figured out, I'd hash out the rules. The idea of being an actual consort still frightened the crap out of me too, so I didn't hate putting it off. Perhaps some sort of Persephone arrangement would work: Six months in Faerie, six months in the mortal world. But I knew that wouldn't quite work either. Time passed so differently between the two realms; I could return to Portsmyth to find years had passed.

And that certainly wouldn't be fair to my child. She deserved at least basic stability during her formative years. At least, that was what all the books said, and I was inclined to believe them.

"You're restless," Ion muttered to me. "What was the point of all those orgasms if it didn't relax you?"

"A snack?" I replied dryly.

"Not for that." He yawned. "Not this time. Some things are more sacred than mere food. This was one of them."

"Sentimental thing," I said, half-joking. For all his flippancy, the incubus could be honorable at times, though it was often via a code of his own making. In that respect, Talivar was a far easier book to read. The elf wore his emotions on his sleeve, at least when it came to me.

"Will both of you please shut up?" Talivar groaned, nudging my ankle with his foot before rolling onto his side. "Some of us have to be kingly in the morning."

I snorted but took the less-than-subtle hint, shifting again. Not a minute later, Talivar's breathing grew rhythmic and quiet. Even Ion faded away into sleep, or whatever it counted as for him. As far as I knew, sleep wasn't something he needed, but I appreciated the effort.

I let my own eyes drift shut, concentrating on the rise and fall of Ion's chest against me. "I love you," I whispered into the darkness, not trusting myself to say it any louder. But it echoed in my mind all the same. As I slipped away into sleep, I might have heard one of them say something back, but it was lost in the haze of dreams, and then I knew no more.

CHAPTER 12

"EGGS?" TALIVAR HANDED ME A platter, hesitating with a spoon, and I nodded, munching on a bit of dry toast. Room service was a Western-style affair, and considering the number of OtherFolk with us, it seemed the most prudent choice.

So I had a stack of enormous, fluffy pancakes on the plate in front of me, both Talivar and Kitsune urging me to eat more. Usagi-san eyed me from the corner, seated in an overstuffed chair and sipping tea, her ears twitching.

Phin and Didi were perched in front of the flat-screen TV, both looking more hungover than I'd ever seen. Staring at Phin's bedraggled state, I couldn't help but think of Ion's question about TouchStone bonds and sexual energy, but in the end, I only shook my head and swallowed another mouthful of syrup-covered pancake.

I'd find out later. Besides, it wasn't like anyone else had complained about it yet, so might as well let sleeping libidos lie and all that. If that was even possible with Phin. His libido was practically a living entity by itself, his appetite quite possibly rivaling Brystion's—and not in a good way.

"So what's the plan?" I asked after I swallowed my latest mouthful.

"You're going home," Talivar said firmly. "By plane. Ion will escort you, and I will remain here to oversee whatever's going on with Melanie. She's not a subject, but if I indicate she's an important personage in my kingdom, they will let it slide, I think."

I let out a frustrated sigh but knew there wasn't much else I could do about it. "What are you going to do about a passport? I didn't bring one with me."

Kitsune inclined her head. "I'm waiting on the paper-work for that now. We'll get you a fake one, of course. If nothing else, a glamour to keep people from looking at it too closely should work well enough."

I polished off another cup of tea, wishing I had a better idea of how to help Melanie at all. Unknowns made me uneasy, and despite everyone's assurances, I would have felt better if I knew what the actual plan was.

Kitsune's ears flicked when there was a knock at the suite door. "Ah. That should be the messenger with the documents now. We had to double-check with the American embassy to make sure we had the details correct." Kitsune stood up and disappeared into the other room as she went to answer it. "What in the hells are you doing here?" I heard her ask.

She shifted away from the entrance to reveal Melanie. She was dressed in her normal street attire, the kimono replaced by torn fishnets and a leather skirt, a belly shirt, and a faux-fur-lined vest. Her red hair was pulled up to tumble artfully down her shoulder.

"Hi," she mumbled, her voice hollow. She thrust her chin out defiantly, eyes softening when she saw me. "Can I at least have breakfast?"

It was a weird request. The way it had been phrased made her sound like a stranger and not the sister of my heart. The tension ratcheted through everyone, even Usagi-san's nose twitching nervously as she watched the scene unfold before her.

I shook my head and realized everyone was waiting on

me to answer. "Of course," I said, waving her over. Kitsune rolled her eyes and shut the door as Melanie shoved her way past the others, her Dr. Martens thumping heavily on the carpet.

"You shouldn't be here," Kitsune said as Melanie took a seat at the table opposite from me and helped herself to a piece of toast. "It's too dangerous in Tokyo right now with Paganini running about. The plan was for you to lie low until we at least got him deported."

Melanie ignored the fox-woman and slathered on a heavy dollop of strawberry jam, proceeding to stuff her face. Her violin case slid from her shoulder to the floor as she chewed. "That's probably true," she said finally, the words seeming to drop hollowly from her mouth. "But then, I hardly think there's any place I belong now, so what difference does it make?"

"Mel." Talivar kneeled beside her. "You know I will always have your back, but what happened—"

"I didn't know," she cut in, staring at the now-empty plate. "But I do now. And I want to help restore it."

"Is your violin fixed?" Ion asked sharply, raising a brow when she shook her head.

"Not exactly. It's been . . . restrained, I guess. Kitsune had it bound so the magic can't escape like before." A sad little smile crossed her face. "I'm normal now. I can't create Doors or tap into the Wild Magic, but at least I can't create any more trouble, either."

"You didn't mention that yesterday in the car," I said to Kitsune. "I would have thought that bit of information might have been important to know, given the circumstances."

The fox-woman shrugged. "And what would you have done differently had you known last night? I would have told you sooner or later, but I didn't see the point in burdening you with it."

"I'm pregnant," I snapped, "not made of glass."

"You carry the potential heir to the throne." Her fox eyes captured me, holding me still. "And that, above all, is most important."

Talivar coughed awkwardly as Ion nudged me out of my stupor. "Well and so, but that doesn't mean she should be locked away," he admonished Kitsune in a gentle tone. "We're all in this together, and my kingdom will be rebuilt in whatever fashion *I* deem necessary."

"Of course, my lord." She bowed her head to him. There was a story there I didn't know, some fate bonding the two of them that went far beyond mere cousins, but I supposed I should be grateful for the loyalty.

"So what is it you propose to do?" Phineas trotted over and helped himself to a sausage link from the plate I held down to him. "If your violin isn't magic anymore, that kind of limits things, doesn't it?"

"To help however I can. To return and face what I must." She bit her lower lip hard enough to draw blood, and I reached out to take her hand. "Nobu would prefer it otherwise, I think, but I can't keep running away. I can't sit there locked in a cage of his making, no matter how bad he wants it."

"Does he even know you're here?" Ion asked, his mouth pursed. "I'll bet not."

Melanie shook her head. "We had an errand to run in Kyoto. I pretended to use the restroom and slipped away. But you know him. He would never have let me come here."

"You can return home with me and Ion," I told her. "We're going to fly . . . tonight?" I verified with Kitsune, who nodded quickly. "At least there, we can reach the CrossRoads directly, for when you . . . well, you know."

"Yeah." She let out a shuddering breath. "I'll somehow figure out a way to get my soul back or . . . I won't. But

I won't find the answers here." I squeezed her hand, her fingers twining about in mine so hard my bones nearly cracked beneath the pressure.

She turned toward Talivar. "And I want to make it up to you too. Whatever I can do. I know I can't pay for what I've done, but I'll do anything you want. Anything you can think of that might help offset this debt." Her voice faded, and she released my hand, rubbing at her eyes.

Talivar watched her gravely, and I knew he was torn between the agony of a friend and the needs of a king. "Let's get through the first part," he said finally. "And then we'll discuss the rest of it. Reparations will be made to the best of your ability."

To her credit, she didn't flinch beneath the austerity of his words, and for the first time, I had hope that things might work out the way they needed to. Even if things couldn't go back to the way they were, we were a family, and nothing would change that.

Kitsune's eyes narrowed at Melanie's words, but she gave a little nod of satisfaction. "It's a start."

"All right," I said. "Let's finish up here, and then if you need a passport too, we'll have Kitsune see what she can do about that." I glanced over at Didi, who was still mostly ignoring us, her face drawn to a video of several men dressed in business suits, all moving in perfect syncopation as they sang. "What in the hell is that?"

"World Order," Didi said, cracking open a Ramune and taking a long swig. "The lead singer, Genki Sudo? He's such an ikemen."

"If you say so," I muttered. "Oh, and I have something for Nobu," I told Kitsune. "If Melanie is coming with me, then you should probably take it to him. I'll go get it; it's in my purse."

To be honest, I wasn't entirely sure what I was supposed to do with Nobu's soul stone, but if we didn't see him again before we left, then it would have to be taken by someone else. Kitsune felt like the right person for the job.

I wandered into the bedroom, slipping out of night-clothes and digging something acceptable out of the pile of outfits Kitsune had brought me this morning. Courtesy of Haru, of course, and though there wasn't a huge amount that would fit, I did eventually find a serviceable long skirt with a waist loose enough to fit under my ever-swelling belly. My bra needed to be adjusted another hook size to accommodate for sore breasts and aching nipples, and I tossed on a fresh T-shirt with something scrawled on it in Japanese that I couldn't remotely read.

But it was soft and large and that was good enough. A quick face wash and tangled finger-brush through my hair later and I was feeling human enough to face the day. I threw the hobo over my shoulder. If we were leaving tonight, I wanted to see about picking up a few small souvenirs.

"And I'm telling you we need to leave right now!" Nobu's voice reverberated through the door as I was about to open it. I froze, his anger a nearly tangible force. This was going to be a shitshow, and I wanted no part of it. If Melanie really had left without telling him . . .

I cracked the door to see Nobu standing there, his wings outstretched in quivering indignation, arms held back by Ion as the incubus was trying to calm the shinigami down. "We already discussed this."

"No, *you* discussed it!" Mel shouted, her cheeks flushed and angry. "*You* decided. You didn't give me a chance—"

"You don't understand." Nobu slumped. "Every minute you're outside my shrine, I can't hide you. My powers don't extend that far." He shrugged away from Ion, pinching the bridge of his nose. "You shine like a beacon. Your power—it's so easily traced, Mel. I could find you the moment I set foot in Tokyo."

Kitsune stood to the side, her ears flickering. She saw me peeking through the door and shook her head, waving me away. Well, of course she wouldn't want me to get between a god and his lover.

I debated if I should lock myself in here and let them sort it out or turn the shower hose on them when the distinctive odor of sulfur crept into the room. Everyone froze and then turned toward the front door of the hotel room as a gentle rapping sounded upon the wood.

"Daemons," Talivar said sharply.

"They're here," Nobu agreed, his face grim as he shoved Melanie behind him.

Kitsune's hand was already on the hilt of her katana, thumb pressing it out of its scabbard by scant inches, waiting for Talivar's command. Usagi-san stood beside her, her nose twitching nervously. Kitsune barked something at her I couldn't hear, and the midwife jumped and stepped toward the master bedroom.

"Knock, knock," something hissed from the other side of the door. My legs quaked in answer. *The Collector.* Somehow Paganini had managed to bring the Devil's repo man straight to us.

"Do please let us in," Paganini's voice chirped from the hallway. "Otherwise we'll have to break it down, and I'm pretty sure you don't want to attract that sort of attention here."

As if in emphasis, a distinct hum of the bow being drawn against the strings of his violin vibrated the door, a miasma of dark promise shuddering through me. Ion took Melanie's arm and shoved her toward me, his golden eyes meeting mine with a fierceness that defied description. His glamour melted away, leaving him dark skinned and crystal antlered, his cloven hooves stamping the floor.

For an instant, it seemed as though Nobu would protest but he inclined his head. "Agreed."

Melanie frowned. "Wait, what?"

"This isn't a fight for you," Nobu said. "Let us deal with this. If you see the opportunity to escape, use it. You do *not* want to be taken by the Collector." Both he and Ion shuddered at the name, exchanging a look that spoke of very specific and intimate memories.

"But—"

"Mel," Phineas said softly, all amusement drained away from him. "We'll take care of this part. You have to follow through on your end." The tiny tip of his horn began to glow. I'd nearly forgotten that as a creature of the Light Path, Phineas could hold his own, despite his small size.

Didi crouched beside him, smashing the bottle of Ramune so she was left with a jagged-looking weapon. "I've got your back," she said. I stifled a giggle at the absurdity of it all, but something told me I did not want to be on the business end of that thing when she got going.

Talivar pulled out his cell phone and barked a few sharp words into it after dialing. "Calling for reinforcements," he said. "The embassy has been notified, such as they are. For whatever reason, there is such a thing as protocol, and they have invalidated it by coming here, particularly after that run-in with Haru." Kitsune's ears flicked toward me. "Go, Abby. You and Melanie. Into the bedroom. Do *not* come out until I tell you otherwise," she commanded, her jaw shutting tight with a snapping command that brooked no dispute.

She gestured at Usagi-san, who quickly escorted me and Melanie into the master suite and locked the door. For such an herbivorous-seeming creature, she certainly looked like she was about to lay down some punches. She leaned up against the door, one long rabbit ear pressed to the wood, the other ear twitching.

"Not fair," Melanie seethed, going still as the knocking grew louder, the music taking an even more sinister turn.

The low rumble of conversation rumbled past the door, Nobu obviously challenging Paganini, and the violinist chuckling. The Collector's deep voice burbled in delight, and then I couldn't tell what was going on. Shouts, swearing, the clash of swords. A rank, burning odor seeped into the bedroom from under the door. Was the place on fire?

"Move," Melanie snapped at Usagi-san.

The rabbit refused to budge, drawing a small dagger from the sleeve of her kimono—a kaiken. "Balcony," she said, her voice clipped.

"No," Melanie refused. "This is not your call."

"Baby." Usagi-san pointed at me and shook her head. Something slammed against the door, hard enough to make the room shake, the flat-screen TV pulling away from the wall. I jumped awkwardly onto the bed to avoid getting brained by it.

Usagi-san crouched by the door as the sulfur smell grew stronger. I gagged against it, losing most of my breakfast in the process. The midwife didn't flinch, holding her position like a statue.

When the doorknob jiggled, she finally turned toward me, her eyes darting to the sliding door of the balcony, her face sweaty and desperate. "*Onegaishimasu*. Please."

Fear fluttered in my throat. Once again powerless to do anything but save myself, save my child. "All right." I sucked in a deep breath before I slipped out the sliding glass door with Melanie, shutting it behind me as the bedroom door splintered. Wood shards slammed into the glass so hard that it cracked. I leaned against the wall, one hand splayed over my belly. My fingers dug into the brick behind me.

Could I climb it? Maybe get to the balcony above? I bit my lip. Of course, we were in the penthouse. There was nothing above us at all except the roof.

I gritted my teeth, eyeing the distance to the roof. Maybe if I weren't pregnant I could shimmy up there fast enough.

Maybe. But not now. And the nearest balcony was at least ten feet away. The ground . . . Well that was stupid to even contemplate. I certainly wasn't going to be climbing down.

I didn't even have a weapon to defend myself with. Still.

"Fuck this," Melanie said, dropping the violin case and removing the tattered instrument.

"What are you— You can't!" I whisper-shouted. "You said you couldn't with it being restrained."

She gave me a half smile, showing me the red thread on the bow. "It's a spell. All I have to do is untie it and the power will be restored. Even if it's corrupted, I can't let them take the brunt of my sins anymore, Abby. I can't."

"But your control . . ." My voice faded. The determined set of her jaw was all too familiar. Short of ripping the thing out of her hands and chucking it off the balcony, I wasn't going to be able to stop her.

"We have nowhere else to go," she pointed out. "You want to wait here while everyone else dies?"

I flushed. "Well, no, but it's not like I can—" My words cut off as someone screamed on the other side of the glass, the sound splitting my ears, a horrible guttural sound of agony. We both startled, staring at each other wide-eyed.

Her face paled, and she sucked in a deep breath. "I'm sorry," she said, tugging on the thread bound to the neck of the violin. It slipped away in the breeze, fate undone with nothing more than a nimble set of fingers and stubborn will. Then she raised the bow to the strings, and the power of the Wild Magic shivered in the air between us.

She struggled to keep the song in tune, the notes swirling about me like something tangible. "Open it," she commanded.

With a heavy swallow, I opened the door, dry heaving as the thick scent of blood and sulfur wafted in on a stale breeze.

Without slowing down her playing, Mel entered the

room, smoke billowing about her. I tentatively hovered in the doorway, my hands raised to my mouth as I took in the remains of the bedroom.

Talivar lay half-sprawled against the wall, groaning as he tried to get to his feet. "Abby, stay there."

A low cry escaped me as I knelt down beside him. "Are you all right? Where's Ion?" I demanded when I saw Phin stagger out from behind a dresser. "The others?"

"Fighting with the Collector, last I saw. Him and Nobu." The unicorn blinked up at me blearily with a tired waggle of his beard. "I'm okay, but remind me to never get on Kitsune's bad side."

I halted, relief shunting through me, but Melanie did not, the music taking shape as a shield, pushing away the smoke. Something crashed in the other room, slamming into the wall with a wet thud and a scream.

"Paganini!" she called out, her voice deep and full of fury. "I'm coming for you!"

The music abruptly changed, and Paganini emerged from the kitchen area, a deep slash on his face making him look half-mad, his lips spread wide a grin of monstrous proportions. Past him, I could only see chaos, furniture twisted and glass shattered, the golden glow of something on fire lighting up the violinist's silhouette. Dimly, I made out sirens in the distance.

Melanie stepped toward the Devil's TouchStone, her playing growing faster, matching Paganini with the confidence of a lifetime of skill. My sluggish mind tried to place the song they were dueling with, but it was somehow beyond me, like reading a menu and having the words slip off the page in dull squiggles.

The power built and built, a mountain of it filling the room, and I retreated instinctively, Talivar crawling past them to find me on the balcony again. "This will be bad if we don't stop it," he said, wiping blood from a cut on his forehead.

"Where's Ion?" I asked again. "And what the hell just happened in there?"

Whatever he said in response was whisked away by a violent gust of wind, the music growing discordant. Melanie was shouting something, but even I could see the Wild Magic was becoming undone, the notes taking on a cutting edge.

Paganini abruptly stopped playing and backed away, leaving Mel by herself, struggling to control it. The silver violin began to smoke, its tarnish of corruption growing.

"This is what happened at the Barras," Talivar said, panic lacing his words. "We have to get out of here before she blows up the whole hotel." He attempted to move into the room, but the wall of magic shoved him back.

"Mel," I screamed. "Stop it!"

"I can't!" She turned and turned, tears streaming from her eyes. "It won't stop!"

Nobu lurched from the bathroom, half the hair from his head apparently burned off. He took one look at what she was doing and staggered toward her into the thick of the music. Grabbing her arm, he pointed at the entrance to the kitchen area. "Door! Now!"

She shut her eyes, and the music changed slightly, the edges of the walls alighting silver and gold, making a Door to wherever Nobu had wanted. Sweating, the shinigami gestured as it took shape, changing it slightly into what appeared to be a Gate. I blinked, wondering when that particular ability had manifested, but there obviously wasn't time for questions.

The minute it lit up, Nobu straightened, his wings outstretched for balance. *I'm sorry, little bird,* he mouthed and shoved her into it.

The Gate slammed partially shut in a wave of magic, the backlash of her power rolling out of it with a clap of thunder, hurricane-force winds pushing me against the edge of the balcony so hard I nearly tipped off.

Nobu glanced up to see me there, tears streaming from his eyes, though if that was simply sadness or the intensity of the heat of Mel's power, I couldn't tell. Before I could even ask what had happened, he was on his feet, shoving Talivar out of the way as he launched onto the balcony and into the air, his wings snapping out.

Behind us came a rumbling roar, a vile, guttering chuff that made my legs go weak, the balcony vibrating beneath my white-knuckled grip. Talivar's jaw tightened. "The Collector!" he shouted above the din, turning toward me with a helpless sort of terror. For a span of several heart-beats, his gaze lingered on my face before resting on Nobu. "Take her out of here! Go!"

Nobu grabbed my hand, pulling me over the edge with him. Together, we fell.

"Goddammit, look up, Abby! Give me your arm!" Star-tled, I did as Nobu said, wincing as he snatched me from the air, his blue-black wings a thundercloud of feathers and wind, as they snapped up and down, trying to regain the thrust needed to push us into the sky.

"Didn't account for the extra weight," he grunted, catch-ing an updraft. "You weren't this far along before."

"Hey, take me back!" I squirmed, punching his shoul-ders. But instead of returning me to the balcony, he kept going, leaving me to stare helplessly at Talivar as we soared past.

"Knock it off unless you want to be dropped," he snapped. "And sorry, but no. With Melanie gone, the Collector will search for another target—and you're the prime one being the only other mortal in the room. Melanie needs you, and I don't have any more time for social niceties. The others can't help where we're going anyway."

"Oh, but I can?" I glared at him, but his face remained impervious. "I hate you," I growled, terror for my friends overtaking any sense of manners.

"Like I care." He shook his head. "My little bird's time is almost up, and I'll be damned if I let her fade away without even a fight. I'm sorry if your feelings are hurt, but besides that, I couldn't give two shits."

My stomach plummeted. "Can't her violin be bound again?"

"No. Kitsune's spell was temporary. It was enough to give us time to get to Hell and throw ourselves on His mercy, should He be willing. Or at least attempt to make another bargain. But Mel's undone that to try to save me and the rest of you. If we don't do something quickly, there will be nothing left of her at all."

"Those daemons with Paganini found us so fast . . ."

"I told you I was not welcome in Tokyo. I'm too easily traced here. But when I realized she had left, I knew I didn't have any other choice." His mouth quirked. "There's quite a bounty on my head these days. That little thing I asked you to retrieve is worth a tremendous amount to the right bidder."

"And yet you trusted me to get it. I'm almost touched."

"I trusted you would do the right thing for Melanie." He said this with a touch of sadness, and I almost felt sorry for him. Almost.

"How long are you planning to fly?" I shut my eyes at the ever-shrinking ground with a hard swallow. "Is there a Gate nearby you could take instead?"

"There is, but it's not one I can open." He snorted. "I'm not sure I'll be able to open any more Gates for a long time. Right now, I'm trying to put some distance between us and Paganini."

"But you're a god, aren't you?"

"Mmm. Maybe not. Not anymore." He winced, and I realized his wings were slowing down, the burn marks on his face scabbing over.

"Are you okay?" I asked. We seemed to be dropping altitude at a slightly alarming rate.

"Hush. I need to concentrate." He struggled to regain an upward motion, grunting with each flap of his wings.

I shuddered at the way the ground lurched up at us, blinking rapidly as I realized Nobu was losing feathers. A lot of them.

"Uh, Nobu . . ."

"I know."

"But your wings . . ."

"I *know*. Now kindly shut up." He huffed again and tried to bank right, only to lose his balance so we fell a few feet. I shrieked despite myself, shivering in the breeze. "Change of plans. I'll try not to drop you. Hold tight. That's it. Otherwise, be quiet while I try to find a place to land." At his words, I clung a little harder to his neck, though I didn't know if I was helping or hurting him. My mind whirled. Everything had happened so fast in that hotel room, and I'd been so helpless. And Mel . . . Even knowing what was going to happen, she'd marched in and at least tried to fight them. I couldn't fault her for that. Still, I sent a little prayer of thanks to Nobu for having his wits about him and stopping the devastation, whatever the cost. If not for him, we all would have died. My nostrils flared wide, thinking about it.

The mist parted, revealing a mountain in front of us. A big one. Nobu grunted, sweat dripping from his forehead, and I could only imagine how uncomfortable it would be with the burns, the blisters starting to weep. But I didn't think he would welcome my attempts to bandage it just now, and we were, indeed, swaying something terrible, lurching from side to side as he adjusted his flight path.

"Fujisan," he said, nodding at the mountain. "I never get tired of seeing it. I'll try to get us as high as I can, but you may have to walk the rest of the way."

"Wait, what?" Before I could say anything else, he let out a rumbling yell, his wings pumping madly. "The rest of the way where?"

"Gate," he gasped. "At the summit." And then he let out a sad sort of cry, as though the very light had gone out of him, his wings exploding like some sort of anime fever dream gone horribly wrong.

The earth hurtled toward us, and he rolled, shifting his body to take the brunt of the crash right before we slammed into the side of Mount Fuji like a sparrow caught in a wind turbine. We tumbled over and over, Nobu twisting around me, even as I balled up tightly against the curve of my belly. I grayed out as we came to a halt, cradled in a snow drift, and a blanket of feathers.

CHAPTER 13

SNOW DRIFTED PAST ME, COATING my face and sending deep chills skittering over my skin. I lay there, mentally tallying the aches and bruises stiffening my joints, wiggling my toes to make sure everything was still working. My lungs burned, pain lancing through my wrist when I pushed on my palm to try to sit up. At first, I thought maybe it was fractured, but after careful inspection, I decided it was just badly bruised.

I ran my good hand over my belly, patting it in sudden panic. From the onslaught of little baby kicks fluttering against my rib cage, I could only assume she was doing well enough. I groaned, shifting away from Nobu. The shinigami had cradled himself around me to shoulder the impact, and for that, I was grateful.

Absolutely livid at this turn of events, but grateful.

I shook him awake, heartsick at the travesty his wings had become, nearly featherless and drooping. I reached out to touch one but hesitated, not sure how to help. In fact, his entire being seemed lifeless, except for the soft exhalations of his breath indicating he was still alive.

He blinked up at me. "Little bird," he mumbled and then frowned as he realized who I was.

"Are you all right? Aside from the obvious." I brushed the snow off his shoulders as he sat up, trying to ignore my own shivers. "Where are we?"

He let out a humorless bark of laughter. "That's a relative question. I'm alive, for now. Same as you. And we're still on Fujisan," Nobu said, craning his neck as though trying to figure out exactly where. "The summit is that way, maybe a few hours climb." He eyed me doubtfully, taking in my long skirt, T-shirt, and loose pair of sandals. "Maybe a few more," he admitted.

"Are you fucking kidding me?" I half exploded at him. Inwardly, I knew our landing here hadn't been entirely his fault. He'd kept me alive and that was no small thing, but the wave of helplessness that came crashing down as I studied the snow-covered mountain was overwhelming and absolute. "Look at me! Do I look like I'm equipped to go hiking?"

"Not really, no." He gathered himself to stand, ignoring the feathers puddling at his feet. "Might as well get started. No point standing around here and freezing to death in the meantime. You can bitch at me along the way."

I gave a helpless little laugh when he stretched out his hand to me, but what choice did I have? "And there wasn't a closer Gate you could have crashed at?"

He gave me an unfriendly look. "Not one the Collector wouldn't have chased you down at. Besides, I wasn't thinking too clearly myself. Under the circumstances, you should count yourself lucky we managed to get here at all."

What the hell was going on? "Wait, what did you mean you weren't a god anymore?"

He let out a barking laugh and stretched out the tattered remains of his wings. "I would think that would be obvious enough. My power is fading, and when it's gone, the god I was will be gone too."

"I don't understand." I let out a gasp as I sank up to my ankles in the snow drift.

Nobu sighed. "This isn't going to work. Here." He lifted

me so I was in his arms again, carrying me princess-style. "Hold on as tight as you can. We're never going to get up there if your toes fall off. At least this way we can keep each other warm."

"How romantic," I muttered, but even I had to admit he was right. "You should probably get that burn on your head looked at. And your wings . . ."

He grunted something noncommittal. "See any doctors around?" He ignored my scowl and rolled his eyes. "Don't be stupid."

"Where did you send Melanie?" I demanded, trying to at least distract him a bit.

"My shrine. It was the only place I could think of, given the situation. And it seems only fair to take on some of the damage she's inflicted. If I hadn't interfered all those years ago . . . Well, who knows what might have happened." He said it matter-of-fact, but there was a distinct edge to his voice that made me think he was hiding his emotions very well. But then I'd never been able to read him. Nobu had a tendency to shut out everyone except Melanie, and I was clearly a poor substitute for her.

"But if she took that power into your shrine . . ." I left the thought unfinished, shuddering.

"Oh, there's no *if* about it," he said. "It's been destroyed. Obliterated into the void, just like the Barras. It's why I'm losing my power: Without a shrine to focus the prayers, well, that's what gives a god his celestial aura and all that jazz."

I pulled away from him in horror, my head snapping toward him. "How can you be so calm about it? To send her there, knowing the Wild Magic was uncontrolled . . ."

His lips twitched in a half smile. "I had the feeling things were going to go badly when I realized she had left for Tokyo. I made sure my priests were gone so no one would get hurt. Hopefully she'll stay put until we manage to get back there."

"And how are we planning to do that? We're on top of a mountain. You're injured, I'm pregnant, and we'll probably freeze to death before we even reach the damn Gate." I stifled the urge to smack him.

"I guess we'll find out," he said dryly. "But we can have that discussion later around a hot cup of tea after we get to the summit. Your choice." The breeze didn't seem to bother him. Maybe he didn't feel the temperature the same way I did, though he was dressed in his usual leather pants and thin-threaded shirt.

Temporarily defeated, we began the steady climb upward again. Snow fluttered down in a breath, warning of a storm on the cusp of becoming a monstrous blizzard. A chill rushed down my spine and refused to leave, my teeth beginning to chatter.

I pulled the jar out of my hobo with his soul stone. "I didn't get a chance to give this to you earlier."

"Careful with that," he hissed, snatching it from me. He held the jar up with a faraway look. "I'll have to make sure Haru is amply rewarded for his loyalty. There aren't many who would stand by their word for someone like me." He shook his head, thrusting the jar into a small bag, which he shoved into his vest.

"So, that soul stone . . . What possessed you to give it to him?" The question was vaguely trite, but I meant it.

He let out a sharp bark of laughter. "It's not that interesting a story. I was human once, same as you. Same as any shinigami."

"And you decided letting a yokai stick his hand up your ass was what, a good idea?"

"Not quite." He paused. "The place the tengu brought you to in Shimabara? I was alive during the time of the real one—during the Edo period, as they call it. I owned a tea house."

I blinked. "You owned a brothel?"

"Of course. It was a good way to make money, to survive the changing tides of history. I was never one to get involved with the power struggles between samurai and merchant lords, so it was much easier to smoke my pipe and sell pretty girls to the highest bidder."

"Charming."

"I did what I had to in order to survive, though that did include some rather unsavory things. Flesh was—and is—simply another commodity. It's traded for money, for food, for a chance to escape the poverty of a family forced to sell their daughters so the sons might be able to eat." A half smile curled his upper lip. "Some even managed to do well, their contracts bought out by powerful men who were easily charmed by a bit of poetry, a flash of thigh . . . and I was there to oversee it all. Not that it was something that could be done overnight," he added. "Those girls needed to be trained from a young age."

"A medieval pimp. How classy. And here I would have figured you to be a traveling musician or something. Sort of what you were with Melanie." I didn't know if I was disappointed, outraged, or some combination of both.

"There wasn't time for anything like that. I liked eating, you know." He sobered, carefully stepping around an outcropping of rocks, his feet slipping slightly. "So do you, judging by your weight."

I rolled my eyes, but let it slide. He was carrying me up a mountain, after all. His skin was paler than I remembered, but there was a determined set to his chin that made me not want to question him about it. What would be the point anyway? We had to press on, or we'd freeze to death.

I looked over my shoulder at the mountain's peak and realized we were following a path of sorts. "Aren't you worried about other climbers?"

"Too cold," he grunted. "They close the mountain to

tourists most of the year, though there are cabins at various stations. If we get stuck, we can take shelter there for a while, but I don't think there will be any food in them."

I squinted through the mist. "Isn't there a Gate just up there?"

"There are others," he admitted, "but those aren't working Gates—more for decoration, really. To mark out the sacred route to the summit. The one on top is the one we need." He sighed, and we continued the climb until it got steep enough that he had to put me down, forcing me to limp behind him as he attempted to stamp down the snow.

"So what's a death god do anyway?" I asked him, trying to ignore the way the cold lanced up my naked toes. The rapidly thinning air was making it difficult to breathe, my head going light and loopy. My limbs shivered violently, and I wrapped my arms tightly about my swelling stomach, as though I might somehow protect my unborn child with the sheer force of my will.

"The name sort of speaks for itself, doesn't it?" Nobu said.

"*Omae wa mou shindeiru*," I intoned, the familiar meme resulting in a bout of my own hysterical laughter interrupted by the clacking of my chattering teeth. "You are already dead."

"Get away from me with that anime garbage," he snapped. "We don't kill anyone, but we know when people are going to die. There's a sort of aura around them, I guess. Like we can see Death approaching. I knew you were going to die before, you know. Back when we made that deal to free Brystion and Talivar, and you drank the water of Lethe. It was on you then, clinging like a shroud."

I shuddered, anger flaring within my chest. "Why didn't you tell me?"

"Would you have listened if I had? You didn't trust me then anyway."

"I don't trust you now," I pointed out.

"Fair enough. Besides, you drank the Lethe water. You would have forgotten it, along with everything else, so what would have been the point?" He shrugged. "The shroud is gone now, though—except for the bit of it every mortal has at any given time."

"And Mel?" I asked pointedly, not sure I wanted to know the answer but unable to keep from needling him about it.

"None of your business," he snarled. "I can't just go around telling mortals when other mortals are about to die. There are rules that even gods have to follow."

"But you *can* go around changing the fates of those you care about? I see." I raised a brow, unconvinced.

"There are always exceptions," he admitted. "And not exactly, no. But I wasn't much good at following rules and laws when I was human. I didn't see much point in changing that once I became a god. My original job was simply to collect the souls of those about to die, to send them wherever they needed to be. It sounds more romantic than it is."

"And then you had a shrine built to you?" I yelped as a bit of rock scraped the freezing bottom of my foot.

"In a manner of speaking," he said. "It only takes a few humans to realize that a place or a being has power, and not long after that they start asking it for things. Prayers followed, and the building of the shrine and then the priests moved in and that was the start of that. Mine is on the humbler side of such things, and I got bored of it quickly. I'm not particularly good with the god stuff, so I wandered the world awhile and ran into Melanie at Julliard during a concert. The rest is history, I guess."

"And at some point you played cards with Haru and gave up your magical ass stone?"

"Something like that." He stretched his arms, the remains of his wings flapping sadly. "Or I let him win, truthfully.

Call it insurance against a time when I thought I might need it. Most mortals who are made into shinigami are desperately trying to move on to their next lives, but I figured that wouldn't even be an option without my soul. I'd be stuck here as a god for the rest of my life, and that suits me fine."

"Does Mel know all this?" I asked, disbelieving.

"She knows it well," he said, his voice growing faraway and fond. "She married me, didn't she?"

I blinked. "Wait, what?"

"We're married. Finally," he said, suddenly smug. "That's what we were doing in Kyoto. She was getting stir-crazy, and I figured I could pick up the paperwork while we were out. It was simple enough to add her to my family registry anyway—nothing fancy like a ceremony. That's why I was able to direct that new Door of hers in the hotel room. We're obviously TouchStoned now."

I felt a twinge of hurt that she hadn't told me, but I swallowed it down, thinking of my own haphazard hand-fasting with Talivar. Sometimes marriages just happened, I guessed.

"But you converted it to a Gate. How did you manage that?"

He shrugged and waggled his fingers at me. "God powers through the TouchStone bond, I guess. I've never tried it before, though; it was more an act of desperation. But it worked, and that's all that matters."

By now, shivers were rolling through my body on a regular basis, my lips chapped and burning. But I could see we were finally approaching the summit. Relief crested over me, spurring me into action. I ignored the numbness of my feet and concentrated on where to step, crying out when I stumbled against Nobu. The shinigami hoisted me into his arms again, his body heat like a furnace beneath the crust of snow settling on his shoulders.

"Slow breaths," he said, carrying me up the rest of the way. The pitch of his voice was off, and I realized he was swaying badly as we reached the top.

He set me down almost immediately and sagged to his knees. The fog and mist swirled below us, rolling in an ever-changing sea of softness. Beautiful, but I couldn't stop to appreciate it for more than a few seconds, my hands stiffening into claws. If we didn't get out of there in the next couple of minutes, I'd be dead, shroud or no. I swallowed hard. Maybe he couldn't see the death shroud on me because he'd already lost that power?

I didn't have time to dwell on it. "So now what?" I asked.

"The Gate. There." He pointed at the torii gate perched on the top of the mountain. Unlike the Gates in Kyoto, this one was gray in color with stone lions guarding it on either side. I'd almost missed it, it blended in with the snow so well.

"Is this thing even on?" I tapped the Gate, eager to get out of the wind. I shivered violently, my hands shaking as I tried to wrap them around me.

He shook his head. "Nope. Truthfully, it has been closed for a very long time. There's a binding on it, set by the guardian of the mountain. God or not, even my failing yokai power probably won't be enough."

"You said 'guardian.' Why don't we ask him?"

"I doubt the old man even wakes up more than every other century at this point. Mountain spirits are notoriously difficult once they're asleep, especially the old ones."

"This sucks." I tore off a bit of my skirt to wrap around my now-frozen feet. "We need to hurry up."

"Yeah," he said, laying his hands on the Gate. It lit up like a firefly for a half second, extinguishing a moment later. "Dammit!" He tried again, and when that didn't work, he strode over to one of the stone lions and punched it in the face. "Wake up!"

Dizzy, I wrapped my arms around my belly, tucking my hands into my armpits as I sagged against one edge of the torii gate, squatting as best I could manage. But even I knew if we didn't get this thing open, there wasn't going to be any chance for us at all. Terror gripped me, but I was so cold I could barely focus on anything but how badly I was shaking.

My eyes slid shut, and I blinked hard, trying to stay awake. My vision glazed over despite the sharpness of the wind, burning my cheeks as Nobu tried to awaken the guardian of the mountain. Had he grown smaller in the time since we'd landed?

"I'm sorry, baby," I whispered to my belly. "I really . . ."

" . . . am."

My head jerked up. I was in my Dreaming Heart. Panic set in as I realized I must have fallen asleep, that I was probably freezing to death. "Wake up, wake up," I slurred, my thoughts clumsy and slow.

Was my Dreaming Heart dimmer? I staggered toward the Victorian, everything growing hazy.

I blinked. The Key to the CrossRoads was still here, wasn't it? In all the craziness of the last few days, I'd completely forgotten about it.

"Key, key, key." Over and over I said it, as though repeating it would keep me from forgetting. Would it even work if I could manage to wake up? Kitsune hadn't thought so, but I had no choice but to try if Nobu couldn't open the Gate.

The door to the Victorian jiggled open, and I lurched inside. Even as cozy as the house had been, it felt terribly cold. Ice was forming over the walls, my breath puffing with each exhalation. Dream or not, it was echoing what was happening to my body with terrifying accuracy.

"Key . . ." I mounted the steps upstairs, slipping when I hit the top one, and skidded into my bedroom. Frost crackled the windowpanes as I ripped up the floorboards and dug out a small Holly Hobbie box, the keeper of my childhood treasures: Rocks, a feather, two seashells from a trip to the beach, and the Key to the CrossRoads.

The heart-shaped gem winked on its chain, flirting almost. *Why have you left me here for so long?*

I snatched it from the box, clutching it in rapidly shaking fingers, trying to fasten the clasp around my neck. Once it was on, it would never come off until my death, but seeing as I was about to die anyway, that was pretty much a moot point. It made an almost audible click as it finally fell into place, the stone lighting up with a soft, singsong note as it settled itself around my neck.

Its power hummed through me—a piece of my past, a piece of my future. A piece of me returned.

"Abby!" My head jerked toward the voice, my body lurching out of the room and down the stairs to the outside. Sonja paced outside the gates, her crimson wings shivering. "What's going on?"

"Open," I gestured at the gates, trembling so hard I could barely stand. The succubus caught me as I began to fall.

The Key to the CrossRoads hummed and my jaw chattered as I tried to answer her question. "Have . . . have to go back. Stuck on a mountain. Fuji. If I don't wake up, I'm going to die. Wake me up. Please," I said desperately, caught between elation and terror.

She hugged me tightly. "Mount Fuji. Got it. I'll contact everyone else. Hopefully we can find you. Now, wake up! Wake . . ."

" . . . up, Abby," Nobu slurred at me.

My eyelids fluttered, the lashes nearly frozen together.

He was partially wrapped around me, as though to keep me warm. His own face was pale still, his lips chapped and windburned. "Awake," I gasped, teeth chattering. "Got the Key."

"The what?" He brushed off the snow and gave the necklace a gentle tug. "Where did you get that?"

"Dreaming." My feet were so numb I could barely stand, clawing my way up the edges of the Gate. It flared to life almost immediately, a crystalline blue-and-silver hue illuminating us in the gathering shadows.

"At least it still works," Nobu said. "I was a little afraid its time in Hell might have broken it."

My fingers stroked the Gate, and an even colder spark shocked its way up my arm. I caught a glimpse of a past I couldn't quite make out, a history of the mountain in images both confusing and beautiful. In layman's terms, this mountain had seen some shit.

But I wasn't there for a history lesson. "Open," I said aloud, my inner voice repeating it, asking, coaxing, commanding, trying to walk that fine line between pushing too hard but not being a wimp about it.

Each Door I'd run across had always had its own personality, and this one was very much asleep and not looking to awaken. The Gate lit up slightly as I continued my requests, the necklace becoming so bright it was nearly blinding. The power rippled through me, filling me with a delicious warmth. The baby kicked in response, and I nearly wept with relief, even as I doubled my efforts.

In that instant, I feared it would overload somehow and break, but then the Gate sluggishly began to respond with a lethargic pulse. It didn't have the same spiderweb feel that Doors had; the magic was definitely different, fighting me. It itched over my skin as if I were suddenly covered in a swarm of bees. Perhaps this is what Phineas had meant about that tickle on his skin, but for me, it felt like I would be stung to shreds if I continued.

"It's working, Abby," Nobu said, his voice weak and distant. My eyes flicked to him blankly, still trying to keep my composure in spite of the power attempting to flood through me like a firehose. Whatever he saw seemed to alarm him, and he took a step back as I continued to punch through the barrier.

A grinding sound, like stone shuddering off its skin, the Gate vibrating hard enough to set my teeth chattering. Something rolled in my belly, rippling.

Baby. The baby was moving. Was the vibration hurting her? I tried to pull away from the Gate, but Nobu had pressed his hand against mine, keeping it there. "Let me go!" I squirmed, but his hand didn't loosen in the slightest.

"Keep going," he said through clenched teeth, frost crusting on his lashes. "We will die if you stop. Your baby will die."

My belly moved again, and every instinct I had urged me to flee. "Fine, have it your way." I pressed my forehead to the Gate, sending it all the power I had. *"Open!"*

And everything went black.

I was tumbling, tumbling, the blackness around me rising in a thick miasma. The crystal at my neck twinkled brilliantly, lighting up my skin in a bluish-white glow. In some ways, that was worse because all it did was illuminate how much nothing there was. Like my nightmares, I simply fell, waiting for the darkness to come and swallow me up.

But that didn't happen, and I was overcome by relief, even as I began to fret. I squinted to see past the light, my hand blocking it slightly as I tried to see if there was anything else out there.

For a moment, I did. Great strips of silver and gold crisscrossed all around me in some infinite dance, moving and weaving as though upon a great loom, sewn into a pattern I certainly couldn't make out, let alone comprehend. Like the CrossRoads maybe, if it were stretched out like string instead of wrapped around the Earth. But it was mostly silver in so much as I had seen, with only the dark tracks of the Wild Hunt that Talivar had ridden. Gold, I had no true knowledge of at all, and here and there shots of ruby red, glittering like blood amid all that silver.

For half a breath, it almost made sense to me. But then it was gone and I was falling again, the tracks sweeping by me as though I were on the Shinkansen, everything blurred beyond recognition. Would the Key know where I was supposed to go? If I reached out to touch one of the tracks would it rip my arm off? Would I end up some-where else entirely? Would I simply fall for eternity?

Something niggled at the back of my mind. A tune? A song? What was it? I shook my head as though to clear it and realized I actually *was* hearing music. But the notes were all warped, like someone playing in the wrong key entirely but close enough to almost be right.

It was better than nothing, though, and I tried aiming for the sound, but it's hard to change direction in a vacuum. In the end, I wriggled my way through the darkness like a tadpole, unsure whether I was getting closer or not.

"Hellooo!" I called out, my voice seeming to reverberate around me, echoing past the music.

The song changed into something almost questioning and then sped up. I hummed a few bars of "Help Yourself" by Tom Jones. "Love is like candy on a shelllllll . . ."

The tune immediately changed to match—still distorted like an unstable carousel but familiar all the same. "Mel!" I cried out, for who else would know me so well, would be playing beyond her means to find me, to press past the corruption of the magic she couldn't control to save me?

"I'm here!" I shouted, the words deafening.

HERE. HERE. HERE. HERE.

Almost immediately, a red cord emerged from the shadows, beckoning me like a lifeline. I took it without thinking, almost blindly grasping it in relief, and it began to shunt me along until I was parallel with one of the gold tracks.

I reached out my hand to the track, letting out a little gasp as I merged onto it, rolling straight through a Gate. Tumbling forward, I hugged my arms around my belly and came to rest in a field of rapeseed, the grass warm and soft and utterly not of the human world. A path ran through it, the field silver-tinged at the edges. I was on the Cross-Roads, then.

"Abby?" Mel's voice came from behind me, weak and strained.

I struggled to my feet, breathing hard, and found Melanie standing there, the violin drooping in her arms. The silver varnish had worn off almost completely; the color now no longer that of burnished wood but more like an old scab.

We staggered forward, the two of us leaning on each other for support. Her red-rimmed eyes peered at me from behind her lavender glasses. "Are you all right? Is the baby all right?"

I patted my belly, wincing at the soreness of my wrist, the numbness of my toes, the chapping of my lips as I wet them with a parched tongue. "I think so?" My hair was damp, my skin clammy, and the ground tilted sharply when I attempted to shift my weight and adjust my balance.

Melanie eased me onto the ground, her hand pressed to my forehead. "You're feverish. We need to get moving. I don't think there's any water here."

"*Mmmph.* Wherever *here* is." I reached up and pulled the Key from my shirt. The glow had faded, its power now dormant, though it still hummed in a vaguely comforting way. "Where's Nobu? He was wounded pretty bad, Mel. His wings—"

"I know." Her eyes welled up, and she hugged me again. "I'm so, so sorry. His shrine . . . It's gone. I fucked up, Abby. I fucked up real bad."

"Well, you did come pretty close to blowing up the hotel room," I admitted. "But I think you scared off Paganini, so it's not a complete disaster. Everyone else survived as far as I know, and I met Sonja in the Dreaming so I'm sure they'll be sending out search parties once she can reach everyone."

"Nobu said you used the Key to force open the Gate, but you overloaded it with power. He tried to follow you, but you were gone, so he returned to what was left of his shrine, hoping you'd somehow found your way to me." She shrugged sadly, biting her lip. "You weren't there, of course, so I went to look for you. As for Nobu . . . He's in rough shape, Abby."

"But he's alive? That counts for something, doesn't it?" I squeezed her hand.

"Yeah. He's resting for now. With his shrine broken, his power is not what it was. He used the last of it to stabilize the violin a bit—that's what allowed me to use it to find you." Her eyes darted away. She obviously wasn't telling me everything, but I wasn't going to press her on it now.

"At least he made it." I got to my feet, my back aching. "How long was I, uh, floating about time and space?"

"I'm not sure. It had probably been several hours by the time Nobu found me, and then I was searching for you for a while. I didn't even think the Wild Magic would work for something like this, but it's all I could think of to do. I'm surprised you heard me, to be honest. It felt like I was playing inside a wet plastic bag."

"Somehow I don't think Tom Jones is CrossRoads playlist material. But it totally should be." I smiled ruefully, shifting again, trying to ease the pressure on my hips as we started down the path. "Who else would it be but you? And now we are here. It's got a nice Elysian Fields vibe to it, if somewhat disappointing in its dearth of vending machines." I let out a deep breath. "Ugh. It feels like my guts are being squished into my chest."

"They probably are," she said. "And the magic chose the place, not me. But we're on the regular CrossRoads—that much I can tell. The magic feels different. Familiar. Like an old friend, maybe."

"Well, that's a relief," I replied, "however you managed it. At least I'm warm and off the damn mountain."

"I think we both did it, somehow. The Key channeled the Wild Magic, even as messed up as it was, and I think that allowed us to find our way here. It seems to be a pocket tucked off the main CrossRoads." My back twinged again, but instead of sitting down, I began pacing, grimacing at the way my thighs chafed. I didn't know whether it was sweat or I'd pissed myself, but it was gross and I kind of hated it.

Her eyes slid to my bulging stomach, which seemed somehow lower than before. "And when are you due?"

"I've sort of lost track of the trimester, to be honest. Every time I travel off and on the CrossRoads, my belly gets bigger. Kitsune brought me a midwife when I was in Tokyo, but how do you account for time when you're spinning outside the fabric of reality?" Another twinge. "Jesus, what's up with these fucking cramps?"

"Ah, Abby?" Melanie cradled the violin and bow in her left arm, her right hand reaching out to steady me. "I had been hoping you might join me on the next part of this particular quest, but I think there's something else that needs to happen first . . ."

My voice grew oddly husky, and I winced against another cramp, letting out a chuckle. "I mean, how long can a field trip to Hell really take? We can make it a girls' night out."

Melanie snorted. "Eternity, most likely. But that doesn't matter right now."

"Ah," I gasped, a sudden rush of pain flushing through my nether regions. Something hot splashed over my ankles, soaking my skirt. My nostrils flared as I met Melanie's awkward gaze.

My water had broken.

CHAPTER 14

"YOU KNOW, IF YOU SUSPECTED I was going into labor, you could have fucking said something," I grumbled. We were on the CrossRoads proper now, following the silver cobblestones as best we could in search of a Door that would take us to the mortal realm.

"I would have thought you would notice before I did."

"It's not like the contractions are particularly consistent," I pointed out. "And my timing's a mess. By all rights, I shouldn't be ready to give birth for at least a few more months. My mind's been a bit occupied by other things, you know?"

She flushed. "I know. And this isn't the way I wanted things to go down." She paused when we reached an intersection. "I could swear this looks vaguely familiar, but if we're not careful, we're going to end up in the Borderlands."

The Borderlands were a sort of chaotic no-man's-land between the Paths, occupied by OtherFolk that didn't always fit in a single category. It generally wasn't a good place to be and certainly not by a woman in labor.

I let out a soft groan, breaking out in a cold sweat. I bent over slightly, panting. "Shouldn't we try to find our way to a hospital or something? I don't want to be dropping this baby in a field like livestock."

"Something tells me we're not going to have that long."

"You some kind of doctor now? Ahhhhh!" This time the contraction came harder, sucking my breath away. "Never mind," I gasped. "Just get me the fuck somewhere I can lie down."

"All right. Change of plans. We'll head toward Eildon Tree. We're bound to run into someone there, and if nothing else, it will be safer than giving birth on the side of the road."

"I don't care if we end up in Satan's basement," I snapped as another contraction hit. "But sure, Eildon Tree. Where is it?"

"This way." She took my hand and led me forward through a series of road divisions, taking each step with confidence. At some point, I realized she was humming bits and pieces of *Hamilton*.

"Everything's legal in New Jersey . . ." I sang, trying to distract myself. "How do you even know where Eildon Tree is?"

"I sense shit like that," she said finally. "Like seeing music with my synesthesia. Since I helped re-form it, I always seem to know vaguely where it is. For something like this, and given the time span, I think it's probably the safest place to be. It is a sacred place to the OtherFolk, after all."

"I guess Ion and the others won't be able to make it in time," I said, my voice suddenly small and scared. Despite all my reading and research, with the change in time, I'd barely gotten used to the concept of *being* pregnant, let alone wrapped my head around the idea of taking care of another person.

In all my wildest dreams I didn't imagine I'd be here on the CrossRoads, giving birth among the roots of Eildon Tree. While I was grateful Melanie was with me, it wasn't like she had given birth herself. If we didn't find someone to help us, it was going to get interesting—and maybe not in a good way.

A rolling wave of nausea slammed into me, and I gagged. Though whether that was simply stress or a normal birth thing, I had no idea. My nostrils flared as it hit me that I was going to have to do this without any sort of pain management most likely. As someone who had had a fair amount of chronic pain—before the accident with my years of rigorous ballet training and afterward, when I suffered from my crippling wounds—I had a fairly high pain tolerance. You had to, to be a dancer. But this was something new.

What if the baby got stuck? What if I was in labor for days? Myriad awful scenarios whirled in my thoughts, every horror story from YouTube births and forum rants suddenly a terrible and true potential thing that could happen. Wrapped umbilical cords, high blood pressure, tearing . . .

Another dizzy spell hit me. "Water," I croaked. "Get me some motherfucking water."

"We're almost there. It's at the top of the hill. Once I get you settled, I'll go find help," she said, her hip taking most of my weight for a few steps. "Jesus, you're heavy."

"It happens when you get pregnant, I hear," I retorted, sighing with relief when the tree appeared out of the mist. This close to it, I could hear its song humming on the wind. I'd been here twice before. One time was during the almost-war between Faerie and Hell. The original tree had been there then, as old as the world itself, an ancient yew standing there coated with tiny white blossoms and wish-rags left by wandering OtherFolk pilgrims.

The new tree had only been there for what I figured was about six months, and if it wasn't as large as the old tree that had been there, it certainly was trying to be. Where the other one had been a rich gray color, its branches sprawling in all directions, this one seemed to be much more organized. Or maybe split.

It was though it had four personalities—one section dark and gnarled, one soft and blooming, one strong and robust and green, and one wild and gold and joyful. In a way, it made sense; the tree hadn't sprung out of the earth organically like its parent had. This one had been nurtured by a madman and then forced to sprout via the Wild Magic. It was bound to have some quirks.

I wanted to ask which one was Mel's, but it felt vaguely rude to do so. I should at least be able to recognize my own friend's magic. I shivered, suddenly hot and cold at once. I paced around the tree as though I might somehow outrun my own skin.

"There has to be someone nearby. I'm sure if we sent word to Faerie, Moira would be here with midwives. Pain control. Something." I hated how frightened my voice sounded.

Surely some sort of birthing instinct should have kicked in by now, telling me what I needed to do? What I should be preparing? I leaned against the bark of the tree, my fingers clutching around a gnarled branch. A wave of helplessness washed over me. Was I supposed to breathe now? Squat? Sit? Everything I'd read in those books faded away until I felt as though I was nothing more than a hollow shell, a vessel for a being, trapped in the maze of my own body.

"I want my mother," I whispered, though I knew that was an impossibility that even the Wild Magic couldn't fix.

I sank to my knees, waiting for the pain to stop. How many minutes apart was I? I couldn't seem to remember the time. Closer meant the baby was coming, right?

Mel hesitated. "I don't want to leave you like this, but I don't know how else to get help. I can't open a Door, not without someone TouchStoning me directing the magic, and it's not working that well anyway."

"I know." I coughed. "I know. And I don't want to attract the wrong sort of attention either. I mean, it's safe enough here for now, but . . ."

There were a lot more daemons that ate babies than I cared to know about. *A lot.* Not to mention Paganini and his ilk were still on the hunt for Melanie, assuming they had found their way out of Japan.

Beneath my hands, the tree thrummed soothingly, like an umbrella had lowered itself over us, and I immediately relaxed. As though we were protected. Did it remember me? Did it remember when I tried to rescue it?

Its EarthSong rose in my veins, bidding me to be calm, and if I caught the barest edge of my mother's smile in it, what of it? I sucked in a deep breath, letting it ease out of me as pain rippled in my lower half.

It was as though a snake constricted itself tightly around my womb, and then relaxing as soon as I struggled to catch my breath. "Oh, this sucks. I feel like I'm going to either shit myself or puke," I said between gritted teeth. "Or both. And— Oh!" Another contraction, this one even harder. "Fuck, how dilated am I?"

"I hope that's a rhetorical question because I'm not getting down there to look." Melanie laid her violin beside me, her face pale. "I'll run faster without having to carry this. I'll be back as soon as I can. Hold on, Abby. You're going to be okay."

I nodded, my fingers clenching tightly along the tree roots. "Now please, please go find someone!" This time I let out a scream, my panting hard and hot. I moved into a squatting position, trying to ease the cramping, and then rolled onto my side, unable to find relief.

When I looked up two contractions later, Melanie was gone, and guilt and fear immediately swept over me. "You have the worst timing, you know that?" I said to my stomach with a halfhearted laugh.

My temperature seemed to vacillate between penguin chilly and living on the sun, my throat a desert. Struggling to my feet, I began to pace again, ignoring the steady drip of dampness sliding down my thighs. Amniotic fluid? Piss? At this point, I didn't much care.

"Sorry for making your roots dirty," I muttered to the tree. It felt rude. For all the Hallmark garbage on TV and in movies, the act of birth was a violent thing, like a mini Big Bang trying to take place within a single body. No wonder it was painful.

I held on to the tree as the spasms built up again and then passed, my legs quaking as I let out another gasp.

"Abby? Abby!"

My mind gibbered with relief at the familiar voice. "Moira?"

My half sister pushed past Eildon Tree, her otherworldly beauty stark and crisp. Standing next to her, I was horribly aware of what a hot mess I was—sweaty, dirty, shaking with the effort of trying to give birth.

Her face grew alarmed. "Oh, my dear. Let's get this taken care of. The midwives are coming; I'm having my men build a birthing tent for you outside the tree. Something to give you at least a bit of privacy." She laid her hand upon my forehead, the coolness of it soothing. "How do you feel?"

"Like I'm going to drop an elephant. Thirsty. Tired."

"Water!" she called, snapping her fingers as a page dashed up with a flagon. Moira took it from her and tipped it toward my mouth. I wanted to guzzle it but could only manage the barest of sips before sinking to my knees as another contraction swept through me. This one felt different from the others—lower, deeper. A burning pressure where there wasn't one before.

One of the elvish midwives arrived then, sweeping Moira out of the way as she knelt between my thighs. "My turn,

Your Highness. No time. Fetch me the cloths from my bag. This baby is coming right now." To her credit, Moira did just that. Even royalty had to step aside for birth.

I lost track of the minutes after that, relief settling in that I had nothing else to think about save to focus on what was happening below. Moira sat next to me, letting me clutch her hand.

I blinked through another rack of pain and realized I'd had blankets pushed under me so I wasn't lying directly on the ground. The midwife bustled about between my legs, clicking her tongue. "Won't be long now, my dear. You're beginning to crown."

"Crown," I said, sipping a bit of water from a goblet someone thrust into my hand. "What a ridiculous word."

"You may feel a bit of burning," the midwife added. "But don't push until I tell you. I don't want you to tear."

"Burning, my ass," I snapped. "It's like I'm sitting on a fucking blowtorch."

"Breathe, Abby. Come on. You're almost there." Moira wiped the sweat from my face with another cloth.

"Where's Mel?" I asked, straining my ears for the tell-tale sound of her music, but I couldn't make out anything except the harsh sounds of my own breathing. And then the pressure upon my abdomen was like a vise grip, and everything blurred.

Pushing. Pausing. Pushing. Pausing. My own voice, cry-ing out as I strained to somehow shift the shape of my flesh around this little body working its way out of me. Another momentary lapse of guilt came as I realized neither Ion nor Talivar were here to share this, but I shoved it away. Nothing to be done for it now.

My body tensed up again, and I struggled to breathe, to remember who I was, my entire being torn away until it was only this. The most complete universe I could be.

"Abby?" Moira said gently as something slipped, warm

and wet, from between my thighs and into the midwife's waiting hands. "It's a girl."

And in the chill morning air, a baby's mewling cry split the dawn even as I burst into tears.

The thing about having babies is that everything about them is extremely messy. Including me. The next few minutes passed by in a blur as the midwife bustled about. Another one appeared a moment later, my baby cleaned up and wrapped in soft cloths, even as the other set about helping me to expel the afterbirth and cutting the cord.

Moira knelt beside me, gently holding the baby so I could see her, though at this point, it was barely a dark-haired head swaddled in blue silk.

"Ah," the midwife tsked. "You have a tear."

I winced, shifting my swollen nether regions. The whole area felt vaguely numb, as though it weren't even real, even as I began to shiver violently. "Stitches?"

"Of course not. That's barbaric." The midwife shook her head, and her fingers lit up in a gentle swell of silver magic. Almost immediately, the stinging stopped, soothed by a cooling flush.

A sigh of relief escaped me, and I glanced toward Moira. My half sister had an oddly tender look upon her face. A twinge of uneasiness ground in my guts. I trusted her inasmuch as we had been through a great deal together—plus, relatives and whatnot—but if the tales were true, the Fae had always had a slightly unhealthy obsession with human babies. Hopefully not the case here.

"Have you thought of a name?" Moira lowered the infant into my arms, even as the midwife covered up my trembling form with another blanket. My mind went blank in a sort of hazy incomprehension, as though I were merely dreaming. Because she was really here and I was suddenly completely responsible for her. Terrified elation shook me, a desperate realization that she was mine and I was hers. It was as though we were the only two beings in the entire world, trapped in a bubble where time had simply stopped.

I stared down at my daughter's face, trying to determine who she looked like, but I quickly gave up, concentrating only on her ridiculously long lashes and perky little mouth.

"Not yet," I said, absently trying to make sense of Moira's question. "I know we sort of threw some names out there, Ion and I—and Talivar too at one point. But she wasn't supposed to be here this soon, so we weren't considering any in particular yet."

The baby opened her mouth, a soft bawling sound that caused my breasts to tighten.

"She's probably looking for a bit of soothing," the midwife said, helping me position her toward my breast. "Your milk won't come in for a bit, but this part is just as important."

The baby turned her head, as if by instinct, and a burning rush jolted through my nipple as she latched on. My eyes fell on the spot where Melanie had left her violin, but it was no longer there. "Where's Mel? I would have thought she might have wanted to be here for this part."

"Ah, well." Moira averted her eyes slightly. "I've stowed her away in my tent. There's a lot of bad blood between her and the other denizens of Faerie right now. It was getting to be a bit on the ugly side."

"Everything she's done for them over the years . . ." Then I sobered. She *had* caused the deaths of many of the residents in the Barras. Maybe there were things that you simply couldn't come back from.

"My lady, let's get you moved some place a bit more comfortable," the midwife said. "We can't have the king of the Unseelie Court think that his consort has suffered from ill hospitality."

"Nothing like the reality of protocol," I said as the baby released my breast, leaving me aching.

Moira and the midwife helped me stand on shaky legs, the other servants quickly cleaning up the cloths and what was left of my skirt. A little ways off a silver tent had been erected in the field, a number of smaller ones dotted about it. It reminded me of the army camp Moira had set up last time I'd been here, and I said as much out loud.

She laughed. "Nothing that intensive, I promise. I simply wanted to make sure you were protected. The Door Maker did mention that you were being pursued; I merely thought it prudent to make sure you would be safe." She inclined her head toward my daughter. "That little bean of yours is technically the heir to the Unseelie Court, after all."

I said nothing to this particular fact. Talivar and I still hadn't decided anything yet, but if such a title helped her to survive, then I would certainly take advantage of it.

Moira led me into the silver tent where an extravagant bed had been set up, complete with enormous bolster pillows. An exquisite bassinet stood within arm's reach of the mattress, and it hit me even harder that this was happening.

"I figured you would want to room with her. Faerie royalty don't always get that opportunity," Moira said ruefully, a hint of bitterness in her voice. I'd nearly forgotten what she'd gone through to keep Benjamin at her side—her love child with her angel bodyguard was shared between families at different parts of the year—and even I'd been forced to babysit him for long periods of time when she had to go to Faerie for various business. I knew now it had been to protect her son, and that was something I couldn't fault her for.

"We'll only be here for a short while," Moira continued. "I've already got a room started for you in the palace, one near those gardens you enjoyed so much, if I recall."

"I wandered the mazes when I had no memories of who I was." I shuddered.

"Ah, well. I'd forgotten about that. Perhaps a view of the forest, instead . . ." She smiled wryly. "But you can wait there until Talivar comes for you. What's left of the Barras isn't worth trying to live in, and I suspect now that you've birthed a child, he'll want to build a castle of his own where you will live."

Her voice continued tripping along, light and airy, as she discussed all things baby and mothering, as though delighted to finally have someone to share her wisdom with. I found myself simply nodding along, the high of the birth finally letting down and leaving me exhausted.

Besides, I had no real intention of heading to the castle with her, but I'd learned enough by now not to voice my thoughts on this matter. Moira was used to having things her way, and it wasn't worth the argument.

"I'll have the servants bring you something to eat," Moira was saying, tucking me gently into the bed. "You did so well, my dear. Rest. And then we'll celebrate Talivar's heir. The kingdom will be ecstatic."

"Shouldn't we wait for him, then?" I asked. "It seems like the news should come from the king." My mouth kicked up into a fond half smile. "It might do the people of the Barras good to see him happy."

"Of course, you are right," she agreed with a nod. "He should be along shortly. Apparently he's still hung up in Japan—something about the destruction of a hotel room? He wanted me to let you know the others are with him as well, but they're all being detained while things get sorted. The embassy had to get involved, but I'm sure he'll manage."

I pinched the bridge of my nose, relief leaving me temporarily exhausted. "He always does."

"Well, anyway, rest awhile. I'll make preparations for travel and everything else." And with that she slipped out of the flaps of the tent, her perfume leaving a lingering trace on the air.

I sagged into the bed, still holding my little nugget of a daughter, who gleefully remained asleep. I decided I should do the same while I still could, but I was rather loath to put her in the bassinet yet and the bed was more than large enough. You could fit an entire army of children in there and still manage to find a spot to sleep.

I curled up on my side, the baby balanced in the crook of my arm, but even as tired as I was, I couldn't quite manage to drift off. My eyes kept popping open to stare at this little thing I'd made. *That Ion and I made,* I corrected myself, seeking out those physical characteristics that would belong to one or the other of us. Ion had been human during her conception, so I wouldn't have expected to see anything incubus or daemonic about her, though I suppose we wouldn't be able to rule that out until later.

But for now though, she seemed ridiculously human, and that was more than enough for me.

"Wahhhh!"

I came to with a jerk, dimly realizing I was wet. Or more to the point, the nugget was wet and squalling as though I'd left her on a doorstep. My breasts tingled in response to her cries, and I was hit with the overwhelming urge to nurse. Still, I was also very aware that we were both coated in baby piss.

I had no idea how long I'd been asleep, and I struggled to move, unsurprised when a servant girl seemed to materialize out of nowhere. I was fairly sure she'd been standing guard outside the tent the whole time.

Within moments, the baby had been cleaned and swaddled again, the bedsheets and my clothes changed. "Will you feed her?" The girl held out the baby to me, and I immediately took her and placed her at my breast, her little mouth straining for a swollen nipple.

Another jolt as she latched on, a bit too tightly, but I shifted awkwardly until we somehow made it work. The girl nodded approvingly. "Your milk will come in soon; that will make things better. I'll make sure the cook puts something in your food to make it more plentiful."

I smiled wanly, my mind already on trying to find Melanie. "I wouldn't mind a change of clothes first—real ones, with support, not just a nightshirt." My eyes dropped down toward my breasts. "They've gotten a little bigger recently."

She flushed in an enchanting fashion. "Of course, my lady. Anything else?"

"Don't suppose you'd be able to conjure me a diaper bag? For traveling?"

She frowned at the unfamiliar word and then shrugged. "I'll see what I can figure out. For nappies and the like, right?"

"Exactly." I smiled. "And perhaps a sling so I can carry her more easily." It almost hurt me to be this deceptive to a true innocent, but Moira would have known what I was going to do, so there was no good in asking her about it. And it wasn't like I could run down to the store for a BabyBjörn either. I would have to make do with what she could provide.

In the meantime, I would eat and recover my strength. If we waited too much longer, we'd be heading toward the castle. I shifted my lower half, testing out the soreness. Whatever the midwife had done was probably nothing short of a miracle. There was no real pain at all, though my stomach was still nearly as large as it had been when I was pregnant.

My boobs, though . . . Well, that was another matter.

"They don't tell you about this part," I said to myself. If my milk hadn't come in yet, I suspected it would be soon, given the way they were aching. And no chance for a magical breast pump. If Kitsune were here, I could have asked her about that. The Barras had been the home of a number of interesting technological hybrids, but at this point, I was going to be stuck doing it the old-school way.

The servant girl returned during my ruminating, bringing everything I'd asked for and more, including enough hot water to fill up the copper tub in the corner. "The midwife says you're not supposed to soak in it yet, but I thought you might want to wash your face and hair. There's a stool you can sit on and I'll pour the water on your back."

My body ached for such a mundanity. It *had* been awhile, and I'd gone through an awful lot the last few days. In my head, I was still calculating: How long do I have? How much do I need?

Glancing down at my nugget, the baby rewarded me with a sleepy sigh. "In a bit," I said, placing her in the bassinet and removing the lid from the tray of food. I nibbled on bits of whatever was there, not really tasting it; it was purely sustenance for now.

"What else is going on out there?" I asked.

"Ah well, Her Highness will be leaving soon to make preparations for your arrival. There's to be a fete, you know. Once King Talivar arrives, of course. There are a lot of Fae who will wish to grant the babe a blessing."

"Sleeping Beauty, eh?" I said, unsure if I should be alarmed at the idea.

"Oh, no, don't worry. *Those* sorts won't be there," she assured me. "And this tent is well guarded, both by spells and by the best knights in the Queen's Guard."

I snorted. "I've seen how good they are, and I wasn't particularly impressed, no offense. Last time they were guarding a dangerous man, he still managed to not only escape but kill me along the way. I hope they do a better job this time."

She flushed, and I shook my head, sorry I'd said it. It wasn't her fault, after all—no reason for me to take it out on her. "My apologies," I said, meaning it. "You can go now. I'll take care of the bathing and whatnot; there's a lot to sort through here."

She curtsied once and bobbed her head, leaving quickly, which made me feel all the worse. Hopefully she would chalk it up to raging hormones.

I ate and drank as much as I could, taking advantage of the hot water to dunk my head in and clean up. The midwife had done her best, but being able to wash myself was a big improvement. There was nothing quite like a bath, even a shallow one like this, to make one feel human again.

The clothes the servant girl had brought me were typical Faerie garments, but at least they were suitable for everyday wear. Nothing that belonged in a ballroom, anyway. I wasn't going to fit into pants for a little while as it was, so the traveling skirt and the bodice, which had easy-opening fasteners over the breasts, looked like a miracle.

"Let's hear it for Faerie style." I wriggled into them, grunting as things settled into place and pulling the shawl over my shoulders. The travel bag was stuffed with diapers, blankets, and a few other odds and ends that were undoubtedly going to be useful. I sucked in a deep breath, more uncertain of anything than I ever had been in my life.

My ears pricked up at a sudden ruckus outside the tent. It had the ugly rumble of a mob in the making. Uneasiness stirred inside me. Was it related to Melanie? And if Moira wasn't here to oversee things, the potential for trouble was much higher.

Holding the baby in my arms, I poked my head out of

the tent. The opening was flanked by several knights on either side. One of them coughed as I took a few steps outside, as though I was going to head for the cluster of other tents.

"I'm sorry, milady. Orders are that you're in confinement until Her Highness tells us otherwise. If you need anything, simply let us know and we'll make sure you're attended to."

His elven features were young and earnest, and I didn't bear him any ill will for simply following the orders he'd been given. But on the other hand, I wasn't a prisoner, and Moira could suck an egg.

"Well as the consort to King Talivar, Moira doesn't have any direct authority over me. I'm a member of the Unseelie Court and, therefore, under that particular jurisdiction, correct?"

He blinked, and I smiled. I'd been in this situation before, and I was well past being manipulated into quietness.

"I'm sorry," he started, but I raised my hand to stop him.

"Never mind that. What's going on over there?" I pointed in the general direction of a flare of witchlight that illuminated a lone tent, surrounded by the dark silhouettes of what could only be some very angry people. Melanie had to be in there.

"Ah," he said. "The Door Maker is being kept inside for her protection. By order of Her Highness." He gave me a wan smile. "Don't worry, you're perfectly safe from her here."

My head snapped toward him as though I'd been slapped. "I'm going to pretend I didn't hear that. Come with me." I stalked off without waiting to hear if he'd follow, but there was a brief hesitation followed by the clink of chainmail, so I knew I had at least a bit of an entourage to protect me.

The grass was damp beneath my naked feet, but it felt soothing upon the chapped skin. A cluster of Faerie OtherFolk were arguing in front of the tent, shoving their way up to the entrance, only to be pushed away by the guards in front of it. I stood on my tiptoes, trying to find the safest way through.

They were elves mostly, of both Courts, all pointed ears and shining grace with carved faces of supreme beauty and elegance. But their expressions of hostility and anger were anything but, marring the illusion. And it wasn't only elves. I saw insect-men and boggles, brownies and smaller Fae, twisted of form and face.

Whatever was going on, it did not look particularly good. I pressed forward, mostly ignored by the mob, and half a second I thought I might actually make it to the entrance of the tent without being noticed.

Until the nugget opened her mouth and let out a shrill cry.

I rocked her, ignoring the sudden silence as all those furious faces turned toward me. "What is going on here?" I asked finally.

"The Door Maker's in there," one of the insect-men grumbled. "She has to pay for what she did. And them Seelie dicks is protecting her."

One of the elvish women sniffed disdainfully. "If you weren't so disgustingly primitive, maybe we could have a more civilized conversation about it. The Door Maker has served us very well over the years. Why destroy that relationship because some of the riffraff were caught in the crossfire?"

The insect-man flinched. "My wife was in there when the Barras blew up. She died. What compensation is there for me?"

"There isn't any," Melanie said softly, appearing at the entrance of the tent. "There is nothing I can do to make up for what I did, accident or no." Her face was calm, but the misery in her eyes when she saw me was a tempest of self-loathing and bitterness.

"Mel . . ."

She shook her head. "Don't. Take your baby away from here, Abby. It's too dangerous . . ."

"She must pay!" the insect-man shouted again.

I pushed past him to stand in front of Melanie. "She will. But how she does so is not for you to decide. Only the king can determine her penance, what compensation she will need to provide. You know who I am, and you know I am dearest friends with the Door Maker."

The insect-man spit at my feet and turned to stalk off, only to be met by the blade of one extraordinarily pissed-off Kitsune. I did a double take, looking through the crowd for Talivar, Ion, or Phineas. Surely if she was here, the others would be too.

The fox-woman's eyes blazed cold fire, her tail swishing, her lips pulling into a terrible grin. "Did you disrespect the wife of the king?" she asked softly, her katana seeming to hum with obvious intent. The crowd of elves around us immediately stepped back several paces, some leaving the area entirely in a quick shuffle that would have been comical if not for Kitsune's murder face.

"Apologies," he said, his mandibles clacking nervously.

I reached out and moved the blade away from his throat. "He has a right to be angry."

She snarled. "Right or not, such a thing could be considered an assault upon the monarchy. There is no room in the Unseelie Court for such acts. You cannot allow—"

"Kitsune." Talivar's voice was sharp and utterly unrelenting, a command of complete authority, and relief flooded me to the point that I nearly toppled over.

She immediately withdrew, sheathing her weapon in a single fluid motion. "Your Majesty," she said, lowering her head. His gaze softened when he saw me, lingering on the baby in my arms, and he paused as though he was going to say something else. He only sighed deeply.

"Door Maker," he said, turning toward Melanie. "Your violin. Please turn it over to Kitsune's custody."

Melanie retreated into the tent and returned with the violin, holding it out to Kitsune. The fox-woman gave Talivar the side-eye but nodded, taking it carefully.

Talivar shifted in his Armani suit, looking vaguely uncomfortable as he addressed the rest of the crowd. "Without her instrument, the Door Maker cannot tap into the Wild Magic. That should ensure the people's safety here until tomorrow when I will pass judgment upon her for the injuries she caused me and mine. Until then, she is to be left alone and unharmed." His face darkened. "Is that clear?"

The insect-man bowed, the others around him doing the same. Kitsune's face grew supremely satisfied. "I will stand guard here," she offered.

Melanie smiled tightly, exhaling as though trying to steady herself. "I'll see you all in the morning, then." She reached out as though to touch the infant, but then thought better of it. "Hello," she whispered, her eyes lighting up. "She has your nose, you know. And that lower lip . . . That's all you."

"You think so?" I flushed despite myself, but I sobered as I remembered why we were here.

Her smile grew rueful. "I would ask to hold her, but under the circumstances . . ."

"Yeah." I marched up to her anyway and hugged her as tightly as I dared. "Tomorrow. We'll get it sorted tomorrow and then tackle this Hell bullshit, okay?"

"Something like that," she muttered, releasing me to disappear into the tent. The rest of the crowd faded away even as Kitsune ordered the other guards to watch the rear and took up her place beside the front of the tent.

I sagged as soon as Talivar and I were left alone, and we

walked to my tent. He trembled beside me, as though he wanted to reach out to touch me but didn't quite dare to do so. Maybe it was the need for decorum among his subjects.

"Ion and Phin are waiting inside," he said, pausing outside the entrance. "Given what was going on, they both decided it was best that I take care of it directly. I'm so sorry, Abby, but weakness in front of the Courts is a surefire way to lose my crown, even at the expense of my wife and the birth of her child." Suddenly desperate, his mouth found mine, kissing me fiercely over and over as if he couldn't quite believe I was here. "When I heard Moira had found you, that you'd gone into labor, I nearly lost it."

He let out a sobbing laugh. "I didn't realize Nobu was going to disappear with you like that. We had no idea where you'd gone, and the political backlash at the embassy was a nightmare. The damage to the hotel, the mess with the Collector . . . Didi stayed behind in an act of good faith to try to help work things out. I hated to leave without fixing it myself, but there was no choice."

"It's all right." I pulled his head toward my shoulder. The nugget squirmed, and I chuckled. "Do you want to hold her?"

He waited patiently as I adjusted the swaddling blanket to place her in his hands. "Oh, she's perfect," he murmured. "I see you in every little curve of her face." He blinked at the rapidly forming tears in his eyes. "And how are you holding up?"

"Trying to figure out this mother thing," I admitted, shifting my hips. "But I really need to sit down. There's a lot of . . . fluids after birth, you know. It's really . . ."

His mouth quirked with amusement. "Of course. And I've monopolized your time out here long enough." With an elegant gesture, he steered me inside, still holding the baby.

I wasn't lying about the fluids. I might not have had to suffer the stitches of a tear, but the uterus still kept to its own schedule. There wasn't a bit of magic in the world that was going to help with that.

I barely stepped into the tent before Ion was there, gently whisking me away toward the bed, burying his face against my neck. I snorted. "Happy to see me?"

"You need to rest," he demanded, tucking me away before pouring me a goblet of water. I let him fuss over me for another minute or so, his fingers sliding over my skin, as though making sure I wasn't about to disappear.

Suddenly I noticed the bruises on his neck and jaw, and a contusion above his right eye. "What's that?"

"Souvenir from fighting with the Collector." He grunted. "I'm mostly sore now, but nothing was permanently damaged, so I think I'll manage. Too bad that asshole got away with Paganini, but there's no way the embassy was equipped to hold such a creature anyway." A bitter chuckle escaped him. "Hopefully those fuckers have returned to Hell for now."

"With any luck, they have no idea Mel is here," I added. "And I am okay. I am here," I said finally. "And so is your daughter."

He stilled, his eyes closing. "I know. I just . . ." His face was a portrait of what I suspect was the terrified realization that he was, in fact, a father.

I gave him a gentle shove toward where Talivar still cradled the baby in front of Phin, the unicorn waggling his beard at her. "Go on," I insisted. "I'm going to take a little nap. Go say hello. And start thinking of a name." I closed my eyes as though that ended the conversation. I felt his gaze upon me for a moment longer and then it faded. I waited a few minutes before cracking an eye open to see Talivar hand her to Ion, both men with the most delighted expressions I had ever seen on their faces.

I stifled a giggle and closed my eyes in truth, allowing them to bond without my interference. Within minutes, I dozed off, only to be awakened some time later by the sudden squalls of a hungry baby.

Bleary, I sat up as Ion handed her to me. The lanterns in the tent were dim and soft. Talivar was passed out in the bed beside me, snoring softly.

My daughter snuffled in a way that had my breasts immediately aching. I unfastened the front of my bodice as Ion watched bemusedly. She was already turning her head greedily, and I helped her find the newly engorged nipple, hissing as she struggled to find the right latch and then relaxing as things seemed to sort themselves out. It was a weird sensation, this pulling. As though I was made of thread and each suck yanked on something deep inside me, so deep I didn't think I would ever find the bottom of whatever it was.

My womb cramped in response. I was pretty sure it was part of the deal with breastfeeding, and with any luck, it would help stop the bleeding that much faster so I'd be able to get out of here. But for now, I'd simply sit and watch my daughter nurse, humming a song that felt vaguely familiar to me, though I couldn't place where I'd heard it. Maybe it was the song all mothers sang to their babies in the dark hours, whispering words of hope and promise and the delicate assurance of a bond that could never be broken.

Somewhere between lullabies and a mild case of spit-up, I drifted off to sleep, cradled in a boat made of stars and the embrace of the two people I loved most.

CHAPTER 15

I GLANCED OVER AT THE KITCHEN clock, noting the hour with a satisfied smile. "Time for a feeding and a bit of a nap." I padded into the bedroom. My little iPod chugged away, softly playing Brahms's "Lullaby" on repeat, and I hummed along. Ion and Talivar were in my bedroom, fixated on the cradle that rocked back and forth, back and forth.

The music grew louder, and I frowned, trying to turn it down, but it kept playing, even when I unplugged it from the speakers completely. "Hey, what's going on? Do you two know how to make this thing shut up?"

But neither responded, the music becoming a cacophony, no longer a pleasantry of notes but a chorus of discordant melodies, mocking and angry. And still the cradle rocked and rocked. I struggled to get to it, my feet moving as if I were in a pool of molasses, thick and slow and heavy. Somehow I reached it, pushing Ion out of the way, peering into the cradle to see . . .

"Abby, wake up!" I startled upward, groaning as my hand brushed over my breasts. They were rock hard, as though they might burst beneath the pressure, and I guessed my milk must have come in. My eyes were half-shut as I fumbled at my bodice, looking around for my daughter, desperate to ease the heavy feeling.

I blinked, staring up at Phin. The unicorn was grim, and a chill ran down my spine. Except for the two of us, the bed was empty, both Ion and Talivar absent. Along with my daughter.

Alarm bells rang in my head. "What's going on? Where's the baby?"

He stared at me, his eyes glowing blue with a brilliant anger I'd never seen before. "She's been taken, Abby. She's gone."

I vomited into the basin beside the tub, tasting nothing but bile, my breath coming so hard and fast I nearly passed out. Moira rubbed my shoulders, holding my hair away from my face. "Slow breaths, Abby. You'll black out again if you don't slow down."

Dimly, I heard her voice as she rattled off commands to servants, guards, midwives. Someone had helped me change my clothes, a midwife assisting to express my milk enough to gain some relief. I was brought food, and I suspect a sedative of sorts, but I was so beyond comprehending what was going on an entire brass band of miniature elephants could have paraded through the tent and I wouldn't have noticed.

Then Melanie was there, hugging me hard as I sobbed into her shoulder. "We'll find her, Abby."

"I don't understand," I croaked out for what had to have been the tenth time. "How—"

"We don't know, exactly," Moira admitted. "A spell of some sort, one powerful enough to break through all the shields I had around the tent, to knock out all the guards and keep everyone in this tent asleep until they were gone."

"Where's Talivar? Ion?" I stared blankly at Melanie. Why weren't they here with me?

"Talivar's gathering a search party to scour the Cross-

Roads even as we speak," she said. "Though there's talk of him calling the Wild Hunt if he cannot find her himself." Her mouth compressed grimly. "Brystion left in a fury. I'm not sure where he went, but I'm sure he's out looking too."

Kitsune appeared at the entrance of the tent, her face troubled as she approached us. Kneeling beside me, she bowed deeply. "I have failed you and your child," she said, her voice tinged with shame. "And therefore, I have failed my king. You may punish me as you see fit."

"Why would I do that?" I lurched to my feet and hurled a floor pillow at the bed. It bounced off the headboard and knocked over the bassinet, spilling the little mattress onto the floor. "I'm the mother who let her own baby get stolen a day after giving birth," I said bitterly. "What kind of awful person does that?"

"The kind of person who assumed she would be safe with her family," Phin said softly. "We're all at fault here."

Moira said nothing but went to pick up the fallen furniture. I couldn't even look at it without bursting into tears, and I turned away. She hissed in air through her teeth. "Abby, look. This was beneath the bassinet."

I shuddered when I saw the feather between her fingers, glinting a familiar black and blue.

Nobu.

"Not possible," Melanie said, shaking her head as she came to the same conclusion. "He's not a god anymore. He doesn't even have wings like this now."

"Then how did it get there?" I snapped, desperation making me sound harsher than I had intended. Moira turned the feather over, but she didn't make any outward commentary.

"Wait, Abby," Phineas said, his ears flicking. "Remember at the Midnight Marketplace, when all this bullshit started? Paganini was there that night."

I froze, swallowing hard. "Nobu's feather. He picked it

up and put it in his pocket. He was here. It had to have been him."

"The Wild Magic," Moira mused, her mien thoughtful. "I don't believe I've seen it used this way before, but I suppose it might be possible. It's a good clue, at any rate." She stood up and handed the feather to Kitsune. "Go tell my brother what we've found. I'll put the word out among the rest of my people."

"Why bother?" I asked, turning to Melanie. "We know where he's gone. He's doing it to force me to make you go there."

"Out of the question," Kitsune snapped. "You're not going anywhere. Either of you."

Moira nodded. "Until we know what we're dealing with—a ransom situation, a hostage exchange . . ."

"Oh, I know what we will be dealing with." Ion shoved his way into the tent, his glamour gone and his tail lashing violently. His eyes flared into a golden nimbus as his gaze lit upon the feather in Kitsune's hand before focusing on me. "Everybody out," he snarled. "Now."

To their credit, they left, Melanie giving my hand a squeeze before she slipped out after Kitsune and Moira, Phineas trotting at her heels. I barely had time to respond before Ion swept me up in his arms, clasping me tighter than he ever had before.

Tears erupted from me, great ugly sobs choking me so hard I couldn't breathe. The incubus said nothing, sparing me any empty platitudes, but I could feel the tremble beneath his skin, the heat of his anger rippling in anguish.

"They took her," I mumbled into his shoulder. "They took my baby. Where were you?" I couldn't help but ask it, the words spilling out of me like an accusation, though it was all directed at myself, a tidal wave of helplessness and self-loathing.

"I was here," he said softly. "Talivar was here. Phineas

was here. You couldn't have asked for three more attentive beings in a single room, Abby. Paganini's control of the Wild Magic is nearly unparalleled, except perhaps by Melanie, but she was asleep in her tent. Even if she had been awake, she did not have her violin to try to counterbalance whatever Paganini was doing. He could not have chosen a better time for his attack." He pressed a quick kiss to the top of my head. "I'll get her back. I swear it."

"I want to come with you," I pleaded, my voice shaking. "What if she's hurt? She's going to be hungry. You'll need me." Left unsaid were far worse possibilities, the ones that turned my brain into gibbering mush.

His thumbs wiped away the wetness from my cheeks. "Not for this, Abby. Paganini is in Hell, you are just a few days post-birth, and there are places I will go that you cannot. I don't want you to see what I will do, but trust me. Trust that I will find our child and I will bring her home to you." He leaned his forehead against mine, the bells in his hair chiming like a promise. "Rest now," he murmured, scooping me up and tucking me into the bed. "I'll send the others in to make sure you're attended to."

Exhausted and drained and dizzy, I rolled into a ball beneath the blankets when he left. I could hear his voice outside the tent, talking low and urgent to whomever was still waiting. I shoved my face into the pillow and wept.

"This is bullshit," Melanie snapped, pacing about my tent. "They need to let me go. This whole mess is mine."

I sat up on the bed, adjusting my clothing and trying to make my aching breasts at least a bit more comfortable. I'd pulled the tangle of my hair into its usual bun, though that was mostly to keep it out of my face as opposed to an actual fashion choice.

Kitsune stood by the door of the tent, her restless eyes

watching Melanie walk pace with an uneasy air.

Melanie rounded on her. "Give me my violin and I'll go."

"I can't," Kitsune said. "Talivar is not here, and his word still stands."

"Don't give me that," Melanie snapped. "You do what you want all the time."

The fox-woman shrugged with an air of sadness. "But I don't go against Talivar's wishes. He is the king. And until he returns, his word is law."

"And what about the word of his wife? Of a mother? Does that not hold any weight at all?" I tried not to scream. Every second I waited here felt like another missed chance, a possibility of rescue slipping away. Taking Ion at his word, I knew he would do his best to find her. On a rational level, I knew it, but every other part of me burned with the need to go after her, even if I failed.

"The wife of a king, yes," said Kitsune sadly. "My duty is to protect you, even from yourself."

Phineas perched on the end of the bed, his head cocked at Kitsune. "Well, you know I always say it's better to beg forgiveness than ask permission."

"That goes for my underwear drawer, I take it," I shot back.

He winced. "I'm saying that if a certain person were to accidentally leave a certain instrument lying about and another person took it . . . Well, who's to say anything is wrong? Just a big misunderstanding. That's all." He shrugged, his eyes closing. "And I'm lazy and old and napping, so I can't possibly talk sense into anyone, let alone a mother separated from her child."

Kitsune made a frustrated sound.

"Please," I begged.

She bowed abruptly. "I have some business at Eildon Tree. Perhaps you'll find it enlightening to go and pray there later." And with that, she was gone, whisking through the tent flaps with a silent grace I could only marvel at.

Melanie's eyes slid toward the tent flap. "I think it's about time to blow this scene."

I let out a shuddering breath. "I'll get some things together. She'll need diapers and blankets and . . ."

"Yes." She pushed her glasses onto her head. "Listen for my signal. When you hear it, head for Eildon Tree. But I'm thinking maybe it would be best if you don't leave out the front. Might buy us a little extra time." Her hand found a paring knife from the breakfast tray that morning and pushed it into my palm, jerking her head toward the rear of the tent.

"Got it," I said. "I'll be there."

She hugged me hard, and then she was gone, shadowing Kitsune's footsteps.

Come sail away, come sail away, come sail away with me . . .

The familiar tune inched its way into the tent, buoyed on the soft notes of Mel's violin playing, and I knew it was time.

Left alone with a dozing Phin, I had quickly packed as much leftover fruit and bread as I could into the makeshift diaper bag the servant girl had left me the night before, testing its weight on my shoulders. I was still bleeding, but I had enough rags shoved into my crotch that it hopefully would be manageable—plenty of extras in the bag, as well, along with a fresh blanket and some cloth diapers.

I'd pushed away the thoughts of what had happened this morning as best as I could, but simply having a plan had set me on fire and given me something to focus on. There had been no sign of Ion, and Moira had told me only that Talivar had not yet returned.

I knew the elf king well enough to know he was probably beyond ashamed that this had happened on his watch, but I knew he was trying his best to make up for it. I had to trust he would understand why I'd left. Not that I had any real idea of how long the road to Hell would be, but at this point, I didn't have any other options.

I slipped the diaper bag onto my back and tossed my hobo over my shoulder. Taking the knife, I poked a hole in the seams of the tent behind the bed. "Quietly, quietly," I whispered, carefully undoing the bits of thread. The cloth was exquisite, of course; I could hardly expect Moira to have a tent made of anything but the best. I almost felt guilty about slicing it up.

Almost.

After waiting long enough to fit my slightly enhanced encumbrances, I did take a quick peek, relieved when I saw no guards at all. In the distance there was a bit of muffled conversation, the clink of plates, the soft thump of horses' hooves as the guards made their rounds.

All the better. If I had to think about it, trying to sneak out in the dead of night like all the fairy tales was probably a bad idea. If everything was quiet and no one else was supposed to be moving around, it would make me stand out all the more. This way, I could potentially blend in a bit. The CrossRoads were open to everyone, of course.

Still. I pulled up the hood of my cloak . No sense in making it completely obvious.

My boots squelched in the damp grass, but I tried to time my movements to the sounds behind me. In the distance, Eildon Tree loomed on the top of the hill. I had no direct means of finding my way into Hell, but the center of the CrossRoads seemed a decent enough place to start, and the violin was calling me there with gentle coaxing. A thick mist swirled around me when I was partway up the hill, making it hard to see past a few feet, so when a figure rose out of the darkness, I nearly shat myself in alarm.

But it was Melanie, her eyes supremely old and sad and full of some emotion I didn't understand. Her lips curled when she saw me, a ghost of her old smile. "I wasn't sure you'd make it," she said.

"Wouldn't miss it." I drew another shaky breath. "You ready?"

Melanie shut her eyes. "All right, then. We'll do this together."

"Like always," I agreed. "So, uh, how do we get there?" I stared at the CrossRoads ahead of us, the silver path lighting up as I scuffed my boots across it. "I mean, have you ever been there?"

She shook her head. "I've opened Doors occasionally for Contracts that definitely went to some pretty shady places, but never into Hell itself. It's not super high on my bucket list, you know?"

I fingered my necklace, giving it a little squeeze. "Well, as long as I've got this, I think we'll be all right. Even if you can't quite make a Door that works, if we find one, I can probably open it. For now, I suppose we'll head in the general direction?"

"Seems like the thing to do." She lifted the violin to her shoulder, idly swinging the bow. We walked around each quarter of the tree, trying to get our bearings. The instrument still had a peculiar sheen to it—almost as if someone had tried to patch up the magic with daemonic shoe polish.

"And see not ye that braid, braid road,
That lies across the lily leven?
That is the Path of Wickedness,
Though some call it the Road to Heaven."

I quoted the poem aloud, remembering Paganini's tantrum in the Midnight Marketplace. "One direction for each Path. Which one did you make? That's the one you have to fix anyway."

"Technically, I fixed the Mortal Path," she said dryly. "Guess there was some spillover of the magic." She pointed her bow to the right. "That way. Something about it seems to have my . . . signature, I guess. It's strongest in this direction." She slipped her violin beneath her chin, her bow poised to play. "I'm not sure what I did before, but if it's too hard for the average mortal to walk, I'll have to smooth it out as I go."

I watched her run her fingers over the neck of the instrument, and I knew this was a fucking terrible idea, but then she stroked the strings with the bow. The Wild Magic rose up and up, surrounding us in a golden bubble of light and music, beckoning the way with a seductive slither. The warped sound of before was gone, the notes clean, clear, and crisply full of power.

"What happened to your playing? It sounds better," I said. "But should you be so . . . I don't know, *obvious* about it?"

"It's not like they won't know we're coming," she said. "Though I wish I knew what the road had looked like before." I cocked a brow at her, and she flushed. "Okay, no, not really."

"Well it's not like we can call an Uber, but a guide might have been a good thing." I frowned. "Where's Nobu? Surely he should have caught up with us by now? You'd think he'd practically be rushing us to the Devil's doorstep to try to get this thing finished, god or not."

The music took a more somber turn. "He's here in spirit, anyway. Hopefully that counts for something."

"That doesn't sound suspicious *at all.*" I shifted my shoulders beneath the weight of the diaper bag, not used to carrying quite this much baggage. "Speaking of . . . I thought we'd agreed not to hide things anymore, married lady."

She flushed. "Fair. I was going to mention it at some

point. And I *will* explain everything—but not right now. I've got too much I need to concentrate on."

I gave her a look but didn't press it. After everything she'd been through, I could tell she was barely holding it together. The last thing I needed was her power unraveling here.

"Honestly, I don't think we'll have any problem getting there," I said. "After all, Hell wants a repaved road and you're the only one who can do it. Getting out, though . . ." I swallowed down a ripple of fear. "Guess we'll have to wing that."

"Isn't that what we do?" She thrust her head toward the cobblestones in front of us. "Look, there—that's promising isn't it?"

The path ahead of us was normal enough at first, but as we followed it, the golden luster of it grew moldy and dim. The cobblestones were uneven, catching at my feet and nearly causing me to lose my balance. The mist grew thicker, trees pressing in close on both sides to tear at our clothes and snarl my hair.

I pushed a branch out of my face, wincing as a thorn caught my thumb. "*Mmmph.* I can see why they might be a little concerned by this, yes."

"Guess I'll start here, then. Hold up. I'll move in front and smooth it as I go. That should make it easier for you to follow."

She raised her violin to her chin, the bow sliding over the strings as the soft strains of "Canon in D" floated past. A strange choice maybe, but she was the one controlling the show.

The power shimmered, silver sparkles falling over us like snow, and I distantly caught the sound of Melanie humming along, her voice in counterpoint to the music. Everywhere the snowflakes touched reacted immediately. The trees withdrew, gnarled roots pulling away, thorns disintegrating into black dust that fluttered away into the mist, a hint of sulfur riding the breeze that suddenly blew up.

"That won't do," Melanie said, her eyes closing. She stopped walking, and the song changed to "Sakura." Perhaps a bit cliché given we'd just come from Japan, but it worked. The cobblestones flattened, becoming smooth and even, a golden hue taking on a shining luster with each step she took. Even the fog itself burned away, leaving the path ahead uncluttered and easy to navigate. On either side of the road, the trees burst into bloom, scattering cherry blossom petals in a haze of pale pinks and white.

"Careful," I warned her, half-joking. "Make it look too nice and you won't want to leave."

"Something like that," she said, her jade eyes peering over the violet teashades in a coquettish flare for half a second before the music began again, this time becoming fast and lively and sounding vaguely Irish.

A chill struck me, ice burrowing into my gut. She was making it look nice because she thought she'd be staying there. I flinched away from the thought but didn't press for confirmation. After all, if I had such power, wouldn't I do something similar?

Melanie stepped carefully around each broken cobblestone, each twisted tree branch, the magic melting away the horror and replacing it with a bit of heavenly wonder, as though the very road was being coaxed into remembering where it might have come from so very long ago. I watched a minute longer and then stretched my shoulders, carefully following my friend as flower petals fell like snow all around us.

"Abby! Mel!" The music cut off as we whirled around, my heart rising in delight to see Talivar riding the golden road toward us on a dark horse, Kitsune riding pillion behind him. Trotting beside them was Jimmy Squarefoot, and above them all was Sonja, gliding easily on wings so red it seemed as if they dripped blood.

The three of them came to a halt, Sonja landing past us. The elf king launched himself toward me, wrapping me in his arms. I sagged, my eyes closing as he covered my face with desperate kisses. "I'm sorry. I'm so sorry."

My fingers drifted over the nape of his neck, soothing him. Out of the corner of my eye, I could see the others giving us a bit of privacy, the three women bent deep in a heated discussion among themselves. From the look on Melanie's face, it was clear Kitsune was giving her a rather strong "I told you so" lecture, but even I could tell she wasn't particularly put out. Things had gone according to plan, after all.

Nonplussed, Talivar shook his head before turning to Melanie. "And you. What the hell were you thinking doing this on your own? Both of you are going to shorten my life span by at least a hundred years."

"You took my violin," Melanie pointed out.

"To *protect* you," Talivar said, pinching his nose in exasperation. "I never had any intention of letting you go to Hell on your own."

"She's doing it for me," I interrupted. "For the baby."

"As for my issue, I didn't think anyone would *want* to help, not after what I did to the Barras . . . all the trouble I've caused everyone," Melanie said.

Sonja snorted. "Don't be stupid. Hell is isolating. It wants you to feel alone. People and souls make dumb bargains when they're desperate." She shook her head, folding her wings. "You're walking right into His trap. Whatever is waiting for you at the end, at least let us be there for you, Door Maker. You've still got more friends than you think."

Melanie blinked back a rush of tears, the violin hanging

from suddenly limp fingers, and she let out a sob, burying her head in Talivar's shoulder. She wept as though her heart would break, and I realized how much pressure she'd been putting on herself all this time. The elf rubbed the nape of her neck, resting his chin on her head.

"Always with the dramatics," Phin piped up from one of Kitsune's kimono sleeves, his head poking through with an eye roll. "We're all in this together—as we always have been."

She let out a half-hysterical giggle as he leaped from the sleeve and gave a little shake of his beard. "That being said, there is a limit for some of us," he admitted. "As a creature of the Light, I can't go much farther than this. Even Talivar can't go all the way down this road."

"Not like this," Talivar agreed. "I'm the king of the Unseelie Court. For me to approach Hell directly . . . Well, it would come across as an act of war. Given all the trouble we had with you and the Tithe . . ." His words drifted off uncomfortably. "I can still attend you as your husband at least part of the way. Hence why I brought Jimmy along."

"I'm truly sorry, Absinthe." Jimmy snuffled. "Do ye have somewhat of the baby's?"

I stilled. Of course. Jimmy had a tremendously powerful sense of smell. Digging through the diaper bag, I pulled out one of her swaddling blankets, choking back a sob as Jimmy planted his piggy snout straight into it and closed his eyes.

"Got it, aye. If she's around anywhere within the next few miles, I'll ken it." His lips parted in what I assumed was supposed to be a reassuring grin.

"Do you . . . Do you smell her now?" I asked softly, trying to brace myself for disappointment.

He shook his head, his tone gentle. "Not yet."

"Well, they wouldn't have come this way." Sonja squinted down the road. "It's been choked up anyway, so he would have taken a Door." Her eyes darted toward Talivar. "We might do the same."

"There's no telling where they would have gone." His nostrils flared, and he took my hand. "Best to stay as a group. Ion is already out this way searching. We know they're waiting for Melanie's arrival. We'll have to trust in that for now." My fingers entwined tightly with his and fought another wave of tears.

Melanie had turned toward Jimmy. "I am so sorry for everything."

"Aye," he said. "I ken ye are. And I ken ye didn't mean it, but—"

"When this is done and Abby's baby is safe, I'll spend the rest of my life making it up to you and others," she said, her chin raised. "I swear it on the Wild Magic. I know I can't fix things completely, but I'll try."

"Aye," Jimmy said. "We'll have a bit of a chat, ye ken?"

She rewarded him with a tearful smile. "All right, then. It's a date."

Kitsune stared at us all impatiently. "Shall we press on?"

"If it helps, I have this now." I reached into my shirt and pulled out the Key to the CrossRoads. It glittered like a star in darkness.

Sonja's dark eyes lit up in response. "This is perfect." She glanced up at Melanie. "Short of TouchStoning her on the fly, that is. Even if we get stuck in a jam, there are Doors all along the road to Hell. Most of them are closed or only open one way, but with the Key and the Wild Magic, well, we have a chance to make things . . . interesting."

"Is there a point to this?" Phin asked snidely, baring his teeth as though contemplating a bite.

She skirted out of range and rolled her eyes. "Yeah, there is. The road to Hell is full of the trapped and the damned, most of them serving out their punishments, all of them dreaming of freedom."

Kitsune stared at her. "So you're suggesting we free them?"

Sonja licked her lips. "I'm suggesting Hell likes order. Chaos makes for interesting bedfellows, and the idea is to be such a big pain in the ass He won't want us a stone's throw away from the Gates of Hell, let alone the lower circles of Hell itself." She turned toward Melanie. "Wild Magic or no, if you really show him what you can do—like let yourself go completely—I guarantee you'll end up in too much trouble. Hell is hard enough to run as it is; you'll be the bullet in a barrel of fish."

I weighed Sonja's words carefully. It seemed too pat, too easy. She was a daemon herself, obviously, but I still considered her one of my close friends. And she would obviously know Hell better than the rest of us would, so there wasn't much else we could do other than trust her.

She looked down. "I want to find my niece. I want my friends back. I want Portsmyth to return to the way it was. And I want that bitchface Paganini to suck a fat one."

"Something we can all agree on," Kitsune said. "Well, I will go as far as I can. Technically, I'm not of Faerie—informal ruler of the Barras or not. Different mythologies and all that. We'll see how they're dealt with." She reached out and plucked a cherry blossom from the air. "While I can't say I mind the overall decoration, it may not be what He had in mind."

Melanie shrugged. "If you're not going to be specific in your directions to the Contractor, you get what you get."

Then she lifted her bow to the strings. "All right. Let's do it." The first few bars started out slow and sonorous and then merged into an oddly fitting rendition of "Ease on Down the Road."

And if we weren't exactly heading to see the Wizard, well, that was fine. I didn't think I was headed home to Kansas anyway. Still leading the horse, Talivar slipped up beside me, his hand finding mine. Fingers entwined, the two of us trailed the others. We were going to get our daughter back.

CHAPTER 16

NO ONE EVER SAID THE road to Hell was short. At least not to my knowledge. Or maybe it was, depending on who you were. But in this case, it was a ridiculous slog. No longer content with tree roots and broken cobblestones, the farther we went, the larger the road became, littered with potholes and piles of garbage.

The mist had mostly lifted now too, leaving us with a view of a desert, dried and desiccated, thick cracks like rivers winding through the landscape. I couldn't tell how long we'd been traveling. Maybe a few hours at best. I'd been forced to pause several times to change some of the cloths I'd had, the bleeding holding at a steady state, even as my breasts had begun to ache something fierce.

Talivar and I had ridden for a while, and that helped take some of the worst of the load off, but in time, even riding became painful, my legs aching fiercely. I was taking a break from riding when the road changed, becoming more urban than before.

Small, squat daemons of a sort I hadn't seen before sat sullenly on the broken remains of a wall, a billboard with a flickering neon sign that was supposed to read "Abandon hope, all ye who enter here." Only part of the neon was broken, so it read, "A dope . . . all . . . who . . . r . . . here."

"Apt," I noted wryly.

"It's not *not* wrong," Phin agreed, trotting beside me for a closer look. The unicorn shivered where he stood, as though the very air attacked him. I stooped to pick him up, holding him over my right shoulder. He was trembling like a neurotic Chihuahua.

The small daemons perked up when they saw us. They were about as tall as my knee, maroon in color, with scales and forked tongues and cloven hooves and all the rest. Like cherubs of the damned, maybe.

"Fresh meat," one of them hissed.

"Finally. I'm so hungry . . ." A larger one bared its teeth at us, bat wings fluttering.

"Can it, bub. Nobody gives a shit," the one closest to us snapped. It studied Melanie with amber eyes and took a drag on some sort of hookah, puffing out a perfect aquamarine smoke ring.

He was definitely chemically happy on something, though I doubted it was anything from the mortal world. I retreated from the smoke on instinct, but Talivar and Kitsune had already moved in front of me.

The smoking daemon pointed behind us as the others hopped back and forth in anticipation. "They're fixing the road, aye? Let 'em through."

Their heads swiveled almost as one, faces lighting up in delight. "Ah, why didn't you say so! With this, we'll start getting clients again."

"Clients," Kitsune repeated, her mouth pursing.

"Clients. Souls. Dinner. Sometimes it's all the same," the smallest one said, grinning up with a mouth of very pointy teeth. "Can we help?"

"Sure you can help, sugar," Sonja interjected before anyone else could respond, returning a rather toothy smile of her own. The little daemon swallowed perceptively. "In fact, I think that's a wonderful idea. We have the Door Maker with us, after all. She's to be His new TouchStone.

Why don't you lot run ahead and let everyone else know we're coming? That way we don't run into any more issues of mistaken identity and whatnot . . ." Her voice trailed away as though it were a polite request, but there was absolutely nothing of a request in it. It was a command, full stop.

The rest of the daemons stared at her and then at Melanie, and without a word, they took off like a shot, little legs pelting the crooked road until they took to the air, amid shouts of "Make way" and "You there, move along!"

Phin snorted. "And the real treasure was the friends we made along the way."

"There now," Sonja said with satisfaction. "That should keep the rats out of our hair for a bit. I don't know about you, but I don't fancy getting into a pissing match with every first-circle daemon out here trying to sow his wild oats or move up in the ranks, you know?"

Kitsune frowned. "But is it a good idea to announce our coming like that?"

Sonja shrugged. "It's not like we could hide it for long. Now people will be looking out for us." She gestured at the road. "Getting this fixed will make for a lot of goodwill among the regular folks that live here, even if you were the direct cause of it being fucked up." She wrinkled her nose. "I wouldn't bring that up, though. It would just confuse things."

"Wasn't going to," Melanie murmured, nonplussed. We exchanged a look, and she shook her head, shrugging.

"Your friend, he don't look so good, aye?" The hookah daemon had wandered back and gestured at Phin, its mouth opening wide in a toothy grin. "Never ate a Light Pather before. If he gets too sick, I'll, uh, be happy to take him off your hands."

"You're panicking at the wrong disco, sister," Phin snapped. "Try it and see how much you like having your ass bit."

It burbled a croaking giggle. "Don't flirt with me like that. I might get the wrong impression."

Phin shivered, burying his head in my shoulder. "I'm sorry," he whispered. "I don't think I can take much more of this. The evil here . . . I feel as though I'm going to fly apart. This is so much worse than whatever was going on in Japan."

I nudged Talivar. The elven king wore a stubborn expression that I recognized all too well, but in this case, he was going to have to give in. "Do you feel the same way?"

He shrugged. "It's not as bad as what he's going through, but maybe a faint tickle. A whisper, I guess. Like a voice trying to lead me down a path I don't want to go." He gave me a wry smile. "I'm not sure it's trying to tempt me so much as perhaps make me an ally of sorts. It's not like I have a mortal soul."

"You need to go back," I said, tugging on his coat. Something suddenly felt all wrong, and I couldn't place what it was. I knew that I had to protect them both. Phin had already given everything he had for me once; I couldn't simply let him sacrifice himself for me now.

"Please," I repeated. "Take Phin and wait for me at Eildon Tree. He'll die if he stays here, and I can't help him. Besides, you said it yourself: If you continue much farther, it will be seen as an act of war."

"And should any harm come to you or your daughter, that's what they'll get," he said darkly, though he took Phin from me, cradling the unicorn in his arms. Phin's bloodshot eyes rolled up toward the back of his head.

Talivar's mouth found mine, lips soft and tender and full of promise. "I will do as my wife wills—for now. But I leave you in the care of Kitsune and Jimmy. They will protect you where I cannot." He called to Jimmy, who had stoically led us along, his nose twitching the entire time.

"Are you good to stay?"

"Aye, Your Majesty." Jimmy tugged on his shirtsleeve, wiping at his dripping snout. "There's a hint of her smell on the breeze, ye ken? But there's a lot of sulfur too. It's mixing things up a bit."

Talivar exhaled sharply. "Keep going, then."

"Until it means my life," Jimmy said, bowing his head. Kitsune did the same, her fingers sliding over the hilt of her katana.

"Now we need to find a Door," Talivar said. "I don't fancy walking all the way back the way we came."

Sonja shook her head. "There should be one around here that will suit."

Melanie stopped her playing as we said our farewells, Sonja leading us toward a dark set of rocks thrusting its way out of the ground in a nearly obscene fashion. Graffiti in a language I didn't understand was scattered about in chalky script.

The daemon with the hookah sniffed. "This place has gone to shit. That Door's been unusable for a while—ever since that Maurice fellow was all up and down the Cross-Roads. Paganini boarded them all up."

Sonja snorted. "Well I supposed that's one way of keeping out the riffraff. Even if it makes it more difficult for everyone else." She wrinkled her nose at the Door. "Probably full of spiders in there."

I shuddered, but Talivar merely tapped the sword at his waist. "I think I'll manage. I'm sure I've faced worse."

"I'm sure." Sonja patted the horse. "I'd take this fellow with you. He's bound to be eaten where we're going, and to be honest, there's not much water." She shrugged at me sympathetically. "Not that I want to make you give up your ride and all, but . . ."

I shuddered. "No, no. I get it. I don't need to see it disemboweled."

Talivar nodded reluctantly. "Fair enough."

Melanie stroked the carved Door, turning toward me. "You sure you want to do this? I can maybe help a little with the Wild Magic, but the Key is, well, the *key* to this part. I don't want to put more strain on your body."

"I think we have to. And we ought to do as many as we can—whichever ones we come across anyway, depending on how difficult it is." I found the canteen I'd packed in the diaper bag and took a long pull. I had to stay hydrated.

Kitsune pressed her lips into a thin line, and she nodded grimly. "I agree. A fox never has one escape route. I see no reason why that should change simply because of where we are."

"All right, then." Melanie gestured to me. "What do you need?"

"Let's see how much this takes out of me, and then I'll let you know." The hookah daemons had quieted down as I approached the Door, one hand outstretched to trace the designs carved into the stone. I had never opened a Door in the Dark Path before; it had a distinctly different flavor from the ones I'd opened in Faerie, or even the Gates in Japan.

A ripple of unease tinged with sulfur seemed to suffuse my skin. I ignored it as best I could, pulling out the heart-shaped Key from where it was tucked under my neckline. It hummed, my apparent intention enough to bring it to life.

The hookah daemons whistled in appreciation. "That's what I'm talking about! Free trade!"

I had no idea what they were talking about, but I would take enthusiasm over being attacked any day of the week, so I took it as a sign of encouragement. The Door itself wasn't particularly responsive the way it normally was in the presence of the OtherFolk, but the edges lit up a darker silver when I gave it a mental nudge. A normal Door would usually open, given the proper encouragement—even one that hadn't been used in a while—but this one had been sealed shut.

Open . . . Open . . .

Mentally, I coaxed it, cajoling it to release its secrets, bare its soul, or whatever the equivalent was for a tangible opening to the CrossRoads. The veil of magic billowed out as I captured the strands keeping it shut. I'd compared the process once to puncturing it with a bit of needle and thread, pulling out the strands before it could sew itself back up.

"Ah," Melanie noted. "Wild Magic was used for this. I can see it now. It's definitely going to be a bit obnoxious. Let me try to help." She lifted her violin to her chin, her eyes closing in concentration as she tapped out a beat only she could hear.

Time, time, time . . . See what has become of me . . .

I hummed along to the familiar Bangles song, bringing up memories of the two of us during college and late-night Brat Pack movie binges. And then the veil shimmered, and I could see the threads quiet down, easily pulled out with the power of the Key.

The Door groaned, and everyone instinctively shifted away from the entrance, ready for an eruption of daemons or an elevator of blood or something. I wasn't sure which. But instead, a soft mumble emerged from the Door as the veil fell away, a golden hue streaking up the sides so the whole thing lit up like a lantern.

Almost immediately, a rush of daemons poured onto the road, pulling a series of carts full of various body parts, sprawled in a mishmash of limb-Jenga and putrefying flesh. I turned away as I got a whiff, trying not to wretch into my shirtsleeve.

"Finally, some good fucking food," the hookah daemon purred, taking another long puff.

"Charming," I said, moving out of the way, *really* not wanting to know what was in the rest of the carts. The last of the daemons piled through, chatting excitedly until they saw the state of the rest of the road. The small daemons escorting us chattered back, gesturing at me and Melanie, and the entire group of new daemons turned to stare at us expectantly.

"Guess that's our cue," Melanie said. "Back to it and all that."

Talivar leaned his face to my ear. "Find our daughter, Abby. If you fail to arrive home within the next day or so, I shall gather my armies and storm the very Gates of Hell, treaties be damned."

"You say the sweetest things," I whispered, suddenly very much afraid. Talivar had been my rock for several years now—my lover, my husband. To go on without him terrified me. But we had no choice. And my baby couldn't wait.

Phin's eyes rolled forward. "If we don't get out of here soon, I'm gonna start barfing rainbows. And not the good kind."

Talivar shook his head, and a moment later, he'd disappeared through the Door, leading the horse behind him as the gold light faded. I sighed. At least I'd managed to save two people I cared about. These days that was no small thing.

Without a word, I gestured to Melanie that we should move on. She stretched her shoulders and rolled her neck, then set off playing another song, her eyes glazing over as the Wild Magic took control again.

I watched her for a minute, slightly awed at the way she gently nudged the magic along with her music—the road straightening out here, bumps smoothing out there, trees retreating and bursting into bloom.

Sonja, Kitsune, and I followed behind her, Jimmy holding my hand. The cart-pulling daemons trailed us, whistling in tune. It made me nervous to have them all behind us like that, but better than in front of us with whatever was in those carts stinking up the place. Melanie must have felt the same because the song changed again, and before long, the entire continent was singing along to a warped rendition of "Heigh-Ho!" I began to question my life choices.

Even when Melanie stopped every hour or so to take a drink or help me open another Door, the daemons behind us cheered. But as the day wore on, her fingers started bleeding, the blisters popping and oozing.

I approached her during one of her breaks. "You're going to have to stop soon, Mel. Your hands need a rest. You'll be playing down to the bone if you're not careful."

She swallowed hard, refusing to look at her hands. "If I stop now, I won't have the strength to start again." Her fingers clenched, a rivulet of blood dripping from her fingertips. It hissed as it touched the brickwork below our feet, and the very road itself made an odd little sucking sound as it absorbed the crimson drops. "This is most likely a one-way trip for me, Abby," she said, her voice husky with loss.

"But—"

She winced. "It's all right. Nobu and I discussed this possibility. It's the only way, Abby. The only way out I have. The only way to save the people I love, and that includes your daughter."

Sonja fidgeted, folding and unfolding her wings. "To be frank, any gift from Hell comes at a steep price."

"As I learned the hard way," Melanie said ruefully, gesturing at her violin. I let her take another mouthful from my canteen. "How much longer do you think we have, anyway? We could be at it for months at this rate."

Sonja peered into the distance. "I don't usually come here by the front door, so to speak, but judging by the landscape, we're getting pretty close to the first circle. I would think your promise to fix the road would end there. Everything after that's internal, and if it takes forever to get somewhere, well, that's practically the definition of Hell anyway, isn't it? Getting there should be easy. Getting caught up in the bureaucracy? Well, that's the whole damn point."

I glanced behind us. We'd picked up a rather substantial parade of daemons and other unsavory creatures, most of them milling about and clearly bored. And that was perfectly okay with me. As long as they weren't trying to start any mischief, they could do as they liked.

Melanie wriggled her fingers and winced. "Let's get this over with, please. I'm ready to be done." She shivered, and then the soft sound of an aria spilled over the crowd, pushing us all into silence.

Her eyes were half-closed as she danced her way forward, hips swaying, hair blowing free. A fresh wave of Sakura blossoms hovered about her in the breeze. It was easy to watch her, moving lightly as a blossom herself, except for the crimson stains on the neck of the violin, already seeping into the wood.

The tiniest of pixies sat on the scroll of the violin. I'm not sure Melanie even saw it. In fact, I wasn't entirely sure it was real; it faded in and out like a spirit so fast I couldn't make out the details. I opened another Door wedged into a rock as Melanie swept past, undoing the Wild Magic sewn into the veil and coaxing it awake.

Another mile. More doors.

My feet were aching, my breasts leaking milk, but aside from trying to stuff a couple of rags down my shirt there was nothing I could do. And then we came to the end.

The road simply halted, easing into an enormous stairway with a platform that spiraled downward to a red gorge below. In the distance loomed a great city made of various circular platforms, like rings nested inside one another.

They lifted and lowered at various intervals, pulsing like the breathing of some sort of animal too large to see. I shuddered and backed away.

Beside the entrance slumbered what appeared to be an enormous dragon, black and covered with moss. It smelled faintly of manure and had a distinctly bovine face, complete with floppy ears and horns. Sonja gave its nostrils a pat. "Don't worry," she said cheerfully. "She won't wake up until the end of the world. She's been here awhile."

"Comforting," I noted. "An apocalypse cow. How quaint."

Melanie snorted and peered over the edge. "It's not quite what I was expecting," she mused. "I thought it would be full of torture and lost souls. Something with a Constantine vibe."

Sonja shrugged. "There are parts of it that are, but souls come through a different intake. You can't go there unless you're part of it—either a soul or a judge—so most of us don't pay much attention to it unless we're part of the Punishment Guild or whatever. Say what you will though: Hell throws one . . . hell of a party sometimes."

Melanie sucked on the tip of her finger before turning to hum the last gold cobblestone into place. The road gave a nearly audible sigh, the edges lighting up with a soft glow. As if it was some sort of signal, the daemons behind us cheered, quickly pushing their way toward the stairs and heading down. The ones with the carts shuffled off the platform lifts, taking their repulsive cargo with them.

Eventually, the last of the daemons disappeared. Even the hookah daemon had fucked off to who knew where. Butterflies tap-danced in my gut. Where was my baby? My breath became rapid, panicked. "You've done what they asked. Where's Paganini? Where's my daughter? Jimmy, can you pick up anything?"

The pig-man snuffled, his eyes streaming from what I

imagined was the overwhelming stench of sulfur and dae-monic nastiness. "Aye, Absinthe. She's near, but I cannot get a direction."

"Abby . . ." My name whispered on the wind, striking deep into my heart.

"Brystion," I breathed, startled as the incubus limped toward us, a crimson collar about his neck, one of his crys-talline antlers cracked and broken. I let out a half sob when I saw his swollen face, the scratches crisscrossing over his black skin, the missing fur from one hind flank. He'd been tortured.

I was running toward him before the others could even react, catching him in my arms as he stumbled, the collar tightening until he struggled for breath. His arms were brittle beneath my fingers, his ribs twisting like the keel of a ship with each labored gasp. He was starving.

A cloaked figure stood behind him. "Let him go, you monster!" I snapped, not caring if it was the Devil Himself. It very well could have been, but then Paganini revealed himself, removing the hood with a little sneer. "I'll fucking kill you if you don't."

"Oh my. Don't want to mess with the mama bear," he mocked, but he did what I asked, the collar going slack. "I do hope you understand. That bullshit in Tokyo was rather vexing. We had to pull a lot of strings to leave the country, and well, I'm afraid things got a bit out of hand when the incubus showed up and tried to kill me. I'm out of patience."

"You attacked the mother of his child," Kitsune said bluntly, her thumb on the scabbard of her katana, pressing gently on the hilt. "You threatened his friends. You tried to kill us multiple times. Whatever did you expect?" She snarled at him.

"I'm sorry, Abby," Ion murmured in my ear. "I tried to get her back. I did." He paused. "They did let me hold her, and she's all right, but . . ."

A sudden squalling wail interrupted whatever he'd been about to say, and I uttered a sharp cry as a daemon approached Paganini. I blinked. It was another incubus, but whereas Brystion had a more deerlike appearance, this one was all goat, with thick black hooves and twisted ram horns. He was wearing a Dead Can Dance T-shirt and holding my baby with a distinct lack of empathy. "Dude. It's making noise again. Can I eat it?"

Paganini waved him off. "We don't need it now. It served its purpose."

Brystion let out a strangled curse, attempting to get up, but Jimmy beat us to it, hurtling himself at the unknown incubus with an enraged squeal. Paganini neatly stepped out of the way of the charging pig-man.

"Fuck this noise," the incubus said. "Catch!" And he tossed my daughter into the air toward the cliff, perhaps assuming Jimmy would attempt to do just that. I screamed as she fell, racing to try to reach her, but even I knew there was no way I could get there in time.

Sonja swept past me, her wings cutting through the air like blades, dipping low to snatch the infant with gentle precision, wheeling high before landing beside me. Her wings remained outstretched as she passed me my wailing daughter, blocking Jimmy and the incubus from my view.

I clutched my daughter, feeling all over her head, her body, her face. Was she hurt? Based on the indignant cries, her lungs were healthy enough at least, though her blanket was soaked through. I let out a soft whimper of disbelief, my breasts suddenly letting down.

Sonja looked behind her and winced at whatever she saw. "I'd head over there by Kitsune," she said, more a command than a suggestion. "I don't think you need to see this part right now." I staggered toward the remainder of our group, Ion limping beside me, but not before getting a brief glimpse of Jimmy tusk-deep in the other incubus's abdomen. A pile of entrails spilled out on the ground before him.

I shivered, but I wasn't filled with a snippet of regret. Jimmy had always seemed a harmless sort of Fae, but I'd forgotten that the Unseelie Court was not known for subtlety. Kitsune met me halfway, flanking us until I found a spot near the Apocalypse Cow. I shrugged off the diaper bag, and Ion helped me change her, holding her so I could wipe her down and swaddle her up in a clean blanket. Without pausing, I pulled up my shirt, my daughter making an eager sound as she found my breast and latched on.

Everything was wet and warm and suddenly right, and I wept with relief. "Thank you," I whispered. "Thank you, thank you, thank you."

"Ah motherhood," Paganini sneered.

Jimmy stood up, blood spattering his face and clothes, his beady eyes fixated in rage.

"Try it," the Devil's TouchStone said, sliding his bow up the strings, the notes vibrating madly. "I'm rather fond of pork chops, you know."

"Don't," Sonja beckoned to Jimmy. "He's not worth it, and his magic will obliterate you."

Jimmy's ears twitched as though he wasn't quite hearing what she said, but his eyes grew clearer. Wiping his mouth, he returned to my side, his entire body trembling. "I've never killed no one before, ye ken? I don't like it much. But the baby . . ." His eyes rolled in a panic, the whites showing.

I smiled, trying not to get even more choked up. "She's all right, Jimmy. Thank you."

Kitsune took him aside, her head lowered as she whispered something into his ear. He made a little whimpering sound, nodding at her words.

Sonja wheeled around on Paganini, pointing at the

infant in my arms. "You go too far. Even we don't punish the innocent."

"No one's innocent," Paganini snapped. "And you're not in a position to negotiate."

"But I am." Melanie stepped past us to confront Paganini directly. She gestured at the smooth, glowing road that stretched out behind us, her bloodstained fingers dripping. "And haven't I done what was requested?"

"Not without a great deal of work on my end," Paganini pointed out. "If you'd come here to begin with, none of this would have happened. This is all your fault."

"Yes," she said. "And I will spend the rest of my life making up for that. What's your point?"

"My point is you still have a debt to pay." He waggled his obnoxiously long fingers, his knuckles bending in an almost-inhuman way.

I stood up, still nursing my baby. "But you said if she fixed the road here, her debt would be cleared!"

"I lied," Paganini said dryly. "Duh." He turned his attention to Melanie again. "Now, are you ready to finally bend your will to His? To become His anchor in the mortal realm?"

"No," Melanie said simply, showing her hands, the violin dropping to the ground with a clatter. Its silver hue faded, the hum of the instrument slithering away with a hiss.

He frowned at the violin on the ground. "You seem rather casual about throwing away the instrument that holds your soul. Even if you break it, it still belongs to Him."

"Maybe." She gave a bitter half smile. "Nobu always told me I didn't need the magic of the violin to play. The Wild Magic was always inside me; the violin simply amplified it. Made it so I didn't have to work as hard, protected my body, made it simple. It gave me the power to create Doors on the fly. I've suppressed it nearly my entire life, using the instrument as an excuse to not go beyond some arbitrary boundary." A soft sound escaped her. "And now I'm done with that." She shoved the violin with the rounded toe of her boot. "You can have it." She lifted her chin in Paganini's direction and locked eyes with him as her foot came down and crunched the violin into pieces.

CHAPTER 17

THE SOUND RATTLED LIKE BONES, splinters erupting into a thousand shards with a sonorous hum. I caught the barest hint of laughter, an echo of Melanie's voice singing, and a glittering burst of light that faded almost immediately.

"You . . . you can't do that!" Paganini exploded, staring at the remains of the violin. "You're lying. Something's not right. Your soul was bound to it. You should have died the instant it was destroyed."

Melanie let out a snort. "'Tis a puzzlement."

I cocked a brow at her, my attention drawn to the broken violin, then to her calm demeanor. There was more going on than she was saying, but I wasn't about to interject myself into this particular fight. Given Nobu's quest for his soul stone it wasn't hard to put two and two together, however they'd managed it.

Sonja shrugged at Paganini. "Think you've been outplayed, TouchStone. But look at it this way: He still retains you, and He's had the pleasure of watching this little drama unfold. Sometimes it's more about the game than the outcome—at least where He's concerned."

"No." The violinist shook his head, his face growing pale as he began to play his own instrument, the music starting to pour from the strings as he moved his bow in rapid motion. "You traded your soul for a violin. That was offset by your paramour for a while, but the debt has been called in."

"And I have returned it," Melanie said, clearly growing frustrated. "I have repaired the road to Hell. The violin is no more. My soul has vanished with whatever Wild Magic was trapped inside it. I have *nothing* else to give."

Spittle frothed from Paganini's mouth, the music sparking a hazy golden ambiance only to turn razor-sharp a measure later. "Then you can give your life."

The power erupted toward us, arrows of Wild Magic tipped with malevolence. I braced myself against it, but even as I turned my shoulder, trying to somehow protect both my baby and Ion, Melanie let out another cry, her tattered fingers raised, her shaking palms somehow absorbing the arrows and turning them away so they dissipated into nothing.

"How are you doing that?" Paganini's eyes burned into her.

"Maybe she's better at controlling the Wild Magic than you are," Kitsune said matter-of-factly, her face pensive.

"Bullshit! No one mortal has that kind of power. That's why we need the instrument to focus it." He played even faster, the notes whizzing by us like race cars on a track of magical air.

But Melanie moved her hands just so, and the notes shattered, discordant and harsh. Her own magic shimmered like a rainbow made of opals. I caught a faint hint of what sounded like a few bars of Led Zeppelin's "Stairway to Heaven," but it faded away to be replaced by the more somber tones of "Flight of the Valkyries."

For a beat, the notes took the shape of tiny warrior women riding winged horses, the music growing louder and louder until we were nearly all covering our ears as the very ground shook with the cadence.

"Enough." The deep rumble of a voice that somehow sounded larger than the Heavens echoed all around us, making my bones ache.

The music cut off abruptly on both sides, Paganini's nostrils flaring wide. Melanie slumped to her knees, her ruined hands cradled in her lap with a soft sobbing moan. My eyes darted between her and Ion, unsure of what to do, but Sonja had already gotten to Melanie, her wings snapped out as though to protect her from whoever stood before us.

I gently poked Ion. "Is that . . ."

He shook his head. "Of course not. He doesn't leave His domain for petty garbage like this. That's Asmodeus, one of His generals." He shuddered. "Do me a favor and don't get involved in this, please. I don't have the energy to rescue you." His mouth curved in a mocking smile, his face still ashen with exhaustion.

I gave the daemon general a sideways glance, but he wasn't paying any attention to me. He had all the charm of one of those medieval wood carvings with the bat wings and the forked tail, almost like a larger version of the hookah daemons. A much, much larger version. But in an Armani suit and touting a pompadour.

"What is all this about?" he demanded of Paganini, pushing the skinny man with a meaty finger.

"Nothing you need to be concerned about." Paganini sniffed, lowering the violin from his cheek. "Doing His work and all that. You know how it is."

"Oh, I *know*," the daemon hissed, baring his teeth. "I know that I just received a phone call while I was in the shower with a certain lady daemon, demanding to know what the fuck was going on up here at the entrance to Hell. What a surprise to find you in the thick of it. My free time is very precious to me, so I'd appreciate an explanation." His eyes flicked around the group. "Mortals, that brother-sister pair of sex daemons, a kitsune, and something else . . ."

"Not just any mortals," Paganini said, bowing gallantly. "I present to you the Key to the CrossRoads and the Door Maker, the mortal He has been chasing for so many years to become His new TouchStone." His voice faltered on the last part, as though he had to vomit up the words.

Asmodeus snorted. "It's a Who's Who of bullshittery is what it is." He chewed on his lower lip and kicked one of the cobblestones, scuffing it slightly. "I see she fixed your fuckup, though. That should get her a few brownie points with the boss."

Melanie blinked out of her stupor. "Wait, what?"

"I thought you would have figured it out already." Paganini pinched the bridge of his nose. "While you did actually mess up the road a bit during our re-creation of Eildon Tree, I may have . . . helped that along."

"Why would you do that?" I exploded, ignoring Ion's warning grunt. "Look at her! She's destroyed now! She'll never play anything again!"

Paganini smirked. "Good. You think I wanted to give up my position to some girl who knows nothing of the world? Who doesn't have a fraction of my talent? Who thinks because she can control the Wild Magic with her music . . ."

"You were jealous," Melanie said softly, staring down at her ruined hands.

"Of course I was," he snapped. "For nearly two hundred years, I have been the anchor for my Lord, was given the chance to turn my music into magic. You think I'm simply going to let Him throw me away because a shiny bauble caught His eye? I did *not* get to where I am today because I let the wind blow me where it would. So I shut down the road, the Doors, all of it. And I told Him *you* had done it. Originally, I was hoping it would piss Him off enough that

He'd give up on you." He smiled miserably and gestured to the now-smooth road. "But as you can see, that backfired."

"Then why chase us down? Why try to hurt my friends? Why not leave me to run away and live the rest of my life in peace?" Melanie's voice shook, a tremulous thread of anger and anguish. "I gave up . . . I gave up everything."

"I was *trying* to kill you." Paganini's upper lip curled. "Using your friends to find you, isolate you, make you question all your choices, all your power. If you were dead, then He would forget you and I'd be in the clear."

"And yet, the fact that someone who you insist has no talent was able to undo the Wild Magic *you* put in place speaks volumes," Asmodeus pointed out, his fingers twitching as though he wanted a cigarette. A second later, he pulled out a vape. "Trying to quit," he said as blueberry-scented smoke wafted about us. "She don't like it."

"Charming," Sonja said, digging through the diaper bag and pulling out some of the rags I was supposed to use for my own bleeding. With a careful hand, she began to wrap the cloth around Melanie's exposed fingers. "This is going to need a healer of the highest order," she said.

"I will never play again," Melanie said, nudging her broken violin. "Ever."

"Well, that's your choice, but if you want to be able to wipe your own ass in the future, then I suggest you get these looked at." Sonja inclined her head toward me. "Abby's already got one baby to take care of, and that doesn't even count the one on her boob."

Ion snorted, and even Mel had the grace to blush faintly, the smallest of smiles playing about her lips. Without a word, she held out her hands so Sonja could reach them easier, wincing as the cloth brushed over the mangled skin of her fingers.

The daemon general took a long inhale on his vape and puffed out the smoke. "Well, I guess that's that, then. Shall

I tell the Boss you're no longer interested in the position?"

"I was *never* interested," Melanie retorted.

"Don't lie. To me or to yourself. It's unbecoming. Of course you were." Asmodeus shoved the shattered violin with a cloven hoof and leaned down into Melanie's face, his expression sly. "The way I heard it, old Long Fingers there dangled a mighty fine instrument in front of you and you didn't even hesitate."

"And I paid the price for that," Melanie said bitterly. "Over and over again." She rubbed the violinist's hickey on her chin against her shoulder. "When will I stop having to pay?" Her voice dropped to a low whisper.

"Well, you know, He's always up for a bargain," the daemon said. "Though at this point, you have very little left to offer. You fixed the road, that's true. And you no longer have the violin He gave you. Though its destruction is rather irritating. He might want you to be responsible for replacing it. Your soul, though . . . Souls are like energy. Their essence can't be destroyed. Displaced, certainly. And it should have returned into you, but for some reason it hasn't. How strange." He snapped his fingers, his voice growing sharp and whiplike. "Come."

She twitched, and it seemed as though she might follow his command, her body wavering like a reed in the wind, but in the end, she simply stood there trembling, the sweat upon her forehead glistening with effort. The daemon commanded her again, sniffing her when the result was the same. She pulled away, but he ignored her. "Ah, that's it. You carry a soul not your own. There's no room for another."

Kitsune's head snapped toward them. "Nobu," she breathed. "I knew that asshole would try something. I had no idea he would go this far, though."

"Called it," I muttered. "I knew that shirikodama thing was going to come into this. He gave it to you, didn't he?"

"It was the only way we could think of to make this work. We both gave up what we loved most to do it. My soul was bound to the violin; there was nothing we could do about that." Melanie glared at Asmodeus. "And perhaps a soul cannot be destroyed per se, but I'll bet anything it can be consumed. Isn't that what the corruption was? I couldn't control the Wild Magic anymore because my soul was being eaten by the violin."

"Clever shinigami," Kitsune said. "In doing so, he removed his own chance at redemption, choosing a sort of half-life between realms instead of being forced to pay his own debt."

"Where is he now?" Ion slurred, struggling to get to his feet. "The Peacock would never do something so . . ."

"Shit." He was fading fast; I had to get him somewhere safe. The sexual-feeding thing would be more than awkward as postpartum as I was, but I'd worry about that when we were out of here. The baby released my breast, and I juggled her in my arms, patting her back gently as she whimpered against my neck.

Sonja rolled up the leftover rags and shoved them into the diaper bag. "He's not looking so good, Abby."

I waved Melanie over, my heart breaking at the sight of her bandaged hands. "Come on," I told her, gesturing my head toward the way we had come. "Let's go home. I think I'm done with this shitshow."

Paganini crossed his arms at Asmodeus. "So that's it? No smiting? No taking her off to the lower circles for conversion?"

The daemon smirked. "You should know better than that. You should know better than anyone." He turned toward Melanie with a toothy grin. "Our Lord never lies, you know. Not really. Deception, sure. Misunderstanding, yes. Miscommunication, definitely. But never an outright *lie*." His eyes flicked toward Paganini. "The same can't be said of mortals. And at this point, I'd say you've repaid us in full."

Melanie blinked, her eyes settling on a shrinking Paganini. "What do you mean?"

"I mean, the amount of collateral damage you managed to produce was amazing." He gestured to our little group with a wave of his slender fingers. "Just look at this little bit of madness right here. Your friends beaten and broken, not trusting you any longer, the death and destruction you caused at the Barras, the years of cowardice and lies. He could hardly have done any better if He had planned it that way."

The daemon's eyes grew sly and slanted. "And He doesn't plan for much when it comes to mortals. A nudge here or there. Envy. Greed. Pride. I'm sure you know the sins well enough by now." He rubbed his chin, his voice growing seductive. "Based on that, maybe you shouldn't leave. Surely you would be much happier here, wouldn't you? We'd fix those hands of yours right up. No need to worry about pesky things like souls . . ."

Melanie shut her eyes, swallowing hard before gently tapping on her chest with her ruined hands. "This soul . . . This soul is not mine to give. It never was."

"You're goddamned right it isn't." Nobu's voice echoed in a high-pitched mockery of itself as a chibi version of the death god emerged from the broken remains of the violin. "If I'd known you were going to do that, I'd never have hidden there, little bird."

"What the fuck . . ." I almost laughed when he fluttered up to perch on Melanie's shoulder, his freshly grown, iridescent feathered wings seeming to shine beneath the reddish light of Hell with an eerie glow. He was dressed in what could only be traditional Japanese samurai garb, looking for all the world as though he'd crawled out of a Kurosawa film, his tiny face smug.

"You have no jurisdiction here, death god," Paganini growled. "This is between our Lord and this particular mortal. All your games thus far have amounted to nothing, and we are exactly where we wanted to be. Except maybe you." He sneered. "The tiny stature suits you."

"It's not about the size," Nobu said, lofting his way toward Paganini's face to kick him in the nose. "It's about what you do with it."

I stared at Kitsune. "Did you know about this?"

"I might have had an inkling or two, yes." Her smile grew cold and fierce, and I briefly caught the edges of a white fox muzzle shimmering over her face. "It's not as though my people aren't tricksters of one sort or another."

Asmodeus gave her an appraising look, his face growing dark as he chewed on his lower lip with his fang. "I could make this into a problem. Technically, you helped steal property that rightly belongs to Hell."

Unfazed, the fox-woman shrugged and smiled just as tightly. "And you sent your people into our territory without a treaty and created a national incident by bringing attention to our headquarters in Tokyo. The number of glamours and amount of trickery we had to employ to keep mortals from noticing and causing backlash was extensive." She paused. "And expensive. Faerie has made good on some of this debt, but we claim the Door Maker as collateral."

The daemon blinked at her. "What?"

"We're taking her as payment for Hell's debt to us." Kitsune shrugged. "If she belongs to Hell, and she was the direct cause of our troubles, well, the debt is on her to pay."

The daemon threw his hands in the air and then dug into his pocket for a cell phone. "This is above my pay grade, and I'm tired of dealing with it. Hold on." He tapped into the phone and turned away, his voice a growling burble that had me wondering if frogs weren't dropping out of his mouth with each sharp syllable. Finally, he shook his head and clicked the phone off with a snap. "All right. I'm going back to bed. This is bullshit."

"What did He say?" Paganini asked, something like fear flickering over his face.

"One, that you're an asshole, and He'd *really* like to see you. Two, He's not going to give up the Door Maker quite that simply. So you all are free to go, and she'll be coming with us."

Melanie stiffened. "No."

Asmodeus shrugged and then grinned. "Well, there may or may not be reinforcements coming to take you into custody, so simply stating your position doesn't make things the way you want them. Let's make it easy on everyone and save ourselves the fuss of a protracted battle."

Melanie threw me a desperate look, biting hard on her lower lip. But when the baby let out a little snuffle, she straightened, her eyes hardening. "Make me," she said softly.

Paganini's face darkened, and he stroked the strings of his violin with his bow. "As you wish."

Asmodeus sighed and added, "Have it your way."

Melanie raised her hands, her eyes closing, and she tapped out a beat. Her voice hummed a counterpoint, but it was discordant and hollow, the notes seeming to echo around us like disembodied ghosts. I caught a vague hint of "Cruel Angel's Thesis," and I had the sudden feeling that the shit was seriously going to hit the fan. *Neon Genesis Evangelion* had been her favorite anime in college, and it evoked some rather disturbing connotations.

Kitsune shifted until she was beside me, her sword half-drawn. "This may go badly," she said in the spaces between the music. "If I tell you to run, do it, Abby." I wasn't sure what had her hackles up, but her tail lashed madly, revealing her agitation. Though what good her katana would be against the Wild Magic, I had no idea.

I gave the Apocalypse Cow a worried look. What if this little shindig woke her up?

End of the world or not, I didn't want me or my friends to be responsible for some retroactive Ragnarök either. Ion groaned, leaning his head against me. "Sorry this is such a cluster. Didn't mean to get captured . . ."

"We'll talk about it later. Let's just focus on getting out of here." Alarmed by his rapidly paling skin, I laid a hand on his brow Sonja's mouth pursed tightly.

"He needs to get to the Dreaming now, Abby. Let me take him so he can heal."

"No," Ion said stubbornly, his arms tight about my waist. "Not going to leave her again. Never . . . Never . . ." His eyes rolled upward, and Sonja nearly fell over trying to keep him from smashing his head on the ground.

"Ion!" I knelt beside him, my hobo sliding off my shoulder. The contents spilled everywhere, but I ignored it as Sonja carefully lowered him into a prone position. From the corner of my eye, I could see Melanie, her brow soaked with sweat. Paganini had begun playing counterpoint, but it wasn't a duet so much as a duel, different rhythms and chords intermixed in an ugly, awful sound.

And then I realized she had unraveled her bandages, moving her hands as though she too were playing a violin. Except she wasn't going through the motions. Somehow a ghostly violin had taken shape, the strings flaming blue and violet with every draw of the bow. Fire flickered all about her, reminding me of the sort of power Kitsune had showed in her fox form.

The music was still discordant, swelling with a cacophony that made me want to clap my hands against my ears to shut it out, but there was no stopping it now. The baby stirred, and I wrapped the blanket partially around her face, trying to cover her ears.

Paganini shook his head and redoubled his efforts, his

elongated fingers a blur against the strings. And yet, his whole body moved like a puppet on a string, as though he was fighting against the very music he was playing.

"She's controlling him," I breathed.

"Holy fuck, you're right." Sonja nearly dropped Ion as she stood up for a better look. Even Kitsune seemed discomfited. Jimmy hunched behind us all, moaning with his bloodstained fingers in his ears. Paganini's fingers grew red and blistered beneath the torrent of notes.

Melanie's eyes remained shut, but there was something trancelike about her, wrapped up in a cocoon of music and magic that only she could understand. I squinted, trying to find Nobu. If there was anyone who could get through to her right now, it would be him, but with his smaller stature, he was lost in the haze.

Asmodeus's grin faded the longer he stood there. "Hey now, that's cheating," he said, reaching out as though to break the connection between the two TouchStones, but the moment his hand brushed over Melanie's form, the magic exploded, spitting like lightning and setting the daemon on fire. He screamed, rolling on the ground as his skin went up in a smoking blaze, only to leave nothing more than a pile of ash half a minute later.

"That's not possible!" Sonja shouted over the din. "He's a daemon. Fire shouldn't be able to hurt him like that."

"It's not normal fire," Kitsune said. "Wild Magic in the shape of flame maybe, but I think this is going to get out of hand." The fox-woman shot me a desperate look. "I don't know if we can even make it out of range fast enough to escape."

Paganini was sobbing now, the skin on his fingers ragged tatters, the appendages little more than bone wrapped in the illusion of tendons. He sank to his knees, still playing, though he foamed at the mouth, and I wondered if he hadn't bit through his tongue.

"Nobu!" I shrieked over the now deafening roar of music. In the distance, a shadow grew over the city below, lightning arcing in all directions. I caught a glimpse of Mel's face as she began to turn about, and her eyes were lit up with a terrible sort of madness.

Our gazes met for an instant, and then we were plunged into darkness.

I was five when I first saw the sprite. She was a little thing, maybe a few inches tall. My child's mind named her Tinkerbell, though her color was all wrong and her teeth were pointed when she smiled. A feral little blueberry of a thing with a potbelly and the wings of a dragonfly.

She danced on the curling scrollwork of my tiny violin, arms swaying as I carefully plucked out the beginnings of "Twinkle, Twinkle, Little Star." She grinned broadly and wiggled her hips.

Even then, I knew she was a dangerous thing to bring into the house. And yet I played on and she danced, only to disappear once the song was finished, my wobbly fingers sliding uncertain and clumsy upon the strings. I had paused, staring at where she'd been, but it was as though she had burst like a bubble, leaving no trace behind.

"Why have you stopped playing, Melanie?" My mother sat on the other side of the room, perched upon her plush sofa with her legs crossed as she flipped through a copy of Good House- keeping.

She licked her finger between each page turn. It was a slow movement, absent of thought. Later, I often wondered if she found the taste of ink that appealing. It wouldn't have surprised me if that's what she lived on, like some literary mosquito, feeding on the pulp of cleaning advertisements and articles about linens.

I remained silent, but my bow was already moving again. The notes squeaked out, and I shut my eyes. Not because I was concentrating but because if I couldn't see her, maybe she wouldn't see me either.

It didn't matter because a moment later, I felt the bony coldness of her fingers cupping my chin, twisting my face so that I was forced to look at her. I was trembling, and the music cut off with a terrified warble, the colors in my mind swirling.

"I'm waiting for an answer, Melanie." Her voice was soft and gentle and terrifying. "Why did you stop?"

"I saw a——"

Her eyes darkened. "Saw what?"

"Tinkerbell, Mama. I saw Tinkerbell dancing on the edge of my violin." She stilled. I knew what was coming next, and a hot trickle ran down my leg. The sharp intake of her breath was the only warning I get.

I'm a statue. Just a statue, and a statue can't be hurt because it's not alive . . .

I heard the crunch before I felt it, the sharp pressure of her Manolo Blahnik heel crushing upon my foot. I screamed as she broke my big toe, but she held my mouth shut so I was forced to whimper against my teeth.

"You don't need your feet to play," she hissed. "And if you lie to me again about seeing things that aren't there, I'll make sure the only way you get onstage is in a wheelchair." She pointed to the violin. "Now play until I tell you to stop. Understood?"

I shook so hard I could barely lift the bow, but I nodded, ignoring the pain radiating from my foot and half up my shin. She retreated to her couch again, leaving me to struggle for another thirty minutes before taking me to the doctor.

One day, *I told myself,* I'll wear shoes so strong she'll never be able to hurt me again.

Pain, bitter and awful and full of loss. All of it exploding out of Melanie in a fit of rage so hot I could barely look at it. A living nightmare made flesh so that we were all forced to relive it. My heart broke for her as I backed away, clutching my baby, Ion struggling to keep up.

"Nobu, make her stop!" I screamed again.

The winged yokai stumbled out of the fiery haze, his eyes wild and frightened. "I can't, Abby. She isn't hearing anything I say."

Behind us, the Apocalypse Cow began to stir, its eyelids fluttering.

"Damned shinigami," Kitsune snarled, staring at it in horror. "This is what you get for messing with the fates of mortals. You've ensured all of our deaths now if we can't contain her!"

"I would not have been so mistaken about that," he retorted, his gaze falling on my hobo, my makeup bag and iPhone still lay where they'd landed, along with the gachapon Haru had given me. Nobu's eyes widened. "Is that what I think it is?"

Cradling my daughter with one arm, I snagged the plastic capsule with its little rubber mascot inside. "Haru gave it to me when I left his . . . office. As an apology."

Nobu let out a burbling bit of hysterical laughter. "Throw it at Mel when I tell you to. And *don't miss*."

"What will it do?" I asked.

He chortled again, but it was shaky and full of fear. "You'll see."

"No pressure," I muttered to myself, trying to will my hands not to tremble so much.

The crescendo of the music built and built, the light growing ever brighter until there was nothing of Melanie but a ball of pure white fire, shrieking into the sky.

"Now!" Nobu shouted, crying out as I let the plastic capsule fly. At this range, I couldn't have missed anyway, but I hurled it at her, blinded by the brilliance of her power. Melanie's form was nothing more than a negative corona burned into my vision.

"Mel!" My voice was swept away in a howling wind.

Something growled behind me, a puff of smoke rolling past as the gachapon was swallowed up by her power.

And then there was nothing at all.

CHAPTER 18

IT WAS AS THOUGH ALL the air had been sucked into a vacuum, collapsing upon itself into silence. The light grew so bright I would have thought the sun was exploding, but after all that build up, the resulting discharge never happened.

Or maybe it did, but it was absorbed and the gachapon shattered, leaving a shadow in its place. A swiftly growing one from what I could tell, an all-too-familiar roar emerging from the chaos.

"The Dragon King," Kitsune said, her tone full of wonder and terror. "The power woke him up."

"The Dragon King, my ass," Sonja snapped. "That's fucking—"

"Gojira," Nobu finished. "Or at least what he's based on. The real thing, as you can see, is far more dangerous than a man in a rubber suit."

I sagged onto the ground, clutching my daughter a little tighter as she let out a sudden cry at the noise. "Oh good. I've released Godzilla into Hell. I'm toast." The kaiju in question immediately made a beeline for the moving platforms, a fiery blue stream emerging from his throat that obliterated a third of the outer ring of the city.

"Believe it or not, we've got bigger things to worry about," Sonja said, pointing at the Apocalypse Cow. The bovine harbinger of the end of the world lifted its head, the air seeming to still all around us. It took one long look at the monstrosity belching a spout of atomic energy into one of the lower circles of Hell, and made a coughing noise that sounded an awful lot like "Fuck, no."

It promptly closed its eyes; the fakest snore I'd ever heard started up, the smoke drifting from its nose dying away. Sonja nudged me. "Come on, we have to get my brother out of here." She and Jimmy helped Ion to stand, the incubus leaning heavily on both of them, his breathing shallow. The pig-man looked as miserable as I felt, and I couldn't blame him one bit.

Nobu and Kitsune ran to where Melanie was lying, sprawled out on the ground. Magic continued to swirl around her, myriad stars turning in time through her hair and over her skin, an echo of tiny notes chiming in time. The blisters on her fingers were gone, fresh and newly healed skin in place of the wounds.

Her eyes fluttered open, and she groaned as Kitsune helped her up. "What happened?"

"You, uh . . . You broke Hell," I said, giving the baby a once-over. Her dark eyes blinked blearily up at me, and I couldn't quite resist the urge to coo. Quietly.

"Astute observation, Abby Sinclair," purred a quiet, masculine voice from behind us. Melanie let out a whimper, and even Sonja stiffened. I knew not to turn around, even without a warning nudge from the succubus.

The power emanating from the cloaked being that swept past us was so virulent and seductive, my mind nearly broke. But I wasn't the focus here, and the Devil strode past us in a cloak of living smoke, beautiful white wings trailing behind him.

"Don't move," Ion whispered.

"Raise your head, Melanie St. James." Lucifer's melodic voice rippled around us. She uncoiled slightly, her chin thrust out in sudden rebellion. He made a motion to touch her forehead, his gloved fingers pausing in the starlight emanating from her. "Ah," He hummed. "You've finally come into your own, it would seem."

"Master," Paganini croaked from a few feet away, his arms crossed to cradle his useless, bloody hands.

Lucifer made an irritated noise. "You will be tended to in time. For now, you will be quiet and let your betters speak, dog."

Melanie stood up, ignoring Paganini's wails, her nostrils flaring.

Lucifer snorted. "It would seem you have outplayed me. All of you. It is not something I will forget," He warned. "But neither will I pursue it." He pointed at Godzilla, who was lasering a horde of daemons brandishing weapons on the other side of the city. "On the other hand, get that piece of shit out of my city and we'll call it even. While I realize this was a movie that never got made, that doesn't mean I feel like acting it out now."

"You'll release me from all debts, past and present?" Melanie asked, her eyes darting toward the rest of us with something like hope flaring to life in them.

"Devil's honor," He said. "I've rather had enough of you, and I would suspect my underlings have as well." He snapped His fingers and a pair of bat-winged horses emerged from the clouds. The unfortunate Paganini was tossed, groaning, over the back of one by a daemon with a cowboy hat. He tipped his hat to Lucifer, and the horses launched themselves skyward, disappearing into the smoking ruins of the city.

"If nothing else, you've provided me with a great deal of amusement." Lucifer's eyes fell on Sonja. "See you next poker night, my dear. Stakes will be double, fair warning."

"As You will," she agreed, inclining her head.

"Careful with that power," He said to Melanie. "Never

know where it's going to take you."

When Sonja raised her face again, the Devil was gone, and she smiled ruefully. "Well, that was a thing."

"You never told me you were that close to Him," Melanie said, sinking to her knees. She began to shiver.

"Yeah, well, you never asked. He cheats like mad, by the way, but don't ever let on that you know." She thrust her chin out in the distance. "How do we get Godzilla out of here?"

Nobu shrugged at Melanie. "If you think you can handle it, we might try a little Pied Piper action. Probably wouldn't hurt to have some backup, though." He pulled out a tiny flute and raised it to his little lips. A puff of multicolored smoke exploded from the tip of the flute. It swirled about as if laughing maniacally before solidifying into Haru.

The little frog-turtle yokai yawned. "Been a while since I was called through one of those." His swirling eyes brightened when he saw chibi Nobu on Melanie's shoulder, and he let out a solitary giggle that grew greater and greater until he was on the ground rolling with laughter. "Oh, it was worth it just to see you like that."

Nobu rolled his eyes and blew it again, and more of the yokai spilled out of the flute until we were surrounded by clusters of the esoteric creatures: A wall with a face. A long-necked woman with a slit for a mouth. A small child holding a bowl. A violin that walked by itself with the mien of a friendly grandfather. The assortment of beings was varied, both grotesque and beautiful, elegant and awful.

They poured out of the smoke until there were so many I could barely count them all.

"The Hyakumono," Kitsune said with a nod of satisfaction. "One hundred yokai. It's sort of our variation of the Wild Hunt. Technically, you're not supposed to look at them or they'll carry you off, but in our case, I think it would only help us." She paused. "Especially since they're here on your request."

The milling yokai sniggered, and the kappa sighed. "Well this has been fun, but I'd like to go home now. Good job summoning the Dragon King, by the way. I didn't think there was a way to wake him up short of an atomic bomb."

"There were complications." Melanie scuffed her boots on the cobblestones. "I lost control of the Wild Magic again, but I think I understand it a bit more now. I don't want to try that a second time, though."

"I can see that. Well, let's start this little parade and see if we can't grab his attention." Haru let out a high-pitched whistle as if to emphasize the point.

Kitsune frowned. "Does that normally work?"

Haru shrugged. "Eh. Usually you have to let him go until he runs out of steam and he'll shrink down, but this isn't a good place for it. What's out there isn't his actual form anyway; it's more of an illusion. We can lead him away for a bit until we can find a Door or Gate or something and go home."

I ran my hand over Ion's forehead, wincing away at the way his skin burned. "We have to get him home *now*."

"I told you I wasn't going anywhere," he retorted stubbornly, reaching out to trace our daughter's head.

"Honestly." Sonja snarled at him. "You're not going to be able to protect her if you die. Come on. They're in good hands now and we can reach the Dreaming from Hell, so don't be stupid."

Reluctantly, he withdrew his hand, and I gave him a gentle shove. "We'll be fine," I said. "Go with her and I'll catch up with you as soon as I'm settled."

"See you in the Dreaming, Abby," he purred, a soft promise vibrating through the words. "Don't keep me waiting long."

"Yeah, yeah, lover boy. Make eyes at her later." Sonja

threw his arm over her shoulder and shook her head at me. "But yeah, I'd get there real soon, Abby." And then they were gone, staggering off toward one of the platforms.

A shuddering breath escaped me. Sonja would keep her brother safe and get him to where he needed to be. One more thing crossed off the list. That only left . . . Godzilla. The Dragon King was continuing to stomp his way through Hell, leaving a devastating destruction in his wake. Did we really want to try to lead that up the CrossRoads?

Staring out across the sea of sand and rocks, I scanned the horizon for anything that could be made into a Door. *If* Melanie retained any of her power to make one, it would be much more prudent to have us simply emerge someplace directly.

My eyes fell on one of the yokai. It was a walking wall with an odd little face peering out of it. Not quite enough for a Door, but maybe . . .

Ah! There was a sliding rice paper door waltzing at the end of the line with a broomstick. I gestured toward Nobu and thrust my head in the rice paper's direction.

His eyes narrowed as he weighed the idea, and he fluttered in her direction. "Allow me to persuade her."

A few minutes later, the rice paper waddled over to us, her face askance. But whatever Nobu had whispered at her had her blushing and nodding.

"I'm not sure I even want to know what you told her, but if it works, that's good enough for me," I said.

"Ah well, since I've been demoted to a mere yokai, I'm going to need a new shrine and a worshipper or two. I simply offered a place in my shrine, whenever it gets built."

"Not a lot of worshippers lined up at the moment," Kitsune pointed out dryly.

Nobu's dark eyes sparkled with an uncharacteristic bit of mischief. "I only need one," he said fondly. "And I've already got someone in mind." His eyes flicked to where

Melanie leaned over to chat with the old man violin, her face full of quiet wonder.

"I suppose only one's enough, if she's your wife," I agreed. "Where will you go?"

"Well, we'll need some place to rest. Her soul requires healing, I suspect," he noted pensively. "My soul. Which-ever it is. And frankly, I think my shrine will do best in my homeland. At least for the initial setup. We'll see what happens after that."

Nobu flew to Melanie's shoulder, tugging on a lock of her hair, and whispered something into her ear. Surprise flashed over her face at whatever he said, her cheeks flush-ing pink.

"Ojiisan," Nobu called out to it before rattling off a series of questions in Japanese too fast for me to follow. The vio-lin stroked its bearded face and bowed in response before leaping into Melanie's arms with a merry little laugh.

Nobu grunted in satisfaction at Melanie. "Do you want to give it a try? The grandfather here will help you, yes?"

Melanie nodded respectfully at the instrument. "If I can maybe channel the magic through him, we might be able to do it."

In response, the violin waved his sticklike arms and grasped his own bow, sliding it over the strings. The dark eyes stared up at her, and he rattled off something in Jap-anese. Her face grew slightly uncomfortable, though whether that's because she understood what he said or because she was holding an actual living violin, I wasn't sure. Either or both were probably true.

"He says he'll play for you if you tell him what you want. You need to be holding him and envision the song, and he should be able to pick up the vibrations of the magic." Nobu alighted on her shoulder again.

"Ready?" I asked her.

She sucked in a deep breath and shut her eyes, humming

beneath her breath, her voice suddenly emerging in a sonorous vibrato. The violin started playing almost immediately, moving the bow in counterpart until it drowned out the sound of her voice all together.

Interestingly enough, some of the other sentient instruments picked up on the song as well, and before long, we had the makings of an otherworldly band. The fact that they were playing a slow version of Blue Oyster Cult's "Godzilla" was apropos.

Nobu and a couple of other winged yokai took to the air to catch Godzilla's attention. "He's cranky," Haru observed, stretching as the giant lizard monster finally shifted his steps to follow our little parade up the gold-bricked road that Melanie had repaired.

"I still don't know why you gave him to me," I said. "Whatever possessed you to do that?"

"Eh. Nobu indicated that you might need a little extra *oomph* somewhere along the way. That's not something he generally asks for, so I figured I would help him out." He popped a randomly appearing cucumber in his mouth and chewed noisily. "Of course, he owes me, but seeing him in that form is almost payment enough. I'll think of something, though."

The Dragon King's roars grew quieter and less demanding as we walked, eventually fading away into sleepy snores as he shrank down. Haru quickly scooped him up in another gachapon capsule, pocketing him away into his shell. "That's that."

"Gotta catch 'em all," I quipped, my body drooping with exhaustion. The baby began to fuss, and I cuddled her a little closer. I needed to go home. We all did.

Melanie shifted her stance, her hands moving in a ghostly echo of whatever the violin was doing—or maybe she was controlling it. The rice paper door moaned, and a golden hue lit up around the entry as she slid open, beckoning us.

"Come away, oh human child," I murmured.

Melanie shuddered. "There! I can't keep it open for much longer! It's a Door, but a Door to nowhere, and it's trying to close!"

Haru marched up to the newly created Door and gave it a slap. "There we go! Everyone in!"

The yokai let out a raucous cheer. Someone had produced a bottle of sake, passing it around as, one by one, they crossed the threshold.

The poor rice paper door began to shake after Jimmy went through, and Nobu said something sharply to her. "She's concerned we're going to leave her behind, but I have an idea. You guys go through first. Kitsune and I should be able to make this happen."

I stepped in quickly, my fingers lingering on the edges of the Door as though I might be able to keep it open from sheer force of will. I let go when Melanie followed swiftly behind me, but I could tell the magic was starting to break behind her.

The violin struggled to keep pace, but the golden hue was fading quickly, even as Kitsune burst forth from the shrinking Door in her fox form to join us, Nobu riding on her many tails. As they slipped through to the silver road, Nobu reached back and pulled hard on the Door's edges.

The rice paper door shrieked as she was pulled inside out through her own body, the opening shutting tight before her.

I stared at her askance. "Well that was awful."

"The only way I could manage in this form," Nobu said. "Unless you wanted to leave her there?"

I shook my head quickly. I had no idea where on the CrossRoads we were, but at least it wasn't Hell. "No. And I don't want to stay here either."

Melanie linked her arm through mine as though to give me some support. "We should be reasonably close to Eildon Tree. That's what I was aiming for."

"I can't walk anymore. I'm done." I let out a groan. "How the hell do we get home?"

"With me." Startled, I glanced up to see Talivar leading a contingent of elven soldiers, armed to the teeth in glittering silver armor. Eye widening with surprise, he dismounted his horse, wrapping me up in his arms. I sagged against him. "Oh, you did it, you did it," he crooned, taking the baby from me to cradle her gently against his chest and planting a tender kiss upon her head. "Rest now. You're safe."

The thought of finally making it *home* flooded my limbs with relief. Normal things like a real bed, my own clothes, a shower. I leaned my head upon his shoulder and sighed. Disposable diapers. A breast pump. A crib. A name.

And maybe some goddamned sleep.

Sonja paced outside the gates of my Heart. "He's settled in your Heart somewhere. I'm sure he's got some haunts you know about?"

"I can think of a few," I replied. "And I'm sorry. It took us awhile to get the baby situated to a point where I could fall asleep long enough to come here."

"Fair enough." Her wings spread as she readied to take off. "Be easy on him," she said quietly. "He's been through a lot." And then she was gone in a flutter of razor-sharp wings.

At the rear of the old Victorian was my overgrown garden, a relic of memories of my grandmother's own garden where I grew up. Here, beneath the willow tree is where I found the incubus, leaning against the bark, his head tipped back while he slowly breathed.

His golden eyes slitted open as I approached. "Took you long enough," he drawled.

"Ah, well. You know how it is. I had a husband to appease, a child to feed, a shower to take," I teased. "Trotting about so quickly after giving birth was a bit of an energy drain. Going to Hell, freeing Godzilla, being carried off by winged daemons, punching through the fabric of the universe, giving birth. It's been a rough week."

I knelt beside him, our foreheads touching. He ran his lips over my cheeks, nibbling gently until he captured my mouth. It was soft and tender, almost uncharacteristically so. Perhaps an indication of the level of his pain and weakness.

"That won't do." I kissed him harder, my tongue slipping into his mouth. He groaned, grunting as he tumbled me onto the soft grass. Normally there would be at least a bit of wooing, but given his injuries, there wasn't much time for the niceties.

He gestured abruptly, and my clothing shredded into nothing, fading in the Dreaming like spirits. My hands drifted into his hair, caressing his antlers with careful fingers. His bells chimed plaintively, but my legs were already spreading, welcoming him as he slid home, both of us gasping. Without prelude, he began to thrust, each movement making me cry out until my voice shattered the moonlight, pushing me over the edge. The first ripples of orgasm washed over me, shuddering, shaking, quaking with pleasure.

He arched his back, his mouth open with half-lidded lust, eyes growing golden and bright and full of some nameless emotion, his face dropping to my ear. "I love you," he breathed. "I love you. Love you. Love . . ."

The ground beneath us shimmered, becoming misty, and we were falling, falling, falling . . .

We tumbled through the Dreaming, past the Cross-

Roads, the two of us entwined, rolling, undulating, and landed right smack onto my bed, Ion slumping against my breast with a soft kiss.

"Sorry it was so fast," he said between kisses. He'd returned to human form, his pale skin flushed with exertion.

"You look better," I murmured.

"I feel better." He flopped onto the blankets, one arm spread carelessly behind him. "That Paganini has always been a bastard. I had to deal with him before when I was there with Maurice's soul. Never been anything other than a major pain in the ass."

"Well hopefully he's out of our hair for a while."

"'A while' nothing," Ion said, rolling onto his side to run a protective hand over my belly, cupping a swollen breast. "More like forever, ideally. Ah, you seem to be leaking."

"It happens." I sat up. My bedroom had been converted into a makeshift nursery by Talivar over the last few days, my apartment newly appointed with myriad luxuries suitable for child-rearing and mommy-pampering. In some ways, it was too much, but I wasn't about to spoil his fun.

None the worse for wear from her stay in Hell, my daughter lay swaddled in a bassinet next to the bed, and I scooped her up. She nuzzled me sleepily, immediately latching on to a newly stiffened nipple. I sighed as the milk let down, and I sat against the pillows. Ion leaned on one arm, stretched out and lazy, as he watched me feed her, a strange look in his eyes.

"Star," he said suddenly. "I want to name her Star. She shines so brightly in the Dreaming, I cannot think of calling her any other name."

"I love it. Let's run it by Talivar," I said, shifting as a light tap on the door startled me to alertness. "And speak of the . . . devil, I guess," I followed up lamely.

"I'm not sure that's the right word," Talivar said, snorting.

The elf king's good eye fell on Ion's prone, naked body with a raised brow. "I see you were successful at bringing him home at least."

"That's one way of putting it," Ion said, stretching, languid and lazy. Talivar didn't rise to the bait, his gaze softening when it fell on my daughter.

Our daughter, I supposed. All three of ours.

"And Star will suit her nicely." Talivar sat on the bed on the other side of me, stroking my cheek. "I don't know about you two, but I need some sleep. We've got a long road ahead in raising her, and we ought to at least get some rest before we start that particular mess."

"I'm just happy to be home. With both of you," I added, shifting over as Talivar toed off his shoes and slid out of his jeans. The elf slipped beneath the blankets on my right, even as Ion stretched out to make room on the other.

My little nugget's mouth drooped open, milk dribbling out of the corner of her mouth with a satisfied wriggle. Carefully, I eased between both men, the baby cradled in the crook of one arm.

And together, we slept.

EPILOGUE

Two months later

" . . . AND THE girl felt a hot flush warm her thighs as she stared into the vampire's dark eyes. Without a word, he fell about the soft pulse of her neck . . ."

Phin's voice droned through the microphone, his voice lilting and bold as he adjusted his spectacles. As far as prose went, I supposed it was okay. The gaggle of women hanging on to his every word obviously thought it was hot shit. And maybe it was.

It brought the customers to the Marketplace in droves, so I'd take it. And it was open mic night, so the crowd was fairly varied. Haru and Didi were there as well, though it was more of a business trip than anything else for them. They were there under the guise of starting up a yokai–OtherFolk exchange program, but I had the vague suspicion Phin was part of that plan too. How much he'd invested in it, I couldn't say. It was none of my business anyway. As long as everyone was happy, they could do what they wanted.

Ion tended bar with an easy manner, and I sat in the overstuffed chair with Star in my arms. Talivar sat beside me on a throw pillow on the floor, his head leaning against my leg as he listened to the story with a bemused look.

As for my becoming his queen, we hadn't quite managed a coronation yet, but I'd started taking a more day-to-day interest in how to actually run a kingdom. Everything was a work in progress, and we'd compromised somewhat by building a permanent Door in the rear alcove that led straight to the newly reassembled Unseelie Court. From here, it was a simple cross of a threshold and I could oversee what I needed, yet still keep a footing firmly planted in the mortal world with Ion and Star.

Kitsune remained my stoic bodyguard, though her duties often kept her on the other side of the Door, but she did make the effort to check in a few times a week. When Star grew older, no doubt her loyalty would transfer, but for now, it was enough.

I sipped from a glass of sparkling water and then set it down on the table beside me. Nobu shot me a resigned look from where he perched on the absolute tiniest of shrines, his diminutive form both charming and deadly. But when Melanie took to the stage thirty minutes later, his face softened, eyes lighting up as though she was the only thing that mattered in the world.

And if her playing wasn't quite as otherworldly as before, there was still a hint of the Wild Magic lurking beneath it all the same, like oil on water, simply waiting to ignite. The violin soared again, music coaxed forward from the strings.

She looked at me through the crowd, and I smiled.

ACKNOWLEDGMENTS

Books may be written by a single author, but as every writer knows, the completion of such a labor of love is only made possible by friends, family, and readers, and this one is no exception.

So here's a nice list of everyone who was kind enough to help me out during the time of this particular writing.

Danielle Poiesz, without whom I'd even be writing this at all. I owe her nearly everything; Piper J. Drake, for many writerly conversations and support; Jim Moore, who has been nothing but kind to me; Staci Myers for beta reading and finding mistakes on things I'd forgotten; Barbie Atkins, artist, beta reader and all around lovely person; Tori Carlini, fellow otome-obsessed fan who came up with Phinder; and Aimo, who has never been anything other than brilliant and utterly amazing.

Special thanks to Atago and Soichiro Oda for their invaluable assistance with the Japanese mythology and many interesting conversations. ありがとうございました.

And of course, to you the readers . . . Without your enthusiasm for these characters and this world, I wouldn't be here. Thank you.

NOTE: I had to take some shortcuts when it came to the of the nuance of the Japanese language for this story. All mistakes are mine.

ABOUT THE AUTHOR

Allison Pang is the author of the urban fantasy Abby Sinclair series, the IronHeart Chronicles and the writer for the webcomic Fox & Willow. She likes LEGOS, elves, LEGO elves . . . and bacon.

She spends her days in Northern Virginia working as a cube grunt and her nights waiting on her kids and her obnoxious northern-breed dog, punctuated by the occasional husbandly serenade. Sometimes she even manages to write. Mostly she just makes it up as she goes . . .

Learn more about Allison and all her titles at:
www.heartofthedreaming.com

www.ingramcontent.com/pod-product-compliance
Lightning Source LLC
Chambersburg PA
CBHW021812110726

47902CB00006B/1754